SUMMONING
SHADOWS

A Rosso Lussuria Vampire Novel

What Reviewers Say About
Winter Pennington's Work

"Winter Pennington's creative mind is a dark and gloriously erotic place. ...The twists and turns of the plotlines are written with the ease of an accomplished author, while the balance of horror and humor is achieved with seemingly effortless skill. Blood, sex, fury, betrayal, animal instinct, true love...they are as intrinsically entwined as the lovers within the pages. It may just be time to go over to the dark side..."—Candia of *Inkubus Sukkubus*

"Pennington has a wonderful talent at writing paranormal stories. Unlike many of the recent books in the genre that have vamps living amongst humans, *Darkness Embraced* has the vampire clan living in almost total isolation. This allows for the focus to be totally on the vampires and the clan hierarchy, customs and politics. Vampires and sex seem to go hand in hand and *Darkness Embraced* embraces the sexuality and sensuality of the main characters and takes them to wild, edgy places..."—*Just About Write*

"[*Witch Wolf*] is a nice mix of urban fantasy with police procedural/ murder mystery. If Pam is your favorite vampire on *True Blood*, you're going to love Lenorre."—*Rainbow Reviews*

"It's a testimony to the strength of Pennington's writing skills that readers never lose track of the plot even as new characters are introduced and others are more fully developed. What follows is an engrossing read involving vampires, werewolves, and some very hot, kinky sex and excitement!"—*Just About Write*

"Kassandra Lyall is a likeable, sympathetic and frequently funny heroine, and Pennington sets her up well amongst a brace of other quirky, intriguing characters. *Raven Mask* is an entertaining novel— highly recommended to anyone looking for a sexy, funny, escapist bit of fluff to bury themselves in for an afternoon."—*The Lesbrary*

"*Darkness Embraced* is a sinfully sexy read. Pick up *Darkness Embraced* and be enthralled."—*Bibliophilic Book Blog*

By the Author

The Rosso Lussuria Vampire Novels:

Darkness Embraced

Summoning Shadows

The Kassandra Lyall Preternatural Investigator Series:

Witch Wolf

Raven Mask

Bloody Claws

Once Upon a Twilight

SUMMONING SHADOWS

A Rosso Lussuria Vampire Novel

by

Winter Pennington

2012

ISBN 10: 1-60282-679-X
ISBN 13: 978-1-60282-679-3

THIS TRADE PAPERBACK ORIGINAL IS PUBLISHED BY
BOLD STROKES BOOKS, INC.
P.O. BOX 249
VALLEY FALLS, NY 12185

FIRST EDITION: AUGUST 2012

CREDITS
EDITORS: VICTORIA OLDHAM AND CINDY CRESAP
PRODUCTION DESIGN: SUSAN RAMUNDO
COVER DESIGN BY SHERI (GRAPHICARTIST2020@HOTMAIL.COM)

Prologue

England, 1810

"You will learn, cara mia, to control your thirst." Renata's honeyed voice washed over the reverberating din of my hunger. The blindfold she'd set in place kept me from truly perceiving her, but I did not need to see her. Even if she had spoken no words, she was my Siren and my queen.

I could sense her where she stood some feet away. A thread of longing and connection pulled tight between us, and I knew she watched me. I could feel her gaze on me as intimately as a caress.

My arms were stretched high above my head, secured by some kind of metal shackles I could not break or slip from. I struggled in vain to get to the woman who knelt at Renata's feet.

Justine.

I could feel the shadow beat of her pulse on my tongue. There was no fear in her, none that I could discern by the steady beat of her heart and breath. She knew why Renata had bid her to kneel, and yet, she did not fear.

Justine was one of the Donatore, a human blood donor among the Rosso Lussuria vampires. She was the only Donatore I had ever met face-to-face within the walls of the Sotto, our underground kingdom.

The blood in her veins tempted me as the fruit hanging from the Tree of Knowledge must have tempted Eve, thick and ripe, tempting and irresistible, begging to be tapped and released.

Yearning echoed throughout my limbs. It made my fingers tingle with the ache to touch Justine, to take hold of her as if she were nothing more than a succulent apple within my reach.

I would have called it desire, but that was too passionate a word. The hunger narrowed the scope of my thoughts into something primal, simple…animal.

My lips burned.

"Epifania," Renata said and the tone in her voice was sweetly commanding. It took effort for me to focus on the sound of it and to resist the urge to fight my bonds.

She had taught me to serve and to please, but my control over my thirst was a hard-won battle I had to conquer myself.

Siren or no, she could not erase the very essence of what I had become when she had given me the kiss of death and rebirth.

You may wonder what it was like, the first night I spent with Renata.

And to that, I can only say this: it was beautiful and terrible.

She made love to my dying body, slowly, gently, artfully, riding my flesh beyond illness and into the throes of ecstasy. When she drove her fangs into my neck, I gave my life to her willingly. She destroyed my withering body in the fire of her passion, shielding me in the cage of her ardor.

On the following evening, I was reborn. I awakened to a world in which the senses dominated. But with the gift came the curse: a hunger I had never known.

It is said some go mad on the night of their first awakening. For me, I can only say that it was the first time I had ever truly felt alive. Even the hunger, in its own way, fanned the bright flame of life.

Renata brought to my lips the sweet wine of her blood. She soothed the fiery, cutting pain that threatened to be the source of my undoing. At the kiss of her blood, at the chalice of her wrist, I found a heaven man had never dreamt of.

The evenings passed, and each night when I woke, Renata was there to abate my hunger and to keep the madness of bloodlust at bay. In time, she taught me the arts of the bedchamber with skill and patience. She revealed to me the beauty and the heaven in being *vampire*.

That night, with Justine at her feet like a loyal dog, she unveiled to me the horror and the hell of it. For those who may think Renata had brought Justine before me as a gift, it was not so.

She used Justine to teach me the dire consequences of my curse. Justine was my blood martyr.

Renata had done her best to prepare me for weeks. Each week, she loosened the shackles she used to bind me, until they were loose enough that I was able to slip them, much to Justine's misfortune.

But Justine had known, too. She had lived in seclusion among the Rosso Lussuria long enough to understand. Though she looked to be a girl of some twenty years of age, she was older than even I, kept youthful and fresh every month by nothing more than a drop of queen's blood.

All the practice in the world cannot spare a vampire her first kill. Some days, I wish Renata had chosen someone other than Justine, for I had known her. I had seen her alive and well. But such had been Renata's purpose.

When I think of Justine now, I remember the husk of her body. I recall the taste of her blood in my mouth, the life I raped from her in order to sustain my own. To further drive forward her point, Renata left me there, kneeling over Justine's body, her blood on my mouth and hands.

The blood of a vampire can sustain and prolong human life. It makes mortals a hardier lot. But I had taken it all from Justine, even that small touch of magic.

Three nights I spent with Justine's body as my only companion. Renata did not seek to comfort me. She did not console me. She threw off the shackles that had held my hunger at bay and barred the door, giving me no room to escape or flee from the lesson at hand.

And when the bloodlust passed, I realized what I had done.

One might believe I bear resentment toward Renata for the harshness of her lesson. Yet, if it had not been for Justine's sacrifice and for what Renata had done, I do not think I would have ever found my conscience again. Every night I woke with Justine's body as a reminder, I gained an ounce of something stronger than the hunger. I regained bits and pieces of myself.

Renata returned on the third night and her guards, Dante and Dominique, took Justine's body away. Renata stood just inside the doorway, freshly bathed and dressed in a gown of black silk, her long waves of hair still damp.

I had not fed in three nights, and though I grew weak, I could feel Justine's blood inside me still. Faint, like an echo, but still there.

Renata gave the order for me to bathe and I went, drawing my own bath and soaking quietly. When I emerged garbed in one of the fine dressing gowns she had provided for me, I found she had not been waiting for me alone. A small human boy knelt in the middle of the room, mirroring Justine's position three nights prior.

"Cara mia," Renata said as she swept her hand out toward the boy.

I paused in the doorway, refusing to step further into the room. The blood in the boy's veins tried to seduce me like panpipes playing in a distant forest, a forest that promised wild abandon. With a will, I shook my head. "No."

"He is there for the taking, cara mia. Will you not feast more than your eyes?" she asked.

As if she had spoken some command, the boy pulled aside his shoulder length honey hair and tilted his head back to offer the line of his neck. He reminded me so of Justine that my limbs trembled. Renata had chosen well, for he looked near enough like Justine to have been her sibling.

I took a shaking step back, and seeing nothing but Justine behind my lids, said, "No."

Renata did not respond, not to me and not to dismiss the boy. She perched on the edge of her bed and simply waited. How much time passed, I do not know, but I knew she waited to see if my will would break.

I fought with every fiber of my being not to lunge, not to give in to the hunger.

When at last she was convinced, she rose and went to the double doors of her room, summoning Dante and Dominique to escort the boy back to safe quarters.

Renata had come to me then, offering the comfort and solace of her body and blood. And so, I learned as she had said I would.

I learned to control my thirst.

Chapter One

America, Present Day

Gold eyes slashed with veins of onyx lightning watched me as I climbed into bed. Her nude body shone like selenite, framed by the black, knee-length tresses of her hair. A small tuft of fur shielded the mound at her groin as she reclined, marvelous and striking. I straddled her, careful of the leathery wings that spread from her back and across the bed.

"You have me at a disadvantage," she spoke with human lips.

"How so?" I asked while I settled my body over hers. I brushed my sex over her, letting her feel that I wore nothing beneath the silk robe. The small node of flesh between her legs stiffened against me and sent a shivering wave of pleasure through my lower body. The black sigil at my wrist tingled with warmth. Once, only a few weeks ago, the sigil had itched and burned whenever I had been close to her. Now, it simply grew warm and tingled ever so slightly.

We were bound together, she and I.

The Dracule, the Great Sires and Sirens of the vampire kind, are a breed unto themselves. Iliaria had never been mortal, and though her current guise mimicked that of human, she was not. She was female, most definitely. The Dracule have a form that is anatomically similar to human, but there are still differentiations. The spur-tipped leathery wings that arched from her back, the long, spaded tail, and the *Nod Dragoste* between her legs set her apart from truly appearing human. It marked her as something beautiful in an otherworldly sort of way. Mayhap for some, it marked her as the stuff of nightmares. For myself, well…

I rolled my hips forward to dance my skin across hers. "Have you any word on the traitor Damokles?" I asked.

It appeared as though it took her an effort to concentrate. She touched my hips to bring my dance to a halt and I obliged.

Damokles had been a very naughty Dracule who had conspired with two overly ambitious Elders to overthrow the Rosso Lussuria Queen, my lover, Renata. Iliaria had initially been summoned by the traitors to kill us. But she had taken an interest in me, and Renata and I had bartered with her.

I took Iliaria to my bed and she spared us. She offered to give me her mark as a truce and symbol of an alliance between us. I had taken it, and so I bore the black flowing lines at my wrist like an elegant tattoo. The mark is Iliaria's name, odd and flowing in the tribal alphabet of the Dracule.

The Dracule tell a story of the beginning of our kind. Menelaos, one of the first kings of the Dracule had taken a mortal woman to his bed. Yet, the Dracule are not a race made for mortal lovers, for bodily lust can awaken in them darker lusts. In the throes of passion, Menelaos had slain his human lover. When he realized what he had done, he wept. The angel Azrael, guardian of death, heard the Draculian king's cries and offered to return the mortal woman to life if Menelaos would give up his own immortality in exchange. Thus, to save his beloved, Menelaos sacrificed his own immortality, and Lilith, the mother of our kind, was created.

The King's Sacrifice, they call it. *The Origins of Vampire*.

It was some hours after dawn and Renata had already died for the day, giving me time to enjoy Iliaria's company. I wore a delicate ring on the middle finger of my right hand, the same side of my body on which I bore Iliaria's mark. The ring was set with a dainty tear-shaped gem. When held to the light, a small prick of crimson showed in the center of the gem's smoky blackness. The ring had been a gift from Iliaria. The gem set within the band is a Stone of Shadows. It is a stone forged from the blood and magic of the

Dracule. Its power cloaks a vampire and protects us from sunlight. Oddly, the Dracule do not have to worry about sunlight or dying at dawn. A lucky lot they are, for the ring was the only power that kept me from dying like the rest of my brethren.

I fingered the ring idly as I awaited her reply.

"I am sorry, Epiphany. I have no word on Damokles's where-abouts."

"It's not your fault," I said, and my words were met with a heavy silence. With Damokles alive and well, we were still in danger. Iliaria feared his hatred for the vampires would rouse some of the other Dracule to rise against us.

Granted, the Rosso Lussuria are not the only vampire clan in existence. There are others like us throughout the world. We simply choose to keep to ourselves, living in our underground kingdoms and away from the prying eyes of humanity. In our daily lives, the Cacciatori, the vampires who hunt for us, are the only ones who venture outside the walls of the Sotto. I should know, for it was the Cacciatori who had kidnapped me and brought me to this world.

It was Renata's mercy that had kept me. I was dying from the consumption when first I had been brought to the Sotto. That was in England, before we made the long and arduous journey to America. For fifty years, I had been Renata's lover and pet. She had cast me out for a hundred and fifty, and I had only recently discovered why. In her own way, she had been trying to protect me. There were those among us who perceived our love as weakness.

Now, I am an Elder. I no longer live a life of servitude. I no longer try to move as quiet as a mouse or cast down my gaze. I am Renata's Inamorata, her lover, her consort, and was declared such before the whole of the Rosso Lussuria. To raise a hand against me is to raise a hand against her.

Inamorata or no, if someone decides they want you dead, I have found they will not stop trying until they succeed. And when one is immortal, they have a very long time to keep trying.

Iliaria's nails dug into the fabric over my hips, bringing my attention back to her.

"You are deep in thought this morning," she said. "Is your little fox speaking with you?"

"Not right now."

Iliaria shifted her hips and her sex pressed against that sensitive spot between my legs. My eyes fluttered closed as a tendril of pleasure unwound within me.

"Epiphany." She released me. "Take off the robe."

I obeyed and loosened the sash, shrugging and sending the silk spilling from my body to pool across her legs.

In the short amount of time that we had been together, there remained certain acts of the bedchamber that Iliaria had not allowed me to perform. She, like Renata, was a dominant by nature, and though they had shared me, neither commanded the other. Iliaria, however, was not the same kind of dominant as Renata. Renata often took the reins of our lovemaking, unless swayed with good reason and the promise of pleasure. Even with the promise of pleasure, Iliaria was not so easily swayed. When I began marking a path down her smooth stomach with my mouth, she caught hold of my hair and forced me to meet her gaze.

"What are you doing?"

I bit back a childish retort fueled by my own selfish frustration. Iliaria would not take kindly to it, nor would I gain any ground with her by using sarcasm.

"Will you not let me please you as I wish to?"

I could feel the emotional battle raging inside her. She knew what I *wanted* to do, a large part of her even wanted me to do it, but some sort of insecurity that I could not fathom kept crawling in the way. She looked away from me, a signal that told me the beast of insecurity was winning.

"I can sense your desire, Iliaria. Why will you not let me please you with my mouth?"

"It is a very intimate act, Epiphany."

I couldn't keep the corner of my mouth from rising slightly. "And we haven't been intimate? I've revealed nearly all of myself to you and Renata."

"That is different."

At that, I raised my brows. "Oh? How so?"

"You are vampires, not Dracule."

"I was a virgin when Renata took me," I said, not quite comprehending what she meant.

"Were that the case," she said, "you would still be a virgin. Do not lie to me."

I sat up on my knees, straddling her while keeping our skin from touching. "Perhaps I should be more to the point; I was a virgin the first time Renata made love to me. I was no longer such when she gave me the kiss of death."

It was true. Renata had given me a choice, something I eventually learned she had not been offered. When she had taken me that first time with the olisbos, a kind of phallic sex toy, she had been gentle, but still, it had not spared me the agony that came with the loss of virginity. To this day, I was ever grateful she had given me a choice and that she had deflowered me before turning me. Had she waited until after my rebirth, my body would have continuously healed and I would have experienced the excruciating pain of that loss every single time she used her toy. I liked some pain in the bedroom, of a certain variety, but the pain of that night was one I preferred to keep a distant memory.

"The act of love between women is nothing new," she said. "It is so among the Dracule, but what you request is not our custom as it is between you and your queen."

"You're beginning to make me feel as though I am asking you to do something vile, Iliaria. I don't like it."

Her spaded tail thumped the mattress below us, a sign of her growing frustration. She released a heavy sigh. "I do not know how to explain it to one such as you."

"One such as me?"

"You are a vampire. You see no shame in it. I am Dracule," she said as if it explained everything.

"Vampire. Dracule. What does it matter? What difference does it make? If I can take you into my mouth and please you, why shouldn't I?"

"It makes me uncomfortable!"

I flinched at her words but didn't give ground. I had seen Renata in her anger. If Iliaria thought she could scare me with it, she was very much incorrect.

"Why?"

Iliaria wiggled out from beneath me, her movements jerky and impatient. "You are acting like a child."

"Your attempts to verbally degrade me because of your own insecurity won't work. You're running from a phantom fear instead of turning around and banishing it."

She stood, slamming her leathery wings around her like a shield to hide her nudity. I wondered if closing her wings that hard around her had hurt, but doubted it. Her eyes narrowed when I moved to lie back against the pillows, mirroring how she had been lying only moments ago.

"So that is it then?" she asked. "If I do not allow you to perform, there will be nothing between us this day?"

It sounded as if she didn't like the idea.

"You're the one who climbed out of bed in a tizzy, not me."

"You upset me."

"I have feelings too, Iliaria, and by rejecting me and something I want to do before even giving it a chance, you hurt them."

"You'll not manipulate me."

"You do realize you're arguing with me simply because I want to bring you pleasure? Can you not at least try it?"

She let out a deep breath. "I do not know, Epiphany."

"We're alone," I said. "It's just you and I. What do you have to be ashamed of? You know I would not intentionally seek to hurt you."

"No," she said. "I do not know that."

"Then give me the opportunity to prove it to you. Have you heard me once complain about anything you and Renata will of me?"

"Again," she said, "we differ."

"What?" I asked. "Do you think of it as an act of submission or something?"

She turned away, and I knew I had finally hit close to the truth. "It is viewed as weakness among the Dracule, Epiphany."

"So is bedding a vampire, to a great lot of them. There comes a time when we have to release preconceived notions and form our own opinions based on personal experience. Wouldn't you agree?"

Her expression turned thoughtful, not as if she were thinking entirely too hard on the subject, but more like she was trying to find the trap in my words.

It was my turn to sigh. "Come to bed," I said, "and have of me what you will."

She put a knee on the side of the bed. "That sounds heartfelt."

"What do you want, Iliaria? Ask for what you desire and I will try to give it."

"Do you mean that when you say it?"

"I would not say it if I didn't."

"I could ask anything from you and you would give it?"

"If it is within reason and within my reach to give, I would at the very least try."

She bowed her body and crawled to me, bringing our faces close. "If I allow you to do this, Epiphany, I will find something that is not so easy for you to do and I will expect compliance when I request it of you."

"Within reason," I said.

"Within reason."

She had let me touch her once, but only briefly. I had learned that in the bedroom, she preferred that I kept my hands and mouth above her waist. It was an odd thing to me, that the Dracule would consider such an act a sign of submission. Then again, who was I to cast stones when the vampires with whom I lived often frowned upon me? I heard their whisperings, still. Becoming an Elder and Renata's consort did not erase them. Queen's whore, they'd begun calling me. Well and good, let them continue to call me what they would. I would not bear the mantle of their shame.

I hoped Iliaria would do the same.

I traded places with her, careful of her large wings. We had learned it was easier with her on bottom, for she had to be cautious of her whip-like tail, which was not solely for balance, but also for defense. The tip of her tail hid a venomous spine-like barb. The venom was strong enough to kill a vampire when dealt a mortal blow, enough to sicken an immortal when dealt a shallow wound. In the bedroom, we'd learned it was more dangerous to nearby furniture.

I knelt between her legs and she did not protest. The fur covering her groin was like silk against my cheek, but it was not the softness of that fur that I sought. It was what the fur shielded I was more curious about.

I traced her with a finger, and her flesh shivered and stiffened in reaction to my touch. Truly, she did enjoy it. Her arousal was a visible thing. I continued to trace her slowly, gently, marking the path of her inner folds with surety and patience.

I pushed my fingers inside her and her body tightened around me. She stretched her arms above her head, her nails scraping across the stone wall.

I found a slow rhythm and she groaned my name.

"What is it?" I asked.

"Too much foreplay," she grumbled.

It was true, she was rigid to the touch. I smeared the honey of her desire across that knot of flesh and her spine bowed.

"For someone so adamantly against this, you seem to be enjoying yourself."

Iliaria's only response was a low, rumbling growl. The growl vibrated throughout my room. It coaxed the hair at the back of my neck to prickle pleasantly.

I pressed my lips against the tip of her then and licked her slowly. At the light touch of my tongue, her body jerked as if she'd been dealt a blow.

"Mmm, you're very sensitive there," I whispered, my breath against her making her shudder again.

"Yes," she said, a growl swallowing most of her words. I managed to make out the words, "vulnerable flesh."

"You'll not have to worry about my fangs, Iliaria. If I must tuck them behind my lips, I will."

If she was going to respond, I didn't give her a chance to do so. I sealed my mouth over her, and her skin between my lips was like a ripe cherry, full and ready to burst. I traced her tentatively, trying to discern what she enjoyed and what she did not. I found that to take all of her in my mouth, I did have to curtain my fangs behind my lips, and the sweet taste of my own blood trickled across my teeth. I ignored it, surrendering myself to her pleasure.

I sucked gently, and she screamed. I paused.

"Keep doing that," she panted. "Lightly, though. Keep it light."

I placed my hands flat against her thighs and continued, minding her request and trying not to apply too much pressure.

At some point, the flow of pleasure took me until I was only distantly aware of the sound of the wooden headboard protesting beneath her grip. I withdrew my hand from her thigh and entered her, eliciting yet another cry. I quickened my pace and the creaking ceased, drowned out by Iliaria's moans. Something brushed the left side of my body, and that too, I ignored until it coiled around my waist and constricted, threatening to crush me.

I pushed at her tail with my free hand, trying to get her to move her tail lower. I didn't need to breathe, but air was something I appreciated, most especially when I had a mouthful of Dracule.

Immortal or no, forced suffocation isn't exactly my idea of a rollicking good time. Iliaria seemed to come back to herself for a moment. She loosened her tail and lassoed it lower across my hips and buttocks.

The closer she came to orgasm, the more tightly her tail cinched around me, and the more I had to focus on her and not being crushed. Being vampire, it would be harder for her to crush my bones, but she was Dracule and preternaturally strong. I was hesitant to discover just where that limit lay.

Iliaria climaxed, her hips bucking and forcing me to rise or lose my hold over her. I followed the movement of her body until at last, she cried out and fell back limply, her tail unfurling from around me.

I collapsed with my head between her thighs and licked clean my blood from my teeth and lips. After a few moments, Iliaria looked as though she was about to say something to me but hesitated.

"What is it?" I asked.

A knock sounded at the door, and Iliaria spilled to her feet out of pure instinct. I found myself standing near the dresser, caught in the midst of sword magic and reflex. In my mind's eye Cuinn stood alert, his ears pricked forward to listen.

"It'sss Anatharic," a hissing voice whispered from the other side of the door. "We have a problem."

"Căcat!" Iliaria said heatedly. "Couldn't you have chosen a better time?"

She rounded the bed while I tied the sash of my robe. She glanced at me briefly, courtesy alone to make sure I was covered, before she flung open the door to admit the Great Sire into my room.

❖

I stood in a hallway narrower than most of the other halls within the Sotto. Anatharic had been correct. There was a problem and it was a very bad one.

The heavy wooden doors that led to the Donatore's private quarters had been reduced to a mess of splintered wood, as if someone had placed a bomb nearby and set it off. Nothing, not even a bomb, should have been able to penetrate the entrance.

"I'm confused," I admitted. "No weapon known to man would allow anyone access into the Donatore's chambers. This area of the Sotto is strictly forbidden to anyone except the queen and her guardsmen."

Anatharic stood just to my right in the less human of his forms. Though once I thought about it, I realized I had never seen him change form like Iliaria. He was tall, taller in Draculian form than he would have been in his other guise. That much I knew. He had his wings folded around his furred body, a stance obviously comfortable to their kind. Only the obsidian fur of his feline-like face and glimpses of the fur on his legs and tail were visible.

His onyx eyes met mine. "I sssusssspect they did not ussse human weaponsss." His speech was slow and hissing, a product of the ribbon-flat Draculian tongue.

"Indeed," Iliaria said.

All three of us had placed a careful distance between ourselves and the splintered doors. Renata had found a mortal witch to place magical wards on the Donatore's keep as a measure to keep the humans safe from the Rosso clan. Neither vampire nor mortal could pass through them without queen 's blood. Technically, the Donatore were nigh undetectable. No one within the Sotto would have heard a sneeze from the other side, the warding went so deep.

How then, had someone found their quarters? To my knowledge, none of the others, save the queen and her guards, even knew how to find it in the labyrinth of hallways. I had only seen it once, when I had accompanied Renata to the door before feeding time. If it weren't for Anatharic's senses, the coppery tinge of mortal blood and the salt of human skin, I might not have even recognized it as the Donatore's quarters.

"The lassst ssscent I had ended here," Anatharic said. His elongated ears swiveled as if he were trying to hear something I could not. The spurred tips of his wings twitched.

"I smell human blood, not queen 's blood," I said. "How do you think it possible that Damokles broke through the warding to attack the Donatore?"

"That I have yet to figure out," Iliaria said, rising from a kneeling position where she had been examining the floor. "We need to go in. If he's destroyed the doors, no doubt the wards are no longer functioning."

I saw Cuinn, my fairie fox trapped in a spirit blade, fold his ears back in the way he had of appearing as a vision in the back of my mind. The sword belonged to me after I had chosen it during a duel, and now, he was essentially stuck in my head and could communicate with me telepathically whenever he wanted to. Which, I had learned, he greatly enjoyed.

Piph, he said, *it could be a trap.*

"It could be a trap," I said aloud. "But we have to do something, Cuinn."

Iliaria knitted her brows in concentration. She raised a piece of wood to her pale face and her nostrils flared slightly.

"It reeks of magic," she said. "Not our magic."

"What do you mean?"

"Not of the Dracule," Anatharic said. "Do you sssuppossse he isss working with a witch?"

That'd explain the door going kerplooey, Cuinn thought.

"I'm going to go wake Renata," I said, concentrating on her. Though I didn't smell her blood, I hoped silently that Damokles had indeed used a witch and not—

I shut my eyes, refusing to think on it. The last time I'd thought Renata gone from me, I'd gone mad with fury. I needed to keep my wits about me.

"Not alone, you're not," Iliaria said. She turned to Anatharic. "Watch this entry. We'll return. Summon if you need assistance."

Iliaria followed me down the winding halls. I tried to keep my pace normal, though my instincts wanted me to run to Renata's chambers. But I knew better. We still didn't know what had happened or what might be lurking in the halls. Running face-first into a monster wouldn't help the situation.

Iliaria kept pace with me, her eyes flicking this way and that.

"You're guarding me," I said, a bit surprised.

"Yes, why wouldn't I?"

I didn't know what to say, and so I shrugged.

Iliaria gave me a strange look. "You are my dragă," she said. "I will always guard you."

It shouldn't have surprised me, really. Iliaria had once used her body as my shield. She risked her life for me every second that I bore her mark. She'd gone against her own people to protect the Rosso Lussuria. She called me her dragă, someone special and dear to her.

I twisted the ring on my finger again.

"If something had happened to Renata," I said, changing the subject, "surely we would have heard the struggle. Dante and Dominique would have called for help—"

"Epiphany," Iliaria brought me up short by catching me by the elbow. "If something has happened to your queen, you are not safe here. You must let me take you somewhere where you will be safe."

"You shouldn't speak of such things," I said, refusing to meet her gaze.

"I want you to be prepared. The devil only knows what Damokles is about."

"Dante and Dominique are not so easy to kill." If they were, Renata wouldn't trust them as much as she did.

"The Dracule are not so easily heard," she said, not exactly comforting me.

The sound of Iliaria's wings clapped open like thunder and the torchlight of the Sotto spun in my vision. The stone wall pressed against my back a second later.

Iliaria's chest rumbled as if a drum played beneath her skin, vibrating against me.

"It's just me." Dante's voice came from the other end of the hall, thick and sticky like syrup.

Iliaria let up, giving me full view of the figure that strode toward us. Dante wore a dark red shirt, darker than the red dyed locks of hair that fell over his eye. His black leather pants were tucked into short boots.

"Where's Dominique?" I asked. "And Renata?"

"Your queen is safe," he said.

Something about his expression made the hair rise at the back of my neck. The corner of his mouth curled slightly upward.

"Iliaria," I said, hoping she would understand.

Whoever was walking toward us was not Dante. I could feel the knowledge crawling like ants under my skin. The fox blade in my hand blazed to life.

Whatever he was, whoever he was, Iliaria was faster. The arm-length blade he'd drawn went clattering to the stone floor as they met. Iliaria took him down in a matter of seconds, her movements a black blur of deadly grace.

"Eeeepiphannyyy," Anatharic's hissing voice sounded behind me, and I turned. He was running down the hall on all fours, nearly as tall as a small horse. His long ears were drawn back against his skull, his wings arched slightly, making his body something smooth and angular as he cut through the air.

I stood there like an idiot, no longer paying attention to the sounds of struggle behind me. Iliaria was questioning the man who looked like Dante. He was screaming as she did something to him.

And Anatharic was making a full-out run for me.

"Get on!"

I didn't comprehend. It was happening too fast. Anatharic leapt in the air like a panther and slammed into me.

For a moment, I was falling in the dark, though I seemed to be falling far too long than was normal.

Anatharic released me and I landed in a heap on the floor.

He caught my arm and jerked me to my feet. "Get up," he said. "Wake your queen. We mussst hurry."

I stumbled toward Renata's great bed in a sort of daze. Relief sang through my heart when I saw her pale visage whole and untouched. With the fox blade in hand, I crawled on top of her. I curled my fingers around the blade until the metal bit deep.

"I need your help."

"Hurry," Anatharic said again. His ears turned in the direction of the doors that led to the hallway outside Renata's chambers, but he came to my side to aid me.

If the man in the hallway had not been Dante, where were Dante and Dominique?

Better yet, why couldn't I hear anything beyond the doors? Surely, I should've been able to hear at least Iliaria. The mark at my wrist still tingled, letting me know she was still close.

Anatharic sheathed his claws and pried open Renata's mouth. I held my hand above it and curled my fingers around the blade. My blood fell to coat her tongue, and Anatharic stepped aside.

Renata gasped the first ragged breath of life, her chest rising sharply as it filled her. Her lids flew open to reveal the dark sapphire and blue topaz fragments in her eyes.

"Epiphany," she said. Unlike the only other time I had woken her by surprise, there was no surprise in her now. Only a calm calculation as she tried to assess the situation. She must have perceived the shock in me, for she locked an arm around my waist as she sat up.

She asked Anatharic, "What passes, Great Sire?"

"We are under sssiege, lady."

"How many?"

"We do not yet know."

Renata's eyes fluttered closed. "It is too early still for the Elders to rise. Have they been attacked?"

"We do not think ssso, lady."

"It seems Damokles has targeted the Donatore," I said.

I felt more than saw the horror of such news unfurl inside her. After the horror came a fine surge of rage that filled her like a thunderous wave, gathering.

"That is impossible."

"Apparently not," I said.

She nodded once, sharply. "Tell me."

"Iliaria believes Damokles used a witch to break the warding."

"Are there any survivors?"

"I don't know," I said. "We hadn't gotten that far. I came to wake you, in case it was a trap. Iliaria and I were on our way here when someone guised as Dante attacked us in the hall."

"Magic?" Renata asked, directing the question to Anatharic.

"Yesss."

"What do we do?" I asked her.

"Go," she said. "Take Anatharic with you and go wake Vasco and those you are able. I will find Iliaria and help her question the witch."

I turned around when the sound of something heavy hit the floor.

"Too late," Iliaria said. She'd flung something at her feet. It took me a moment to realize it was a man's body. His sandy hair was cropped short to his head. Once I took in the attire that mimicked Dante's, I knew it was the witch.

I could not hear his heart beating, though neither could I discern the killing blow.

"He took a vial of poison before I could question him," Iliaria said.

"What of Dante and Dominique?" Renata asked. "Have none of you seen them?"

I shook my head.

Iliaria said, "Not yet."

"Epiphany," Renata said, her voice cool and calm. "Go wake Vasco, Nirena, Vittoria, and Vito." She turned to Iliaria. "Will you go with her?"

"I will."

I didn't know how comfortable I was leaving Renata alone with Anatharic. Iliaria might have known him, but I didn't, not that well.

"I think you should come with us," I said. "If they're still here, is it not better that we don't separate?"

Renata watched me with a thoughtful expression for several moments. "Very well," she said. She rose and retrieved a blue silk dressing gown from the armoire. Considering I was still nude beneath the robe, I went to Renata's closet and pulled on a pair of dark breeches.

As I was more concerned with Vasco's well-being, I didn't bother trying to find the rest of my clothes.

❖

Vasco was fine, as untouched as Renata had been. As were Vito, Vittoria, and Nirena. We stood once again just outside the doors to the Donatore's quarters. We had neither been attacked nor had we found Dante or Dominique. Where on earth were they?

Renata started to step past the splintered doorway and Iliaria and Anatharic blessedly stopped her.

"We'll go in first," Iliaria said.

Renata, strangely silent and compliant, nodded. Vito and Vittoria took up the rear, their swords drawn at the ready. Vasco and I placed Renata between us, and Nirena followed at our heels.

The last time Renata had boldly strode into a room, she'd stepped right into the middle of an ambush. Tension made my shoulders tight.

After rounding a corner, Iliaria said, "We're clear. They're gone."

She and Anatharic moved, and I was able to see the ruins of not only the Donatore's quarters, but of the Donatore themselves.

They had been dragged from their rooms and cornered at the end of the hallway like a herd of cattle. It was such a grotesque mess that my mind didn't want to make sense of the bits and pieces of flesh and limbs. Blood splattered the walls, and bits of skin dangled from the walls as if someone had thrown them there with a meaty slap.

I averted my gaze and turned into Renata. She put her arm around me, knowing I didn't have the stomach for such violence. This close to the confetti of human bodies, the smell of meat, blood, and bile was metallic and sour in the back of my throat.

Renata touched my hair. "The Dracule can deal a fair amount of damage," she mused. "Yet, this does not appear to be the work of your kind."

I heard Iliaria inhale, drawing more than air into her lungs. "Magic, again."

"A magical explosive?" Nirena asked. She passed Renata and me to closer examine the scene before us.

"Are all of them…" I let my question trail off. Of course they were dead. Every single one of them. The Donatore could not withstand that much damage and survive.

I didn't need to ask myself why Damokles would target them. They were our blood source, and without them, we would starve.

It was simple really. So simple that we should have thought of it and saw fit to better protect them.

I could feel Renata's dread like a knot in my stomach. Outwardly, she remained every inch the queenly figure, her head held high as she projected an air of confidence and composure. But we were connected, and I could taste her fear.

"Sì," Vasco said. "All of them, sorella."

"I know *why* they targeted the Donatore," Nirena said thoughtfully. "What I don't get is *how* they found the Donatore. Do you think it possible they've been working with more than one vampire?" she asked Renata.

"None save Dante, Dominique, and I know the way to this place. It does not make sense."

He used the witch to track mortal blood, Cuinn said, and I passed his words on to the others.

"What do we do?" I asked aloud, though I was speaking with Cuinn. "They've effectively burned our crops."

Ah, but ye see, they've burned your crops with magic. In my mind, I saw Cuinn's black lips curl into a fox's version of a smirk. *Magic is reversible. Ye've only to find a witch to reverse the spell.*

Reverse it? I asked.

Aye, he said. *If the Donatore were killed with magic, they can be remade with magic.*

"Epiphany?" Renata asked.

"Cuinn said to find a witch to reverse the spell."

"That does not help us much," Renata said.

Vasco spoke up. "It might, actually."

"You know of a witch, my silver prince?" Renata asked.

"Sì, I do. If she's still in the same location. One of the Stregheria, actually."

"We can take you to find her," Iliaria said. "Our means of travel is safer and less costly when it comes to time."

I was trying very hard to focus on their faces and not on the graphic remnants of the Donatore around us.

Play violence I could handle; serious violence made me ill. Yet another thing that set me apart from my brethren.

"But what of Dante and Dominique?"

We can try ta track them, Cuinn offered.

How?

Remember when we tracked the Great Siren?

I did remember. Cuinn had somehow led me to investigate the hallway without actually leaving Renata's room. It was a sort of projection that had to do with his ability and not mine.

I remember. Do you suppose that will work?

It may take some time, but aye, it should. I'd not recommend doing it here, though.

My chambers are safe, Renata's voice flowed softly through my mind.

I startled, not aware that she'd been eavesdropping. It was decided that all of us save Vasco, Nirena, and the Dracule would return to Renata's chambers and wait while Cuinn and I tried to locate Dante and Dominique. Vasco, Nirena, and the Dracule would search out a witch to aid us.

On one hand, I was relieved that I would not be waiting idly. On the other, I worried for Vasco and Iliaria. Would they find the Stregherian witch, and even if they did, would she help our clan?

Cuinn explained to me that the Stregha were similar to him, albeit, they were, "half-blood Fata offspring." Still, I felt as if I knew little about them. How intimately had we worked with them in the past?

I can't tell you that, Cuinn said, *but your queen's doors are spelled to admit only those she has invited. That's Stregha magic at work.*

Is that what kept them from attacking Renata, do you think?

Aye, he said, *their witch might not've been powerful enough to break the warding on her room. It's…"* He seemed to be searching for the word. Finally, he said, *It's more intricate than the warding on the Donatore's doors.*

I was tempted to ask, "How so?" but didn't, figuring if I did, I was in for a lengthy explanation that probably wouldn't have made sense to me anyway.

Chapter Two

Vito and Vittoria stood just inside the room, guarding the two entryways. Both were garbed from head to foot in black: black boots, black pants, black tunics, and black hair. The only contrast to all of that blackness was the mirroring paleness of their skin and their clear, crystalline blue eyes. They were twins and though not identical, it was obvious with a glance they were biological siblings.

Renata sat in the high-backed chair tucked into the corner of her room by a small glass table. She watched me calmly and I could feel her gaze like the cool light of the moon, a bright beacon to my heart.

I crawled into bed. The last time Cuinn had taken over my senses, only Renata's grip had kept me from falling on my face. I crossed my legs and rested against the pillows as I tried to make myself comfortable. Renata came to the side of the bed.

Leaning over, she pressed her full lips to mine, and one of her hands rose to cup my jaw. Her tongue brushed past my lips and encouraged my blood to sing. Under her kiss, my mind too felt pleasantly cloudy as if I had drunk too much wine.

She drew away and murmured, "You taste of her."

I didn't know what to say. Most days, I had time to wash Iliaria from my skin before Renata woke. It was a measure of respect. It was different when she shared me, for the two were sharing me in the moment, but to know that I'd been making love to the Dracule while Renata *slept*…

A sharp pang of guilt gnawed at me, not because of what Iliaria and I had done, but because of what might've happened to Renata while Iliaria and I had been preoccupied with each other.

The thought made me feel guilty.

Renata smiled softly. No doubt, she heard my thoughts. Whether I willed her to or not, she was my queen, my Siren, and there was no door within me she couldn't walk through.

But our powers were a double-edged blade, for I could sense her emotions and knew that in some part of her, my guilt pleased her. She would not allay me of it. Rather, she reveled in knowing I cared deeply enough about her to feel guilty.

I placed my hand over hers and her skin was cool and smooth against mine. The length of her tapered fingers twined with mine.

I let her have it, all of it; my guilt, my concern, my relief. It was hers.

"When you are done, cara mia, we will remedy your predicament," she whispered against my cheek. The promise was enticing, and I resisted the urge to reach out and touch her. Now wasn't the time. Along with the pang of guilt, she knew too the steady flame of unquenched desire within me.

I nodded, slightly, sensing Cuinn's impatience despite the fact that he did not give voice to it. Renata moved away, and I focused on Cuinn, closing my eyes to concentrate.

The first time Cuinn had helped me to "see" without my eyes, he'd done it relatively quickly, but this time he made an effort to be more patient and to instruct me.

Seeing as we do not know where they are, it will take more concentration from the both of us to find them, he said.

Cuinn had once used this ability to find Iliaria when she'd been summoned to kill the Rosso Lussuria. He'd sensed danger and woke me, and because he had sensed her, it was easier to find her in the labyrinth of hallways. Dominique and Dante would not be so easily found. They weren't a threat, and without that sense of danger, Cuinn had to work harder. We had no starting point, so I was not sure how exactly we were to find them.

What if they had been taken from the Sotto? What if there was nothing to find or sense? I did not like the thought. Dante and Dominique were more than pretty muscle; they were two of the best guardsmen Renata had ever had. I liked them, as much as you can like someone who keeps you at arm's length for two hundred years.

We may need your queen's help, Cuinn murmured through my mind, *to use her ties to them as a compass.*

"Renata," I whispered. "We need your aid."

She sat on the bed beside me and took my hands in hers again. "I will do what I can. I have not sensed them, so I do not know how great a help my ties as their Siren will be."

One thing at a time, Cuinn said. *Just 'cause she doesn't sense them doesn't mean they're not there. We'll focus on one of them first, then the other, to avoid being pulled in two different directions if they're not in the same place.*

But, I thought, *if Renata does not sense them, that could mean—*

It could, Cuinn said. *It does not absolutely.*

If Renata had been awake and they had been hurt or murdered, she would have felt it. If they were safe, why couldn't she sense them? Didn't the fact that she couldn't sense them mean their lives had probably been snuffed out? If they had died before she woke, there would be no life for her to sense.

As much as I disliked the thought, it was a persistent one.

Piph, it was Renata's voice that called me back. Her fingers tightened around mine, and though she said no more than my name, I knew she had heard my thoughts.

Ye need to focus, Cuinn said softly. *It may mean nothing. It's easier for a Siren to sense her vampires when they're in distress. If she can't sense them, they should be okay. For now, at least.*

I thought I understood what he meant and let out a breath. I let myself fall into a quiet darkness, finding a place within myself where each thought sank like a coin to the bottom of a still pool of water.

Now, Cuinn said when it was time.

I let myself think of Dominique again. Where was he?

The smell seemed to start in the back of my throat. I know no other way to explain it. It began from somewhere within me; the hint of iron, of cool stone and burning torches, the old stench of human sweat.

Atta girl, Cuinn thought, *keep it going. Follow the thread.*

This time, his magic was nothing like it had been when we had discovered the Dracule. Then, he had known where to find her; the signature of her energy had been so strong. Trying to find Dominique was like trying to find a pebble in the snow.

Renata held my hand tightly. When she released her energy, I felt a thread pull tight between us. My skin grew warm with the flood of her power, as if someone had thrown open the doors and let in an autumn wind, though I knew this wind had nothing to do with any natural element.

Renata focused the energy she gave me and I'd never felt something so strange and unusual. So many threads seemed to spiral like a web from the base of her power, all of it contained within her. Was that what it meant to be Siren?

If Renata was a spider, she navigated those threads adeptly, swiftly sorting through them until she came upon the connection, the link that she desired.

It was then the vision flared to life, igniting to life behind my lids. The torchlight came into view as the vision in my mind sped up, following a thread that led down a stone hallway lined with dancing torches. When the vision paused at the small cell, it took me a moment to realize that I knew it. It was the holding cell I had been in two hundred years ago.

Dominique moved out of the shadows. He raised his face in a line of torchlight and his gray eyes shifted as if he sensed something and looked to find it.

I opened my eyes and the vision shattered. "He's locked in the purgatorio. And he's alone."

I do not know who had first begun calling the small prison that the Cacciatori used to keep their captive humans the *purgatorio*. Having been held prisoner in such a place, I can honestly say it's less a purgatory than a level of hell filled with despair and darkness.

The Cacciatori hadn't needed to hunt for humans in some time, since we had plenty of healthy Donatore, so there were no mortals being kept there. It was only Dominique, and though I knew where he was, it left me with another question: Where was Dante?

Renata stopped me when I started to get up.

"I could not sense Dante," she said, and her gaze was tinged with a fear that twisted my stomach into knots. "We will wait until the others return to release Dominique. He appeared unharmed, as far as I could tell, but I'll not have us walking into a potential trap." Her voice had taken on a frosty edge, and I knew she was trying to contain her worry.

I let out a breath and fell back on the bed. It was reasonable, practical, and thoughtful to wait for the others, but how long would it be until they returned? And if it was a trap and Damokles was somewhere nearby waiting for us to find Dominique, would he kill him for sport if we took too long to show our faces? If Renata couldn't sense Dante, our best chances of knowing what had happened to him rested with Dominique; that I was sure of.

But I was not queen. Renata was, and if she wanted to wait, we bloody well waited. I bowed slightly and said, "As you will, my lady."

Vito and Vittoria remained at their posts by the doors, neither saying a word in agreement or disagreement. Given our low numbers without the others' aid, I did not think they disagreed.

What seemed an hour later, though it was probably far less, Anatharic and Vasco returned only a few moments before the others to announce that they had indeed found Vasco's Stregherian witch. Iliaria manifested with Nirena and an unfamiliar woman I pegged as the witch.

Renata had taken her seat in the high-backed chair in her room. Had we not been under attack by Damokles and his henchmen, I knew she would have preferred to greet the witch elsewhere, as it was more politically correct. Yet, we still did not know if Damokles remained within the Sotto. Cuinn, of course, did not sense anything. When I pressed him to explain why he could not sense anything, he pointed out the fact that Damokles had been working with a witch and that there are many ways to cloak one's presence. It made enough sense that I let it go.

"My queen." Vasco knelt before Renata. "I introduce you to Savina, the Stregherian witch of whom I spoke."

Savina was a woman of modest beauty. If I had not known she was one of the Stregha, I would have thought her no more than a mortal woman. She was not as striking as many of the Rosso Lussuria. The thick mane of her dark hair was bundled and clasped at the back of her head. Her honey and olive kissed skin was garbed in a simple dress the color of deep merlot. The curves beneath the material were lush and soft; she was not portly by any means, but her hips widened slightly by the fullness of age and motherhood, and I wondered how many children she had.

The witch moved to kneel beside Vasco where Renata could see her fully. Her voice, when it came, was smoky and heavily accented.

"You seek my aid, Queen of the Rosso Lussuria?"

"Rise, both of you," Renata said and they did so. Savina was not so much taller than I, perhaps an inch or two. "Will you aid us?" Renata asked her.

Savina said, "I am here, am I not?"

"You sound none too thrilled about that," I spoke without giving thought to my words. I moved where Savina could see me.

Her lustrous gaze met mine, and even with the distance between us, the blood in her veins sang a sweet siren song of life and crimson promise.

It had been many years since I had been in the presence of a woman who was truly alive. I had no doubts in that moment that, immortal or no, the Stregherian witches were human enough.

"Colombina, are you well?" Vasco asked.

I hadn't realized how intensely I was gazing at the drum that beat in the side of Savina's neck. With an effort, I peeled my gaze away.

"I believe your vampire wants to take a bite of me," Savina said.

"I am well," I said, addressing Vasco.

"Yet, you do not deny the call of my blood?" she asked.

I straightened my spine and met the look of challenge she gave me unflinchingly. "Should I? I am what I am. I am a vampire, and witch or no, you smell very much like a feast."

Iliaria cleared her throat, I think to disguise a laugh.

"You'd do well keeping in mind what I am when you begin to think I smell like your supper."

I inhaled a slow breath to steady myself, inhaling flickers of emotion permeating from Savina.

Her words had been harsh and what lay behind them was harsher: complete and utter distaste.

"She does not want to be here," I said.

"And who are you to speak my mind?"

"Now it is you who wishes to take a bite out of me. If you are so displeased, why are you here?"

Savina opened her mouth to speak when my vision of her was superimposed with the sight of Cuinn. Cuinn rose to his paws, drawing his ears back with a snarl.

Watch it, witch.

A muscle in her jaw twitched, giving the slightest indication that she had heard him. "Vasco, you did not tell me one of the Fatas was among you."

"It is not important," he said.

"Enough," Renata said, sounding tired. "You have said you will aid us. What aid can you give?"

"Vasco has told me of your troubles," Savina said smoothly, sounding politic. "I can reverse the spell."

"Why would you help? I asked.

"Because I can," she said, and I got a very strong sense she wasn't offering to help because she cared, but for some other reasons. Maybe she just wanted to show off her powers.

"We need to get Dominique first," I said. "There's no telling how long this could take. He's still alive. Surely, restoring the Donatore can wait until he's with us again."

"You have found him?" Nirena asked.

"Dominique, yes. We've not yet found Dante. We can't. Renata can't sense him. We've been waiting to retrieve Dominique on the chance it's a trap of some sort."

Vasco's sword sang from its sheath. He stood armed and waited for Renata to give some instruction. She nodded and I retrieved the fox blade from the bed.

"Anatharic," Iliaria said and ordered him to take the rear.

Vito moved to the main doors to be near his sister. As they had before, the Elders in tow put Renata and me in the middle. This time, Savina joined our little hunting party, standing on the other side of Renata so that she was between us.

I spared her a glance.

"If you're worrying about me," Savina said, sounding defensive, "don't. I've no need of your weapons."

I held my tongue. I wasn't worried about arming her. What worried me was whether or not she could be trusted.

❖

The hallway of the purgatorio appeared empty.

"No one else is here," Iliaria said after taking a cautious look around.

Anatharic was on all fours beside me, the length of his tail swaying gently. "Coward," he said, half-growling and obviously referring to the fact that our intruders had disappeared.

Our little hunting party descended further down the hall and rounded a corner to find the cell where Renata and I had seen Dominique. Vasco tried to open the cell and jerked roughly on the lock when he realized it was latched.

"It will not open," Dominique's voice grumbled from the shadows.

"Dominique," Renata said, relief making her voice soft. "Are you well?"

"I am, lady, aside from their silly parlor tricks."

"They've spelled the door," Vasco said.

It was the only thing that explained why, when he tugged on the metal lock, he could not break it. A human, of course, wouldn't have been able to break it. But Dominique and Vasco should have been able to do such a thing easily.

Savina parted our throng. "I'll do it."

Vito and Vittoria stood near the sharp turn in the hallway, quietly guarding and keeping an eye lest Damokles returned. Nirena was just as silent, standing in a spill of flickering torchlight that made her long hair glisten like fine spider silk. Her violet eyes met mine, and though I'd never quite figured her out, there was something different about Nirena; different in a way that had nothing to do with vampirism.

Savina examined the lock and confirmed that it had been spelled. When she summoned her magic, a warm breeze picked up in the hallway. She murmured no words of incantation, merely tugged on the lock and pulled it open.

Those standing closest to the door moved aside to allow Dominique to make his way through. He knelt in his very modern black jeans and white T-shirt, the tail of his dark hair falling over his shoulder as he bowed his head.

"Forgive me, my queen."

"Where is Dante?" she asked.

"I do not know, my lady."

Renata nodded sharply and pressed him further. "What happened, Dominique?"

"We heard noises in your chamber hall, my queen. Dante went to check. When he did not return, I left my post in search of him. That is when they grabbed me."

"How many of them, do you reckon?" Vasco rocked back eagerly on his heels.

"I do not know. They caught me unaware." Dominique shook his head as if shaking away a buzzing thought. "At a guess, I'd say four of them. I did not see Dante."

Iliaria cursed so heatedly that for a moment I thought she'd drive her fist through the wall. She did not, thankfully. "They are toying with us." Her voice was an angry hiss.

"What do you mean?" I asked.

"I think she means," Vasco said, "that because Dominique is unharmed and yet the Donatore do not remain so, that this has become a game of proving their ability to infiltrate our clan and hurt, or spare, whomever they choose.

"But what of Dante?" I asked. "Do you think they would have killed him just for sport?"

Iliaria considered my words. "I do not know," she said. "Damokles hates vampires and murdered his own sister for being the lover of one. If that is any indication—"

"There is the chance that they are using him to gather information for further use against us." Nirena stepped away from the stone wall and circle of light, sending a ripple of energy through the air.

"There is that," Iliaria agreed.

Renata took rein of the situation. "The other Elders will wake soon. It will be easier to find Dante with more of us looking for him. Do you have a problem with restoring the Donatore before our Elders wake?" she asked Savina.

"No."

We left the hallway of the purgatorio, for which I was relieved. My memories of such a place were not so terrible, but I had not seen it in two hundred years and didn't much care to see it again. I remembered a man who had beseeched Renata when I had been held there. He had knelt on the rough stone. His face had been dirty and his eyes hollowed from lack of sleep.

"Please, great lady, I have a family to provide for, mouths to feed..."

I remembered her cold response. *"As do I."*

Whatever became of his family, I do not know, nor do I know what became of him. Like as not, he became nothing more than food in our bellies, as the Donatore were chosen with care and the man had been too desperate, lost in his concern for his family. Too desperate to survive meant he would've been all too eager to run away and return to the life and love he had known. For that reason alone, he would not have been chosen as Donatore. Those that became Donatore became such consensually and were, more often than not, mortals who had nothing to lose in the human world.

I did not know this, Piph, Cuinn's androgynous voice whispered, tempered with compassion. He was a part of me, my little fox, and when I remembered something, he shared in those memories.

It was a very long time ago, Cuinn.

Aye, he said, *and though you serve her, you are not like her.*

His words made me focus my attention on Renata.

Her magnificent eyes met my gaze and held it. The midnight fragments in her irises were nigh black in the dancing torchlight, shadowing the soft ocean blue flecks like Caribbean waters and a starry sky. The expression she gave me was unreadable.

I am not as strong as she is.

Nay, Cuinn said, *'tis not that, Epiphany. You do not share the same cold practicality.*

I severed the eye contact with Renata, afraid that she would hear.

For a long time, I did not understand it—her cold practicality. I did not comprehend how she could seem so cruel, and yet, she showed me compassion when I had not asked for it.

A hand touched my hair to tuck a curl gently behind my ear.

Light and dark run through us all, Renata said.

CHAPTER THREE

We made it safely back to Renata's chambers, and she left Vasco in charge to oversee the Donatore's restoration. Those that were not with his party overseeing the restoration stood guard in the adjoining room. Soon, the Elders would wake and they would need to feed. It may seem unusual to some, to take such great lengths to restore the Donatore. If the human world was nestled so close above us, why did we not just send the Cacciatori to hunt for more? Many of the Donatore have been with our clan long enough to have never known electricity or seen an automobile. They had been gathered throughout the years, slowly, cautiously, like lambs taken by unseen wolves in the night, to become our glorified cattle, our forever source. It would take many, many humans to replace their numbers to provide sustenance for the entire clan.

We didn't feed directly from the Donatore. Their blood was taken every day and brought to us in a dining hall. It was all very civilized, all things considered. We didn't know the Donatore as people, but as food sources.

If we wished to remain unbeknown to the world above, we could not hunt and kidnap mortals in such great numbers. We would have to replenish our crops slowly, which was impossible. Renata could only stay the Elders and Underlings for so long before they would go mad with thirst and seek the world above of their own accord. Driven by a lust for blood, they would be as animals. It would drive us into the mortal world, making us targets.

I had to admit, it was a clever plan. Damokles had hit us where we would be most weakened by the blow. If we could not restore the Donatore, I feared to think of what would happen.

All would be lost to chaos. The streets of Bolivar, the nearest city, would run red with blood. The Cacciatori for the nearest clan would inevitably seek us out and destroy us, one by one, in an effort to stem the chaos.

I fell back on Renata's bed with a sigh.

"You are becoming more thoughtful in your age, cara mia." Renata roused me yet again from my thoughts.

"What do you mean, my lady?" I asked.

She sat in front of her dressing table, and her reflection met mine in the looking glass. The smile that curled the corners of her sensuous mouth was knowing and mysterious.

"Ah," I said. "You've been listening. Do you ever grow bored with that, my lady?"

She did not offer a response and instead set about unwinding the black strands of her braided hair. She brushed the glistening waves until they fell in a veil of silk to her waist. I stifled a warm shudder at the memory of her hair on my naked skin.

Renata laughed, albeit quietly. Somewhere in the back of my mind, I caught Cuinn's amber fox eyes rolling lightly.

Vampires, he grumbled.

Do not pretend I've not noticed where your particular interests lay, Cuinn. You may be closer to my thoughts than I'd like, and I may not truly hear yours unless you direct them to me, but I am an empathic vampire and have sensed a stirring of curiosity in you.

Needless to say, Cuinn closed his yap.

I don't know why, but he didn't want me to tell Vasco. Oh, Cuinn pretended not to like him, and he'd never actually broached the subject with me. He didn't have to. I'd gradually begun to notice the subtle change that took place in Cuinn's demeanor when Vasco was around. Not all of the time, but every now and then, I caught it—the way he became just a bit more impish when Vasco was around. Almost…flirty.

My thoughts circled around one another like sparrows flitting in flight. I kept thinking of the Donatore. I hoped Savina had not boasted falsely when it came to her abilities.

When first I had come to the Rosso Lussuria, I had myself been under the impression that they were nothing more than mortal servants who did our bidding. It is not so, in reality. Yes, they are servants of sorts, and to many, no more than cattle, no more than food. For that reason, we lived in a sort of segregation; Donatore and vampires, adjacent and separate. In fact, the only mortal I had ever known to spend time away from the Donatore's quarters had been Justine.

Justine.

I shut my eyes, blocking out the sight of Renata's bedroom.

Shortly after Justine's death, I had learned of the segregation. The only mortals the Elders, not the Underlings, had any contact with were those imprisoned in the purgatorio. The rest lived in their own underground community among other Donatore.

Which was how Renata had found me and how Rosabella, another Elder, had found her pet Underling, Karsten. Though Karsten was no more, taken by Iliaria when she was summoned to execute our kind. No one seemed particularly disturbed by his loss. Rosabella had been more horrified by the Dracule than distraught by his death.

It seemed as if such events had transpired months ago, but it had only been a little over a week. I had not forgotten that Rosabella had voted against me becoming an Elder, had not forgotten the look of disgust she'd given me when she'd found out I was bedding one of the Great Dracule.

Like so many other things, it was not easy to forget.

I never thought to ask Renata why she had chosen Justine.

The bed moved and the back of her soft hand slid across my left temple.

"I chose her to wait on you because she agreed and I felt you would find comfort in another human's presence."

"She agreed to wait on me at your behest, but did she agree to die for me when you turned me, Renata?" I had never asked it of her, ever.

"She knew what she risked," Renata said, her expression cool and blank.

She traced my jaw with the tips of her fingers. "You have more questions," she said, her touch tender. "Ask."

"Did she serve you as I serve you?"

"No."

"Did she desire to?"

Renata raised her shoulders in response.

"You are playing coy, my lady. She did your bidding thinking it would gain her a place in your bed, did she not?"

She leaned over me, bringing our faces close. Her hair enclosed us like a canopy.

"You are becoming entirely too adept at discernment, cara mia."

Renata's sinful lips were close enough that a breath was all it would take to close the distance between us.

"You played on her desire for your affections and then cast her to my fangs," I whispered.

"I gave her what she wanted."

"To die?" I asked.

"To be embraced by a vampire, no matter the consequences."

Renata kissed me, and all thoughts of Justine vanished under the command of her lips. Her hand moved along my body, sliding between my legs and pressing against me. My hips rose at the contact and I moaned.

I broke the kiss, trying to clear my mind. "Should we be doing this now?"

Renata sank to her knees beside me. She caught my wrists in her hands and pressed my arms high up above my head to pin them to the coverlet.

"Can you think of anything better to do, cara mia?"

I groaned as her energy washed over me like a seductive wave that promised to drown me in the depths of pleasure. Her gaze was bright with power when it locked with mine. She was hungry for more than sex.

She kissed me again until my head reeled with desire.

"Take it," I whispered. "Take me."

Renata grabbed two handfuls of my tunic and tore it open down the middle.

"I shall, my sweet." She eyed my body as if it were a delicious feast. The intensity of her desire and hunger made me ache pleasantly.

She bowed her head and her mouth moved on me again. Her kisses fell like velvet petals on my skin. She undressed me slowly, working every inch of my flesh with her fingertips and teasing me with a light caress of nails. She cupped my breasts and squeezed them, gently coaxing my desire from embers to flames.

She pulled me to the edge of the bed and knelt on the floor between my legs. I reclined on my elbows to watch her. She rested her arm along the line of my thigh and traced my inner folds with a faraway expression. The tip of her finger slid over that sweet spot near my cleft, and I gasped, my head falling back.

Renata kissed my thigh, barely a brush of lips, no more. I gazed down the pale line of my body to find her faraway expression had been swallowed by another. The look in her sky-ocean depths said one thing and one thing only: *Mine.*

Always. Whether I thought it or said it aloud, I don't know. Renata bowed her head and set about claiming me with her mouth, licking and sucking until she reduced me to a mess of small gasps and moans.

I was close to that sweet edge. My thighs trembled as every muscle in my body contracted against the pleasure. I was on a precipice, about to fall—

Someone cleared their throat.

For a moment, Renata hesitated and I thought she would stop, but she was queen and my lover. She did not have to stop.

The sigil at my wrist tingled, letting me know who made attempts to interrupt us. Renata bit me, her fangs piercing me as she fed at my sex. I cried out when she pushed her fingers inside me and the orgasm came upon me like a clap of thunder, a storm that brewed in my blood and broke like lightning through my limbs.

When it passed, I lay back boneless, seeing stars behind my lids. Renata licked my blood from her lips. Her voice, when it came, held a thread of irritation in it. "I do not like being interrupted, Dracule. Such would be a good thing to bear in mind when next you enter my chambers unannounced." She withdrew her fingers from inside me and I cried out again.

"I thought you would like to know that while you were busy fucking, the Stregherian witch has restored your precious Donatore."

"You dare to criticize me?" Renata rose from her kneeling position, standing to all of her height. Her expression was a dangerous one. The tension in the room jumped a notch and flushed my skin.

Iliaria took a threatening step in Renata's direction. "When I criticize you, you will know it."

My skin flushed even warmer, as if their anger was a burning brazier filling the room with heat. Renata took a step toward Iliaria again and I'd no idea what she intended. I didn't care to find out.

"I don't take kindly to threats, especially not ones coming from—"

I sat up. "*Enough!*" The word erupted from my lips, cracking like a whip in the tension thick air.

They both looked at me as though I'd just appeared.

"Lest you forget in your bickering," I said. "I am a woman, not an object. And if you failed to notice, which you obviously seem to have done, Renata was *feeding*. If she hadn't needed to feed, she wouldn't have initiated anything to begin with. Wasn't that obvious?"

I clambered out of bed and tugged on my trousers. Renata reached out to touch me, and I stopped her by holding up my hand. "I do not advise touching me right now, my lady."

"You are feeling our anger toward each other," she said, more statement than question.

"Yes, and if you want me to stop feeling it, I advise you both to get it under control."

Renata let me pass without trying to touch me. I pulled a loose tunic from the trunk in her closet and slipped it on over my head. An empath feels other people's emotions almost as though they're her own. I was no different, and I was especially close to these two angry, passionate women. I didn't want to do something stupid because of their anger with each other.

When I returned to the room, the energy in the air was better, less stifling. There remained an undercurrent, but Iliaria had taken a non-threatening seat at the dressing table, and Renata sat calmly poised on the bed.

"Some of the Donatore did not survive," Iliaria said conversationally enough. "Their minds were too far broken by the original spell and they had to be destroyed."

"How many?" Renata asked.

Iliaria appeared thoughtful. "A dozen," she said, shrugging. "No more."

Renata nodded. "Was there any word of Dante?"

"No. None of the Donatore saw him before they were attacked. They confirmed Dominique's story. There were four of them, two witches and two Dracule. I suspect one of the Dracule was Damokles."

"That's awfully unsettling," I said, still unnerved by the fact that Iliaria and I had been awake and completely unaware of what had happened within the walls of the Sotto. "So do we assume they've taken Dante for information or that Dante has possibly betrayed us?"

"Dante would not do such a thing," Renata said. "His loyalty has been unwavering for centuries. Why would it waver now?"

"Love or hate," I said, remembering something Vasco had once told me, "or something to gain."

Renata stubbornly shook her head. "He would not, Epiphany."

"Still," I said, "it is a possibility to consider, nothing more, my lady. In a predicament such as this, how could I not think it?"

"She's right, you know," Iliaria said. "More than ever, those you trust should be questioned."

Renata stood. "I know Dante," she said. "I will worry about the strength of his loyalty and oath later, but now I am more concerned with finding him. I am his queen, I should be able to sense him, and thanks to the witch your kin conspire with, I cannot even sense my own vampire."

"There's still Cuinn," I said.

I felt Cuinn stir at my mention of him.

"Yes, there is Cuinn, and had he been able to sense Dante, we would have sensed him when searching for Dominique, Epiphany. I did not sense a thread for Dante," she said.

"I didn't remember," I said.

The clap of wings startled me and I turned to find Anatharic, Vasco, and Savina near the doors.

There was blood on Vasco's shirt.

"What'd we miss?" he asked.

"Where's Dominique and Nirena?" I asked.

"Tending to the Donatore and making ready for when the Elders rise," he said, his gaze slipping to Renata. "My lady?"

"Dante is still missing," she said. "How do you suppose we find him?"

Vasco appeared thoughtful for several seconds before he whipped around in a dance-like move to Savina.

"No," Savina said. "I've helped your clan already, vampire. I've granted your boon. You've no more promises to dangle over my head."

"We were friends once, Savina."

"Once does not mean now, Vasco."

"I helped you and yours in your time of need," he said.

"Sì," she said, "and I am forever grateful, but you'll not charm and manipulate me into risking my neck any more than I already have."

"Why do you despise us?" I asked, honestly perplexed.

She turned to glare at me. "What business is it of yours?"

"I'm curious, is all. You seem to bear quite the grudge against our kind, and yet I can't fathom why."

"What grudges I bear and do not bear is none of your concern, vampire."

"I have a name," I said. "You're more than welcome to use it."

"Savina's family was attacked by Il Deboli," Vasco said. "Might I remind you, Savina, that was centuries ago. We are not your enemies, nor are we Il Deboli. I told you then and I tell you now, Il Deboli go against our laws. They do not follow the true ways of our society."

"You're not exactly my amigo, Vasco."

Vasco shook his head, his expression somber. "Only of your own doing, Savina. You chose to give up our friendship when you found out what I am."

Savina didn't reply. In fact, she averted her eyes as if looking at him pained her. After several moments, she finally said, "You loved my brother well."

"I tried to save him, Savina," Vasco said, his voice tempered with kindness. "You are not the only one who suffered at his loss."

"No," she said and her voice was so soft it was nearly inaudible, "but I am the only one that lost both of you."

Vasco spread his arms. "I cannot change who I am, Savina, no more than you can. I am sorry that I could not love you the way I loved Emanuelle."

Savina flinched slightly. "You could have been honest with me instead of playing me for a fool."

Vasco sighed. "How could I have been honest with you when it was a struggle being honest with myself?"

"You have a son."

A long silence stretched throughout Renata's chambers. I caught her gaze. She had been surprised, too. I daresay, all of us were, Vasco most of all.

He stood before Savina, completely frozen with shock, wrapped in a preternatural stillness.

"*What?*" He seemed to return to life, his limbs moving. He took Savina by the shoulders. "What did you just say?" He shook her with an expression of shock and awe.

"You have a son, Vasco," she repeated.

"Do not lie to me!" Vasco shook her again, and this time, she winced.

"You have my word!"

"One night," he said. He cursed in a slew of Italian that was indecipherable to me. "We lay together one night, centuries ago. How can this be true?" He searched her face as if he'd find the answers there.

"Sì," she said, and then responded in more Italian than I could catch.

Bloody hell. At least now I knew that the witches were long-lived as well and that Vasco had been with her a long time ago. Possibly before he'd even been turned.

In my mind, Cuinn opened his long snout, his tongue curling slightly. He yawned as if the whole thing bored him.

The two exchanged more fervent words until Vasco had a white-knuckled death grip on her shoulders.

"Why?" he asked, his eyes were alight with the question. "Why did you never tell me this thing?"

"We were not meant to be, Vasco. You made that abundantly clear. I sought only to spare your son the knowledge of your disgrace."

Vasco hissed through his fangs and abruptly shoved Savina back. She stumbled but did not seek to defend herself. She didn't need to.

He turned his back on her and his long hair fell over his face like a curtain.

I went to him then. "Vasco," I said gently.

Pain. So much sorrow. I didn't think Savina knew how much her unkindness wounded him, how much the keeping of such a secret hurt him. So many years had passed and he had never known that he had a son. I touched his wrist lightly as I tried to bring his attention to me. He ignored me as if I was not there.

I moved around him, for he was taller than I, and though he was slender, my point was not likely to come across as well hiding behind Vasco.

I glared at Savina. "You're a fool."

"You would say that, vampire. You who are one of *them.*"

I drew my lips back in a snarl that revealed fang. A cool hand touched my arm, and I met Vasco's bright eyes. He turned to Savina.

"But my titles, my estates, my inheritance," he said, "all those were good enough to keep, good enough for your impoverished family. But not good enough for me to be in my son's life."

An icy prickle of calm went through Vasco. I didn't know if it was some trick of his powers or simply that I became more aware, but it seemed even his touch on my arm grew colder.

"You always were a privileged snob," she said. "It does not surprise me that you would throw such a thing in my face."

"If you knew an ounce about the man that stands before you, you wouldn't say things like that." I stepped toward her, and the only thing that stopped me was Vasco's icy grip on my arm.

"Of course you would not see it," she said and then added a couple of Italian words I didn't recognize. She waved a hand in the air at Vasco and me. "You are very much alike."

"If you're going to insult me," I said, "at least have the courage to do it in a language I understand."

"*Whore*," she began, but before she could finish, Vasco's sword rang from its sheath in a song of steel.

The tip of his blade was suddenly beneath Savina's chin, denting the tender skin.

"Watch your tongue when speaking to her. Epiphany is more of a lady than you ever will be."

A wave of anger washed from Savina as she glared over the sword at him.

"If you're going to draw blade on me, you'd be wise to use it," she said, her voice low.

Vasco sheathed his sword in a practiced move.

An expression of triumph settled across Savina's features.

"We are done here," Vasco said. "You have overstayed your welcome."

She didn't like that. "You still need my help," she said.

"If this is how you repay a favor in kind, then no. We are better off without it."

"You'll not find your vampire without me."

"You said you would not help us and I tire of these games, Savina."

I shook my head, drawing Vasco's attention.

"What is it, colombina?"

"After all these years, she still wants you to need her, Vasco."

"I do not," Savina lied.

"You're lying to yourself, lady. Aye, you do. You don't like that Vasco is sending you off. You want him to beseech you, and he won't. If you truly knew him, you would know that."

"Of course he would not," she said snidely. "You were always too good for that, weren't you, Vasco?"

Renata said, "Anatharic."

"Yes?"

"Would you kindly see to it that the witch Savina is returned safely to her homeland?"

When Anatharic approached her, Savina backed away from him with a look of disgust and distrust.

"I can find the way myself."

"Then by all means," Renata said, eyes blossoming with power. "Do so. Sooner, rather than later."

"Are you threatening me?"

She stood. "Your services are no longer required."

Savina cast a look to Vasco. "You'll need me," she said, believing her own words. "Before all this is over, Vasco, you'll need my aid again. Remember that when you come crawling back on your knees for it."

In the blink of an eye, she was gone, leaving no trace that she'd ever been with us.

No trace, except for the sorrow emitting off Vasco's tall frame. I touched his arm. "Are you well, my brother?"

He relaxed a fraction under my hand. "As well as I can be, colombina."

"She meant to unsettle you, Vasco."

"I know."

"Do not let her. It makes no difference now."

He shook his head with something close to regret in him. "It makes all the difference, Epiphany. My own flesh and blood is out there somewhere."

"Will you try to find him?"

If Vasco decided to try to seek out his son, if Renata granted him permission to do so, it was a dangerous task to undertake.

Vasco said aloud what I had fairly much been thinking. "It would be dangerous to leave the sanctuary of the Sotto."

"It would, but there is a way, my Silver Prince, if you decide that finding your son is something you must do," Renata said.

"Even then," Vasco said, "there is the danger of being mistaken as Il Deboli."

"Yes."

"I will think on it."

"Simply let me know when you decide. The Cacciatori can ride out with you. That should greatly diminish the risk." Renata inclined her head to indicate the conversation was over, at least for the moment.

It wasn't a bad idea. The Cacciatori were the only vampires allowed to venture outside the walls of the Sotto, but they did not often venture outside the vicinity of Renata's rule. It was rare that any Cacciatori traveled on lands not ruled by their ruler. If it was to be done, it could be, as clans were not allowed to be at war with one another, but safe passage somehow had to be established.

"Now what are we going to do?" I asked.

"The Elders should be awake now," Vasco said.

"So they should," Renata said. "Vito, Vittoria."

They stepped forward in unison.

"Yes, m'lady?" Vittoria asked.

"Gather the Elders."

❖

We left the banquet hall for the Underlings that required sustenance and met instead in Renata's private sitting room. We drank the blood of the Donatore from a heated earthenware pitcher. As there was no electricity in the Sotto, the pitcher sat on a stand above a dancing flame to keep its contents warm. Renata sat in her chair, her long legs crossed while she idly nursed her glass.

Severiano downed his glass and reached for the pitcher to pour himself another. It was a task that, had an Underling been present, would've been required of them.

A task I once would've been required to do.

But my days as an Underling had passed. Though the chair brought close to Renata's was more modest in appearance, I sat beside her now and not on the floor at her feet.

Severiano's hawk-like features drew quizzical, as if he wanted to ask a question. Smartly, he didn't. He waited for Renata to proceed with explanations.

And whilst we waited in silence, Gaspare shot darts at me with his eyes. He'd become incredibly fond of doing that.

Vasco handed me a glass and I took it, sipping the restored life of the Donatore. It tasted no different, which surprised me somehow. It seemed like being terribly dismembered should have some effect.

"Dante is missing," Renata said at last.

"Missing how?" Lorrenzo asked. Alessandra placed a hand idly on his thigh in what appeared to be a warning of sorts. Both were quite afraid when it came to Renata. Then again, both had seen what she was capable of.

I looked to Gaspare. I couldn't help myself. He had been publicly tortured by Renata for openly attacking me in court when I was undergoing the trials to become an Elder. He glared at me.

Unfortunately, age does not always result in maturity.

They were still not happy, those Elders who had voted against me. Rosabella kept sparing glances at Anatharic and Iliaria, who stood on the outside edges of the room, both a part of and apart from the conversation. Vito and Vittoria had taken up the long couch to dine, for they too needed to feed.

In a calm voice, Renata explained the day's events, making an idle gesture with her hand as she beckoned Dominique to step forward and explain his side of what had transpired.

Rosabella raised her brows when he was finished. "And this comes as a surprise to you, Padrona? Your own pet keeps one of *them* in her bed."

I felt Iliaria stir behind me and move toward the center of the room closer to where we sat. Renata raised a pale hand to halt her.

"Remember your place among the Rosso Lussuria, Rosabella," Renata said dangerously. "I am queen here, not you." She tilted her head slightly. "Or do you need reminding?"

"I do not need reminding, Padrona."

"So I thought." Renata turned away. "Severiano, my huntsman, gather the Cacciatori. We know not yet where they've taken Dante, but we will discover."

Severiano placed his empty glass on the table and slipped from his seat to his knees. "As my queen wills." He bowed his head in a measure of respect.

"You really suppose we'll find him using the Cacciatori? For centuries, the Cacciatori have only hunted human prey," Lorrenzo said.

Severiano raised his head then, his gaze keen and alert, his features as sharp and stoic as the bird of prey they mimicked. "You doubt my abilities, brother?"

"Powers not used develop rust."

Renata stood and everyone in the room fell silent. Sognare, who hadn't said a word the entire time, began paying more attention to her, his thin lips drawn in a tight line above his long beard.

"By all means," Renata said, "if you wish to argue, do so amongst yourselves, but do not let it distract you from the task at hand, gentlemen. You are Elders and Cacciatori, and you've prey to hunt."

"I will go with them," Alessandra said.

"And I." Vasco nodded.

Nirena took a long sip of her drink. She arched a pale brow when everyone turned to her. "Is it really a question?"

So it was decided. Rosabella did not offer to go, which didn't surprise me. Gaspare enlisted himself as part of the hunting party, and Sognare did not offer to go. With his gray hair and wrinkled skin, he appeared to be the oldest among us, and though he was vampire, Sognare's powers were more of the mental variety. I had never known him to be much of a physical fighter.

When the Rosso Lussuria established the Sotto on American soil, the area was chosen carefully. We were near enough to the humans to hunt them, should we ever need to, and far enough away not to be noticed. For decades, the Delisle family had tended to the nearby stables we used when we needed to go into the human world.

The vampires that rode out as the Cacciatori were Elders and old enough to remember the world when horseback was the preferred method of travel.

I should know, for it was how they had taken me.

All Elders, aside from Vasco, left to prepare for the hunt. Dominique, being Renata's guard, would stay with us.

Something doesn't feel right, Cuinn.

Aye, he said, *I feel it too.*

If the Dracule can travel between the realms with the same ease the Stregha have, surely, our chances of finding Dante are slim.

That is what I reckon. I've been trying to understand, Epiphany. They attack your Donatore, your food stores, and your queen's guardsmen...

What do you think?

In my mind, Cuinn offered a fox's equivalent of a shrug, his head dipping below the line of his shoulder blades.

I think they're targeting your queen. Think about it, he said.

I'm bloody trying! But it doesn't make sense, Cuinn. None of this does. They did not harm Dominique. Why would they take Dante?

Bait.

I turned to find the face that went with that voice. Renata touched my hand. She covered my palm with hers.

Bait, Epiphany.

Out loud, I said, "Vasco, don't go."

"I have to," he said, his gaze compassionate. "It is my duty, Epiphany. I am the best swordsman among the Rosso Lussuria. I must go."

"You needn't go if it's a trap."

"If we have any hopes of uncovering Dante's whereabouts, I must."

I stood too abruptly. "You've known all along that this is a trap?"

"I will go with them to even the ssscore," Anatharic said. He crawled around the side of the couch so that I could have a better view of him. Though, as large as the Dracule were, both in human and their more animal form, they were hard to miss with or without furniture in front of them.

"And I will stay here, with you and your queen." A hand touched my shoulder. Iliaria's touch sent a tendril of warmth tingling down my arm to hum in the flowing black lines of her mark.

I felt like a fool. How could I have not seen it? But how could we be so certain it was a trap?

'Tis the only thing that makes sense, Piph. Like as not, they'll expect your queen to be among the hunting party.

"And if they don't, Cuinn? What if they expect Renata to be here?" I turned to her. "Why do we not ride out with them, then? Surely, the higher our numbers, the better?"

"You think in terms of war, Epiphany. One must think strategically. The Dracule are a strategic lot, as you've seen. We mustn't show our hands too soon," Iliaria said.

"She is a vampire queen, Epiphany, not a human king that holds the front lines charging into battle. Part of the reason we are Elders is to be the first line of defense for the clan," Vasco said. "For our queen. If we die, the queen must carry on for the rest of the clan."

"Anatharic will stay close to him," Iliaria said.

Anatharic turned his feline face to her. "Ssshe can sssummon me ssshould anything happen."

Renata touched my wrist and her fingers circled my skin like silken shackles. "Our options are sorely limited, cara mia. If it is a trap, walking into it is the only way to find out."

I sighed heavily and fell back into my chair.

Inamorato or no, Renata was queen, and I had little say when it came to her decisions.

"What would make any of you think we'd find them in the human world in the first place?" I grumbled.

It was Iliaria who said, "They'll be waiting for our move. They attacked your humans in hopes of destroying them all and forcing your hand to hunt."

"And so we wait here, twiddling our thumbs, while the others put their lives at risk?"

"No," Vasco said, "you wait here where you are safe."

"I take it if I ask, I can't go?"

"Would you really leave me?" Renata asked.

I gazed at her for several long moments. I knew what she intended with her words and they hit their mark.

I couldn't leave her alone, not after what had happened earlier. "No."

Renata touched a stray curl of my hair and tucked it behind my ear in tender affection. "You are my consort," she whispered. "What makes you think you would not be valuable to the Dracule were they to get their hands on you?"

"Indeed," Iliaria said. "If I was to lure you out to expose yourself, taking your consort would be one way to do such a thing."

"So you see, Epiphany, you, as well, must remain under guard."

"Well, I don't like it."

"And you think I do?" Renata asked, continuing to toy with my hair in a distracting manner. She wound a spray of it around her finger and tugged lightly. "This is what it means to be a ruler," she said almost idly, tracing the side of my neck, "with every crown comes the weight of it."

"Under these circumstances," Iliaria knelt before me, her gaze intense and sincere, "a ruler must remain idle and protected."

"While the Elders risk themselves in a silly ploy that we're not even sure will work," I said.

"They know what they risk, Epiphany."

"What some of them risk." I shook my head, thinking of those Elders who had not volunteered to travel among the Cacciatori's band.

"Let the court deal with them," Renata said. "They know they will not be held in high esteem for their lack of action."

Vasco came to me then. He took my hands in his as he knelt before me. "Do you lack confidence in me, sorella?"

"No, Vasco. I care for your safety, though."

"Then believe me when I tell you I will return to you." He grinned wickedly. "You tasted my memories once. You know what I am capable of."

It was true that I had once tasted Vasco's memories. He'd given them to me as a gift before I'd dueled with Gaspare, for he was a far better swordsman than Gaspare. It was rumored he was the best among the Rosso Lussuria. With the Wall of Swords available at our disposal, it said something of his skill, for most of the Elders knew some sword work.

It soothed me, but only somewhat. The knowledge that Damokles had evaded capture not once, but twice now, was still there.

I nodded, having nothing more to say, at least, nothing that would've been a comfort to him.

Vasco rose when the door to Renata's private sitting chambers opened. Severiano bowed his head. "All is ready, Padrona."

"I will return." He stooped to kiss my cheek. "I promise."

With that, he left to join the Cacciatori. Silently, I prayed to whatever Gods listening that his promise was one he would keep.

CHAPTER FOUR

I am a lover, not a fighter, as the saying goes. Silly as it may sound, I have seen the midst of battle. I have heard the ringing of steel on steel and seen the faces of treachery and rage. I have seen the blood of conflict anoint swords and pool from bodies.

I have watched the light slip from a traitor's eyes while I thrust a sword through his heart and found that there is little in killing that pleases me.

But sitting in Renata's bedchambers, I did not know which was worse: battle or the tedium of waiting. Time seemed to have slowed to a crawl. The Cacciatori would return before sunrise; in that, they had little choice. Exactly when before sunrise was a mystery.

I shut my eyes. If they did not return by sunrise, it would indicate that something had gone terribly wrong with their plan.

"Epiphany," Renata called to me. She took a seat at the circular glass table. "Bring the board and pieces."

I reacted mostly out of instinct, rising from her great bed and opening the wooden cabinet doors to retrieve the game. I set about setting it up, grateful to have something to do, even if it was nothing more than a minor distraction from my worry.

I caught Iliaria watching me with an expression of perplexity.

Renata gestured for me to sit and we began to play. Iliaria moved closer to watch over my shoulder as Renata moved a milky white playing piece closer to mine. She took her time about it, seeming to have an endless patience with the game. She always did.

There was no way I was going to win. I never did, unless she let me, but I certainly had improved in the years that we'd been playing.

Renata had always told me I was too quick to sacrifice pieces. Much of the time, my attention wavered and I cared little about winning. This game, I was not so impulsive. I completely submerged myself in the distraction it provided.

Iliaria placed a hand on my shoulder when I was about to place my crystal knight on a square on the playing board.

"You are cheating, Dracule," Renata said, offering a half smile.

Whether Iliaria was trying to guide my attention or not, Cuinn took the opportunity to help me out.

Wrong move, Piph. Try the rook.

I saw it then, Renata's white bishop perfectly aligned to seize my knight.

I took his advice, using my rook to eliminate the threat.

"Cheating?" Iliaria asked. "How so?"

Renata narrowed her eyes knowingly.

"Three against one?" she asked. "That is how you intend to play this game, is it?"

I mumbled a quick apology and she laughed.

Renata leaned back in her chair with a look of challenge and mischief. "By all means," she motioned toward the board, "consult your counsel." She inclined with a wicked smile. "If you think you will win against me, Epiphany."

You willing to test that, o'queen ?

Renata mused, "How shall we sweeten the reward, hmm? What does the victor of this game receive?"

"What do you want?" I asked.

She touched my cheek and heat rose to my face. "Mmm, well, I already have you. That leaves little to ask for, doesn't it?"

I swallowed around my echoing pulse. "What you mean is that I'm already willing to do anything you ask of me, thus you have little to achieve by beating me in a game of chess other than a certain sense of satisfaction?"

She gave a sweetly cutting smile. "Precisely."

"Finding a reason to retreat?" Iliaria asked, a tinge of teasing in her tone.

"No," Renata said. "I will play a game against the three of you. We'll merely decide upon a boon at a later time. Agreed?"

"Agreed," Iliaria said.

I thought Renata would ask to begin the game anew, but she did not. We played against her, the three of us, and it turned out to be quite a lengthy game. Cuinn and Iliaria began doing most of the work. One would think of a party of three against one that the larger party would have the upper hand. We didn't, considering Iliaria and Cuinn were at odds with each other every time our turn came. When I took Cuinn's advice, Iliaria complained. When I took Iliaria's advice, Cuinn cursed up a storm until my ears rang.

Renata sat in her chair, thoroughly amused as our mess unraveled while she took piece after piece until our king was left with little defense.

In the end, she won as she had predicted.

And I daresay, out of the three of us, Cuinn was the least happy about it. He rambled off in my head about *if only ye'd done this* and *if only ye'd done that.*

Take comfort in the knowledge that whatever boon she asks will be of me, not you, Cuinn.

With that, he ceased.

After our game, time crept by sluggishly again. I sighed, returning to recline in Renata's bed while she and Iliaria conversed in hushed voices. They spoke of the Dracule. Iliaria suspected Damokles was trying to assemble a following among them, if he hadn't done so already, and that the Rosso Lussuria was but one of the many clans he was targeting.

"If that's true, then surely we should find out for ourselves if any of the other clans have had similar experiences or attacks?" I said.

"Indeed, cara mia. You are correct. We should endeavor to find out if this is simply an affront to our clan or vampires as a whole." She rose to open the door to a small cabinet nearby and retrieved a leather case from inside. She opened it and unraveled the scroll within, spreading it across the table.

I had no idea how we would go about such a thing, for clans in general had very little contact with one another. That's not to say that we were at cross-purposes, only that we tended to keep to ourselves. I was again uncertain as to how safe passage would be established.

Renata spoke, reading my thoughts. "Under certain circumstances, a ruler is allowed to move between the clans and seek sanctuary if they need to do so."

"So you couldn't send an ambassador?" I asked. "You would have to go yourself?"

"Yes."

"If Anatharic and I were to take you to visit one of the clans, would you be allowed to assemble a small party?"

"According to our laws, yes. So long as I am present and have reasonable cause, they cannot declare us Il Deboli." She shook her head. "But it is difficult to predict the outcome of these things. I cannot say with utmost certainty how another ruler will react."

"Still," Iliaria said, "it might be worthy of the try. Anatharic and I can carry a few of you and move easily between the realms. It would be best to keep our numbers as small as possible, not only to keep the threat of attention at a minimum but to assure that we can evade capture if we need to."

"How many can you carry at a time?"

"Effortlessly?" She seemed to think about it for a moment. "Two at the most. I'd say three, but I will not be as quick carrying three bodies."

"Do you suppose Anatharic will agree to it?"

"Yes."

"Then it's settled," Renata said. "Come the next nightfall, we'll leave for Bull Shoals and request an audience with their king."

They began discussing who would accompany us to meet with the clan of Bull Shoals. The scroll on the table turned out to be a hand drawn parchment map. Though it was old, it was accurate, indicating the numerous vampire clans speckled throughout the

American continent. The clan of Bull Shoals was some miles from the Arkansas-Missouri border. It was the closest clan to our own, and judging by the guide marks on the map, it was located in the midst of the Ozark Mountains.

"Great," Iliaria said, "they're located in a tourist attraction."

"Yes and no," Renata said. "The lake resort is here." She turned the map, tapping it with the tip of her lacquered nail. "The clan itself was established many years before ours and is located in a set of caverns the humans have never and will never discover."

At that, Iliaria raised her brows skeptically.

Renata smiled slowly. "We are not the first clan to have used the aid of the Stregha centuries ago. The pathway and entrance to the caverns is terribly difficult to find, let alone navigate to gain admittance."

"Being so close to a resort poses an opportunity to their hunters, I imagine."

"It does."

No doubt, many a soul had gone missing while wandering their campgrounds at night.

"If I am to carry you there, I will need specifics. Do you know where the entrance is?"

"Yes."

"You will have to guide me, lest we end up on a cliff edge."

"Ah," Renata mused, carefully rolling the map and sliding it back into its leather case. "That is where we will need to be if we are to gain entry."

"This sounds a bit precarious, my lady."

She shrugged. "It is the only way that I can perceive."

"Do you know their ruler?" Iliaria asked.

"Yes and no."

"What does that mean?" I asked.

She placed her hand over mine, her eyes like dark sapphires in the flickering candlelight. "I met Augusten centuries ago, very briefly, before he left Roma to establish the clan here. I have not had any association with him since."

There was a stumbling sound on the other side of the bedroom door. Renata and I looked at each other before Dominique's voice filtered through.

"Padrona, they have returned."

Renata did not raise her voice when she said, "Let them in."

Dominique opened the door and Anatharic entered the room, standing to all his great height on his hind legs. He carried something swathed in a cloak in his arms.

Renata stood without hesitation and made her way toward him.

"Place him on the bed."

Anatharic did so as the others began to spread out through the room. Nirena's white-blond hair was speckled and matted with blood. A cut on her cheek had healed, but where the cut had been, the blood was just beginning to dry.

Vasco strode into the room behind the others. A few specks of drying blood decorated his brow and cheeks too.

My heart soared with relief. He smiled and came to me.

He wrapped an arm around me and murmured. "I keep my promises."

I touched his hand when he drew back. "I'm glad you do."

I turned my attention from him and the others and to the still figure laid out on Renata's bed. She sat beside the figure and ran a hand through his dark red hair. Renata murmured his name and my chest tightened.

"They bound him to a tree so that he would burn come sunrise, my queen," Nirena said. "He had been tortured when we found him."

"You were right to bring him back," Renata said and I could feel her closing down as she put a steady hand over her emotions.

She unwrapped the cloak from around him and revealed his bare torso. His chest was lined with old blood and numerous cuts, some deeper than others.

In the middle of his chest was a larger cut, a cut shaped into an unmistakable X. I had once worn the same X between my shoulder blades.

The room turned in my vision, and Vasco caught my elbow when my knees gave out from under me.

"Renata," I said, feeling the blood I'd drunk earlier spin uncomfortably in my stomach.

"I must try to heal him, Epiphany."

Vasco pulled me to my feet and held me close to his chest. I let him without protest. I let him comfort me while a sense of dread continued to unfurl within me.

Neither Vasco nor Renata addressed the sense of my dread or its cause, but I could feel empathically that they too felt it. They too thought about it and had an inkling of what that mark cut into Dante's chest meant.

While Renata tried to heal Dante, I wondered how it could be possible. Surely, Lucrezia could not be alive out there somewhere. Renata had executed her, she had taken her heart and head. She had left nothing salvageable of her body.

Witches, Cuinn muttered, *always playing with darker magics than they should.*

Renata lowered her shields and the room crackled with her energy like a biting wind. Slowly, she narrowed that energy, shaping it and driving it none-too-gently into Dante. I let Vasco's tall frame ground me against the tide of emotions that swelled within me.

I pray it is not true.

Aye, Cuinn's ears flattened behind my closed lids. *But 'tis better to be well prepared of the possibility than to deny and live in ignorance. A danger foreseen is half avoided.*

A ragged breath shattered the silence and Dominique and Anatharic were suddenly beside the bed to help restrain Dante and keep him from thrashing about.

Renata stepped away with something akin to defeat. Dante's green eyes were wild and completely unlike him. There was nothing recognizable in his gaze. He bared his teeth at Vito and Vittoria when they approached to help and then he began to scream, a high-pitched and panicked sound that vibrated inside my ears and made me wince.

It was then I knew that Dante's captors had broken his mind.

❖

We learned from those who had ridden out among the Cacciatori that they had ridden hard through the woods in pursuit of a cloaked figure, presumably one of the witches that had been working with the Dracule. The cloaked figure had led them to Dante, bound by silver chains to a large tree.

It had been a trap, an ambush. Severiano recounted three Dracule. With Anatharic's help, they'd fought them into retreat. Damokles had not been among them.

"Scouts," Iliaria said. "If they retreated, they were scouts, nothing more."

"Why set an ambush only to retreat?" Vasco asked.

To that, Iliaria shrugged. "Your guess is as good as mine. Perhaps he is biding his time and testing the abilities of your warriors."

"Or he's preoccupied doing something else," I said.

No one disagreed with me.

Dante had been taken to a holding cell, for his protection as well as the protection of the other clan members. With his mind so broken, none of us knew what he would do. Renata could heal him bodily, but she could not repair the damage done to his wits. We could only hope that with time, he would awaken from his madness.

Lorrenzo shifted where he sat on the sofa beside Allesandra. He hissed through his teeth when he moved his leg as if it pained him.

"You are injured," Iliaria said.

"Show us," Renata said.

Lorrenzo raised the leg of his breeches to reveal the nasty gash along the length of his calf muscle. Iliaria knelt to inspect the wound and he backed up as far as his seat would allow.

"You have a Draculian barb in your leg. If we do not remove it, it will not heal."

"I thought your barbs were toxic?" Renata asked.

"The skin sheathing the barb is," she said, probing his wound despite his fear of her and making him wince. "Luckily, the Dracule missed and did not get a fatal shot. Anatharic, I need your assistance."

Anatharic unfolded his wings from around his body and knelt with her.

"Hold him down," she said to Allesandra.

Allesandra obliged while Iliaria and Anatharic set about removing the barb from Lorrenzo's calf. Anatharic used the tips of his claws to slice the wound open wider and Iliaria plunged her fingers into the wound to find the implanted barb. Lorrenzo protested, but let Allesandra hold him down.

"This is going to hurt," Iliaria warned him, as if her digging in the wound hadn't, and then she jerked her hand back. Blood flowed in a rivulet down Lorrenzo's leg and he screamed, but Iliaria had already pulled free the barb. She held up a sharpened spine longer than my hand.

"Would you like to see?"

I moved closer to her, because honestly, I did. She handed the barb to me and I examined it, tracing the bloody length. Beneath the blood, the barb was as white as bone. It sharpened at the tip like a dagger. Tiny teeth traveled down the length of it to a widened base.

"There is no way to pull it out delicately," she said. "Once embedded in the skin, it is a snug fit." She indicated the direction of the serrations. "It cuts and tears flesh on its way out, no matter how you pull it."

"I see that."

"So it is only lethal if it is a mortal wound?" Vasco asked.

"Yes, the toxin can kill a vampire if the blow is to the heart."

"That is useful to know," he said.

Iliaria took the barb from me. "It's no longer toxic, as it's no longer attached and the skin sheath has already been broken."

"May I keep it?" I asked and everyone in the room gave me an odd look at the question. Iliaria shrugged and handed the barb back to me. It was fascinating, though I couldn't put my finger on why.

"What will happen to the Dracule?" Lorrenzo asked.

"In regards to the loss of the barb?"

He nodded.

"Another will grow back."

She sighed and tossed aside the long train of her brocaded coat. The Draculian attire, when they wore it, was a combination of both modern and outdated. It was specifically tailored to fit their bodies, at least Iliaria's was. The back had perfectly stitched openings to give her wings freedom. Her tail, on the other hand, was usually hidden beneath folds of fabric.

She pulled back the slightly spaded tip of her tail to expose a barb much longer and sharper than the one that had been thrust into Lorrenzo's leg.

Vasco gave a low whistle. "That's a great deal larger than the other."

"I'm older," she said as if that explained everything. In a way, it did.

"I hadn't known that the size of the barb was dependent on age."

"Now you do," she said and sent her tail flicking back beneath the folds of her coat.

She stood. "You should bind the wound to prevent further blood loss. You may feel some symptoms of the toxin, but your body will heal now that the barb has been removed."

Lorrenzo looked a bit out of sorts but acknowledged with a nod that he was listening and understood. Even if he hadn't understood, Allesandra paid rapt attention to Iliaria's instructions.

Renata dismissed the Elders, all save Vasco, who reclined at ease on the sofa with his long legs crossed at the ankles.

"What a night," he said, almost as if he were talking to himself.

"There is more, I'm afraid."

He fixed me with a questioning gaze and I looked at Renata for permission to speak. She gave it, with a slight nod.

"We've been discussing matters, and it's been decided that we'll travel with Iliaria's and Anatharic's help and approach the King of Bull Shoals."

At that, Vasco appeared somewhat surprised.

"Truly, my lady?"

"Truly," Renata said. "I believe it is the only way for us to uncover whether or not Damokles and his toadies are targeting vampires as a whole or simply our clan."

Vasco swung his legs to the floor and leaned forward. He propped his elbow on his knee, resting his chin on his hand. "Not that I disagree with you, my queen, but how do you suppose the king will take our arrival at his gates?"

At that, Renata raised her thin shoulders. "I've no idea."

"If we do not take that many, we will be able to evade capture even from the king if necessary," Iliaria said. She asked Anatharic, "Do you have any qualms about this?"

"No."

"Who will you send?" Vasco asked.

"It is more a question of who I will take," Renata said.

Vasco's eyes were filled with calculation. "Do you think it wise to risk yourself?"

"Wiser than sending an ambassador, yes."

"You believe the King of Bull Shoals will honor our laws?"

"I do," she said, "unless he has changed that much in a few centuries."

"Not an easy call, my lady."

All of us agreed with him.

They finished discussing matters and Renata appointed Vasco to choose who he would take among the Elders. He gave the question some thought.

"Vito and Vittoria have skills better suited for defending the clan," he said. "They are some of our strongest fighters, but I think, my lady, given their loyalty, they're the ones you would want to leave behind to protect your throne."

Wordlessly, Renata encouraged him with a nod to continue.

"Severiano is a good huntsman," I added.

Vasco shook his head. "A good huntsman and a bad politician, he doesn't have the patience for it. Nirena," he said. "Nirena is politically savvy and a good fighter."

"Then we will take her with us," Renata said. "We will leave for the clan of Bull Shoals next sundown and see just how deeply this threat goes."

"What about Dante?" I asked. "The mark?"

"The mark does not necessarily mean anything, cara mia. I know you fear the worst, but many cuts happen during a torture session."

"So you believe it is purely coincidental, my lady?"

"I do not know," she said, surprising me a little with her candidness. For a moment, I feared she would deny my fears altogether.

"Do you think it's her?"

Renata's features softened with sympathy. "I cannot say. The hand of logic would prompt me to decline the idea, but at the same time it encourages me to consider the possibilities. The Dracule have been working with witches, and though I think the chances incredibly slim, cara mia, I will not deny it altogether."

"Thank you," I said.

She reached for me and I took her hand. She gave my hand a reassuring squeeze. "We can but wait and see what strands unravel, my love."

"Sì," Vasco said. "The unfortunate way of politics, sorella. One step at a time, a lot of watching and waiting."

I sighed. "I hate bloody politics."

Chapter Five

As sunrise drew near, Vasco, Vittoria, and Vito decided to bunk in my bedroom. My room was closer to Renata's bedchamber than the Elders' sleeping quarters and more accessible if we needed them. Technically, Renata's room was the safest in the Sotto, and though Iliaria and Anatharic could travel quickly by their own means, everyone agreed it was a more convenient location if I personally had to wake the others.

Renata wanted me to wake her after the sun rose.

She had not chosen another guard. At Iliaria's behest, Anatharic stayed in the sitting room off of Renata's boudoir. Dominique hadn't liked the fact that Renata hadn't chosen another guard. Dante was like a brother to him and I could tell, though he hid it, that he worried for him. But Renata was his queen and he worried for her as well. His worry dropped a few notches when Anatharic agreed to keep vigil at Iliaria's request.

It struck me as odd, how compliant Anatharic seemed to be toward her. I decided to ask about it when I wasn't so overwhelmed with everything else.

"Epiphany," Renata beckoned to me from her great bed.

I went to her and when she drew me close, I rested my head on her shoulder and reveled in the feel of her, of feeling sheltered in the circle of her arms.

"Dracule," Renata said, bringing my attention to the fact that Iliaria stood watching us from the center of the room. "Will you join us?"

"Is that a request?"

"Please," I murmured, "don't start quarrelling. There's been quite enough of that this day. Come to bed, Iliaria."

"Is that what you want, Epiphany?"

"Yes, that's what I want. If I didn't want it, I wouldn't have asked. This silliness must stop. I don't have the patience for it. I want to lie between the two of you, to feel safe and protected and loved. So get over here and stop it."

Iliaria merely blinked at me.

I let out a breath of air in a huff to show my impatience. Renata's laughter came slowly, trickling softly throughout the candlelit room.

"Well," Iliaria finally said, "when you ask so kindly. How can I decline?"

I snuggled into Renata's luscious form and buried my face in the bend of her neck. The bed dipped as Iliaria crawled in behind me. She laid her body against mine and her arm slipped around my waist under Renata's.

Well played, Piph, Cuinn said with a victorious smirk.

Cuinn…

Aye, aye, I know, he grumbled. *During vampire cuddling time, bugger off.*

His words were enough to make me chuckle aloud. Renata drew back enough to look at me.

"You seem to be in good spirits, considering."

"Well, it is *vampire cuddling time,* according to Cuinn."

Iliaria snorted behind me while Renata smiled lazily and traced the line of my jaw with her fingertip. "We'll have all day to do this, cara mia."

I slipped my arm over her waist and began to trace tiny circles at the small of her back. "That sounds lovely."

"Mayhap we'll do more than cuddle, if your Dracule does not find it disagreeable?" Renata said with a baiting tone.

"I was upset with your timing, Queen."

"How is my timing now?" Renata asked. "Would today be a good time for you? Or would you prefer for us to spend the entire day bored and doing nothing more than waiting for an attack from your kinsmen?"

Iliaria's tail thumped the mattress as I sensed her agitation rise.

"Renata," I said softly.

"Hmm?"

"I think we should establish a rule that the bed is a quarrel free zone." Iliaria's tail twitched again and I added, "As much as either of you may dislike it."

"Perhaps that is a good idea," Iliaria said, her voice low and threatening.

"Do you think you can accomplish that, Dracule?"

"Renata," I said again.

"What, Epiphany? I am merely asking a question."

"You are baiting her, my lady."

This time, Iliaria's tail actually thumped my leg.

"If you keep your mouth closed, perhaps," Iliaria grumbled.

Renata laughed. "*Perhaps* if I find something to put in it, I will."

I blushed, though I was not certain why. I didn't think either of them realized they argued not so much because of their differences, but because of the ways in which they were very much alike. They were both proud and dominant, and neither was readily willing to submit or cede to the other.

Of course, I did not say such thoughts aloud. I didn't have to.

"I will not argue that," Renata said. "Your Dracule tries to impose her will on me by presuming I should think and act as she does."

Iliaria sat up, carefully drawing her wings back so that she didn't hit either of us with them. "And you are constantly testing me and trying to see how far you can push before you get a rise out of me."

I worked myself out from between them and started climbing out of bed.

"Epiphany, where are you going?"

"I'm going to take a bath whilst you two settle your differences."

Renata let me go. I left them both in her bed, arguing in hushed voices with each other about who started what and how they started it.

Women, Cuinn said, sounding as exasperated as I felt.

I really couldn't disagree with him.

❖

When I rose from the bath wrapped in a heavy linen towel, Iliaria and Renata had finally stopped arguing. I found Iliaria still in bed, reclining against the mound of pillows and seeming at ease next to Renata.

Renata's gorgeous features were slack and unmoving, dead as she was due to the time of day. I made to retrieve the fox blade and Iliaria brought me to a halt. "Wait."

"Yes?"

"Come here."

She'd removed the long coat she had been wearing earlier to reveal the fitted blouse and breeches underneath.

"It must be very difficult dressing," I said, making idle note of it.

Iliaria rose from the bed. As if she was not already tall enough, the slightly heeled boots made her even taller. She towered a good head above me.

"Dressing does take some assistance at times."

I moved behind her and found that tiny buttons traveled in two vertical lines down her back, beneath each of the openings for her wings.

She peered over her shoulder at me. "Many of the Dracule do not bother with much more than a cloak."

"Why do you?"

"I am not like many."

I touched the base of her tail and the seamed opening with a fingertip. She shuddered slightly under my touch.

"I need to wake Renata."

"Do you remember this morning when I told you I would ask you to do something you would not enjoy?"

I sensed a trap in her words, but failed to see what it was.

"Yes?" I asked, openly suspicious.

Iliaria was fast, mayhap faster than any vampire I'd known. She grabbed a handful of my hair and pulled me in tight against her body. The breath caught in my throat at the sudden contact.

"I want to take you while she sleeps." Her mouth slid hot across my cheek to whisper in my ear, "I want her to smell me on you when she wakes."

She held me pinned so tightly against her body that I felt the *Dragoste* between her legs stiffen in arousal against my belly. I breathed her name, but she did not release me.

"I told you I would find something you would not like and that I would ask it of you. You do not like the idea of disrespecting or angering your queen, do you?"

"No."

"But you will do it," she said and it was more of a statement than a question. She raised the linen sheet at my thighs. "You will do it for me, for our bargain?"

Piph, Cuinn said, *your queen's like to get her hackles up at this…*

Would she? Perhaps, but I did not think she would harm either of us for such a trespass. She would be heated, oh yes, but it was doubtful she would be angry enough to risk our alliance with the Dracule.

"Your answer, Epiphany? Will you consent or be forsworn?"

She put me in quite the predicament. On one hand, I had given her my word. What she asked of me was within my reach to give. On the other, she was true to hers and had found something that was not easy for me to give, for the consequences would swiftly follow. Renata did not have to cross the Dracule to punish me.

If I renege on my word, she will never forgive me.

Cuinn sighed heavily. *You're the one with the shovel.*

"I will not be forsworn," I said aloud.

Iliaria smiled widely enough to reveal the fangs on both her upper and lower jaw. Her obsidian-stroked gold eyes filled with lust and dark promise.

She pulled the towel off me, forcing me to stand nude before her. The warm candlelit air kissed my skin as my hair slapped in wet strands against my back. Iliaria unfastened her breeches and pushed me roughly to my knees on the stone floor.

"It took me a while to truly understand that you do not feign pleasure solely for another's enjoyment; you really do relish a firm hand."

Her grip in my hair twined tight, her nails digging into my scalp.

"I have held back," she said, her tone serious. "I will be no imitation of your queen, Epiphany, but I am Dracule, the first of your kind, and from henceforth, I will require the same courtesy and respect that you show to her. Pull them down."

I understood what she asked of me. I gripped the band of her pants and worked them down her tail and legs. She did not have to speak the orders to make her second request known. I had played such games with Renata for centuries and understood all too well what was expected of me.

Iliaria used the grip she had to hold me up high on my knees. I kissed the knot between her legs and flicked my tongue against her hard tip. She spaced her legs apart as much as the breeches around her ankles would allow. I licked her sex. The muscles in her arms tensed, echoing in the grip that held my hair.

Iliaria let out a groan when I took her into my mouth. She relied on the grip she had in my hair to control my movement, pushing and pulling me ever so slightly above her sex.

When she climaxed, she blessedly released my hair to avoid ripping it out with the force of her orgasm. Her hips twitched as she gripped my shoulders. The taste of her coated my mouth like sweet honey.

I started to move away when she hauled me up as if I weighed nothing.

"I did not say I was done," she growled.

Iliaria kicked off her boots and the material at her ankles and lay me down on the bed next to Renata. She nestled her lower body between my legs and rolled her hips forward to glide her sex across mine. She teased me with her body until she pressed herself more solidly against me and I struggled to remain passive and not roll my own hips with hers. Iliaria raised up on her hands and drew back slowly. Her sex clung to mine like a mouth. She rocked her hips lightly and I writhed beneath her.

Her hips rose and fell, gradually picking up the tempo. She clawed at the pillows behind me and slammed her body against mine in a way that was almost too much pleasure, almost too much pain. I screamed and she covered my mouth with hers, her tongue sliding hot and wet past my lips. Somewhere during the kiss and the harsh dance of her hips, she brought me to orgasm.

She spent herself and collapsed on top of me. Her wings fell flat, their span nearly wide enough to blanket the bed. Slowly, she raised back on her hands and arched her spine in a way that disconnected the union of our flesh. Her skin clung to mine, and as she eased off me, another noise escaped me and I clawed at her shoulders.

She rose to her knees and drew her wings in close. She made to climb off me and I touched her hip, tracing the sculpted curve.

"Wait." This time, I was the one that made the request.

She waited, watching me with those strange black and gold eyes. Without the tide of pleasure to overwhelm me, her mark at my wrist tingled when I touched her. I touched her anyway, tracing the smoothly muscled plain of her stomach and the skin that stretched perfectly over her hips. I lowered my hand to play in the velvety fur above her groin.

Iliaria's lashes fluttered in pleasure. "Did I hurt you?" she asked.

I laughed lightly. Renata would have never asked me such a question. She knew me well enough and how to read my body so adeptly that she did not have to.

"No," I said. "No, you did not hurt me, Iliaria. When will you realize that you do not have to hide from me?"

I slid my hands up her body until my palms were flat against her ribcage, beneath the swell of her breasts.

"I do not want to be her," she said, her voice hushed.

I knew what she meant. "You are not."

"I do not want to be your master."

"I did not ask you to come to my bed as my master."

"Then what do you want, Epiphany?"

"For you to be yourself."

"That is all?"

"What else would I want?" At that, she did not respond. She climbed off me, ignoring my hands on her body. She stood and wrapped her wings around her like a cloak.

"Wake your queen."

I retrieved the fox blade and cut a long wound in the open palm of my hand. I ignored the fiery rush of pain and went to Renata's still form on the bed. Iliaria helped open her mouth and I curled my hand into a fist.

The touch of Cuinn's magic unfurled within me like a tiny star, suffusing my limbs with warm energy. That warm glow dripped with every drop of blood that fell from my clenched fist.

Renata gasped the breath of life, her pupils nearly drowning in the topaz and sapphire flecks of her eyes. She sat up as Iliaria moved away from the bed. I waited patiently for Renata to gather herself and to come to her senses. It didn't take her long.

When her pupils returned to a normal size, I started to move away and Renata caught me by the wrist. "Epiphany?"

"I delayed her," Iliaria said before Renata could ask anything else.

I daresay Renata surprised us both with her reaction.

"Why?" she asked. "If it was only to have time alone together, you could have made a simple request for it."

"Epiphany struck a bargain with me earlier this day."

Renata turned to me. "Is that true, Epiphany?"

"Aye, it's true."

Renata appeared most interested. "And what was this *bargain*?"

I wasn't too keen on telling her, but she had asked, and she was my lover, so I did. If revealing our act in the bedchamber bothered her, not only did she not show it, she seemed to find it hard to believe.

"You would not allow her to pleasure you with her mouth?" Renata seemed as confused as I had been.

Since Iliaria did not bother to reply, I did. "That was the bargain," I said. "In order for me to please her with my mouth, she told me she would find something I would not like and ask me to do it."

Renata pulled me into her lap and snaked a long arm around my waist. Her dark expression made my pulse speed.

"Mmm, but you enjoyed being *delayed*, didn't you? And now I shall have to punish you for your insolence and for taking such great pleasure in going against my orders." Her lips moved against the sensitive skin of my neck and I shivered visibly.

"I'll leave," Iliaria said.

"On the contrary, I think you should stay, considering the role you played in her rebellion."

Renata buried a hand in my hair, but where Iliaria had held back, Renata pulled my head back roughly to expose the line of my neck. I gasped.

"Did you dominate her?"

"Yes."

"And she delighted in it?"

"Yes."

"So." Renata tugged harder on my hair, gradually bowing my spine until my breasts rose and fell like offerings with every breath I took. "Now you see that I do not abuse her. I do not do anything to her that she does not enjoy."

My body tightened with the need to feel her. Renata's breath was warm against my breast. She kissed me lightly and then sucked, taking me into the hot cavern of her mouth and teasing me on the cusps of her fangs. I groaned and she bit down, piercing my skin. She drew back to watch the blood as it trickled in a steady stream down my body.

"Correct, cara mia?"

"Yes."

If Renata hadn't had such a grip on my hair, I would have looked at Iliaria to see what expression she wore. As it was, I couldn't move.

Renata smiled darkly and used the arm she had around me and the hand she had in my hair to lift me. For a moment, I thought she was carrying me toward the bath, and then I realized, it was not so.

Renata yanked a tapestry down from the wall and pushed my back up against it. Her smile was both cruel and sweet.

"Raise your arms."

I did, without question or hesitation, and Renata clamped the silver shackles she kept hidden by the tapestry about my wrists. When she drew away, I was not left suspended, for which I was grateful. Though the shackles held my arms up high, my bare feet pressed against the floor.

Renata went to the armoire, pausing before opening it. "You should stay, Dracule."

Iliaria looked at me, desire and hunger in her gaze. She may not have wanted to be like Renata, but I saw in her the same dark craving. Chained to the wall, I was helpless, and something within her, I knew, enjoyed the sight of it.

And for the first time in the bedroom in what seemed ages, I felt a genuine flicker of fear.

It was not being shackled to the wall that brought about those stirrings. Renata would strip me of any guard I had before Iliaria, and I did not know how the Great Siren, who battled herself, would react. Was I afraid of Iliaria? In certain ways, I was afraid of them both.

Renata returned from the armoire with a dainty knife in her hand. She pressed the line of hard steel flat against my cheek.

"Do you remember this?"

I did, for it was the same blade that she used to cut me when we played even darker games, before she had cast me out for such a long time. Fear fluttered like tiny moths in my belly. She had cut me only once since I had returned to her bed. Once, and then only to erase the scar Lucrezia had carved into my flesh.

I shut my eyes, reminding myself that the game we were about to play was one of trust and consent. My voice trembled slightly, "Yes, my lady."

Iliaria said, "She is afraid."

"That is the point, Dracule."

Renata turned the knife in her hand, the sharp point of it tracing an invisible line down my cheek and following the curve of my jaw.

"Why would you subject her to this if you know she is afraid?"

Renata leaned in close and her breath was hot against my cheek. Her knife continued its steady descent, whispering softly across my skin, down over the beat of my pulse and neck.

"Are you afraid, Epiphany?"

"Yes, my lady."

It was true, I felt fear, but with it came the steady rush and hum of desire. The two feelings mingled inside of me, until I could not tell where one began and the other ended. They swam together in my veins like two leviathans in the deep, twisting and gliding, rippling and twining in an eternal dance.

Fear or desire? I could not discern which I felt more strongly.

Renata's blade danced over my chest, pricking my skin and making my nipples taut. The tip of it bit into the tender skin on the side of my breast and I gasped, jerking my arms involuntarily and making the shackles above me clink and sway. The pain was immediate and stinging. The area flooded suddenly with warmth. She cut me slowly, carefully, assuring that I felt every parting of skin. Blood trickled steadily in a descent toward my navel.

The candlelight blurred like a flickering star in my vision. I did not fight the pain. I exhaled and gave myself to it. The mastery of pain is not in the fighting of it, but in the acceptance of it, the surrender.

"I suggest you watch carefully, Dracule. As hard as you may try to understand her, you do not."

Renata took my nipple into her mouth. Her tongue played against me in lazy circles. She sucked gently, working me exquisitely and forcing my limbs and muscles to slacken as my body melted and surrendered to the pleasure she invoked. I felt the blade against my other breast. The flat steel slid back and forth to shadow the movement of her tongue.

"Please."

In perfect synchronicity, Renata bit down, catching me between her teeth, and the tip of the knife pricked me again. I cried out, falling even deeper into the wet darkness she summoned.

Renata kissed me gently, her mouth sealed against the side of my breast as she licked the blood from my skin, tracing the already knitted wound with her tongue. Her mouth followed the path of my blood as she drank it, though not once did she forget the knife in her hand. Its tip cut lightly over my hip when I forgot it, and I startled, jerking on my bonds again.

I spread my legs and rested my head back against the hard wall.

Renata nipped at the skin below my navel. "Are you ready, cara mia?"

The sweet flow of desire weighed heavy within me. I no longer felt the flicker of fear or the awkward fluttering of it in my belly. I felt calm at last. The two leviathans no longer struggled but became one as desire swallowed fear.

"Yes."

Renata did not ask me if I was sure. She took me at my word and began the game in earnest, cutting me over and over. At times, her blade was quick and dancing and I felt the pain after the initial cut. Other times, her hand was lingering and steady, so that I felt the creeping crawl of the blade as it parted my skin with aching sluggishness.

Always, she soothed me with her mouth, nursing and salving my wounds with her tongue and encouraging my desire to rise after its painful descent.

When she was done, I felt weightless and surreal, as if she had given me some sort of mind-altering drug. And I wanted her desperately.

"Her body is an instrument, Dracule, and like any instrument, you must learn to play it to truly hear the sweetest music it is capable of producing."

I heard the knife fall to the floor and knew she was done with it. Renata would not stop to put anything away. She would not risk snapping me out of the pleasant state of mind she had put me.

The tips of her fingers brushed the skin between my knees and I opened to her. She caressed me tenderly, exploring me effortlessly before easing inside me. I moaned as every muscle within me tightened at the coaxing of her hand.

Renata raised my thigh to her hip, and I used the shackles at my wrists to raise myself and lock my legs around her waist. She pressed me back against the wall and kissed me, deep and unhurried. The taste of my blood was everywhere inside her mouth. The rhythm of her hand mirrored her tongue as she penetrated me. She pushed into me as deep as she could go and withdrew slowly.

She pulled back, pausing for only a second to find the angle she wanted. Her thumb slid across me while her fingers worked inside me.

Her silken lips met mine again and I opened to her, moaning her name. When she brought me, it was a gentle and luxurious thing. I hung loosely, barely able to keep my legs locked around her hips.

Renata laughed and took me down.

"Please," I whispered.

"Please what, cara mia?"

I gave her a look to let her know I didn't believe she hadn't read my thoughts. She knew what I wanted.

"Very well, then," she said. "But I think now it is time your Dracule joins us."

Renata sat on the bed and held me in her lap. I kissed her neck, opening my mouth and sucking lightly. I felt more than saw Renata direct her attention to Iliaria.

"What say you?"

Iliaria echoed Renata's response to me. "Very well."

I felt Iliaria move up behind me before she drew aside my hair and her mouth moved at my shoulder, persuading me to moan against Renata's neck. Renata handed me off to Iliaria while she rose from the bed to remove her gown.

I touched Iliaria's face and pulled her mouth down to mine. She returned the kiss briefly, letting me feel the sweet drag of her fangs before drawing away from me completely.

"You will not hurt me." I searched her face, trying to understand why she had pulled away.

Iliaria gave no response aside from a blinking stare. Renata came to us, and for what seemed like several minutes, they stood, facing each other. Strangely, there was no tension between them, only a quiet knowing.

Renata trapped me between the two of them. She touched a dark lock of Iliaria's hair, and for a moment, I thought she would lean over me and kiss her.

Renata must've caught the image, for she startled and looked down at me with an expression of surprise. She laughed and placed her hand against the side of my face. "Cara mia, cara mia," she chided.

Iliaria may not have read my mind, but it wasn't hard to guess what I'd been thinking. She shook her head at me. "That would be a very bad idea." She held me against her as she moved toward the bed and crawled across it on her knees toward the middle.

Renata laughed again as she lay down beside me. She reclined on her side and propped her chin on her fist. "You do me an injustice, I think," she said to Iliaria.

"I am going to pretend you did not just say that."

"You do not believe that I could bring you pleasure?" Renata asked.

Iliaria's tail twitched and swayed.

"Renata…" I said.

Renata grinned widely enough to reveal her fangs. "Hush, dolce mia. If she was not so easy to tease, I would not do it."

Iliaria was a blur of movement. She straddled Renata and pinned her wrists to the bed with a victorious smirk.

Renata's eyes narrowed as she frowned and pushed against the hands that held her wrists. Iliaria used her upper body to apply more weight. "Do you really want to test your strength against mine?" Iliaria asked.

Renata pushed her arms up again and still only managed to gain a modicum of ground before Iliaria shoved her back down.

"You will lose," Iliaria said, "and I do not think you will enjoy that. You both wonder why I hold back. Do it," she said to Renata, "put your strength against mine. All of it."

Renata said, "No."

"Perhaps I should dominate you then, just to prove my point."

"You are more than welcome to try," Renata said. "But proving your physical prowess and strength does not mean you will dominate me."

Iliaria leaned in close and whispered, "Then perhaps I should seek your lover's aid, hmm?"

Renata laughed. "What makes you think, Great Siren, that Epiphany will help you?"

"Epiphany?"

"Eh?"

"What do you think?"

"Yes, what do you think, cara mia?"

What did I think? I wasn't sure.

"She is unsure, Dracule."

"And I think you underestimate her."

"I'm not quite sure what either of you are talking about," I admitted, aroused but aware of a dangerous undercurrent.

"It's a very simple question, my sweet."

"Well, I don't get it."

Renata gave Iliaria a look that said, "see, I told you so."

She tried to get up and Iliaria shoved her back down again.

"Do not be hasty. She has given neither of us an answer, unless, you are scared?"

"I am not scared of you, Dracule. Epiphany is not a dominant by nature. You cannot expect her to be what she is not."

"Give the girl a chance to speak for herself. What is your answer, Epiphany?"

"Let me see if I'm following you; you're asking me to dominate Renata? To help you dominate Renata?"

"Yes."

"I…" I looked at Renata. "What do you want, my lady?"

At my response, Iliaria stared at me with something close to exasperation.

"You really do not have any desire to be in control?"

"I'm not sure what you mean…to dominate? No, not really."

"You have no desire to have your wicked way with her while I hold her down?"

"Is that what you felt when I was chained to the wall?"

Iliaria's eyes darkened and her lashes fluttered as if the memory played inside her mind. "Yes."

"Very much so," Renata mumbled.

I looked at her then and thought on their words. With her arms stretched above her head, she was beautiful, but Renata was beautiful anyway.

I crawled to them both and knelt, sitting back on my heels. I touched Renata's stomach and her muscles twitched against my hand. I traced the hourglass curve of her figure.

"What do you want?"

Renata smiled softly at me and said, "Discern it."

"Iliaria?"

"Yes."

"Release her."

Iliaria let go of Renata's wrists. She sat back and folded her wings behind her.

Renata watched her with a heated stare, taking in every inch of the Draculian flesh in front of her.

"Contrary to what you may assume, I am not repulsed by you, Dracule."

"I will not let you dominate me."

I felt something then, a tendril of emotion from Renata.

"I don't think she wants to dominate you, Iliaria. I think she's curious about you," I said.

"Does that bother you, cara mia?"

I blinked. "Why would it?"

Iliaria looked very suspicious. "Curious…in what way?"

"Not in a way so bad as you seem to be thinking," Renata said.

"Now I am confused," Iliaria said.

I touched her arm. "You know how you make love to me?"

"Yes…"

"Will it bother you to stay where you are?"

I wasn't sure how to put the request any more mildly than that, and I didn't think Renata would approve of me just blurting it out.

"Aside from your strength, there are other things I'd rather you prove to me, Great Siren."

Iliaria looked as though Renata had hit her over the head with something, the surprise was so blatantly written across her features.

Was it really that difficult for her to imagine that Renata was *sexually* intrigued by her?

Renata laughed and smiled darkly. "Do I make you nervous, Dracule?"

"Absolutely not," she said. "I am surprised by the request, is all."

"Why?" Renata seemed genuinely curious.

"You are really asking me that question?"

Renata shrugged. "Why not?"

"If you two can agree to be equals, things might go a little more smoothly here," I said. The expressions on their faces told me plainly, they weren't following my line of thinking. "She's not asking you to dominate her, Iliaria, and she doesn't want to be dominated by you and vice versa. Correct?"

Neither disagreed. "Then why can't you both just agree not to play a game of dominance with each other? Just because you're in the same bed doesn't mean you can't touch each other, and that if you do, it's not a sign of submission from one or the other. That's a silly way of looking at things. Pleasure is pleasure."

Renata smiled slyly at that.

Iliaria said, "I do not trust her."

Renata's smile faltered. "I do not comprehend why you do not trust me, Dracule. What have I done to earn your distrust?"

When Iliaria did not answer, I sighed.

"Renata?"

"Yes, Epiphany?"

"This grows tiresome."

Iliaria let out a rumbling growl that made me flinch. Renata's eyes widened when Iliaria grabbed her by her thighs. Iliaria pushed them apart and Renata didn't fight her.

Iliaria rolled her hips and pressed her sex against Renata's. Renata made a surprised noise low in her throat and clawed out, seeking something to grab hold of. She caught my arm, her sensuous lips parting as she dug her nails into my skin.

I watched as Iliaria continued to roll her hips, dancing her skin against Renata's, her frustration and anger making the dance more passionate and less controlled. Renata's nails bit more deeply into me and I made a sound of pain for her. She opened her eyes and guided me to her.

"Where do you want me?"

Before Renata could give me an answer, Iliaria said, "In front of me."

Renata gave a nod in agreement and I swung a leg over her, my stomach over Renata's, able to watch Renata's face as Iliaria moved against her.

Iliaria wrapped an arm around my waist, not once losing the strange chaotic rhythm she had chosen. Granted, she was much gentler with Renata than she had been earlier with me.

I moved until her body nearly cradled mine. Iliaria reached around me, her fingers dipping between my legs as she circled my clitoris.

"Very nice, Dracule," Renata half moaned. "Very nice, indeed." Whether she referred to Iliaria's choice in position or what Iliaria was doing between her legs, I wasn't sure.

Iliaria pressed her face behind my ear and chuckled, making my skin prickle all over. Her finger began sliding back and forth, rolling my clit in a way that made me nearly lose my balance. I dug my toes into the blanket in attempt to keep myself on my knees.

Renata touched my thigh, clawing me lightly. Her hips moved between my legs while Iliaria moved behind me, against me.

Renata caught me by the wrists, raising her hands. "Brace yourself on me. Put your weight in my hands."

I blinked and realized, even while being pleasured, Renata's mind was still going as she figured out the mechanics of the position we'd chosen. I did as she bid me and she took my weight, stretching my arms high above me and canting my body at a slight angle.

"Dracule," Renata said.

Iliaria stopped playing with me, but I could still feel her moving behind me like something slinky and liquid. I tried to turn around to see what she was doing.

"Tsk, tsk." Renata called my attention back to her.

"I don't understand," I said.

"You will soon enough."

Iliaria pushed inside me from behind and I cried out, my hands curling into fists where Renata held them. Iliaria pushed into me, rough and sudden, before withdrawing and teasing me with the tips of her fingers.

She slid between my legs in a manner that became less teasing and more purposeful. Her gentle fingertips began to trail in an entirely new direction until I felt them tickling along the line of my buttocks.

I tensed.

"Ah, ah," Renata chided. "Don't tense, cara mia. It will hurt worse."

Iliaria's fingers slid over me and I tensed whether I wanted to or not.

Iliaria actually stopped moving to ask Renata, "Has she not done this before?"

"Actually," Renata smiled most mischievously, "I don't believe she has. Have you, Epiphany?"

"No, my lady."

I'd never really thought to give it a try and Renata had never done it to me.

Iliaria's breath was warm against the back of my neck while she stroked me between my cheeks. I shuddered for her, in fear and excitement. A thousand nerves tingled pleasantly throughout my lower body. "Take your queen's advice."

"That is?"

"Don't tense. And remember, I am holding back."

Iliaria didn't give me time to decide. She pushed her finger inside of me roughly enough that she didn't have to fight my body. She simply conquered it.

Much to my surprise, my first reaction when she pierced me was to make it stop. It hurt. It hurt more than Renata's blade parting my flesh.

But I couldn't make it stop. Renata's hold on my wrists turned from helping to hold me up, to helping Iliaria to hold me in place.

Iliaria began to pull out of me before pushing into me again.

This time, I cried out in protest.

"Stop fighting, cara mia."

I looked at her through half closed eyes. Her hold on my wrists loosened, just enough that I didn't feel so trapped and helpless.

"Relax."

Iliaria had stopped moving again. "Close your eyes, Epiphany. You are hurting yourself by fighting."

"You know how to do this, cara mia."

I drew in a deep, calming breath and let it out slowly.

"Gently," I said. "I can handle it, but you cannot be that rough, Iliaria. Not there."

I felt her fingers teasing my entrance before she slid inside of me again. Her thumb and fingers squeezed like a gentle vise, and this time, I moaned, tightening and shuddering for her.

"Better?" Renata asked.

I nodded and Iliaria resumed in a way that I found much, much more bearable. She made a conscious effort to be gentle when I requested it. She took her time with it, and when her fingers moved inside me again, I was able to relax and sink into her. Renata released one of my hands. The subtle plunge of Iliaria's fingers continued while she moved fluidly behind me and against Renata. Renata reached between my legs as she too began to pleasure me. Her finger circled and flicked against me until my body tightened around Iliaria and the sensation of them both inside and around me brought me with a long, shuddering moan.

Iliaria did not withdraw when my climax passed. I bent and kissed Renata's stomach, licking and nibbling on as much of her skin as I could reach. Her muscles grew rigid beneath my touch and when she came, she buried a hand in my hair, crushing my curls as she groaned. Iliaria followed a moment later and we slowly collapsed against one another in a satisfied heap.

CHAPTER SIX

I sat in Renata's high-backed chair with a crystalline glass of Iliaria's blood in my hand. Her blood was stronger than the Donatore's, richer and more refreshing, like a cup of perfectly steeped tea. At least, the memory I had of tea in my father's house.

Home. It seemed so long since I had thought on it. How many years had it truly been since my father had put me on his knee and spoke of my mother? Had I been six or seven years of age then?

I brought the glass to my lips and rolled Iliaria's blood on my tongue. I tried to recall the taste of tea, the smell of the bitter herbs tickling my nostrils. I tried to remember the feel of the porcelain cup in my small hands.

What would my parents have been like if they had both lived? My memory was that of a child's, not a woman two hundred years on.

"Mayhap that makes them all the more precious, cara mia, that they are not tainted by age."

She came to me and rested her hand on my bare shoulder. I had not bothered dressing or covering myself. It was still some hours till dawn, though Iliaria had retired to the other room. Unlike vampires, the Dracule required a certain amount of sleep to function.

Renata's lacquered nails swept lightly across the skin at the base of my neck and I shivered.

"Perhaps," I said.

The Rosso Lussuria itself had never been my home. I had not realized that until the day Renata had cast me from her bed.

She was my home.

Vasco was my family. But the rest of the clan moved around me, past me, without ever becoming part of me.

Renata stooped to kiss my cheek. She ruffled my hair affectionately and I watched her disappear into the bathing room, hearing the rush of water as it filled the tub.

I sighed and downed the glass of Iliaria's blood. Partly, I think she offered it to me because she felt bad for hurting me.

How's your arse? Cuinn asked cheekily.

It's well, Cuinn. Thanks for your concern.

What's bugging...err...troubling ya, Piph?

What do you mean?

Why so melancholic?

I thought about it and shook my head.

Honestly, I don't know.

You can talk to me, Piph.

I know, Cuinn.

I shut my eyes, blocking out the sight of Renata's bedroom. I saw Cuinn behind my lids, his fox eyes gentle and compassionate.

I know what's really bothering ye. It's all right to admit you're scared.

Admitting I am afraid doesn't make it better.

Cuinn sat on his haunches, proud and straight and taller than any fox I'd ever seen in the wild.

I won't let anything happen to you, Piph. If those big ol' bat-beasts mess with ye, they'll be getting my bollocks in a twist, and trust me, they don't want to do that.

I laughed. *Leave it to you to paint such a colorful picture. I'll certainly keep that in mind.*

Do, he said. *And keep your chin up, lass. You're depressing the holy feck out o' me.*

I'll try, I told him, *but only for your sake, O' Great and Mighty Fox.*

Making a mock o' me, are ya? Not wise considering I've saved your fangs more than once already.

Me? Make a mockery of you? Never!

I folded my arms on the table in front of me and rested my head, shutting my eyes to block out that dizzying flicker of firelight.

I heard Renata emerge from the bath and turned my head to find her. She was dressed in an exquisite gown of blue velvet so dark it was almost black. I remained hunched over the table. The expression on her face turned quizzical and for some reason, I started laughing.

Once I started, I found I couldn't stop.

She continued to stare at me, and the longer she stared, the harder I laughed. "Epiphany?" she asked. "Are you drunk?"

I buried my face in my crossed arms again and laughed, really not certain what was so funny, but finding the fact that I was laughing over essentially nothing rather amusing.

Renata took the empty glass from me gently, as if afraid I'd protest her taking it. "Perhaps next time you should drink Iliaria's blood more slowly."

"Aye," I slurred, watching her set the glass on a dresser nearby. I could feel myself swooning a bit. "I seem to have caught the googlies."

Renata paused, canting her head. "The what?"

"The giggles." I started laughing again, unable to stop. "Ah, the giggles!"

Not so fortunately, my laughter had woken Iliaria. She emerged from the other room appearing none-too-pleased with me.

I bit my bottom lip and tried with everything in me not to start laughing again. If I did, I wouldn't stop. Her staring so intently at me did not help my inner battle.

"My, my, you don't look happy," I said.

I made a choking sound as I tried to catch the laugh that threatened to slip out. I shut my eyes tightly, as if it would help to keep the laughter from bubbling up again.

I saw Cuinn, and something about the fox Fata being stuck in my head became the most hilarious thing in the world. I could no longer contain it. I fell back on the bed, laughing.

I heard Iliaria ask above my laughter, "What the devil has gotten into her?"

"Your blood, Dracule. It's made her drunk."

"The moon will rise soon," Iliaria said. "We cannot take her to Bull Shoals like this."

"It should wear off before then," Renata replied smoothly, then added a bit uncertainly, "I hope."

"Bull Shoals?" I asked, gasping. "What kind of bloody name is that? It sounds like bullshit!"

"Epiphany," Renata said and her tone was firm and serious as if she were trying to reprimand a restless child.

"Yes, my lady?"

"Hush."

"I apologize, my lady, but…" I thrust my arm in Iliaria's direction, pointing a finger at her. "It's her fault, you see. She's the one that felt bad about sticking a finger in my arse and decided to share her blood."

"Epiphany," Renata tried again. "If you do not lower your voice, I will gag you."

I growled but did as requested. I shut my mouth and crossed my arms under my breasts, not at all thrilled with the command.

"She has drunk my blood before and this has not happened."

"She has *sipped* your blood before, Dracule," Renata said. "This is apparently what happens when one decides to drink it at a gulp."

"Gulp," I said. "Such a strange word…"

Renata turned her back on me and opened one of the armoire's drawers.

I sat up. "My lady?"

She stopped beside the bed and said, "Epiphany, open."

"Open what, exactly?" I inclined with a whisper. "Open… sesame?"

Renata raised a black velvet sash between us and I frowned at her.

"You really believe she will listen to you when she's in this state?" Iliaria asked.

"Epiphany," Renata said, her voice making my name a dangerous purr.

I opened my mouth.

To her credit, she was gentle when she tied the sash in a knot at the back of my head. Gentle or no, having a mouthful of cloth like some kind of horse with a bridle was not comfortable or on my top lists of favorite things.

Renata grabbed the material stretched over my cheek and used it to raise my gaze to hers. "You are not to remove this until I bid you do so. Understood?"

With some reluctance, I nodded.

"Good girl."

I fell back against the pillows with a heavy sigh, feeling irritable and not in the least amused.

Renata and Iliaria left me to myself. Renata pulled the door to the sitting room closed behind her, though I could hear her voice faintly when she addressed Anatharic. No doubt, they would discuss the coming visit to the clan of Bull Shoals.

Nude, alone, and gagged, I entertained myself by watching the dance of candlelight. I stared at it for a long while, and most likely due to the effects of Iliaria's blood, I found it no longer made me dizzy, but that I was quite enchanted with it. The flame moved like a woman dancing sensuously, throwing her arms out and sending shadows of the canopy's posts to writhe on the wall.

Renata had not bound my hands. I could have very well removed the cloth tied about my head, but even in my dull state of intoxication, I would not disobey a direct order.

If I removed it, she would know and would only find something less pleasing for me to endure.

Lover or not, she was still my queen.

Cuinn was silent, leaving me alone with my thoughts. I raised my wrist, tracing the black curling lines of Iliaria's mark. She had told me when she had given me her mark that I could use the sigil to summon her. I wondered how it worked. I thought of her and the sigil tingled with warmth.

I whispered her name in my mind and the sigil tingled even more fiercely, as if tiny ants were crawling from the black lines and out over my skin. I resisted the urge to drag my nails over the mark.

"Epiphany," her voice called from the other room, "stop it."

Satisfied to have figured out exactly how it worked, I set about finding suitable attire for the excursion to Bull Shoals. I considered wearing a gown, as many of the clan rulers were old enough to remember when the notion of a woman wearing leggings or trousers was unheard of and unladylike. But in the end, I decided against it.

I was far more comfortable in the pants. I tugged on a pair of black velour leggings and slipped a white camisole over my head. It took longer than I expected to find a shirt that was both elegant enough to pull off in court and yet comfortable enough to fight in, should it come to that.

I threw the olive green top over my head, tying the laces at my elbows and collar into bows. The sleeves spilled out from my elbows and I moved my arms in a sweeping motion, confirming that they were not too wide to get in my way and not too tight to constrict my movements.

I found a pair of stockings and boots and sat on the stool in front of Renata's mirror. It wasn't until I saw my reflection that I realized my hair was a wild, frizzy mane. I picked up Renata's brush and frowned, unable to figure out any way of brushing around the cloth she'd set about my bloody head.

"Cara mia."

I hadn't heard Renata enter. She took the brush from my hand and placed it on the table. She loosened the knot at the back of my head and set the thick strip of cloth alongside the brush.

"Are you feeling better?"

"Yes," I said.

Renata opened a small jar and scooped out an apple-scented pomade. She spread a thin sheen of the ointment throughout my hair, taming it and making the curls appear shiny and smooth. She pulled my hair back into her hands, tying the tail of curls off with a black ribbon.

"There," she said, admiring her work with a measure of satisfaction. "Perfetto. Rise," she added.

I stood and turned in a slow circle.

"Suitable," she said. "Practical. It will do."

"Thank you, my lady."

Her eyes sparkled. "It would be more appropriate for you to wear a dress."

"I will if that's what you want."

She shook her head, the waves of her hair reflecting blue highlights. "No." She placed her hand at the small of my back, sliding it downward over my rear. "I prefer this. It pleases me." Her lips brushed the curve of my ear and I shivered for her. "It has the added advantage of being highly distracting."

"A distraction to you, my lady, or to others?"

She slipped behind me and her arm snaked around my waist as she pulled me back against her and turned us to face the mirror.

"Both." Her breath was warm against my neck. "Do not play too coy or too bold tonight, cara mia."

"What shall I play, my lady?"

"Quietly confident," she murmured the words against my skin as her mouth traced a path across my shoulder.

"As you will."

"The moon rises, dolce mia. Shall we?"

She offered the crook of her arm and I took it, resting my hand at the bend of her elbow.

The tension of daylight lifted as the moon rose over the land above the Sotto. I did not need to see it to know it. Every vampire feels the weight of sunlight and the lifting of it when darkness crawls over the land. It is a survival instinct. Even while I wore the Stone of Shadows, Iliaria's ring, I could feel its weight lift and fall beyond the shield of magic.

"It is time," Iliaria said from the doorway.

Renata nodded. "Dominique."

Dominique suddenly stood in the doorway that led to the outer halls of the Sotto.

"Yes, Padrona?"

"Summon Vasco and Nirena."

He bobbed more than bowed. "As you wish, my queen."

We waited in the sitting room while Dominique summoned Vasco and Nirena. Anatharic was still in his Draculian form. His bottomless eyes followed me unnervingly when I sat down.

After a few moments, I realized he was watching me intensely as I took my seat. Whatever thoughts he had whilst he stared, I really didn't care to know.

❖

Dominique wanted to go with us.

"My lady," he said, trying to persuade Renata, "they took my brother. They attacked me. Should I not travel with you so the King of Bull Shoals can hear the recollection of the events from my own mouth?"

"Could I, I would take you, Dominique."

"My lady," Dominique pleaded.

"It is not my decision, Dominique. The Dracule can only carry so many of us. We are traveling light."

"If we carry them together," Anatharic said, "we could carry him with usss."

Iliaria held the map in her hands. She rolled it in a practiced move and tucked it into a pocket of her coat. "We can make it work, Anatharic."

"We will have to climb from the bottom."

Iliaria nodded. "Yes."

"Climb?" Renata asked.

The two Dracule shared a look and Renata eyed them both with some suspicion.

"You've already investigated the entrance to their clan?"

"Yes. Anatharic did while I was resting. It seemed unproductive to have us both guarding the room when we needn't go in blind."

"I can go?" Dominique asked.

"Yes. Vito and Vittoria are aware of their duties while I am gone. Severiano will hold my throne. They do not need you here, Dominique."

I felt Dominique's relief, though he did not outwardly show it. He had been Renata's guard since long before I was born. It made sense that he didn't want to leave her side, especially when we had no idea how the King of Bull Shoals would react to our visit.

Anatharic and Iliaria told us to stand in a circle and link hands.

It was a great deal different traveling in such a way, despite the fact that the only experience of their travel that I had was when Anatharic had protected me in the hall. I held Iliaria's hand and felt the steady pull of her magic, felt it merging with Anatharic's and circling us like a small storm.

The spinning sensation stopped abruptly and my feet found solid ground, though my insides felt as if they were still spinning dizzily with the rush. Wind touched my face, blowing curls of my hair loose from the ribbon.

The murmur of water lapped at rocks below us and the dark sky above was speckled with stars. A sliver of moonlight reflected off the black water nearby, and a pang of longing gripped me.

Centuries. It had been centuries since I had felt the wind, since I had seen the night sky, the stars, the moon. I couldn't remember the air ever smelling so good, so sweet, so…natural.

I stepped away from Iliaria and Renata and touched the side of the rocky cliff, feeling the jagged stone slide smooth and sharp against my palm.

"It has been longer for us, colombina." Vasco's hand rested on my shoulder, calling my attention back to him and the others.

"I cannot remember the world ever seeming so alive, Vasco."

"Sì," he said, "you have never seen it with your senses. It is something mortals take for granted."

A bird called from somewhere high up in the trees, seeming closer than it really was. I turned my attention away from the lake and to the woodlands that surrounded us. I hadn't realized I'd taken a step toward the sound until Renata called me back.

"Epiphany," her voice was gentle. "We have other matters to attend to, dolce mia."

"Anatharic and I will carry you each to the opening, one at a time," Iliaria said.

"Why not teleport?" I asked.

"It isss easssier to climb," Anatharic said.

Nirena shrugged. "I will go first."

"And I," Dominique said.

Iliaria and Anatharic went to the base of the cliff. Nirena and Dominique mirrored each other, looping their arms about the Dracules' necks as they clambered onto their backs.

I had never seen the Dracule climb. They were quick and agile. Anatharic in his more animal form was quicker than Iliaria, as he used his claws to puncture the stone, where Iliaria used her hands and the spurs of her wings to get the grip she sought.

They ascended the mountain until they were nearly specks in my vision.

Something heavy and solid landed on the ground beside me and I jumped. Iliaria laughed, rising from her kneeling position with her wings stretched out behind her. Anatharic followed, using his wings to cup the air as he landed.

"Can you fly?" I asked. "Truly?"

Iliaria grinned widely. "Would you like to find out?"

Renata and I were next. Iliaria positioned herself against the wall and ducked so that I was able to loop my arms about her neck.

She climbed, her movements smooth and sure and without hesitation. She slipped once, and growled. Her tail jerked to the side, aiding her upward swing as she reached for a handhold. The spur of her wing bit the stone and aided her in regaining her footing.

"It is not as easy as it looks," she grumbled. I wasn't sure if it was a statement or an apology of sorts.

"I imagine not, especially when you're carrying someone on your back. Should I hang more loosely?"

"You are fine," she said. Though the line of my body pressed tightly against her back, she seemed to have no trouble maneuvering her wings around me.

We made it to the mouth of the cave and I realized why they could not teleport with us. The walkway leading into the cave was too narrow and we had to form a line simply to stand. An invisible pressure pushed against my skin.

Magic, Cuinn said, *to ward off humans. Any human that comes near the cave entrance shall not see it or pass through it.*

What would happen if they were to try?

They would not, he said calmly, *the magic itself is a deterrent spell. They'd feel an unease so tight in the pit of their bellies they wouldn't want to. It's a spell the Stregha learned from the Fatas, to remain unseen and unfound.*

I peered into the cave, trying to see further, when Iliaria said, "I'll get him."

I turned just in time to see her dive over the cliffside. I rushed toward it and Renata caught me by the wrist, assuring that I did not topple over.

It is hard to describe the Dracule in motion, for they move quickly, even for a vampire's sight. What I saw was Iliaria's wings held close to her body in the dive and the clap of thunder when they opened, catching the wind, her feet touching the ground, barely.

I daresay, Vasco didn't even see her coming, for when she grabbed him around the waist and pushed off the ground, he screamed. By the time they made it to us, tears of laughter rolled down my cheeks.

Iliaria landed, rolling unceremoniously to break her fall. She caught Vasco before he rolled right into us and knocked us all off the narrow walkway. She was laughing, too, a strangely deep rumbling peal of laughter that sounded odd coming from her human lips.

Vasco sprung to his feet and dusted off his breeches. "What, colombina? You've never heard a grown man scream?"

"Like that?" I asked. "No, Vasco. I have *never* heard you scream like that. If the clan of Bull Shoals didn't know we were here, I imagine they do now."

Vasco fussed with his attire, obviously more than a little embarrassed. "Brava for such a graceful landing," he muttered.

Iliaria made a choking sound as she suppressed a laugh. "Had you not been flailing like a little girl that would not have happened."

"We ssshould dessscend now," Anatharic said as he eased beneath a low hanging arch and down the narrow walkway to follow the descent that spiraled toward the cave's belly. Dominique waited for Renata's command. She nodded, indicating that yes, we should follow. Anatharic dropped to all fours after having to duck through several low hanging stones. I walked between Renata and Vasco, the only person in our party that did not have to duck or bend. Iliaria took the rear, so that our party was placed between the two Dracule.

If a person didn't know the cave had been spelled so that the humans would not find it, it became obvious when the pathway steepened so that even if they had, it would not have been a tourist attraction. There were too many precarious steps and treacherous footholds.

Anatharic called us to a halt. "The path is broken. There's a gap up ahead."

"Another reason the caverns are fitting," Renata murmured.

Large stalactites dripped like massive stakes from the center of the cavern's ceiling.

"What about dropping down?" I asked.

"You have not looked over the ledge recently, have you, colombina?"

At Vasco's words, I peered over. The drop was not so terrible that it would cripple a vampire, but the stalagmites stretching upward from the cave's floor were an entirely different matter. Oh, we'd probably survive, skewered or no, but I did not think anyone in our party was exactly keen on testing the idea.

"What about climbing, then?"

Iliaria shook her head. "The walls are too slick with humidity. It would be too difficult to gain a hold."

"Flying?"

"There isss not enough room."

"Anatharic is right," Iliaria said. "There's not enough room to gain any momentum in here."

"Then we jump," Nirena said from behind Anatharic. "Can you leap so far, Great Sire?"

"We ssshall sssee."

"Back up!" Dominique called. "We're going to need room to make the leap."

One by one, we scuttled back up the path, trying to give Anatharic the space he required. I was far enough back I couldn't see the space they were jumping over, but if Dominique said we needed more room, we'd do it.

Out of all of us, the Dracule had a better chance of making the leap given their stature. Though the others were in the way, I heard Anatharic take his running start on all fours. A few seconds later, I heard him land softly on the other side of the gap.

"I'll go," Dominique said, and I knew he had stopped Nirena from trying to make the jump before him.

His booted feet slapped the stone on the other side.

"It's wider over here," he called. "Nirena, give yourself more of a run before jumping."

We backed up some more.

Nirena made it, then Renata. Vasco was up next and since we were closer, I was able to more clearly see where exactly it was we were jumping.

My stomach lurched. "Vasco, I can't make that. I'm not as tall as any of you."

"You will make it," Iliaria said behind me.

"I can throw you over, colombina?"

"I'd rather you not."

He patted my shoulder with a smile. "You will be fine." He turned and ran, leaping over the break in the path with the ease of a sprinting gazelle.

It was my turn and I frowned.

"It is not about your reach, Epiphany. It is about your speed. You are a vampire. You can make this leap."

It really did not look physically possible.

She's right, ya know. You'll certainly not make it doubting yourself.

"If you say so…"

Iliaria pulled me back up the path. "Here," she said. "You need even more of a running start than the others. Now, run."

I did.

The cavern streaked in my vision and when it came time to jump, I faltered and misjudged. I leapt too late and fell, trying to catch the ledge with my hands and slipping on the wet stone.

A hand caught my wrist.

Vasco grinned down at me. "You didn't think I would let you fall, did you?"

I gazed down over my shoulder at the spike-riddled floor.

"Sì," he said, hoisting me up with ease. "That would not have been pleasant."

"Thank you, Vasco."

"Always, sorella."

Anatharic led the group down the last several feet of pathway. Iliaria made the jump easily behind me and caught up with the rest of us.

The floor was thick with stalagmites of various sizes, so many that there was absolutely no way of navigating to the mouth of the narrow tunnel without stepping through them. Anatharic used his body to push against the stalagmites, toppling some over and giving us a path through the perilous field.

Finally, we made it to a tunnel.

"Do you know where thisss leadsss, Queen?"

We could hear the sound of water flowing from somewhere beyond the tunnel.

Renata said, "Follow the water, Dracule. That will lead us to the clan of Bull Shoals."

The tunnel was a great deal longer than I reckoned and uncomfortably small, and though none of us had too much trouble walking through it, the walls were so close it was impossible not to brush against them. Every so often, we had to carefully round corners and ended up with scrapes in spite of our careful efforts to slip through. Blessedly, we were not reduced to crawling through on our hands and knees.

The sound of water grew louder, echoing from the chamber beyond and throughout the tunnel, which spit us out into a much vaster room. Stone draperies hung in thin sheets from the ceiling, appearing as though all it would take would be a gentle breeze to send them swaying. Pillars lined the room, some as high as the ceiling itself and some like small phallic altars. A single lit torch in one of the pillars illuminated the brown and tan stone formations around us.

"Well," Vasco said, rubbing his elbow as if he'd knocked it against the wall on his way out of the tunnel, "by the looks of it, I'd say we've made it."

A man's voice startled all of us to attention. "State your purpose!"

Vasco grinned back at me like some kind of wicked cat. "See?"

"Aye," I grumbled. "We've made it."

The Dracule pushed us into a tighter group as Renata responded. "Inform your king, Keeper of Bull Shoals, that the Queen of the Rosso Lussuria has arrived and wishes to gain an audience with him."

There was a moment of heavy silence before the sound of stone grumbling against stone emitted throughout the cavern.

"Are you armed?" the man called.

"Sì," Vasco called back. "We would be foolish to stumble into your territory without means of protection."

"As you say," the man's voice called out again and several cloaked figures stepped out from behind their hiding spots until a dozen of them surrounded us.

I daresay, the King of Bull Shoals was either paranoid or simply employed more guards than Renata had ever thought to consider.

They were all cloaked from head to foot in black garb, their faces shrouded and hidden from sight. A dozen crossbows with silver tipped arrows were aimed in our direction.

"I suggest you not draw any of those weapons. Do not draw and we will have no reason to fire."

"Very well," Renata said, encouraging Anatharic and the others to move aside so that we could both see the person speaking. "We will give you no cause to attack."

The figure raised his bow in Anatharic's direction. "Who are they and why are they here?"

Anatharic gave an unhappy growl, and the figures around us stirred, some of them training their bows on him.

Iliaria said his name and he quieted.

"They are Dracule and a part of the matter that I wish to discuss with your king."

One of the figures stepped out of the circle of guardsmen, and a woman's voice came from her shadowed hood. "That cannot be."

The woman drew back her hood to reveal a pretty face with high cheekbones and wide, doe-like eyes. She lowered her crossbow as she inspected Anatharic and Iliaria.

"Istania!" the man called. "What are you doing?"

"If they were going to kill us, Gulliver, they would have already done it."

The woman, Istania, came closer to our group and knelt before all of us. She placed her crossbow on the ground beside her.

"I am Istania, Elder and huntress among the clan of Bull Shoals. They have sent word of your arrival to our king, Queen Renata. I will take you to await his audience."

The rest of the figures followed her lead. She smiled with genuine sincerity and political politeness that made her dark green eyes seem gentle and kind.

"Move aside, Gulliver."

Istania gestured to an area between two ivory pillars. "This way, if you please."

Stone grumbled against stone again as two other figures pushed open a stone doorway.

Thus, we were ushered inside with a small army of armed Bull Shoalians marching silently behind us.

CHAPTER SEVEN

Istania and her party led us through a clean and narrow hallway. Beyond the hidden stone door, the cave was much more obviously inhabited. Stone steps had been carved where the paths sloped, and stalagmites and stalactites had been cleared away, all save the ones too large to move. Istania indicated a long stone bench, and we sat down to wait. Small burners had been placed atop wide pillars throughout the room, casting a soft light. Our sight is keener in the dark than a human's but when a vampire hunts in the dark, we rely more on other senses than eyesight. Most of the Rosso Lussuria preferred light on a normal basis. Clearly, the clan of Bull Shoals did as well.

I sat between Renata and Vasco, and only Iliaria and Anatharic did not take a seat. They stood like deadly guards at each end of the long bench. The stone was damp and cool beneath my clothes.

I thought Istania would strike up conversation with us, but she didn't. She waited with us without offering as much as a peep. When she caught me watching her, she didn't smile. Her features remained steady and focused.

Some minutes later, a cloaked figure pulled aside a linen hanging to reveal another doorway. "The king will see you now."

He held the hanging in his hand and stepped aside to permit us to pass through.

❖

"Queen Renata," Augusten called from his throne as we entered the throne room, "to what do I owe such a pleasure?"

The others in our party fell back to allow Renata to walk ahead. I slowed my pace, remaining near enough to see her profile.

"King Augusten." Renata's voice was politic and honey smooth. Her lips curled in a smile that made her eyes sparkle invitingly and she curtseyed, appearing every inch a monarch paying courtesy to another while she did it.

King Augusten was dressed from shoulder to foot in black leather. He rose from his throne, the dark ringlets of his hair clinging to his forehead and offering only flashes of the silver circlet at his brow. His face was clean-shaven and masculine, his jawline strong, and the arch of his nose unmistakably Greek.

"So," Augusten said as he moved toward Anatharic, assessing him without bothering to hide it. "I have heard that you wish to speak with me and that you arrived at our humble abode with two demons in tow." Augusten made his way down our line to observe us. He hooked his thumb under his belt as if it were a habit. As he passed, the others bowed their heads in respect.

"Feigning ignorance does not become you, Augusten. You know as well as I what and who they are."

I lowered my gaze when King Augusten stood before me.

"True, but why they are here, with you…" He waved a hand in the air. "That I do not know, Queen Renata."

"Allow me to enlighten you," Renata said. "We have been attacked by their kinsmen. The Great Sires standing before you are our allies."

Augusten's leather boots were still in my field of vision. He stayed silent for a long moment.

"Who is she?" he asked. "She does not appear to belong with your party, Renata. Your guardsman," he said, gesturing idly toward Dominique, "your beauty and political brains," he gestured toward Nirena, "and your cunning warrior," he said, nodding at Vasco. Augusten reached out to touch me, placing his calloused fingers beneath my chin and lifting my face.

Iliaria's tail slithered across the stone floor and I felt her agitation rise. She didn't like Augusten touching me.

"What are you?" the king asked ponderously. His chocolate gaze searched my face. "A present, perhaps?"

"She is mine, Augusten. Epiphany is *my* Inamorata."

"Ah," he released me and I did not lower my gaze. "I had heard some years ago that you had taken a woman as your pet. This is her?"

"Yes."

"Do you love her?" he asked and it seemed like a terribly odd question for one monarch to ask another.

"Yes."

"And you," Augusten moved toward Iliaria. If he was scared of her, he did not show it. "You were unhappy when I touched her. What is the girl to you, Great Siren?"

"She is my dragă."

"She is your lover, too?"

"Yes."

"I suspect if I touch her again you'll rip my arm off and feed it to me, no?"

Iliaria wisely did not respond.

"What of you, girl? Do you speak?"

I kept Renata's advice in mind and tried to speak with subtle confidence. "I speak, my lord, when I am spoken to."

"Where ever did you find this one? You've the hint of an accent, girl. English?"

"Yes, my lord."

"Ah, and I'm guessing you're far older than you seem. How old are you?"

"Two hundred, my lord."

"She has a sweet tongue, Renata."

"More than you will ever know, Augusten."

King Augusten beamed at her in good humor. "Come," he said, and the cloaked figures that had moved to stand against the wall moved to escort our party. "We shall discuss and dine. Let it never be said that the King of Bull Shoals lacks in hospitality toward a neighboring queen."

The tension in the air seemed to slacken like a rope let loose as the king and his party led us to a room designated for the king's private dining. When I moved to sit at the table, Augusten spoke to me. "Come here, girl." He held a chair out from the table expectantly.

I cast a glance at Renata and she offered a slight nod.

Humor him, cara mia.

"Thank you, my lord." I offered a brief curtsey and sat. The king took his seat at the head of the table while Renata took hers across from me.

Augusten clapped his hands together twice, and two cloaked figures moved from the line they had formed against the cavern wall and disappeared through an archway that led to another room. When they returned, two men and two women garbed in white linen robes followed subserviently behind them. Their white robes were sheer enough to leave little to the imagination. They were quite obviously nude.

"I believe our customs differ slightly," Augusten said, sparing a glance at Renata. "The clan of Bull Shoals prefers the fruit straight from the tree." He smiled as one of the women knelt before him. He swept aside her pale hair to expose her neck.

Augusten struck like a snake, and much to the woman's credit, she made only a small sound of pain at the bite.

I silently reminded myself of the lesson I had learned with Justine.

A woman knelt before Renata, her brown hair spilling from the hood and covering her breasts. Renata grabbed the woman by the arm and pushed her onto the table. The woman's hood fell back to reveal a face that was soft and doe-like. Renata jerked her head to the side, exposing her neck.

"Cara mia," she said.

The rapid beat of her pulse sang to me and I followed its song. I bit the side of the woman's neck, and when I bit her, Renata pushed up her gown and sank her teeth into the pulsing drum high up on the woman's inner thigh.

I flushed with jealousy and the girl beneath me squirmed uncomfortably, drawing me back to myself. I still had not released the wound after biting and had only bitten down harder when the jealousy surged through me. I unsheathed my fangs from her skin and sealed my lips over the wound as her pulse pumped her blood eagerly into my mouth.

Renata held my gaze while we fed. I sensed more humans being ushered into the room, heard their gasps and startled cries when our party found a place to bite.

It is just food, cara mia.

I shut my eyes again and drank.

Renata drew back first, dabbing at the corners of her mouth with a square of crimson cloth.

I pulled myself away with an effort, swallowing and licking the blood that had dripped onto to my lower lip.

When the others were done, Augusten raised his hand and his cloaked guards led the light-headed humans back through the archway.

Augusten smiled at me when he asked, "Did you enjoy?"

I forced myself to return the smile as politely as I could. "Yes, my lord."

He patted my hand on the table. "Good, that is very good. Queen Renata." He turned his attention to her, but kept his hand unnervingly on mine. The urge to move my hand away from his was instinctive. I was wise enough not to move, however, for fear of insulting him. "We have matters to discuss. You mentioned a particular problem with their kinsmen?"

Iliaria and Anatharic, again, had not taken the seats offered to them. They remained standing. I felt Iliaria move up behind me. The weight of her hand rested on my shoulder. Wisely, Augusten took note of it, and removed his hand from mine.

I silently thanked Iliaria.

"Yes," Renata said, her attention shifting from Iliaria to Augusten. "Some of the Dracule are rising against the vampires. They attacked our stores and tried to burn our crops."

Augusten leaned back in his seat, appearing thoughtful. "And what do you want from me and mine, Renata?"

"To warn you. If you have not already been attacked by the Dracule, there is a chance that you may be." She shook her head, waves glistening in the candlelight. "We have not yet figured out if they are targeting our clan alone or if this is a move against all of us, Augusten."

For what seemed a long while, King Augusten did not say anything. He pushed his chair out and rose. "Come," he said and the others at the table started to stand. "No," he said, glancing at them. He looked at Renata and then me. "You."

It was Vasco who protested. "We will not leave them alone."

"Vasco," Renata said, only his name. Vasco dropped back into his seat, obviously not thrilled with her command but obeying without quarrel.

Renata offered her arm to me and I took it while Augusten led us away from his dining hall.

"You truly believe the Dracule are gathering an army to attack our kind?" he asked Renata.

The hallway he led us through was dark and tunnel-like, lined with a few burning torches.

"An army?" Renata shrugged lightly. "I am not so certain they are gathering such strength in numbers, Augusten, but I do know they have made moves against us, and from what I have heard, they may move against neighboring clans."

Augusten stopped at the end of the hall, bringing us to a halt behind him. "We have not been attacked, Queen Renata. Why should I show concern if we, the Bull Shoal, are left untouched?"

"How long do you suppose it will stay that way, my lord? Do you not believe us?" I asked. "The Dracule that have banded together do not despise merely our clan. Their leader despises all vampires. I would not think for a moment that when they are done with us, this war will dissipate. They will more than likely move to conquer another front."

"And you know this how, little one? Perhaps it is only your clan that is in their line of sight and not ours. If we raise hand, then we will draw attention to ourselves. What you ask of me, you ask of my people."

"Noble and wisely spoken, Augusten, but by not raising hand with us, you may harm your clan more. What then?"

Augusten placed the tips of his fingers against his temple as if we were giving him a headache. "I must think on this, Renata. I cannot be rash. Will you stay and pass the day here?"

"One night, Augusten."

"I will consult my Elders and send word to the other nearby clans," he said. "You will have my decision come next nightfall."

Augusten clapped his hands together, and one of his hooded guards moved through the archway in front of us. His guardsmen knelt.

"Yes, my lord?"

"I will need ink and parchment," he said.

"As you wish, my lord."

His tall guardsmen disappeared.

"It is dangerous to send out riders, Augusten. We took a risk simply coming here."

Augusten turned on his heel, expecting us to follow. "I do not have to send out riders, Queen Renata. You should know me better than that."

Renata spoke to his back. "Then pray tell, how do you mean to contact the other clans?"

"I have my ways."

Augusten pushed aside a large rock with ease, admitting us through another doorway.

The room we emerged into was lined with wooden shelves and rows of books. His guardsmen stood near a high-backed chair of brownish-red leather. Augusten sat, crossing his legs and taking the tablet and parchment from his guard.

He gestured toward the leather couch across from his chair. "Make yourselves comfortable."

We did so as Augusten dipped a long quill in the inkwell his guard held and began to scribble a series of short notes, tearing the parchment and rolling it carefully.

When he was done, he dismissed his guard with a bow of his head. I caught a glimpse of the man's face beneath the hood. He appeared young and boyish, with a wisp of blond hair that cast his blue eyes in shadow. He looked like a teenager.

The boy returned carrying a small gilded avian cage. Augusten opened the latch and retrieved a large-eared bat from inside. The bat clambered up Augusten's sleeve, appearing docile but inquisitive.

"Would you like to hold him?" Augusten asked, catching my obvious interest in the little creature.

"May I?" I asked, feeling somewhat childishly excited at the prospect.

Augusten had me cup my hands together and placed the teacup sized creature with its crown-like ears into my palms. Its fur was creamy and soft and dusted with colors of coal and ash. The bat turned in my hand, its beady black eyes assessing me mildly.

"I always thought they were blind," I murmured, feeling the bat watching me. "But you're not, are you?" I asked it.

The bat chittered softly.

You're seriously not thinking about keeping that creepy fuzzy thing as a pet, are ye?

So what if I am, Cuinn?

It's a flying rodent, he said. *Wouldn't ye prefer...oh, I don't know...a puppy or something?*

The bat made a fuss, squeaking and chittering as if it'd heard Cuinn's insult.

Actually, he's not a rodent.

Augusten stroked a finger down the bat's back when I handed it back to him, and when it quieted, he tied the little piece of rolled parchment comfortably around the bat's neck, showing considerable gentleness with it. I sensed the bat quite liked Augusten.

Augusten raised the bat in his hands and I felt his shields part like a curtain. His power caressed my cheeks, tickling strands of my hair and sending them dancing.

The bat chittered again before flying away.

"Clever, Augusten," Renata said. "You've used your power to bespell bats." The corner of her delicious mouth twitched in bemusement.

Augusten retrieved another bat from the gilded enclosure. "A handful," he said, "no more. It's far more efficient than traveling."

Augusten placed another of the bats in my hands. This time, he did not let me hold it long. He secured the parchment, and then took it, raising it to meet his eyes, calling his power, and sending it flying off with the others to fulfill its mission.

He sent five bats in all, each to carry their master's messages to the nearby clans. He rose and handed the empty cage to his guard.

"Now, we shall wait and see," he said. "My guards will escort you to your chambers. We will dine once more on the eve and I will give you my answer."

Istania and another of his guard appeared in the doorway to escort us to our rooms for the night.

"My thanks, Augusten."

He nodded at Renata, waving his hand. "It is nothing."

I curtseyed slightly and probably a bit awkwardly since it wasn't something I was accustomed to doing, as it was not obligatory among the Rosso Lussuria. "It is appreciated, my lord."

"I have shown the others to their chambers," Istania said. "I will lead you to them and to your own private quarters, my queens."

Queens?

I glanced uncertainly at Renata, who smiled sweetly and knowingly. Surely, I had not heard Istania right.

We were escorted to our chamber, which was an odd, circular shaped room. The ceiling and floor had been cleaned of any debris or natural formations. The stone walls were smooth, as if they'd been polished, and a wooden doorway had been established along the western wall, separating our room from the others. A large, elaborately carved canopy bed graced the center of the room, draped in blue and black silks. A menacing creature was carved into the headboard, its sharply triangular face and horns pushing out toward the room, framed by intricate carvings of small flowers.

Iliaria was sitting on the bed when we entered.

"They have posted guards outside our doors," she noted with mild indignation. "Anatharic will be staying in the room with the others. I will stay here with you."

"I would do the same were they guests in my Sotto, Dracule."

"I know," Iliaria said. "As would I, but I do not trust their guards to keep you safe."

When it came down to it, neither did I.

A gentle knock sounded at the door, and I waited for Renata's nod of approval before answering it.

Istania held a bundle of clothes in her arms. "The king requested I give you these." There was no distaste or displeasure in her that I could sense, only a subtle calmness. "That door there," she gestured with a dip of her head toward the only other doorway in the room, a doorway I had suspected led to a closet of some sort, "leads to your own personal bath. If you require anything else, do not hesitate to ask one of the guards posted outside your door. We do hope you do not take their presence amiss, as they are for your protection as well as ours."

"No insult has been taken," Renata said smoothly, tipping her head in thanks.

Istania mirrored the gesture and held the clothes out. Truthfully, I wasn't certain they would fit and if they did, I didn't know how Augusten managed to find clothes for us on such short notice. None of us had thought to bring a change for ourselves. Istania left and I set about making myself useful and putting the garments away in a wardrobe just beyond the door leading to the bath.

When I had completed the task, I took in the bathing room. It was spacious, and though the clan of Bull Shoals had probably altered it, the spring-fed pool appeared to be a natural occurrence. Beautifully crafted brass lanterns were placed on stands throughout the room, flickering and reflecting off the surface of the water.

"It has its own quiet charm, doesn't it?" Renata asked.

"It does. Have you spoken with Vito or Vittoria?" I asked.

"Yes. All is well. There have been no further attacks."

"The others aren't questioning their authority for the time being?"

Renata's mouth curled slyly. "Not with Severiano at their backs, no."

"That's good," I said. "Will we return on the morrow's evening?"

"I suspect," she said, "it all depends on what word Augusten receives from the neighboring clans."

"What if they've been attacked, my lady? If the Dracule are targeting all of us, what then?"

"What do you mean, Epifania?"

"Should we not band together as Damokles and his henchmen have and fight back? It would be easier to eliminate the threat if we stood together as vampires."

"Mmm," she murmured, toying with a curl of my hair that had broken free, "that is why I believe Damokles is targeting one clan at a time. It is far easier to bully one than it is three."

"I do not want to put any of the other clans in danger, my lady, but I don't think this is a battle we can fight alone. The Dracule have heard rumor that Damokles seeks to convert even more Dracule to his cause as we speak."

Renata sighed, releasing the lock of my hair. "I know, cara mia."

I changed the subject, feeling we would gain no more ground on it. "Well," I said, "if we are staying here for the rest of the night and throughout the day, what exactly are we supposed to do?"

She smiled mischievously. "Dolce mia," she said in a purring voice. Her arms slipped around my waist as she pulled me in against her. "Have you not learned by now that we have little problem finding something to do?"

I placed my hands on her shoulders, rising on the tips of my toes when she bent to kiss me.

"What will you, my lady?"

She tugged the ribbon in my hair loose, sending the weight of it spilling and swaying freely down my back. "We will get to that."

She kissed me and her lips were tender and sweet.

As it was Renata's night, Iliaria left the room and went to sit with the others. Renata took my hand and guided me to the bed. I went willingly into the circle of her arms, feeling at home and at ease despite the unfamiliar surroundings. For a long while, we simply lay there, idly exploring one another. Renata toyed with my hair and I traced circles on the small of her back.

She pushed my thighs apart with her knee and I moved against her, sliding up and down on her thigh and circling my hips. I buried my face in the bend of her neck and her hand sank lower down my body. She squeezed and I moaned when her nails dug into my skin.

Renata tugged at the back of my shirt and I rose to let her draw it up over my head. She pulled the garment off and cupped my breasts, guiding me to her mouth. She nibbled and teased my breasts in a way that made me shudder with pleasure.

"Mmm, I have always liked that about you, Piph."

She bit the side of my breast, her fangs piercing me. I gasped as she sealed her mouth over the wounds, sucking lightly.

When she drew away, I asked, "Liked what, my lady?"

Renata sat up and pushed me onto my back. Her hand marked a path up my chest before she dragged her nails over me from my neck to my waist. My eyelashes fluttered closed while she touched me.

Her hands played over my hips. "You do not hide yourself in the bedroom."

I smiled slightly. "You never asked me to."

She began peeling my leggings off. "No," she said, a flicker of something impish passing through her gaze. "No, I want to see all of you."

And she did, tossing the leggings aside and spreading my thighs. Renata lay back against the pillows and pulled my lower body onto her lap. Her fingers splayed me and she watched her hand while she traced me. She played over a particularly sensitive spot and I clawed at the blankets.

Renata laughed softly. She pushed her fingers inside me and my muscles responded, cinching as I moaned at the feel of her. She worked me with a slow and steady hand, and while she did so, she continued to watch me, to watch her fingers as they moved in and out of me. She eased out slowly. When she pushed into me again, it was harder and less controlled. I cried out softly and shoved my hips toward her hand.

She shifted, curling her body against mine. She eased out of me again as she spread the honey of my desire over my most sensitive spot.

She brought our faces close, still flicking and playing between my legs. Renata pressed her lips against mine in a kiss that was deep and sensual. Somewhere during our kiss, I spent myself, crying out my pleasure against her lips.

When I tried to raise Renata's gown, she pulled me into the circle of her arms. I didn't resist her and lay with my head on her shoulder.

"Not yet," she murmured against my hair.

I nodded without asking why. When she wanted me to please her, she would let me know. She always did.

Some minutes before dawn, I heard the door between the two rooms open quietly.

Iliaria stood at the foot of the bed watching us with her strange eyes. Her features were pleasantly blank. "Anatharic thought you might want this," she said making her way to Renata's side. "Were it not so close to dawn, I would not have interrupted."

She held her hand out, palm up. Renata sat up quietly and when she saw what Iliaria held out, she looked at her in surprise.

"Is he certain?"

"Yes, put it on."

Renata took the slender ring with its small cloudy gem from her. She slid the Stone of Shadows onto the middle finger of her right hand, the same finger on which I wore mine.

"Are you certain?" she asked.

"I would not give it to you if I was not," Iliaria said. "It is by far easier than having Epiphany wake you with blood and blade."

"It is," Renata said, giving her a sidelong glance. "But it means I will be awake throughout the day, Dracule. You will have to share Epiphany."

"You tell me what I already know."

"The Great Sire has my thanks," she said.

"We must speak of strategy," Iliaria said. She sat on the bed to face us both. "Anatharic and I have those that are loyal to us, those that we may call upon and trust if we need to."

"At the moment, things are dependent on what word we receive from the clans Augusten has sent word to. This is not yet a full-fledged war, Dracule."

"Not yet, but we must prepare. Damokles will make this a war, Renata. He is picking at your clan solely to find weak spots."

"And if he has attacked no others?"

"We must convince them to stand with us. It is only a matter of time until he attacks the others. The vampires must show a united front in this."

"We need to form an alliance," I said. "But how? If they haven't been attacked, they have no physical proof we speak the truth. How do we convince them to fight what they will essentially believe is our clan's battle and not theirs?"

"It would be easier if Damokles has attacked another clan," Iliaria said, seeming frustrated. She shook her head. "I do not know. We must consider the possibility that he has not and what to do under those circumstances."

"What would you do, Dracule?" Renata asked.

"The only thing you can do, that I can discern. I would form an alliance with those clans willing and that believe this is not solely your battle to fight."

"Those may be few and far between."

"I know. Would that there was some way to convince them otherwise. I believed Anatharic's and my presence would be sufficient evidence that you are telling the truth, but King Augusten seems hesitant to believe."

"Mayhap," I said, thinking furiously, "Mayhap it's not about convincing them that we're telling the truth."

"What do you mean, cara mia?"

"We've been going about this arseways since the start. Instead of convincing them that we're telling the truth, we need to convince them they should form an alliance with us, regardless."

"How?" Renata asked as she searched my face. "They are not going to join and fight with us if they do not gain something in return by forming an alliance with the Rosso Lussuria."

"Precisely," I said.

"Most every clan has their own wealth." Renata lay back against her pillows. "I cannot sway them with riches. What then do we have to give them in exchange for an alliance?"

I fingered the Stone of Shadows on my hand. "Power," I said. "We offer their rulers power." I looked at Iliaria and asked, "Can it be done?"

She cast her gaze to the ring on my hand and I knew she understood my thoughts. "It will be."

Whether the clans believed us or not, we would find out how far their rulers would go for a taste of the power that our allegiance with some of the Dracule rewarded us. If it was enough to persuade King Augusten, it just might be enough to persuade the others.

❖

We passed the day talking politics instead of making love. Iliaria sent Anatharic away to contact the Dracule that were loyal and true to them. It was through them we would gain another Stone of Shadows and use it to sweeten the pot of an alliance, starting with King Augusten. Iliaria and Anatharic could make more, but each ring the Dracule made came at the price of blood and power.

It was decided that each Dracule that lent a Stone of Shadows to a ruler would become an overseer of sorts, in that they would remain in contact with those vampires who took the deal. Why wouldn't the Dracule keep watch on those with whom they shared their gifts? It was not purely a selfish move on the Rosso Lussuria's behalf, but a cautious one on behalf of the Dracule.

Shortly after moonrise, Istania and two cloaked guardsmen knocked on our door and escorted us before King Augusten. Renata and I had bathed and changed into the garments given to us by the king himself. The dress I wore was a gray several shades darker than the gray of my eyes. The bodice of the dress cinched like a corset and was lined in whirling black velvet designs. The sleeves fell low on my shoulders, leaving my neck, collar, and a good portion of my back bare. Once, I would not have worn such a gown for fear of revealing the scars the Elder Lucrezia had left on me. But Renata had healed them and I could wear the dress proudly.

When Renata was done tying the stays, she stood back to admire the dress.

"Very alluring," she said, smiling softly.

The gown Renata wore was white and flowing with glimpses of aquamarine silk beneath it. She kissed me and drew away and I fought not to sway back into her touch.

"We have a king to meet with."

"So we do, my lady."

I turned to make my way to the door and found Iliaria just inside it. Her strange gaze flicked from me to Renata. What she thought or felt, I don't know. So many emotions came off her at once I couldn't tell which was the strongest. I went to her anyway. I touched her shoulder and when she did not back away from me, I stood on the tips of my toes and offered a kiss.

"I told you once, Epiphany, I do not want your pity."

"A kiss is not pity. A kiss is my way of saying that I care."

She kissed me, but it was brief. A brush of lips, and nothing more.

Iliaria stepped out of the room ahead of us and I sighed.

I felt Renata's hand at the small of my back. "It is hard to please us both, I know. The Dracule is far more sensitive than she's willing to admit."

"Yes."

"You will find a way, cara mia."

"Are you so certain of that?" I asked. "One moment, I believe I understand her, and the next, she throws my understanding out of reach."

Renata gave me a knowing smile. "You discerned how to please me, Epiphany. Of course, I am certain."

She offered her arm and I took it, resting my hand in the bend of her elbow.

As it turned out, King Augusten did not arrange for us to be escorted to his throne room. Instead they led us to the same dining room in which we had dined the night before. When Renata held the wood and leather cushioned chair out from the table for me to sit beside her, Augusten did not complain or usher me to another seat.

"Have you enjoyed your stay?" Augusten asked Renata in a tone that was almost perfunctory.

"We have, Augusten, thank you."

Augusten raised his hand, indicating to his servant guards to bring in the first and only course of our meal—the humans we had fed on the night before.

I felt his gaze upon me as the humans in their sheer white garb spread through the room.

"You look resplendent this evening, Lady Epiphany. You wear that gown well."

"My thanks, my lord," I said, making sure that my tone was detached yet at the same time polite.

I wasn't so certain why Augusten kept singling me out or why he seemed to be paying a great deal more attention to me than was courteous. I sensed strongly it had to do with Renata's presence, as if, in some way, he was trying to unsettle her.

Yes, Renata's voice purred in my mind. She caught the wrist of the woman who nearly passed us. The woman seemed to react out of instinct, offering her wrist subserviently. Renata bit her and she gasped but did not struggle or draw away.

I waited quietly for Renata's instructions.

When Renata raised her mouth from the blood servant's wrist, her gaze was filled with power like a raging sea stretching toward a beautiful blue sky. Before I could feed, Renata sent the woman on her way. She used the hold she still had on her wrist to guide her from between our chairs.

Renata drew aside the long curtain of her hair and said, "Cara mia."

A rush of excitement filled me and I licked my lips, wetting them as I rose from my seat. Renata caught my hands in hers and pulled me into her lap. Her hands slid up my thighs beneath the dress, splaying over my buttocks and stroking me encouragingly.

She tilted her head and I bent to place a kiss upon her pulse. Distantly, I was aware of what transpired, aware that somewhere in the room, Iliaria watched us, aware that not too far from us, King Augusten stared, his gaze fixed like a dart in my back.

I didn't care. Whatever game he and Renata played was their own, though I knew I was most assuredly being flaunted; a part of me was thrilled at the fact that Renata so brazenly claimed me as hers.

I opened my mouth and pierced her, taking some of the life she had taken from the woman into my own body. I kissed her neck while I drank from her, sucking the wounds lightly. If I made some show of it, it was not intentional. I swallowed slowly when my mouth was full, full of blood like molten lust.

Renata did not touch me any more than was appropriate and when I was done, I rested my head on her shoulder, feeling so content I feared I might somehow begin to purr. She raised a hand and stroked my hair back from my temple.

"Lest there be any question left to ask, Augusten, Epiphany is mine. She is my Inamorata, my lover, and my pet. Not yours."

The king had the decency to feign surprise. "You insult me, Queen Renata, to think I was under any other impression."

"Do not think a circlet of silver at your brow will keep me out of your head, Augusten. I have one weakness. It is not silver and it is most definitely not one I recommend you seek to exploit."

Augusten was quiet for a long moment. "As you say, Queen Renata."

Renata took hold of the conversation and changed the subject. "Have you heard word from the other clans?"

"Yes."

"And?" she prompted.

"No other clan save yours has been attacked by the Dracule."

"As I imagined. Do you know why, Augusten?"

"I do not," he said, leaning back in his seat. "For all I know, Renata, this could be some ploy of yours."

"It is not." Renata turned her head and I followed her gaze. Istania sat at the other end of the table. "What do you think?" Renata asked her.

Istania's eyelids flickered slightly before she addressed King Augusten. "She is not lying, my lord. There has been truth to their words ever since they entered our caverns. Either that, or they believe their own lies."

"We're not dissembling," I said. "We have been attacked twice by Damokles. The Dracule managed to infiltrate our clan and to turn some of the Elders against the throne. The traitors have been punished, but Damokles has proved by attacking our Donatore and my queen's personal guards that he still lives and fights."

"Why would he choose your clan alone to attack?"

"I do not know."

"Augusten, have any of the clans you sent word to ever had an alliance with the Dracule?"

"Not that I know of, why?"

"That's why they're attacking us," I said, understanding Renata's line of thought and addressing her. "You told me once, you knew the Dracule. And Vasco had a Draculian lover. We've been… entangled with them in the past?"

"Yes, cara mia."

"Ah, but that leaves another question, Queen Renata. You did not request that I send word to any clans that have ever had an alliance with the Dracule. I would not even know where to begin." After a long silence, he finally asked, "What do you want, Renata? What do you ask of the Bull Shoal?"

"An alliance."

"You do see the trouble with that, do you not? If we form an alliance with you, we side with you and your battles become ours."

"This battle will become yours whether you like it or not," Iliaria said, her tail swaying and sending a pebble scattering across the stone floor. "Which is why the Rosso Lussuria come to you with an offer that sweetens the deal." She raised her hand and Anatharic stepped forward on his slightly arched legs. He uncurled his furred hands and left a slender ring with an elegant smoky stone before Augusten.

Augusten eyed the ring with some suspicion. "How long?"

"A year," Renata said.

"That is too long. Six months," Augusten said, clearly wanting to pick up the ring, though he left it on the table.

"A year, no more and no less, King Augusten. Were you in my position, you would seek the same."

"You say the girl is your lover?" he asked.

"She is."

Augusten raised his gaze to Iliaria and said, "But she is yours, too. I have seen the way you look at me when I look at her. You are both protective of her."

I wasn't really certain why King Augusten was so concerned with whose lover I was. It seemed a strange thing to be concerned about and made me uncomfortable.

"She is my dragă," Iliaria said.

"Nine months," Augusten said after staring at me for a moment longer, and I relaxed a fraction as the subject changed. "I can give you no more than that, Renata."

"Ten."

Augusten smiled. "You drive a hard bargain."

"We need your help, Augusten. I would not be here did we not. If the Dracule is left unchecked, this war will find its way to your doorstep. An alliance will benefit us both."

"Ten," he agreed. "On one condition."

"Name your condition, Augusten."

"Take Istania and some of my guard with you."

Istania's eyes widened a fraction, and I knew Augusten hadn't consulted her.

"We will take your spies."

Augusten reached for the ring and Iliaria was suddenly there, holding it. "When the moon rises on the tenth month, this will be returned." She turned the ring between her fingers, the white gold band sparkling faintly in the fire light. "Unless you desire to barter again."

When Augusten nodded, she gave him the ring and he slipped it onto his finger.

A ruckus sounded from outside the dining hall. A man's voice boomed abruptly through the passageways, the words echoing in my ears. "Halt!"

Augusten and Renata exchanged a look as every guard in the room drew a weapon. Vasco, Nirena, and Dominique were suddenly on their feet, their weapons drawn. Istania too had drawn her bow.

Feet scuffled against the stone floor before they sounded again in frantic slaps as if someone were running.

"Halt!"

Istania waited for her king's orders, her bow aimed at the doorway.

"Augusten," she said. "They're getting away."

"Go," he said. "Apprehend the intruder."

In the blink of an eye, she was gone, taking two of the cloaked guardsmen with her.

"My lady?" Vasco asked.

Renata offered the barest of nods and Vasco and Nirena went.

Dominique stayed behind and no one, not even his queen, questioned him. I knew he would not leave her side, even if she ordered him. I believe that knowledge alone stopped Renata from ordering him to join the others.

I was wearing the fox blade in a sheath at my hip. Strangely, it was the first time the blade had not magically ended up in my hand at the first sign of a threat.

Cuinn?

Aye?

Do you know what passes?

Cuinn roused from his sleep. His maw opened as he yawned widely, the tip of his tongue curling.

'Tis not the Dracule, and considering whoever it is was trying to flee, they don't seem an immediate threat.

Voices sounded from the other room again. The sound of someone's air rushing from them filtered into the room after the clear sound of a punch landing against someone's body.

"Move!" Istania yelled. "Give me a clear shot!"

Another grunt and the sound of someone's foot splashing in a small puddle. The cavern walls shuddered as a body crashed into one of them.

"Step aside!" Istania's voice carried over the others.

Vasco's voice rose over hers. "Wait," he commanded. "Wait!"

All sounds of fighting ceased.

"Do you know this man?"

"Get off me!" a man said in a thick English accent I didn't recognize. "Get her off me!"

"Nirena?" Vasco asked.

"Not yet, Vasco. Who are you?"

"Does it matter? Get off me!" he said, his voice hoarse and panicked.

"Not until I know who you are and why you were spying."

"I didn't come here to hurt anyone!"

"Why were you sneaking around?"

"He's telling the truth," Istania said.

"Look at him, Nirena," Vasco said.

"Let him up. Let the guards escort him before King Augusten."

I didn't hear Nirena get to her feet, but I heard a small pained sound emit from the other room, telling me someone was injured.

King Augusten pushed his chair back. He looked mildly disinterested when he said, "I suppose we should go see what all the commotion is about."

The guardsmen that had not followed Istania into the other room surrounded Augusten, doing what guards were meant to do and using their bodies to safeguard their king.

The fight to apprehend the intruder had broken out in a wide hallway. As they had done with our party, the guards had their bows fixed on a figure slouched against the wall holding a hand to his chest. The metallic scent of blood hung heavy in the moist air.

Vasco stood several feet away from the figure with his sword point resting along the line of his leg. Blood was smeared on Nirena's gown, as if she had used the material to wipe a blade clean.

Istania kept her crossbow aloft and sighted on the man before us.

"Spying on vampires is a dangerous hobby," Augusten said, his voice smooth and detached. "I will ask you one question and only one. If you answer falsely, you will be executed by my guardswoman. Why were you spying?"

The man shifted against the wall, his hands coated in the blood spilling from the wound high on his chest.

"Because the Rosso Lussuria vampires need my help." He raised his face defiantly, his azure eyes filled with stubborn courage.

Out of the corner of my eye, I saw understanding dawn over Vasco's features.

King Augusten spared a glance at Istania and Istania tipped her head. Yes, he was telling the truth.

Augusten moved in a blur of black leather. A sword rang from his sheath; the man against the wall raised his hand and swept it in an arc through the air. Augusten's sword went flying, clanging against the stone before he could point it fully at the injured man.

Vasco gave a choked sound as if he was trying to restrain a laugh. All faces in the room turned on him.

A wave of irritation rippled from Augusten. "Do you know this man?"

"Sì," Vasco continued to laugh. "Ah, sì. I believe I do. And you know me, if I am not mistaken?" he said to the man on the ground.

"Sì, padre."

Vasco sheathed his sword and strode forward. He held a hand to help the man up. "Does your mother know you have been following her?"

The man's eyes, a startling mirror image of Vasco's, narrowed. "No."

Augusten raised his hand in a gesture and his guardsmen turned their bows on Vasco. Istania hesitated, briefly, before she too directed her weapon as her king had ordered.

Renata stepped forward. "Augusten..."

"You should have told me you brought one of the Stregha into my kingdom, Renata."

"We did not know we were being followed, King Augusten."

Augusten turned to Vasco. "Is that so? This man says he is your son, but you are a vampire. How is that possible?"

"It is so, I did not know we were being followed. It was a very long time ago, King Augusten. Stregherian witches do not age as mortals."

Cuinn answered my silent question. *They're descended from Fata blood, remember?*

The Fatas are immortal?

Aye, and if the Stregha have enough of our blood in their lineage, they age very slowly.

So some of the Stregha do age?

If the magic in their blood is weak, aye.

Istania spoke in Vasco's defense as she lowered her bow. "He is telling the truth. He did not know the boy followed him," she said. "And I think if the witch meant any direct harm he would have done more than disarm you, my lord."

Augusten nodded and the guards lowered their bows one at a time.

"You say the Rosso Lussuria needs your help and that is why you have been following them?" Augusten asked, then said, "Stand up, boy."

"I am older than some of the vampires in this room. Do not call me a boy." He rose with some difficulty, grimacing as it obviously pained him to rise. Vasco stepped back when he realized his son was not going to take the hand he offered, though he uncertainly hovered nearby. The man pressed his hand more solidly against his chest in attempt to staunch the flow of blood and winced.

"No," Vasco said, a thread of sadness in his tone. "You are a man fully grown now. I am sorry. I never knew. I want you to know that had I known, I would have found you."

"It doesn't matter," the man said. "I've found you."

"How?" Vasco asked.

"As you said. I followed my mother. She's always been tight-lipped." He coughed, spitting on the cave's floor with an expression of disgust. "And was even more so when she left to help you. I knew something was amiss."

"And so you took to spying on her?"

Vasco's son grinned widely, and a pang of sorrow and regret made my chest tight. I felt Vasco's emotions like they were my own.

"Sì. My mother quite despises you," he said, wincing again, his chest rising harshly as he fought to breathe. "I know she's withdrawn her aid."

"It was requested that she withdraw her aid," Vasco said. "Do you need a healer?"

"I'm healing. Your vampire just dealt me a deep wound."

I flicked my gaze to Nirena, who didn't bother to apologize or even look terribly sorry.

"My mother is a fickle woman," he said. "She never wanted me to know you. Well, I know you now and I know your clan is in trouble."

"Why would you offer your aid?" I asked.

"I am not like my mother," he said. "I have gifts she does not possess."

"What gifts are those?" Augusten asked.

"I can see the true nature of a person."

"And what do you see?" Vasco asked, inching closer to him.

"In you? I see strength. I see loyalty and honor and humor. I see pain and sadness and a man not held back by life's misgivings. I see a man that fixes his heart to the compass of love, not retribution and hate. My mother cannot see past her own wounds," he said, leaning against the wall and letting it bear his weight. "She never has. I would come to know you, if you would allow it."

I looked at Vasco then and though he made no noise, tears trickled down the paleness of his cheeks in the firelight.

My chest grew tight again.

Vasco smiled sadly. "I would like that."

"Well," Augusten interrupted, "now that your little family reunion is settled. Shall we carry on with more pressing matters?"

Renata kept her gaze pinned on Augusten when she said, "Vasco, take your son to your quarters and have Nirena heal the wounds she's dealt him."

"I do not need healing," Vasco's son protested.

"You will," Nirena said, "and only I can heal what I've dealt."

Vasco laid a hand on his shoulder. "What is your name?"

"Emilio," he said. "My name is Emilio, father."

Vasco slipped an arm around Emilio's waist and helped guide him to his chambers while Nirena and Anatharic trailed behind.

Chapter Eight

King Augusten escorted us to his private study to continue our discussion. "I will send some of my guards with you when you take your leave," he said to Renata. "As I said I would and as a show of reinforcing our newfound alliance. Tell me, what will you do with the other clans? Will you travel to them as you have traveled here?"

"I do not yet know," Renata said, though she seemed to consider it. "It is dangerous."

"It is," Augusten said. "As it was for you to come here, but you came anyway. Why? It has been long since we last met. What made you think I wouldn't have you captured and imprisoned?"

Renata smiled coyly. "I did not think you had changed that much in some hundred years, Augusten. You were always more fair-minded than that, I think."

Augusten toyed with his facial hair. "Was I so easy to read, even then?"

"Yes."

"I would have formed an alliance with you without the bribe, you know."

"I know," Renata said, "but I too try to be fair."

"The others won't be like me. Some, perhaps, but not all. We know one another of old, but there are those you do not know, Renata. I've met King Circen of the Reve Noir clan. He will not be easily convinced. Might I offer you some advice?"

Renata raised her brows, but said, "If it pleases you, Augusten."

"Let me send word to them again, all of the surrounding clans. Set a date to meet with each of the rulers on neutral territory. Queen Helamina of Ravenden expressed a certain amount of interest. I think she will be easily wooed into an alliance. I can only guarantee you safe passage to Helamina's territory, as she is a friend of old. What will you?"

"Send word to Queen Helamina, if you will, and we will go from there."

"Shall I send word that she should expect a visit from you?"

"Do you trust her?"

"Yes."

Slowly and obviously slipping into thought, Renata nodded. "We might as well."

I spared a glance at Iliaria.

"If King Augusten sends his men, we cannot carry all of them," she said.

"Not to worry, Great Siren," Augusten said. "There are those among us that have their own preferred methods of travel."

"So it is decided?" she asked, her gaze sliding from Augusten to Renata. "We will go speak with this Queen Helamina before returning to your kingdom or reaching out to the others?"

"So it seems," Renata said.

❖

It did not take long for Istania to fetch us with word from King Augusten. A few hours passed, at the most. It seemed awfully quick for the message to have been delivered by bat and so I wondered how Augusten had contacted Queen Helamina. Istania and a handful of Augusten's guards escorted us to meet with him again. Vasco's son, Emilio, was whole and healed.

We were led to another circular chamber. There was a small reflective pool of water in the middle of the room. Unlike the others, the room was not lit by any torchlight. Two of the guards that headed our party procured lit torches from outside and carried them in. Augusten stood before the pool. At the edge of the pool, water droplets splashed down into it, sending the reflected torchlight flickering as if the water itself had caught on fire.

"Queen Helamina awaits your audience, Queen Renata." He swept his arm outward, gesturing toward the pool.

"Is Queen Helamina a fish, Augusten? I do not understand."

"Gulliver," the king said.

Gulliver tossed back his hood and went to the edge of the pool while Augusten spoke. "I told you, there are those within my clan that have their own means of travel."

"Ah," Renata said, watching Gulliver as he placed his palms flat over the open pool. The pool rippled as if he'd thrown a stone into it, and a small breeze of power made the curls of my hair cling to my damp cheeks.

Gulliver stood back and bowed his head. "It is done, my lord."

"A veil parter," Renata murmured, "how quaint. I did not know the clan of Bull Shoals boasted of such power."

"Some powers are best not boasted of."

"Hmm," she mused. "Your secret is safe with me, Augusten."

"Good," he said. "I'd hoped you'd say that. I will send five of my men and women with you. Istania, Gulliver, Titania, Anicetus, and Liberius. Each of them possesses skills that will aid you, have you need of them. And…" Augusten turned, waving forth another cloaked guardsman. The guardsman carried something covered in a cloak of exquisite crimson. "This," Augusten said, "is for you, Lady Epiphany."

For the second time in my life among the Rosso Lussuria, I was not sure how to react. Renata tipped her head slightly, just enough to let me know that I should indeed accept Augusten's present.

The guard handed the large item to me. As soon as I took it and its weight hefted in my hand, I knew what it was.

"My lord?" I asked, perplexed.

"You seemed to have taken a liking to them, no?" Augusten asked with a boyish smile. "Worry not, lady. It is only a gift. The cloak too, is yours to keep."

I sank into somewhat of a curtsey, as much as I could whilst holding the cage. "I cannot thank you enough, my lord."

"No thanks necessary," Augusten said. "It is my pleasure. Take good care of him and do not forget to let him out to hunt at night."

I was not exactly sure what motivated Augusten's gift, but I was not so foolish to believe it came without strings.

Gulliver moved to face the small body of water and raised his hands to his chest, as if he were about to pray. His hands parted and the water parted with them, forming two walls of water that stood on either side of a pathway leading to a doorway.

Emilio grumbled, "I could've done that."

Vasco put a hand on his shoulder. "No doubt, but why waste the energy when there's someone else to do it?"

The walkway was narrow, not as narrow as the entrance to the Bull Shoals kingdom, but narrow enough that we could only walk two at a time. Anatharic and Istania took the lead and we fell in behind them. Iliaria placed me between herself and Renata, while Vasco and his son walked behind her. Gulliver and the rest of Augusten's guards took the back of our line.

Emilio said, "Wait," and started working his way up toward the front of our group. Renata, Iliaria, and I formed a single line so that he could pass. "Let me lead with you," he said to Anatharic. "As a precaution. I can help if we come under attack."

"Asss you will, Ssstregherian."

Nirena and Dominique moved to allow Emilio to walk beside the Great Sire.

"We will pass through the doorway and into the clan of Ravenden," Gulliver said. "Queen Helamina will have sent others to await us on the other side."

Anatharic and Emilio led. When Anatharic reached for the door handle, Emilio stopped him, holding a hand above it as if he was checking to make sure it wasn't spelled. He opened the door and light from the other side spilled outward, making the dark walls of water glisten around us.

Emilio stepped through first and one-by-one, we followed suit, entering the kingdom of Ravenden.

CHAPTER NINE

A large brazier burned in the center of the room, casting a circle of dancing light and shadows. Unlike the cave the Bull Shoalians called home, the clan of Ravenden was more similar to our Sotto and obviously built by human slave workers some centuries ago. The walls of Ravenden were of a natural stone streaked gray and white. The firelight bounced off them, making the quartz shimmer like diamonds in a veil. Great stone pillars stood at each corner of the room, trees carved into their marble bodies, and atop each tree perched a raven, the crest of Ravenden.

"Well," Vasco said, "we should have company by now, shouldn't we?"

"One would think," Nirena said.

Istania drew bow and the others did too, as if she had given them an order.

"Something is amiss," she whispered.

I glanced back. The doorway we had come in through had disappeared. Gulliver and Istania were the only two guards from Bull Shoals that bothered removing their hoods. The others stood tall and mysterious.

Iliaria and Anatharic shared a look. Iliaria nodded and they moved in opposite directions. There were two doorways marked by torches, but each of the doorways was without actual doors. It didn't seem the most private place for a quiet entrance. Surely, if the clan of Ravenden was around, they would have heard us by now.

Iliaria's nostrils flared as she tried to catch a scent on the air. I placed my hand on the pommel of the fox blade.

"Someone should be here," Gulliver said.

"Unless we have walked into a trap, Bull Shoalian," Renata said, giving him an unfriendly look.

"I swear on it, this is no trap of our making."

"No," a woman's voice called from everywhere and nowhere. "It is of ours."

I placed the gilded cage on the ground as quietly as I could. The night was suddenly alive with a symphony of hissing steel.

All those in our party stood armed, and yet, nothing happened.

Iliaria had drawn both of the crescent-curved blades of the Dracule.

"Morina," she said. "Doing Damokles's dirty work, these days? I knew you were ambitious, but I had thought you better than to be his bitch."

A tall figure emerged from the darkness at the back of the room, stepping into the circle of light from the brazier. At first, I thought it was some trick of light that made her appearance so strange. And then I realized I saw her truly. Her hair was streaked black, white, and ash gray. Draculian wings stretched from her human back, arching above her shoulders. One of her eyes was covered by a large patch. The eye left uncovered was crimson with branches of the same onyx lightning that decorated Iliaria's gaze.

"Now, now, Printessa." The Dracule smiled widely, revealing all four of her fangs in a sort of grinning snarl. "Is that any way to greet an old friend?"

It was not noticeable, but I felt Renata startle beside me. I wasn't sure why.

Iliaria moved from the doorway and closer to the Dracule. Morina kept the brazier between herself and Iliaria, not exactly hiding behind it, for she was too tall in stature to do that, but it did seem she was making an effort to do so.

Istania moved to my right and Gulliver and another followed her as they flanked out. The two other Bull Shoalians covered the doorway Iliaria had been investigating.

The rest of us stayed as we were. I let the point of the fox blade drop toward the ground and waited. It seemed no one was too keen on charging into battle just yet.

"What did he offer you, Morina?"

"Offer?" Her one red eye blinked. "Why would you think he had to offer anything, Printessa?"

"What did Damokles offer you in order to gain your services to his cause? Power? He has none to give."

"I do not need Damokles's power or his promises to seek to right a wrong committed long ago."

"Aah." It was Iliaria's turn to smile, dark and mysteriously. "So that's what this is? Come to defend your wounded pride? Or should I say, your wounded eye?"

Morina hissed through her teeth. Her face crinkled frighteningly, but Iliaria stood her ground. "You took something from me, Printessa."

"Fool," Iliaria spat the word. "It was your own doing. When will you see that?"

Fury passed over Morina's features. "Never."

"So be it," Iliaria said, raising her hands and the two sickles to her sides in invitation. "Come dig your own grave, then."

Morina started to lunge, but before she could get around the brazier, the sound of a crossbow to my right snapped and sent an arrow whirring through the air.

Morina was fast. She heard the arrow and tried to whirl away from it. She used her wings to shield her body against it and succeeded in knocking the arrow off its course and skittering across the smooth floor.

But while she was busy deflecting Gulliver's shot, Istania took hers. The arrow penetrated her neck and Morina cried out like an animal screeching.

Another of the guards let loose. This time, Morina caught the arrow before it pierced her heart. She jerked the arrow free of her neck and seemed to ignore the gush of blood that spilled down her chest. She spoke through clenched teeth. "You are all making me *very* angry."

Emilio raised his hands and a ball of flame leapt to life between his open palms. "There's more where that came from."

Morina growled her challenge at him.

Piph, Cuinn whispered in my mind, *she said the trap is of their making. I do not sense anyone else, though. She's alone and trying to make ye think it's an ambush.*

Why would she be alone? I asked him. *That bloody well doesn't make any sense.*

He offered his version of a fox's shrug and said, *Beats the pumpkins out of me.*

Emilio's flame stretched and moved as if it were shaping itself into something. If I was going to stop the fight that was about to ensue, I had to do it now.

Renata placed a hand on my shoulder. I think it was to warn me, but I stepped forward anyway.

"Emilio," I said. "Cease fire."

He glanced uncertainly at me and I reached up to touch his arm. He let out a breath, and as he did so, his flame shrunk to a plume of smoke.

"Wise," Morina said. "But why stop now? We're just getting started."

"If you really wanted to kill us," I said as I walked toward her and felt the tensions in the group behind me rise high like a tide threatening to pull me back. My legs trembled ever so slightly, but I forced myself to continue toward Morina anyway. "Why did you come alone? Why not ambush us?"

"Does it really matter?" Iliaria asked. "The fact that she is here and stands against us is evidence enough of her treachery, I think."

"It matters, Iliaria."

Morina's one eye-lid flickered.

"You wonder why I approach you," I said.

"Terrific," she growled. "A telepath."

"No," I said and knelt before her, far enough away that if she made a move to hurt me, I was certain Iliaria could stop her. "An empath. Why do you attack us alone when, Dracule or no, you are outnumbered? You cannot win a battle against the lot of us."

"An empath, even better. The last time I ate an empath I had indigestion for a week."

"Then you know I will not go down so smoothly, though perhaps it says something of your skill when it comes to women, Dracule."

"I didn't mean it in that way," Morina said, her one eye narrowing slightly.

"I'm sure you didn't. So tell me, why do you seek to attack us when you are alone and outnumbered? Surely, if you were working with Damokles and his horde of toadies you would have come with a small army at your back."

"Who says I have not?"

I turned the fox blade in my hand until the flat of the blade caught the light and drew her attention to it.

"An empathic vampire with a spirit blade." Morina laughed darkly. "You do make interesting *friends*, Printessa." She was still gazing at the sword when her eye widened. "You," she said. One moment, she was staring at my hand, at the ring, I think, with an expression of surprise and horror, and the next, my blade went clanging across the floor.

Morina disarmed me in a matter of seconds. For a split second, my vision went dark, and then Morina pulled me hard against her, the point of steel a sharp threat at my throat.

When my mind made sense of what had happened, I realized that Morina had grabbed me and used her Draculian ability to travel between the worlds to shift us to another place in the room. She'd pulled me further back in the room, away from the others and their weapons, and held me in front of her like a shield.

The expression on Iliaria's face was one of fury.

"So this is her?" Morina asked, the tip of her blade threatening to prick my skin. I went very still as my heart hammered like a drum against my ribs. I tried to calm myself to no avail.

Morina's blade cut my skin, sharp and stinging. A trickle of blood slid down my neck. "Answer me!" she screamed over my shoulder. "Is this her, Iliaria?"

"Is she who?" Iliaria asked, her voice deep and growling with anger.

"Don't try to riddle me," Morina said, pushing her blade even harder against my neck. This time I winced and she grabbed a handful of my hair to keep me still. "Is this the vampire you're bedding? The one that has seduced you with her charms?"

"I do not feel that is particularly any of your—" Her blade threatened to bite deeper, and I stopped talking.

"You must be an excellent fuck." Morina's lips moved at my ear, her breath hot. "To sway the allegiances and gain the passions of a Draculian Printessa. Is she as gentle as you'd hoped, vampire? Does she make sweet love to you in the night?"

I wasn't sure how to respond so I didn't. Morina didn't like that, and she jerked roughly on my hair and placed her blade higher up on my neck, against my beating pulse.

You've got to get her to let ye go, Piph.

I don't know how, Cuinn.

Aye, you do. Use your empathy. Use your skills, lass.

I shut my eyes, blocking out the sight of Iliaria's fury.

Renata's voice whispered through my mind, *Play your fear for all it's worth, cara mia.*

I met her gaze from across the room. I understood what she wanted me to do, though I was not so certain it would work on Morina. Renata wanted me to use my fear to extort and distract a Great Siren.

Not so difficult to do, considering my heart was still beating as if it'd jump out of my chest and flee without the rest of me. I raised my trembling hands and touched Morina's arm. "Please," I whispered.

Morina buried her face in the bend of my neck, though I knew she watched the others to make sure they did not move against her. She inhaled deeply against my skin and I did not fight the tremor of my limbs.

"Do you play so weak and helpless for her?" Morina's laugh vibrated against my neck, and I wasn't pretending at all when I cringed and squirmed against her.

She held me tighter, her arms like metal shackles around me. "There are rumors floating around about you," she murmured.

"Queen's consort, Draculian lover." Morina's steely fingers circled my wrist as she raised my hand, turning it to reveal my tattoo. "Oh, you must like her indeed, Printessa, to have given her your mark."

Iliaria was deadly silent.

Morina nuzzled my hair and I bit my tongue and tried to focus on something else, anything other than her face so close to mine. My fear amused and encouraged her. It wasn't exactly helping or distracting her.

"She's right, you know," she whispered at my ear again. "I could not best her in a fight."

"Then let me go."

"So soon?" Morina asked. "I'm not likely to do that, *love*, for as soon as I release you, they'll be on me like vultures." Her lips were pressed so close to my ear that I felt her smile.

"Why are you working with Damokles?"

"I'm not," Morina said. "I'm working for myself. You see, your Draculian *lover* there has taken something from me, 'tis only fair, I think, that I take something from her."

"You would not dare," Iliaria said.

"Watch me," Morina said and several things happened simultaneously. Morina spun me in a dance-like move, her wings spreading out to shield us both. She caught both my wrists in her hands and spun me to face her. She used the grip she had to raise the wrist that was bare of Iliaria's mark to her face. "Know that when I do this, I take great pleasure in it," she said, and then she bit me.

Iliaria screamed, "No!"

But it was too late. Morina's fangs sank down to my bones and I screamed too, screamed at the fiery pain of it, screamed where her mouth and power burned against me like a white hot flame that threatened to sear my flesh away.

❖

Piph. Something tapped my side and my eyes flew open.
Aye, Piph. Get up.

I turned my head, using my hands to push myself upright. Cuinn's orange and coal face seemed larger than it should've been.

That's it, come on.

"Cuinn." I sat up, trying to see past his visage. "Where the bloody hell am I?"

In your head. Where else?

There was nothing, a vast nothingness, save Cuinn and me. A soft orange glow surrounded him, illuminating the darkness around us.

I felt dizzy and sick. "Why?" I asked.

You're unconscious.

"Morina," I said, remembering. "Renata, Iliaria. Cuinn, the others!"

Pipe down! There's not a thing to be done now.

I grabbed him by the ears and pulled his face to mine. "Cuinn," I said, a bit more sternly than I'd have liked, but in the moment, I didn't particularly care. "Cuinn, you have to wake me."

Cuinn didn't struggle or attempt to fight off my hold while I clung to him. His features turned gentle and compassionate. *I cannot, Piph. The Great Siren's drained you close to death. I cannot wake you here.*

I panicked, uncertain what to do. Would she kill me? Would I feel it if she did? Or would I forever be lost in this place of nothingness?

If she was gonna kill ye, you'd be dead already, methinks.

"Then why am I unconscious and where are the others, Cuinn? Do you know where they are?"

Regretfully, Cuinn shook his head and sat back on his haunches. *Nay, I do not. As for why you are unconscious, you remember her biting you, don't you?*

"Yes."

I'm sorry, Piph, Cuinn said, momentarily losing me. I wasn't sure what he was sorry for, and then he stepped forward and bumped my left hand with his snout. *Look, lass.*

I did so. There, on my wrist, were flowing black lines. The letters were more sharply tipped in places than Iliaria's mark, but that's what it was: a mark. I raised the sleeve of my gown and found the dark ink-like sigil merged with another. A long branch of flowing black veins that traveled around my arm and up toward the bend of my elbow like an elegant vine. I checked my other wrist and sighed with relief when I found Iliaria's still embedded in my skin.

"How?" I asked Cuinn. "How can she mark me? I already bear Iliaria's mark."

It does not seem to matter. She's done it anyway. That and more.

"What more, Cuinn?"

She's tied herself to you, Epiphany.

I blinked, trying to understand. "I don't understand, Cuinn. She's tied herself, how? I'm tied to Renata because she's my Siren, and I'm bound to Iliaria through her mark, and I'm tied to you through the sword, but you make it sound as if Morina's done something different in the way of binding..." I raised my arm. "Why does this travel all the way up my arm, Cuinn?"

She's tied her soul to yours.

"That's possible?"

Aye. A bit like a Siren ties a piece of herself to her vampires. Only, this is a Great Siren we're speaking of and essentially she's made it so that if anyone hurts her, they hurt you and vice versa.

The carnelian glow of Cuinn's power began to dim.

"Cuinn?"

The blackness seemed to stretch and grow, threatening to swallow him.

Time to wake up, he said. *I'll be with ye when ye wake, Piph. I'm always with ye. Never forget that."*

As if I could, I thought sadly.

CHAPTER TEN

I woke with skin pressed against my lips. A hand cradled the back of my head and held me upright.

"Rise, vampire. Rise and drink."

The hum of fresh blood was a promise against my mouth and seduced me. It awakened a fiery hunger at the pit of my belly and tainted my thoughts. Driven only by instinct and need, I did as I was told. I bit that sweet wrist and honey blood welled between my lips, coating my teeth and tongue before I swallowed.

I raised my hands and held that wrist to my mouth, drinking the nectar of someone else's life. Even if I had wanted to stop, I would not have been able to do so. My hunger was too great a void and the only objective I had was to fill it.

Metallic and velvety, stronger and richer, in some part of me I knew it was Draculian blood. In some part of me I recognized Morina's smooth alto voice when she had bid me to rise and drink from her. In some part of me, I knew I should've cared, but in the throes of a gut-wrenching hunger, I didn't.

Morina continued to cradle my head while I drank from her. Her blood pooled at the corners of my mouth, dribbling down my chin as I frantically tried to take in more than I could swallow.

"That is enough," she said, but still, my hunger had not abated. Still, I did not stop.

She grabbed me by the hair, jerking my mouth from her skin and forcing me to swallow.

"Enough! You'll drink yourself into a stupor, vampire."

I licked the blood from my mouth. "If I am now your prisoner, lady, a stupor does not sound so bad an idea."

Morina smiled cattily. "So soon you resent me, vampire? We've not yet had the pleasure of becoming well acquainted enough for that, I think, but not to worry. There will be plenty of time."

She released me and stood tall and straight, her wings relaxed behind her. I sat up in the bed she had placed me in, trying to think as Renata would have encouraged me to do in such a situation. The only light in the room was a fire that burned beneath the mantel of a beautiful fireplace. Plum and burgundy draperies covered the canopy. Though not necessarily exquisitely furnished, the room was warm and cozy and well kept, making me think that it was someone's home. Or had been, before Morina had brought us here.

"Where am I?" I asked.

"Here for now," Morina said. "That is all you need to know."

"Where are the others?"

"The clan of Ravenden, I imagine."

"You have brought me here against my will. They will come looking for me," I said.

"Terribly sorry, but that's mostly the point," Morina said. "I have faith they will come looking for you, vampire. Precious as you are." She reached out, touching my cheek. I recoiled, glaring at her. Morina seemed to find that amusing, offering a low, rumbling laugh that sounded like some great cat's purr.

She lunged forward, catching me by the wrist. She jerked my arm toward her and I didn't fight. She was Dracule, and vampire or no, she could've torn me limb from limb. I wasn't willing to find out just how much damage a vampire could withstand from one of their kind.

Morina pushed up my sleeve, baring the tattoo on my arm, revealing her mark as if she thought I didn't know it was there. "But when they find you, as they will, there is nothing they can do to me." She jerked my arm up higher. "If they hurt me, they hurt you and vice versa, vampire." She tossed my hand away from hers suddenly and abruptly, as if it disgusted her. "That, I think, will keep them from doing anything stupid."

"Why me?" I asked.

"Because," she tilted her head, "she values you."

"Iliaria?" I asked. "Why do you despise her?"

Morina smiled sweetly, unnervingly. It didn't match the look of hatred in her crimson eye. "That's a story for another night, *love*." She lowered herself, putting her face close to me. I didn't give ground, forcing myself not to reveal my fear and disgust. "Now, while you're in my keep, you'll behave, won't you? I'm showing you courtesy. The room is nice, is it not?" She touched my hair, petting me in an idle manner that set my skin to crawling. I bit my tongue and shut my eyes, trying to block out the sight of her. But she continued to pet me, stroking the curls of hair back from my face. "If you try to flee, I will find you. If you try to contact Iliaria, I will know. I will not be as courteous if you fail to heed my words."

Gratefully, she stepped away from me and motioned to the room. "You are free to explore, so long as you remain within the walls of this castle. I will only give you that warning, vampire. Do not displease me. This is a paradise compared to what lies in store for you if you disobey."

And with that, she left, leaving me alone with a wave of anxiety that threatened to spill in tears from my eyes.

Don't, Piph, Cuinn's voice whispered soothingly. *It's not worth crying about.*

But it was too late. I stifled a sob and buried my face in the pillow to keep from making any noise. The last thing I wanted Morina to know was that she had the power to upset me, but I couldn't stop the overwhelming flood of dismay that came over me.

I thought of the others and wept.

❖

In the days that followed, there wasn't much to do. I had learned to live without certain luxuries among the Rosso Lussuria, but I had never really reckoned how blessed I was living in Renata's kingdom. Being trapped in Morina's prison made me aware of the small blessings the Sotto provided. Sitting in my chambers in

Morina's castle, I found myself wondering if I would slowly be driven mad by sheer boredom.

Cuinn tried to keep me company and did his best to keep me distracted. He attempted to strike up conversations with me, but more often than not, I found myself at a loss for words and not in the mood to converse. I wanted to be alone with my thoughts, and when Cuinn figured that out, he left me with them.

For the most part, Morina had become completely standoffish. She entered my chambers only to provide me with enough sustenance to keep me alive. She brought her freshly spilled blood in an ornate chalice studded with rubies. She had not offered me her blood directly from her wrist since the night she had taken me. Strangely, she didn't seem keen on the idea of touching me again. For that, I was thankful; for she no longer sought to stroke me as some stray animal she had found and decided to keep. On the other hand, her increasingly cold demeanor left me feeling more and more the prisoner I was.

We talked, sometimes. Though when I tried to engage her in conversation, she spoke as little as possible.

"What day is it?" I asked.

"It does not matter."

And since she wouldn't tell me, I found other ways to keep track of the time that passed, marking the wall beside my bed with ash from the fireplace. I hid the markings behind the spill of the heavy draperies.

Wherever I was being held, the sun did not seem to rise here. Not once did I feel its pull beyond the shielding power of the ring. The only way I could surmise that a day had indeed gone by was when Morina came with her blood.

Three days passed, and even though she had given me permission to explore, I didn't have any desire to do so. It was as if, by exploring my *cage*, I was more a prisoner somehow.

On the fourth day, the boredom broke my resolve. I paced my chambers, catching glimpses of my disheveled and unkempt hair in the mirror. I wanted a change of clothes and a bath. It'd been too long since I'd had either.

I slipped from my room and walked around a banister at the top of the stairwell. I could smell a fire burning from somewhere downstairs and took the stairs as carefully and quietly as I could.

If Morina had brought me to a castle, it was not a very large one by any means. There were no great and spacious rooms. In fact, it appeared to be more of a castle-like country home than an actual medieval keep. No pictures or tapestries hung on the walls. No family crests indicated family history. The furnishings were minimal and dingy. The cold stone floor was bare of any carpets. The only decorative touches to the place were a few wall sconces used for lighting, and even those were drab.

I touched the rough wall, letting it slide beneath the tips of my fingers as I descended the stairs.

Laughter, love, joy…in the back of my mind I heard music, or perhaps, I felt it singing in my blood. I don't know. The night seemed suddenly alive to my senses. I could smell the sweet and savory scent of meat roasting, could hear bubbling laughter ringing and pulsing like an echo in the stone. Once, this place had been someone's home. The walls whispered memories of celebration and cheer.

And then my hand trembled lightly. In some part of me, I was aware I had stopped on the steps as I let my power find what it would.

The memories had their way with me, rolling ahead in time. A door crashed open, there were screams, and terror gripped my chest. I forced myself to stay focused, to not lose the threads of memory that came to me.

There was violence and bloodshed. The walls continued to whisper their secrets, and as much as I wanted to pull away, to stop them from telling me their tale, I did not.

A group of men had come seeking shelter from the rain and were turned away, so the bandits took the place by force.

Not just the home they had taken by force…the women…

I pulled my hand away, stifling a shudder of rage and disgust.

"What do they say, empath?" Morina stood at the foot of the stairs in a pair of dark breeches and flowing gray shirt.

"What did who say to me?" I asked, taking the last few steps.

Morina put her arm out to block my path. "The souls that linger here, vampire. What did they say to you?"

"I'm not sure what you mean."

She narrowed that one red eye at me as her lips pursed. "I do not like being lied to. What did you see, vampire?"

"Why does it matter?" I asked incredulously. "Why does it matter what my power has discerned?"

"Never mind." Morina moved away and I caught her arm.

The look she gave me was so scalding and frightening that I drew my hand away immediately. She said nothing more, turning on her bare feet and making her way down the hall as if I no longer stood in the same room.

"I need a bath and a change of clothes."

Morina paused, her body tense. "And you expect me to do what, exactly? To go out and fetch buckets of water and a spare change of clothes for you?"

"What was it you said you were being? Courteous, was it?" I scoffed. "I fail to see it, considering."

Morina moved so quickly I felt the disruption in the currents of air before my back met the wall behind me.

"No wonder she fancies you so." She pinned me with her hands on my shoulders, her face dangerously close. "You are no better than her."

"And that means what, exactly?"

"Privileged," she said. "Here you are, my prisoner, and you expect me to wait hand and foot on you?" Her grip tightened painfully. "You've some gall, vampire."

"I don't like being dirty." I kept my voice low. "I'll fetch the bloody water myself, if I must."

Morina growled and released me, and when she turned her back on me again, I wisely kept my mouth shut.

Bit testy, isn't she? Cuinn asked. *Then again, I suppose if all you had to do was sit around licking yerself like a cat you'd not be worrying about providing your prisoners with a proper bath.* He snorted.

A bit? I thought. *Mayhap, more than that.*

Aye, they seem to be a temperamental lot.

I didn't necessarily disagree. Iliaria certainly had her *somewhat* temperamental moments. Though they seemed to be mild in comparison with Morina's.

I let out a sigh of frustration and fought the swelling wave of emotions that welled within me. It was pointless to cry or scream. The only thing I could do was try to accept the situation for what it was, as much as I loathed it.

If Morina didn't kill me in a fit, whether she'd marked me or no, I had a chance of survival, of seeing Renata and Iliaria again.

I decided to explore in earnest to keep myself occupied. I avoided taking the same path Morina had taken down the hall and instead found myself in a relatively spacious, yet dreary sitting room. The curtains over the windows were dirty and tattered. The fireplace looked as though it hadn't been used since the previous owners had lived here.

It was empty. Lifeless.

Even the Sotto of the Rosso Lussuria, a kingdom of vampires, danced with more life than the prison Morina kept me in. Did she live in this sorrowful place?

The rest of the castle was in the same state of dire neglect. Cobwebs hung from ceiling corners. Dust clung to unused wall sconces. Old wooden furniture was brittle and unpolished. I wondered how long Morina had been using the home. More so, I wondered why she only seemed to be putting certain rooms to use.

It made little sense.

I found a dry rag draped over the side of an empty basin in one of the downstairs rooms. Morina would not let me leave or bathe or even take the time to keep me company whilst she held me prisoner. Well and so, I would make use of my time even if it was spent in doing something as mundane as cleaning. Besides, I was already dirty.

You're really going to clean? Cuinn asked, sounding amused.

I've nothing better to do. Why not?

You're being held prisoner and you decide to clean your prison, Piph? That doesn't seem a little strange to you?

It's not the first time I've been someone's prisoner, Cuinn.

And do you think you'll win Morina's approval by doing such a thing?

It couldn't hurt to try, not that I really care.

As it turned out, I didn't win her approval. Hours passed as I tidied the place up as best I could with the aid of a dusty old rag. It looked better, by some. Unfortunately, most of the dust just settled back into different places.

I stood on a chair, trying to reach a cobweb high in the upper corner of the sitting room when I heard Morina grunt.

"What are you doing?" she asked.

"The best I can to tidy the place up with a dodgy bit of cloth."

"You don't need to do that," she said and turned to walk out of the room.

"What else am I supposed to do?" I asked. Standing on the chair allowed me to look her in the eye. "This is dreadful, and I'm like to go mad from sheer boredom! You kidnap me. You feed me your blood. You mark me and bind my bleedin' soul to yours and you're using me as bait to attack my lover. Why?" I threw the rag down in a huff and crossed my arms over my chest, trying unsuccessfully to contain my rage and hurt.

"This isn't the first time I've been someone's prisoner," I said. "But always, it was with a purpose. What purpose do you have aside from some silly grudge you're holding toward Iliaria? I know her and I know that whatever you're holding against her, it's ridiculous and childish and petty," I spit the last word at her, safe in the knowledge that if she hurt me, she hurt herself.

I stood behind her mark like a shield. The thought alone made my lips twitch with the urge to smile. I had no doubts that Morina saw what I was doing.

"Bold words," she said, her voice even and cool. "Bold words for one who knows nothing."

"What did she ever do to you?"

"She wasn't the same woman twenty years ago."

"Bloody fuck," I said, exasperated. "Who is? People are different every day."

Morina didn't respond, just looked at me with that implacable, blank Draculian stare.

"You're an angry woman, Morina. Angry and hurt. That's no way to live."

"Who are you to tell me how to live? You know nothing!" She yelled, her face contorting in rage and her tail whipping across the stone. "*Nothing!*"

"Well," I lowered my voice as hers rose, "I might know *something* if you told me. Did you ever think of that?"

"No," she said, putting her hand up in the air. "No, I know what you're doing, vampire, and it will not work."

"Suit yourself," I said. "As Iliaria said to you, dig your own grave."

Morina shook with rage, and for a moment, it rolled off her and flushed my skin to the point where I feared she would stride across the room and strike me.

But she didn't. She folded her wings around herself, as if using them to enclose her anger.

"Do not talk to me again," she said. "For your safety, do not talk to me."

"Why do you keep distancing yourself from me more and more?" I asked. "Why the drastic change, Morina? When I woke, you were more than happy to pet and stroke me as if I was your dog."

The chair was suddenly no longer beneath my feet. Morina shoved me against the wall, hard enough that she knocked the air from my lungs.

Her hand clenched around my throat.

"I...told...you...not...to...speak...to...me." Her voice dropped to a growl as she lowered her face to mine.

I spoke over the strength of her fingers. "Why, Morina? What are you so afraid of if I do?"

Morina hissed and flung me aside. I hit the floor hard, catching myself on my elbows. When I looked up, she was gone.

I sat up and rested my back against the wall, trying to will myself not to feel anything. I imagined an empty room and the blackness that had surrounded Cuinn and me in my head. No windows, only walls. No cracks, no light. Nothing, I wanted to feel nothing.

❖

Time, yet again, seemed to have slowed to a crawl. I let the drapery slide back into place, obscuring the ash-marked tallies I'd left on the wall. I wiped my hand on my gown.

Nearly a week and still I had not heard a word from the others. Still, they had not found me. I made my way across the hall. Morina had not yet complained about my visitations to the balcony there.

The crescent moon hung high above, casting a soft glow on the courtyard below. I curled my arms over the banister and stared out into the night. At least here, I didn't feel so much like a prisoner. I had the illusion of open space, of freedom.

I imagined what the dead gardens below would've been like had they been maintained. What flora would have grown there? What kind of fragrance would cling to the night breeze? I breathed in slowly, inhaling the earth's perfume and finding it crisp and woodsy. I listened to the wind rustling through the high branches of nearby trees, allowing nature's rustling music to distract me from the thoughts in my head.

"Here," Morina said from behind me.

Morina placed something on the floor just inside the doors and I approached to see what it was. She'd placed an old pail of water between us.

"Thank you," I murmured.

Morina ignored my thanks. She gestured toward the bed, refusing to meet my gaze. "There is a change of clothes. I believe they will fit." She picked a box up off the bed and held it out to me. "Here."

"What is this?" I raised the box and the sweet floral smell from inside it hit me. "Ah," I said, before she could answer. "Soap. Thank you again." I glanced at the clothing she had laid out on the bed, a pair of drawstring cotton slacks and a black T-shirt. It was not what

I would've chosen to wear, had I been given a choice, but it was certainly better than the soiled gown I was wearing.

"Wait," I said gently before Morina had a chance to walk out. Surprisingly, she halted without snapping at me.

"I need your assistance, please. It took my queen's help getting into this gown; it's going to take some help getting out of it."

I thought for sure she'd tell me to go bugger myself. At the least, that she would turn me away without a word.

She hesitated and then, finally, nodded sharply. I raised my hair and turned my back to her. Morina moved tentatively, brushing my skin as she loosened the laces of the bodice. When it was loose enough, I tugged on the sleeve and the gown spilled off my shoulders. Morina's fingers stopped working at the gown and I felt them hovering over my bare skin.

"I can remove it now, thank you."

Her hand curled unexpectedly around my throat and she pulled me back against her, her thumb digging into the tender skin under the curve of my jaw.

I felt her breath against my ear. "You are my prisoner," she said, her voice low and dangerous. "You do not bid me to do this and to do that and then dismiss me as if I am your lady-in-waiting."

Breathless with surprise and tense with agitation, I found my voice. "I never meant to imply such a thing, Morina."

She jerked me upward, her grip forcing me to rise onto the tips of my toes.

"Take the gown off."

When I didn't move to do as she requested, she growled, a sound that was purely predatory and animal and brought a rush of fear over my flesh. Her hands clawed at the front of my gown as if she would tear it off me.

"Stop," I said, and then thought better of my words and added hastily, "Please, I'll do it. You don't have to rip it off me as if I'm some cheap harlot."

She pulled the sleeve of the gown down my left arm, baring my breast and part of my stomach. "Take it off." Morina's hand loosened around my throat, allowing me to stand flat on my feet.

Her nails scraped across my neck as she removed her hand, and I cringed.

"Fear." She drew a loud breath through her nose. "The purest rush of fear I've smelled on you yet, vampire." She circled me like a great cat ready to lunge on its prey. Her tail flicked gently behind her. "This is the last time I ask. Take it off."

I drew a deep breath and raised my gaze, willing myself to remain in touch with the defiance I had felt when I'd confronted her before and not to cower in fear.

"This is what you want?" I asked, shoving down the other sleeve and pushing the gown slowly down my body. "A prisoner and a play thing, or simply to relish in my vulnerability, my humiliation, and my fear?"

"The latter will work just fine," she said, smiling cattily, and blessedly moving away from me to sit in a dusty chair tucked against the wall.

Morina watched me undress and her face was an expressionless mask. If there was any hint of desire in her, I did not feel it. If there was any malice in her, I didn't sense that either.

I relied on my empathy and felt something I'd never felt from another woman—*emptiness*.

She felt empty, empty of desire, lust, emotion, anger. All of it was gone, as if she'd blinked it away or flipped some switch inside her head that made it disappear.

Even Lucrezia, sociopath that she was, hadn't seemed empty when she'd threatened to torture and force herself on me.

"Bathe," Morina said, and I bowed my head in defeat and sank to my knees.

If Renata had asked me to do such a thing for her pleasure, I would have done so for her gladly. I probably would have even done such a thing at Iliaria's request. But Morina was not either of them, and her purpose was not for pleasure. She was my captor. I was her prisoner.

I dipped the cloth and soap into the pail and bathed in silence, making as little of a show of it as was possible. I tried to imagine that Morina was not there and that I was not being forced, but it was impossible. Thanks to the binding she had placed on me, the bond that she had forcibly forged between us, I felt her and the vast emptiness within her. I pondered what could make someone so empty. Even the vampires among the Sotto have a difficult time turning their emotions on and off. I would know, for as with Lucrezia, I have sensed their true feelings despite what they have projected. There was always something beneath the mask. Always. It was disconcerting to be so near a living being so bereft of life.

"Your anger, Morina, has burned everything else inside of you," I said, no longer caring if she took it upon herself to punish me. Being with her was punishment enough.

I forced myself to look at her, shoving my fear into the darkest corner of myself. Morina said nothing, nor did she make a move toward me. Her lack of a response inspired me to carry on.

"Would she be proud, do you think?" I asked. It was a shot in the dark, a guess, nothing more than that. Why else would she be so attached to the place? Why else would their spirits still linger here?

Morina flinched at my words, not noticeably so, but enough that I knew my words had hit their target. A few paces were all it took for her to reach me.

Morina struck me with the back of her hand, knocking me to my knees and forcing the corner of my mouth into my fang. The blood welled at the contact and I spit, tasting Morina's blood in my mouth and feeling the wound close as fast as it was made.

"Do not speak of her!"

"You wanted to know what the house told me," I said, feeling her anger as my own. "It is sick of sorrow and violence. If you want to make her happy, bring life back to her home."

I felt something then; a light weight on my shoulder like someone had walked up behind me and rested their hand there. A shiver trickled down my spine before a small flicker of emotion ignited like a lit candle. Its warm glow inched across the room, touching and enveloping me…

Compassion.

Whatever it was, whoever it was, the memories came upon me so vividly that the room in which I knelt disappeared behind the curtain of them.

"Partly memory," a woman's voice whispered. The room was the same and yet, different. The coverlet on the bed was pristine, its bright red and gold colors nowhere near as dull as in the present. A curtain moved and a spill of sunlight stretched through the room. I crawled back out of instinct and pressed myself into a shadowy corner away from the two doors.

"Do not fear," the voice said, though the body it belonged to was nowhere to be seen. *"Try harder, vampire. Try harder to see me and you will."*

I was not sure how I was supposed to try to see something I could not, but I searched the room anyway, trying to find her.

Something near the bed caught my eyes out of my peripheral vision. I saw the outline of a white dressing gown, lace spilling at her collar and wrists. As soon as I saw it, the image became stronger, more solid, and more real.

Her eyes were dark and wide and lined with thick lashes. Her cheekbones were high and round, framed by a mane of black curls. She was petite, probably not much taller than I. Her stature gave her a certain air of fragility that the strength of her bone structure denied.

"Now do you see?" The edge of an accent graced her tone, though she spoke English clearly enough to understand.

Slowly, I nodded at the figure near the bed.

"She stays in hopes that she will see me again, that she will feel me, but it will never be so, it is not meant to be."

"I don't know what you mean."

"He does," the woman said.

Cuinn slipped up beside me, pressing the line of his body against mine where I huddled. His fur was soft and real against my skin and I buried a hand in it, burning orange against my white.

Cuinn genuflected in a measure of respect. *"Aye, lady. I do."*

"What are you?" I asked. "Are you a ghost?"

"I am that which has passed through the veil."

"How am I able to see you?"

"Your abilities allow you to gather and absorb emotions and memories, vampire. His abilities," she motioned to Cuinn, *"his*

abilities help you to part the veil and to see beyond it, for he is one of the Fatas and that is what they do."

"And what are you?"

She's a White Lady, Piph.

"What is that, Cuinn? A ghost?"

Yea and nay, he said. *A White Lady is the spirit of a Fata witch that will not rest. The tragedy that befell this place has forever tied her to it, to protect it and its inhabitants.*

"Like a banshee?" I asked him.

Aye, similar to a banshee.

I wanted to ask more questions, but the White Lady spoke before I could begin.

She looked so sad when she spoke. *"She was not always as she seems, vampire. Perhaps you can help her..."*

Her image wavered in my vision. "Wait," I said. "How?"

Come on, Piph. Time to go.

"But wait!"

I woke with a start, bolting upright in the chambers I had been using as my own. A fire danced in the fireplace, sending crooked shadows to writhe and stretch against the stone walls.

My wits were scrambled. I was no longer certain what was real and what wasn't. Surely, I hadn't dreamed that Morina had forced me to abase myself before her and that a spirit of a witch from the past had presented herself to me. I was a vampire. I didn't have dreams.

I touched my hand to my chest to clutch the collar of my gown, but instead of the exquisite gown King Augusten had given to me, my fingers brushed a spill of lace.

A rush of adrenaline sang through me and I clambered out of bed. The gown swung around my legs and fell in a sheet of white past my ankles.

Cuinn, I thought, the voice in my head conveying my panic and uncertainty.

The door to my chambers opened as Morina admitted herself. In her right hand, she carried the gold and ruby chalice that contained her blood.

Cuinn didn't respond. Morina took one look at me and the expressionless mask she usually wore slipped as her features contorted, first in pain, and then in fury. The chalice fell from her hand and clinked across the floor, her blood pooling on the cold stone.

Morina crept toward me, slowly enough that I could visually keep track of her for once. "Where did you get that?"

"I don't know."

She continued to cross the room, making her way around the bed to get to me. If I thought I could have outrun her, I would have. But she was Dracule, and if I tried to run, she would catch me.

When she was close enough to touch me, Morina grabbed my elbow and jerked me to her. I put a hand up, catching her shoulder.

"Where did you get that?" In the heat of her fury, her voice was beginning to rise again.

"I…I don't know!" I stammered, my heart pounding a warning that something terrible was about to happen.

She jerked me again, pulling a muscle in my shoulder that made me cry out in pain. I tried to draw away from her, and her grip only tightened considerably.

"You've been snooping around," she growled. "Where did you find that? I didn't tell you you could wear anything you wanted to. I left clothes for you. Where are they?"

I didn't know, and in the face of her fury, propelled by my own fear, I fought and struggled against her. I tried to break her hold on me, and every inch I gained, Morina caught me again, her grip even harsher and more bruising than the last as I tried to fight her off with my arms.

She gripped me by both elbows and tugged to pull me to her.

I don't know what came over me. The only thing I could think was that I did not want her to pull me any closer to her, and when she made to do so, I lost it. I fought her hold like a wild animal, no longer concerned with being hurt if I struggled against her. I sought one thing and one thing only: to get away.

I kicked and wriggled wildly. Any part of her body that I could hit or kick, I did. I didn't care how angry it made her. I knew I had to get away. During the struggle, Morina lost her grip on my elbows. In the back of my mind, I knew Cuinn had jumped to his feet. As soon as my arms were free, I felt it in my hand, the old familiar reliable steel of the fox blade.

The blade blazed to life nearly as bright as the fire burning in the room. It glowed with a light of its own, casting its own shadows along the walls.

Morina growled, low and deep, a rumble that felt as though it made the very walls tremble.

Cuinn yelped, *RUN, NOW!*

I did. I ran for the door, and as soon as I made it to it, I felt Morina behind me. I turned, raising my arms above my head and sweeping the fox blade down through the air at an arc. Morina jumped back from the blade and I hit the stairs, taking two and three at a time.

I opened the door at the end of the stairs and ran into the night. The grass crunched and pricked sharp under my bare feet and I ignored it as the blood thundered in my head. The white gown tangled around my legs and I grabbed a handful of it, using every ounce of strength and speed that I could to try to outrun a Dracule.

I didn't get very far. Morina hit me from behind and her weight took me down at the edge of the trees. She grabbed my wrist and jerked my arm, disarming me and sending the fox blade out of my reach.

"I told you not to leave the walls of the castle," she said, pushing my arms up behind my back. "Do you really think you can survive out here on your own? Do you really think you can survive *without me?*"

"It was a chance I was willing to take."

"Foolish girl," she growled, her mouth uncomfortably close to my ear. "No matter where you go, no matter how far you run, I will find you."

"Why are you doing this?"

Morina yanked me to my feet without answering. She kept her steely grip on my arms and steered me back toward the castle. For the first time, I got a good view of it. It was a small keep, secluded, surrounded by land and trees. The outside was as dreary and unkempt as the inside; a blanket of ivy climbed one side of the stone wall, and I wasn't sure if the ivy was protecting it or trying to pull the rocks into ruin.

Morina shoved me. "Go."

I thought about the fox blade, but knew she wouldn't stop to retrieve it. It didn't matter. Wherever I went, so too did the sword. It was part of Cuinn's magic. It would find me again, when I needed it. That, even Morina couldn't stop.

Morina guided me back through the castle. When I hesitated to move as she bid me to, she pulled my arms up higher behind my back until the pain forced me to oblige. She led me down a long hall and past another sitting room. The room was aglow with a single lamp that had been lit and placed atop a table beside a long sofa.

"So this is where you've been hiding, my captor," I said.

Morina pushed me again and I stumbled. Only her grip on my arms kept me upright. The sitting room led to another hallway, one danker and darker than the rest. She continued to guide me through it. At the end of the hall, the stone beneath my feet slanted downward, until I realized she was leading me to a place beneath the castle itself.

Down and down we went, making our descent into the dark belly of the castle. Strangely, I wasn't afraid. A certain helplessness came over me, and with it, a measure of surrender.

"I'm reminded of a story the Sumerians tell," I said. When Morina did not silence me, I continued. "Perhaps you have heard it? The Descent of Inanna. It is the story of the Goddess's journey into the Underworld and of her sister, Ereshkigal. Seven things she carried on her person, each representing her power. At each of the seven doors, she was stripped of something precious to her, her crown, her ring, her measuring rod, her garments—"

"*Queen of Heaven*," Morina snorted. "Haughty and arrogant."

I wasn't sure if she was talking about me or Inanna. "If Inanna was haughty and arrogant, why would she have abandoned her temples, her wealth, and her status to make the descent into the Great Below in the first place?"

"What you forget, vampire, is that Inanna attempted to enter with her wealth and her status. It was her sister who forced her to enter the Underworld in nothing but her own skin. It was her sister who stripped her of those things and forced her to bow low. Comparing yourself to Inanna does not put you in my good graces." She shoved me again, as we had both come to a halt. "Now, move."

"I am not comparing myself to Inanna," I said, "not really."

"Then what do you hope to achieve by telling your little story, vampire?"

"I'm comparing you to Ereshkigal. You may strip me of everything I know and everything I own. You may tear this gown from my body, but there is one thing you can never ever take from me, Morina."

"And what is that, vampire?" she asked, sounding perversely amused.

"My self-respect," I said. "Inanna allowed Ereshkigal to strip her of material things, for she knew it was the only way to descend into her sister's kingdom," I said. "And you seem to forget that slaying Inanna was not easy for Ereshkigal. It has always seemed to me that the two were bound. Ereshkigal grieved when the judges of the Underworld ordered her to execute Inanna. For three days, Inanna's corpse hung from a hook in the Great Below, and during that time, Ereshkigal howled in endless pain. You have bound us, Great Siren. I walk into your Underworld knowing that we are one and the same now."

Morina growled and turned me, gripping both my wrists in one of her hands as she opened a door at the base of the hall. She shoved me through it and into a private dungeon, but she did not release me. She guided me toward the back wall. I had time to glimpse the shackles hanging there before she spun me around to face her.

"Then," she said, her breath moist against my cheek, "shall I do this properly?"

She grabbed a handful of white lace at the front of the gown and tore. The cloth hissed, giving way to her strength as if she tore paper. Strip by strip, she peeled the gown from my body, leaving my skin naked and bare to the dank air. When she raised that one crimson eye to look at me, I did not cower.

"And so, I am brought low, once again. Does it please you, my captor, my sweet Ereshkigal?"

Morina kept that one eye focused on my face, pieces of the gown fallen like ruined petals at my feet. She took my wrists in her hands, and when she raised them, I didn't struggle. The line of her body pressed against mine as she shackled me. The first shackle clicked shut, hard and uncomfortable against my skin.

"Stop talking to me like that."

"Does it displease you so, Great Siren, to be spoken to with such respect?"

Morina growled but ignored my mocking. She reached up to shackle my other wrist, and the movement put the skin of her collarbone close to my face.

Oddly encouraged, I inhaled deeply and the scent of her hit me like leather and night blooming jasmine.

Morina pressed my wrist into the rough stone and went stock-still. I turned my face into the bend of her neck and though I did not touch her, I could feel the ghostly beat of her pulse against my lips.

"What are you doing?" she asked and her voice was still a growl, but a breathy one. I wiggled against the wall and as if it was nothing more than reflex to her, Morina pressed her hips to my naked stomach in effort to pin me and keep me from moving. If she meant to abate my wriggling, it did not stop me entirely. She put her weight on my wrist until a jagged stone bit into my skin and I felt the first trickle of blood.

Morina's breath against my hair came short and clipped. Her sex stiffened against me. A thread of desire unwound between us. I wasn't sure if it was her desire or mine that I felt. In some part of me, some distant part unrelated to empathy, I felt mildly appalled that my body reacted so strongly.

But in another part of me, a part of me that seemed much closer to the surface, that unraveling thread sent all other thoughts floating away like a leaf in a flood.

I kissed her neck lightly, and her entire body strung rigid in resistance. I tried to slip my hand from between her grip and the wall, but she didn't budge. I rested my head against the wall, though my lips ached to kiss her. If I had thought she would not withdraw, I would have. But I knew whatever was happening, it was a delicate dance and I had to tread cautiously.

Morina's eye was closed, and even in the dark, the patch was a striking contrast against her skin. Her features around the patch were tightly drawn, as if in pain. Her lips pressed together and a muscle in her jaw twitched.

I shifted my hips, making my stomach move against her again, and this time, a shudder went through her. Her eye opened, and she quickly shut the last shackle about my wrist.

"Clever," she breathed against my cheek, "but not clever enough. I'll not be seduced, vampire."

"You chose me for a reason, Morina."

I could still feel her arousal against my belly. "I chose you because you are *her* lover."

"No," I said. "Not just that. You chose me because I remind you of yours."

Morina hissed and pulled away from me. When I blinked, she was gone and the lock on the cell door clicked shut behind her.

You're playing a dangerous hand, Piph.

I'm playing the only one I have.

CHAPTER ELEVEN

A merry tune woke me from my slumber. I pushed aside the covers and retrieved my slippers and shawl, guided by the sound as I made my way down the staircase. My brother Tristain sat on the floor near the fireplace playing a small stringed instrument that had been my gift to him for his natal day. He fumbled, plucking the wrong note, and attempted to recover from his mishap by singing a bawdy song over it. Our family encouraged him, yelling out suggestions, clicking their tongues, and slapping their knees in a din of revelry.

"Well!" Tristain stopped playing when he caught sight of me on the last steps of the stairs. "There's the sleeping beauty now! Planned to sleep the day away, did you?"

"With all this racket? Hardly." I smiled sleepily before I went to the window to peer outside.

"Your beast's not yet come, dear sister. We've seen neither hide nor hair of him."

Him, they thought. And why not? It was far easier for them to believe that the *creature* I was bedding was a man, at the least. Thankful though they were when the Dracule had come, they were more grateful they weren't the ones in my position.

"Honestly, Andrella," my sister said, "you seem to have grown an unusual fondness for the *thing*."

"Hush, child." My mother scolded her. She took me by the hand and led me from the room. "Do not listen to her," she said. "She is young and stupid. She doesn't know what you have sacrificed to protect your family, Andrella." Her features were drawn in sympathy. She patted my hand, as if trying to console me.

"You really don't understand, do you, Mother?"

"What do you mean, Andrella?"

"It's not so great a sacrifice," I said, taking my hand away from hers when we made it to Father's study. "I never intended to marry, not as Camilla does. And the beast you deem so monstrous, is not a monster at all to me."

"You're delusional, child. Do you hear what you're saying?"

"Yes, Mother. I know what I'm saying, and no, I haven't lost my mind. I've never been like you, like any of you." This time, it was I who took her hands. I cradled them between us. "I'm leaving, Mother."

"With the *beast*?" She looked at me in horror and shock.

I sighed. "I knew this wouldn't be easy. I love you dearly, but I cannot stay here."

I would pack and be ready tonight, and when Morina came, I would ask her to take me away. I had been thinking of it for weeks and now, after so much thought, I had steeled myself against the nerves and inevitable protest of my family.

I remembered her in the gardens, her skin reflecting the moonlight. Her eyes like beautiful red roses with black veins. I had never expected it to happen. I had never anticipated falling in love with her. Now, when I thought of her, I remembered that night in the gardens and it felt as though my heart would burst.

I had known then, after we had made love under the blanket of stars, that I felt the stirring of love in my breast.

"You're mad."

"No," I said. "I'm in love."

I embraced my mother briefly. "I am sorry, Mama, but this is what I want. This is the way it must be."

She scowled and did not return my embrace.

I shook my head sadly. They had never understood, nor would they ever. I was nothing more than a tool, an instrument, no different than the one Tristain played.

I left to pack my things.

"Tristain!" My mother's voice called from study. "Tristain!"

My brother's large frame appeared in the hallway before I could reach the staircase.

"She's mad, Tristain!" I heard my mother's hurried steps behind me as she called my brother. "Tristain, she is going to leave us! She is going to leave us for that *thing*!"

"You must be jesting?" he asked.

"Step aside, Tristain."

He did not.

"I said step aside." I raised my hand, the power unfurling from within me. The sconces in the hallway extinguished.

"No, sister."

I drew my hand back, feeling the magic pool in the center of my palm like warm honey. I flung it outward toward Tristain, and something heavy hit the back of my head, sending the world rolling in darkness.

❖

I jolted back to myself in my cell. The shackles clanged above me and I cried out as they bit into my wrists. I felt as if I were losing my mind.

"Andrella," I whispered, recalling the dream. Though I knew it wasn't a dream, of course.

"*Vampires do not dream.*"

Movement in the corner of the cell caught my attention. The same woman I had seen some nights ago stepped away from the wall. Again, she was garbed in a gown of flowing white.

"Am I in vision again?" I asked.

"*Yes. In a manner.*"

"Where's Cuinn?"

Down here. Where the hell else would I be?

Cuinn moved, and I felt the weight of his fur against my bare feet.

I kicked him lightly, and he grumbled.

"So you were going to run away with her?"

Andrella nodded, though she looked troubled. "*Yes.*"

"What happened after you were attacked?"

Andrella spread her arm out, indicating the cell around us. "*The same unfortunate thing that has happened to you.*"

"Your family wasn't like you?"

"*Witches?*" she asked, coming closer. "*No. They both feared and relished my power. And because of that, they didn't want me to leave with her.*"

"How?" I asked. "How did you meet her?"

Andrella tilted her head to the side, appearing as real and solid as Cuinn.

"*My family thought it happenstance, but I summoned her. I wanted out,*" she said. "*In the beginning, that was all it was. Morina knew that, but somewhere, somehow...*" Andrella shrugged. "*We fell in love.*"

"Why show me that particular memory?"

"*Because, empath, if anyone can understand, it is you. Morina is not always as she has been. What you see now is nothing more than a shadow of the woman she was.*"

"Then why not show me who she was?" I asked. "Why show me the memory you just did?"

"*I want you to understand what I was willing to risk for her.*"

I felt like she was offering tidbits of information, breadcrumbs for me to follow. It wasn't enough.

"If you want me to understand, I need to know more. You didn't die at your family's hands. I already know that."

"*No,*" she said, that one word a soft whisper. "*The men that attacked us here, that was unforeseeable. Morina has hunted every single one of them to avenge my death. Yet, she still blames herself.*"

"Why? If it was unforeseeable, why? How could she blame herself?"

Andrella averted her gaze. "*When I asked Morina to take me away, she was not ready with an answer. I fooled my family into believing that I no longer had any association with her whatsoever, that they had 'cleansed the devil out of me.'*" She sighed and my heart ached for her, for whatever she must have gone through. "*But when she came, she was not sure of us. She was not sure of herself.*

She was not sure of a witch and a Dracule. That is why she blames herself, vampire, and blames others for her loss. She blames herself because she left me, and by the time she had decided, it was too late. She blames others because she cannot deal with her own guilt."

"You could have run away without her," I said.

"*I could have, but I did not want to.*" Andrella came close to me and the air felt colder, though, as a vampire, I should not have been able to feel the cold. She touched my cheek tenderly, her fingers icy and real. "*You can save her from herself, vampire. That is why she chose you.*"

My eyes stung with unshed tears and my heart ached as if it would never cease. "I don't know how."

"*You will find a way.*"

"I miss my home, Andrella. I miss those I love. I want to get out of here. How am I supposed to show compassion to the one that has brought this hell on me?"

"*Do you know how Inanna made it through the Underworld?*" she asked.

"How?"

Andrella gave a wistful smile before she leaned forward, touching her forehead to mine. Her hand sifted through my hair, setting goose bumps over every inch of my flesh.

"*Through. The only way out, dear girl, is through.*"

I wanted to ask her what she meant, but before I could, a key turned in the lock. The door opened and torchlight spilled into the room, shattering my vision and piercing my skull with its brightness.

When I could open my eyes without wincing, I made out Morina's outline in the doorway. For what seemed several minutes, she simply stood there with the chalice in her hand.

She glared at me with unfeigned intensity, as if I had done something terrible and vile to her. She growled and threw the chalice against the wall in a fit. The blood spattered on the wall and the smell of it permeated throughout the small room and roused my hunger. I fought my bonds as the razors in my belly threatened to tear me apart from the inside out. Morina slammed the dungeon door behind her and I cried out in desperation.

I let my head fall forward, willing myself not to waste energy fighting. If the bonds were enough to have held Andrella, a witch, I knew they were enough to hold a vampire.

"There goes my only means of feeding, Andrella," I grumbled and hoped somewhere on the other side, she heard me and knew my displeasure.

Cuinn certainly did.

I told you, you're playing a dangerous game.

I ignored him and instead, wondered what would happen the longer I went without sustenance. Which would happen first, would I go mad or would I lose consciousness? Madness, it seemed, wasn't so terribly difficult to come by.

The hunger pains were excruciating. They started low in my abdomen and began to spread outward, outward through my limbs, through the branches of my veins. Every muscle in my body constricted in agony until I was vaguely aware of aught else. The muscles in my legs trembled weakly as I tried to keep my feet under me. The metal clamped at my wrists bit into my skin in a cold, unyielding embrace. My head lulled forward and I groaned, unable to keep it up any longer.

Somewhere above, I knew Morina sensed my plight. But she didn't return.

Starvation was its own particular brand of torment. Cuinn tried to keep me focused, to keep me from fading away from reality.

Piph, ye must contact Iliaria, he said. With my eyes closed, he loomed behind my lids. *If ye don't, there's no telling what could happen.*

She won't let me die, I thought. *If I die, she dies.*

Piph, he said, clearly trying to talk some sense into me, *I don't think the Great Siren cares if you drag her down with you. I think she's been there for a very long time already.*

You think Morina's trying to commit suicide?

What do ye think, lass? You're the lover and Inamorata of the Queen of the Rosso Lussuria and of a Great Siren. Ye've got the entire Rosso behind your back and their allies as well as your Draculian lover. For Morina, it's been a swan song from the start.

If I contact Iliaria, she'll try to kill her.

Then let her try. You don't think ol' bat wings can hold her own?

My lids felt too heavy to open, but a certain peacefulness washed over me, a calm acceptance.

NO! Damn you! No! Cuinn's voice rang in my head, making my skull pound again.

Cuinn, please, just let it be, I begged.

I will not. He was angry now. *You're really going to give it all up? If you die, Piph, I die! I'll be lost forever,* he said, and this time his voice was soft. *I don't want that. I don't want it for either of us, Piph, and sinking on Morina's ship isn't worth it. You'll never see Renata again, never see Iliaria, or Vasco.*

And if I contact Iliaria and Morina gets here before she does? I'm probably better off.

Bundle o' shite!

A rumble of thunder sounded from above the dungeon.

Piph, that's not thunder...

The wall at my back shook and I rolled my head back against it, listening. The ground trembled again and rippled beneath the soles of my feet.

Starved and confused, I couldn't wrap my mind around it. Was it an earthquake? Was Morina doing something up above? Was the ivy outside finally pulling the castle to ground for good?

I heard the door open, heard the tumble in the lock, but the light blinded me and I couldn't see who it was. I didn't have to.

"Cara mia."

I felt her familiar touch against my cheek and wept like a child. Renata took me down gently. I wondered if it was another delusional vision prancing about in my head. But if it was, I didn't care. If I sank into oblivion with Renata's vision in my head, at least I saw her once more before the hunger broke my mind completely.

She scooped me into her arms and stroked the hair at my temple. I saw her beautiful face through the slits of my eyelashes and sighed, trying to hold my eyes open, to hold on to the vision.

And then pain, fiery and real, seared to life in my chest and I screamed with the last bit of strength I had left. Which was considerably a great deal more than I reckoned, for once I started screaming, I couldn't stop.

Renata touched the place just beneath my ribs that hurt. Her hands slid through something warm and wet coating my skin.

"Vasco!" she yelled, her voice unstrung and high, carrying through the prison like a great bell ringing. "Vasco!"

The pain traveled higher, higher up in my chest, burning my organs and sending quills of fire through my body. It felt as though I was being torn apart from the inside out. I tried to scream again, and this time, I didn't have the breath for it.

"Sì, my lady?"

"Order them to stop, now! All of them!"

I didn't know what was happening, but something was wrong, terribly wrong. Renata moved my arm, and that one little movement stole an empty scream from my mouth. She whispered my name over and over, until I focused on her face again.

"I am sorry, cara mia, but you must feed," she said and pulled me upright none too gently.

I tried to scream again as she pressed my face toward her neck. I bit down with as much strength as I could muster, trying to drink like she told me to. But the pain was too much, too excruciating to even draw a breath, it felt as though every rib had been broken and turned inward to pierce me. I was too weak and wounded to take hold and my lips slipped off her skin.

"Can't," I murmured.

"Istania," I heard Renata say before the darkness descended again, "fetch Emilio."

❖

My head pounded. I sat up in the bed and reached up to rub my temples. Why on earth did I have a headache?

"Cara mia, you're awake." Renata rose from a nearby chair.

"And I'm still in this forsaken place," I said, noting the familiar surroundings. The same dark drapes with the same fireplace burning.

"Yes. We did not think it would be wise to move you so soon."

I reclined against the pillows. "What happened? Where's Morina?"

"She's in our custody." Renata sat beside me. I took her hand and pulled her closer, relishing the feel of her and breathing out a sigh of relief.

"Is this real?"

"Why wouldn't it be?"

"I've been losing my mind in this place."

"You were starved when I found you." She held me close to her, close enough that I could feel her heart beating against my chest. "I'd feared I'd nearly lost you, cara mia. Trust me, it was very real and very harrowing." Her arms tightened around me. "This is very real," she murmured against my hair.

I wept, the tears sliding freely down my cheeks. I wept, and while I did, Renata held me. The door opened while I was crying and the sigil on my right wrist tingled slightly.

Iliaria crossed the room and came to us, to me. Her body pressed against my back and I wept while they both held me.

When I was done and my tears had passed, Iliaria touched my shoulder. I turned my face and brushed my lips across her hand. I didn't know what to say but I found myself unable to stop touching them both. I had to touch them to convince myself they were real.

"There is someone else that wishes to see you," Iliaria said, rising slowly. I let her draw away as she went to the door to let someone in.

Vasco's face lit up despite his tears and my heart felt lighter, more sure.

"Vasco," I said, my voice choked.

"Save your words, sorella. We have much to discuss. I only wanted to see for myself that you are alive and well."

He walked around to Renata's side and she got up to give him room to embrace me. Vasco bent over and I got to my knees to meet him halfway. His arms encircled me, strong and firm, brotherly and affectionate. He placed a kiss atop my head.

"Sorella, the next time you think to play nice, a little advance warning would be appreciated."

That old familiar Cheshire cat grin spread across his features when he stepped away.

"Aye," I said. "It really wasn't the greatest idea, was it?"

"No," he said. "How do you feel, sorella? Do you feel well enough for more visitors?"

I blinked. "Who else is there?"

"Queen Helamina is very interested in meeting you, cara mia." The corner of Renata's mouth twitched, and I reached out to touch her. She took my hand, twining her fingers with mine.

"It sounds as though there's a story to be told. Why did it take so long for you to find me?"

"Ah, that," Vasco said, "that was unfortunately Damokles's doing. He apparently decided to turn around and start picking on the clan of Bull Shoals. King Augusten didn't take kindly to it."

"Damokles followed our trail to them?"

"It is more than likely so," Renata said. "He heard that the Rosso Lussuria were seeking to make alliances. The reason Queen Helamina and the others were not waiting for us was due to an intrusion."

"What do you mean?" I asked.

Vasco answered. "Damokles has been assembling an army of sorts, recruiting Dracule and vampires alike. They attacked the clan of Bull Shoals as soon as we had left it and Queen Helamina's realm as soon as we arrived. But," Vasco said, grinning again. "Queen Helamina already knew he would attack and established a perimeter around her clan with her guards, giving us safe passage."

"But what about Morina? How did she slip past the guards and how did we not hear anyone?"

"The clan of Ravenden is a large one, too large even for us to hear everything within its walls. Helamina only appointed guards to the places where she had seen in vision that Damokles's party would attack."

"In vision?"

"Queen Helamina's powers are precognitive," Renata said. "She can see certain events before they happen. And though she saw the attack that would unfold, she did not foresee your abduction, cara mia." She touched my cheek as if in apology.

"Sì," Vasco said, "and any time she tried to find you, she could not. We tried everything. Iliaria tried to sense you. Renata tried to sense you. Queen Helamina tried to see you. Nothing. The only knowledge we could gather was that you were safe, as neither Iliaria nor Renata felt your death."

"Then how did you find me?"

Again, he grinned. "This, colombina, you are going to love." Vasco went to the corner of the room and returned with something cupped in his palms.

"King Augusten's bat?"

"Sì," he said. "Renata noticed it was acting unusual."

"Vasco, I don't even know where I am or what country I'm in. How could the bat have found me?"

"It was a group effort," he said. "Renata and Iliaria sensed you last night, sensed the life slipping out of you." The bat tried to crawl out of Vasco's hands and he let it down. It wobbled across the bed to me, crawling up and stopping in my lap as if it were quite content to be there. I stroked the back of its head between its ears and it chittered lazily. "My son, Emilio, is the one who figured out that the bat was trying to tell us something."

"Did he teach it to talk?" I asked.

"No," Emilio spoke from the doorway. "I entered its mind. It's a relatively simple spell, once you get the hang of it."

"And the bat knew?"

"Sì."

"How?"

Vasco shrugged and looked to his son. Emilio mirrored him. "At a guess, it's forged some sort of telepathic bond with you that you are not aware of."

"I'm not sure I understand," I said, gazing down at the bat. "If it's forged a telepathic bond with me, wouldn't I know?"

"Not necessarily," Emilio said. "A lot of animals are highly intuitive, naturally gifted with psychic ability. It doesn't mean it's a personal bond, I suppose, but given the way it was behaving, I'd say it will forge a personal bond with you, if you allow it."

"Hmm, I suppose, either way, that I owe you my thanks, Emilio. Thank you."

"You are welcome, lady."

"You're in Romania, by the way," Vasco said. "Some part of it, anyway."

"Some part of it?"

"There's a spell surrounding the castle," Emilio said. "Have you not noticed that the sun does not rise here?"

"I noticed, but I wasn't certain if I was sane or not."

"Have you seen her?" Emilio asked.

"Seen who?"

Emilio came closer to the bed.

"The White Lady."

"So," I said, falling back and startling the poor bat. I placed my hand near it. It shambled into my open palm and I raised it to my chest. "She's real after all?"

"Oh yes," Emilio said. "She's the one who told me how to save you."

"Piph," Renata said, "do you feel any different?"

"Aye," I said. "But why do you ask?"

Renata leaned forward and touched my neck. She pulled out a necklace and held it in front of me. At the end of the chain dangled an amber gem.

"What have you done, Emilio?" I asked, my chest tight with fear and dread. "Where is Cuinn?"

Emilio licked his lips, as if he was nervous. "It was the only way," he said. "Your Dracule tried to bind you as the other Dracule had, but she started dying with you. We were losing all three of you in the triquetra of power. It was the only way I could save you."

My throat felt like it was closing and tears pricked my eyes. "Not Cuinn," I murmured. "Not him!"

"Well, consider me touched," a familiar lilting voice said. A figure moved at the foot of the bed and rounded the large wooden post.

Cuinn sat back on his haunches offering a fox's version of a ludicrous grin. "So, ye'd come to care for me after all, aye? Enough to miss me if I were gone?" He canted his head slightly, a wily look in his gaze. He raised his large and fluffy tail and said, "What do ye think, lass? Care for another pet?"

I slid my gaze to Renata, who smiled mysteriously. "He's real too."

"Bugger!" Cuinn exclaimed, leaping onto the bed and forcing it to dip under his weight. "Why'd ye have to go and tell her that, Queen?"

Renata shook her head at him.

Cuinn came to me. He tilted his head downward, his large ears flopping forward. "I'm not sharing a bed with that thing."

I reached out to snatch hold of his ears with my free hand. "Oh, Cuinn," I said, tugging his head to me and placing a kiss on the top of it. "Shut up."

Cuinn snickered. It should've sounded odd coming from a fox, but it didn't. Coming from Cuinn, it sounded just right.

"You're larger than any fox I've seen," I said to him, scratching his ears affectionately.

Cuinn flopped over on his back to offer his furry belly. His head lolled back and his tongue dangled out of his mouth when I scratched his tummy.

"I've been waiting a long time to feel again," he said. "Lugh's balls, that's the spot!"

"How?" I asked Emilio.

"The Fatas are immortal," he said. "Truly immortal. There is not a thing in this world that can kill them. The Dracule can be killed. Vampires can be killed. Even we witches have our bane, and some of us grow old with time, but the Fatas are a wild magic and cannot be destroyed."

I stopped stroking Cuinn's stomach. "If recollection serves me well, you tried to tell me that if I died, you would as well, Cuinn."

"It was just a wee little white lie," Cuinn said with a smile.

I pinched him and he yelped. "That's for lying to me."

Cuinn frantically licked the part of his stomach that I had pinched. He looked up at me with narrowed eyes. "I'd do it again if it'd keep you from giving up."

"I know."

I clutched the necklace and Cuinn's amber gem. "If you're here now, what about this?"

"He's still partially bound to the stone," Emilio said. "We've just pulled him from it and bound him in this realm."

"That makes so much sense," I said, letting him know with my tone that it didn't make any sense at all.

"There are still traces of my magic in the stone, make more sense?" Cuinn asked.

"As much as it needs to make, I guess."

"We have much more to discuss," Renata said, letting me know with a glance that she was sorry for interrupting. "For the time being, we will stay here. I will make the appropriate arrangements for you to bathe and change your attire. Then we will meet with Helamina and Augusten downstairs and discuss the rest of our matters."

As far as a plan went, it sounded like a good one to me.

Renata did as she had said she would. I rose and put the bat in its gilded cage. Cuinn was at my heels, keeping me company while the others left to set about whatever duties Renata saw fit for them.

"So how does this work?" I asked him. "How are you here in the flesh?"

"The witches bound us together as the Dracule are bound to you," Cuinn said, following me like a dog back to the bed. "When they bound us, it pulled me to this side of the world."

I remembered Andrella's words about Cuinn being able to move through the worlds. "Can you still move between the worlds?" I asked him.

"Aye and nay," he said. "I can still use my powers here, but I'll never be able to go back to the place where I was. I was bound there, remember? Vasco's witchy son broke that binding."

Cuinn curled up against me and I draped an arm around him. "That's a good thing, though, right?"

"A very good thing," he said. "I didn't mind it with you, Piph. You were the only one that made existence there tolerable."

I smiled. "I'm sorry I can't say the same for you in my head, Cuinn."

He snapped at me and I laughed, shoving him to the floor.

Chapter Twelve

True to her word, Renata managed to procure a bath and water for me to bathe. The tub was brought up to my room and filled before the fireplace. Cuinn curled up at the foot of the bed, and neither Renata nor I bothered to usher him out of the room. Fata or no, he had been in my head. A little nudity didn't seem as intimate as that.

A change of clothes was brought for me, and I was grateful to see that they were mine, though I imagined Renata had asked one of the Dracule to take the risk of returning to the Sotto to get them, I was grateful.

I sank into the tepid water and rested the back of my neck against the tub. I couldn't remember the last time I had fed, but strangely, I wasn't hungry and the pain that had nearly driven me mad had gone completely.

"How is everything at the Sotto?" I asked. "Was our clan attacked when Damokles attacked Bull Shoals and Ravenden?"

"Oddly not," Renata said, coming to kneel beside my bath. The clear water was familiarly scented with rose.

Renata touched my shoulder and I dipped my head to fully saturate my hair. When I sat up, she set about scouring my hair with a thick liquid soap that smelled of milk and honey.

"Where'd they get that?" I asked as the unfamiliar scent tickled my nostrils.

"Queen Helamina," she said, "there are those in her clan that venture more deeply into the human world than we do."

"It seems all our clans function very differently."

"It depends on the abilities within the clan." Renata rinsed my hair with a small pitcher. "There are a few among the Rosso that have the ability to pass unseen, but if one vampire is able to leave the Sotto, the others would want the same freedom to do so. There are those in Queen Helamina's realm that shroud themselves from the humans exceptionally well."

"How is Augusten after the attack?" I asked.

"He's here," Renata said. "You're welcome to ask him yourself later."

"So Queen Helamina and King Augusten are both here?"

Renata offered a brief smile. "Yes, and we've sent word to as many clans as we can reach. Iliaria and Anatharic have managed to sway some of the Dracule into joining us."

I traced Iliaria's sigil at my wrist, which now branched, as Morina's did, up to my elbow.

"She cares about you a lot, you know," Renata said.

I gazed at my wrist and arm, finally allowing myself to take in the binding Iliaria had placed on me. Her mark appeared very similar to Morina's now. Both had the same vine-like appearance and traveled up to my elbows, but there was one major difference and that was the sigil of their names tangled up in the base of the mark.

Iliaria had bound me to her as deeply as Morina had in an attempt to save my life. I knew she wouldn't have done so if she didn't care a great deal for me.

"I know," I said, feeling quite moved in that moment.

Renata toyed with a wet curl of my hair, appearing most thoughtful. "Do you love her?" she asked. I couldn't sense any jealousy in her.

I placed my hand over hers. "Being away from the both of you has given me a considerable amount of time to think. Yes," I said. "Yes, in a way, I do."

I wasn't sure how she would take my words, but I couldn't find it in my heart to lie to her. Besides, she would see beyond any lie I told her.

"You knew that though, didn't you?" I asked.

"Yes."

Renata rose and offered me a fresh linen sheet. I wrapped it around myself and stepped out of the bath. I twisted my hair over the bath to wring out the excess water before getting dressed.

The clothes that had been brought for me were simple and comfortable, a pair of knee-high flat boots, black leggings, and a loose-fitting aubergine tunic.

"What happened to the sword?" I asked Cuinn while I slid on my boots.

He yawned widely before grumbling. "It's still yours when you need it."

That seemed answer enough.

When I was done, I followed Renata downstairs. On the way out of my chambers, I noticed Anatharic and Vasco just outside the room across from mine.

I didn't need to ask what they were about. They were obviously on guard duty. I was fairly certain I knew who they guarded.

"There's a balcony in that room, my lady," I told Renata.

"Aye," Cuinn said beside me, "that's why Emilio's bound her to the room." He grinned. "Karma's a bitch, isn't she?"

Karma or no, I didn't feel particularly sorry for Morina.

King Augusten rose from his seat on the sofa when we entered. The woman I guessed to be Queen Helamina remained seated, though she examined me with some scrutiny. The scrutiny in her gaze didn't seem to match the rest of her. The words *lovely* and *cat-like* came to mind, but her hair was long and blond and fell to frame a body that was slender and petite and a face that was only slightly angular with a tapered chin. Her chartreuse gaze was mesmerizingly feline-like.

"Lady Epiphany," Augusten said, bowing slightly. "We are glad to know that you're well."

"Thank you, King Augusten." Cuinn's weight settled against my leg, but I turned my attention to Queen Helamina.

Renata made our introduction. "Queen Helamina, this is my Inamorata, Epiphany."

Helamina rose. When she was close enough to reach out and touch me, Cuinn gave a warning growl, sounding more like a perturbed dog than a fox.

"And this, I presume, is your Fata, the one who saved your life?"

"Yes, my lady." I placed a hand lightly on Cuinn's head and he inclined at my touch. "This is Cuinn."

"He's mighty large," Helamina said.

"Have ye ever seen a fairy fox?" Cuinn asked.

"No. Until now."

"Ah well, we're a big lot. Best left unprovoked, too."

Queen Helamina seemed more amused by his threat than anything else. "I'll take your word for it, Lord Fox," Helamina replied smoothly, managing not to sound as if she were teasing him with the title.

Cuinn's ears pricked forward pleasantly.

"Careful, Queen Helamina. You think he's big," I said, "his head's bigger than the rest of him."

Helamina smiled and it was friendly and pleasant. I wasn't sure what I had expected, but pleasantness from another vampire queen certainly hadn't been it.

Cuinn put his ears back in delayed reaction as my words sank in and turned a glare on me that was supposed to be intimidating. I ruffled his head affectionately and whispered, "It's true, and you know it."

"We have matters to discuss," Renata said, taking a seat on another sofa that had been brought into the room. I sat beside her and Cuinn hopped up to sit with me.

Of course, I didn't really expect him to curl up on the floor, especially not in a room full of vampire royalty. Cuinn considered himself an equal, and none of us argued or attempted to burst his bubble of confidence.

Discuss, they did. Mostly, they talked about strategy. Queen Helamina spoke of her visions and informed us that she knew Damokles would strike again.

If we waited long enough, she was sure he and the Dracule helping him would attack us here, at the castle. I wasn't sure I wanted to stay much longer, but I had little reason for protesting or disagreeing with the decisions of those who outranked me.

"We have word from the clans of Phoenix, Malvern, Jardin Dieux, and New Orleans. They will fight with us when the time comes."

"Has Damokles amassed so many followers as that?" I asked Queen Helamina.

"He has gained enough loyal devotees to attack both Augusten's and my clan simultaneously," she said. "That I find worrisome."

Augusten nodded his agreement. "As do I, but it is more a matter of cutting the serpent's head off, I think."

"Well," Iliaria said from the doorway, drawing our attention to her, "when targeting the serpent's head, best you make certain it doesn't grow another."

"She's right, I'm afraid," Renata said. "Yet, how do we defend ourselves without our actions of defense being seen as a threat to the Dracule as a whole?"

"Those not aligned with Damokles's agenda will already know it is not an affront to them."

"Ye better give them a scare," Cuinn said. "Let them know the vampires won't sit idle when they're trifled with. It's the only way."

"Then," Helamina said, "we're all in agreement? We stay and fight?"

One by one, Iliaria, Renata, King Augusten, and even Cuinn nodded. I let out a sigh. Never, in all the time that I had been with the clan, had the Rosso Lussuria had cause to go to war.

Now that we did, I feared the price of it.

❖

Renata did not press me to tell her what I had endured. Granted, being Morina's prisoner could have gone far, far worse than it had, but I did not wish to speak of it or divulge what I had gone through. Not yet, anyway. I had only spent a week and a day as her prisoner, but strangely, it felt as far more time had passed.

In the days that followed, I thought of her. I thought about confronting her, and every single time the thought crossed my mind,

I did not act on it. I remembered when I had tried to speak with her before, remembered that it had all came to naught. Too, I thought on the White Lady's words. If there was some way that I could help Morina, I didn't see it. The more distance I placed between Morina and me, the better. It was not cruelty or apathy in regard to her, not necessarily. It was a matter of distancing myself from who I had been as her captive and remembering who I was.

With the distance between us and my thoughts percolating, I began to feel a measure of pity for Morina. It didn't happen overnight. It was not until some days later I gained enough distance between myself and the events that had transpired that I began to remember things other than how I had felt. Namely, Morina's pain and the grief she masked in anger.

Iliaria did not feel pity for her. She made it abundantly clear that whatever Morina was going through was her own doing. In a way, she was correct. But I don't think she had seen as much as I had. I didn't feel she had all of the pieces to the puzzle that was Morina.

Then again, when it really came down to it, I didn't think I had all of the pieces, either, and I found myself over thinking it, wondering if Morina was truly as bad as she wanted to be. A part of me wanted to lean toward compassion, whilst the other part argued and pointed out the fact that Morina had taken me and left me to die.

But she had been willing to die with me. I wasn't sure what to make of that.

Cuinn glanced up at me while we walked the castle grounds. Anatharic followed. He was far enough away to give us the illusion of privacy, but it really was just an illusion. When I'd first requested to take the bat out and release him to find food, Renata had hesitated. The only reason she yielded to my request was through her own sense of compassion. She knew that if she did not let me roam somewhat freely, I would begin to feel as captive with her as I had with Morina. And so she let me leave, so long as Anatharic played the role of my unobtrusive guard. Well, as unobtrusive as the incredibly tall Dracule could be.

"You're going to have to help put the entire puzzle together, ye know," Cuinn said almost idly and I knew he'd been eavesdropping on my thoughts.

"I know, but I don't think I'm ready to face her again just yet."

Blessedly, he seemed to understand. I had learned that Cuinn could still communicate with me telepathically. Fortunately, for the most part he'd respected my wishes. We had both decided to leave the telepathy for situations where we needed it.

Since he had become physical in our reality, he had not left my side. Once or twice, I had thought he was not there with me, but when I looked I found that he was. Strangely, I didn't mind. After the scare of nearly losing him, I gained a greater appreciation for his company.

Renata, Iliaria, and Vasco managed to keep themselves busy as they made arrangements with King Augusten and Queen Helamina for the other clans to join us. I didn't think the small castle would hold everyone, but I had faith they would find a way for it to accommodate the lot. Vito and Vittoria and the rest of the Elders had joined us. Even Gaspare, whom Cuinn cunningly suggested using as Draculian bait. Alas, although Renata found his suggestion amusing, it was not meant to be. It was apparently déclassé to single out only one of your Elders and to use them, in Cuinn's words as, "giant bat-beast fodder."

I knelt in the dry grass and opened the latch on the cage door. The bat didn't take much encouragement to climb the bars to the cage's opening. He climbed onto my open palm and I set him off in search of food.

Cuinn watched him with an expression of mischief and fascination.

"You're not going to eat him one of these days, are you, Cuinn?"

"Ah, no." He shook his head as he lay in the grass beside my feet. "I wouldn't eat the little bugger. Too many sharp and wee little bones get stuck in your throat and—" He made a terribly loud hacking noise that made me laugh.

I sat beside him, watching the bat flap its wings wildly and dive for a small flying insect I couldn't see.

"That's a comfort." I grinned. I laid my hand on his back, feeling the rise and fall of his breath. It soothed me and I felt a bit of tension leave my shoulders. He stretched his front paws out in front of him like a lazy cat. "This is better, Piph. It is so much better." He gazed at the night sky above us. "If I wasn't so peeved at Ol' Patch for almost killing ye, I might thank her."

I ruffled his ears. "I know, you hooligan. I'm just afraid it won't stay this way."

His mouth opened wide as his tongue curled in a yawn. He dropped his jaw onto his forepaws. "Ye gots to have faith that we'll give 'em a good arse kicking."

"I hope so," I said. "But the conflict seems childish. Is it really worth their lives and our lives to fight over something as stupid as one man's ideals or his hatred for another?"

"Why not?" Cuinn asked. "Mortals throughout the centuries have been doing it for ages for land, for wealth, for power, for hate, for lies. It just makes the beasties no better than the mortals. We've no choice but to defend ourselves, and we've every right to do just that."

He was right, of course. Damokles didn't give us any choice but to prepare to fight back, and I couldn't blame anyone for defending themselves. Still, it seemed petty and wasteful. And ungrateful, ungrateful of the gift of life.

The bat flew back to us when he was done hunting and landed on Cuinn. Cuinn startled, but didn't protest and neither did the bat when I picked him up to put him back in his gilded home.

I stared up at the castle as we approached it. I was glad Renata and Iliaria and Vasco were there, but I was ready to return to the Sotto, for things to return to normal and not to be at the brink of war.

I was ready to go back to the Sotto, and I realized for the first time I did actually consider it my home. The knowledge startled me a little, for I had always considered Renata my home, but somehow, at some point, I'd begun thinking of the Sotto that way.

Renata descended the stairs when we walked in. I didn't know if she sensed my thoughts or read some expression on my features, but she came to me and slipped her arms around my waist. "Soon, cara mia. Soon, we will shake the dirt of this place from our feet."

I wrapped my arms around her and she held me more tightly whilst I sank into her. For now, the piece of the home I found in her and the others would have to do to combat the dark fear that set within my breast while we stayed within these walls.

"Soon," I said, "whole and safe and soon."

As far as prayers went, it was one of the sincerest I had ever made.

❖

Despite so many vampires in so small a place, I found myself restless and unable to keep to my room. The sun didn't rise, and thus no one slept. The others stayed well away from my chambers, namely because of who I shared those chambers with, but Renata managed to find ways to keep herself occupied as she conspired with King Augusten and Queen Helamina and our Draculian allies. They arranged for our allies, friends of Iliaria and Anatharic, to bring the Donatore we would need. Renata chose those who were loyal to her and who enjoyed her service to come to the castle. Queen Helamina chose among her humans, and King Augusten chose among his. It was not only war we had to worry about, but necessities and taking care of ourselves while we prepared for it.

I walked with Cuinn in the dead gardens under the light of the waxing moon. The vague memories that I had picked up from Andrella clouded my memory and made me feel somewhat melancholic, no matter how much I tried to shake them.

I stopped to sit on the stone bench and Cuinn silently followed. The night was alive with the hushed whisperings of the others within the castle's walls. I turned my gaze toward the balcony that overlooked the garden.

I still had not approached Morina. I was gazing at the balcony, thinking on her, when Cuinn got to his feet and put his body in front of mine. A noise of warning tumbled from between his black lips.

Gaspare swaggered into the clearing as if he sought to claim ownership of it. Just the sight of his walk inspired me to roll my eyes, but I resisted the urge. He fingered his dark beard idly, a gesture he often reserved for when he was prowling pretentiously around the court. His black pants were tucked into a pair of impractical thigh-high boots. The only color on his person was the shine of the sword hilt at his hip and his pale skin that peeked through the edges of his black jacket.

He stopped and looked at me as though I'd just appeared.

"Don't pretend you didn't know I was here, Gaspare," I said, knowing his oblivious and arrogant saunter was all for show. "What do you want?"

He smiled and there was something petty and cruel in it. "Your tongue grows bold, little rabbit."

"And your games grow tiresome, Gaspare."

Cuinn stayed between us, stating his loyalty. If he unsettled Gaspare, aside from staying where he had stopped at the end of the pathway, Gaspare didn't show it outwardly.

Gaspare tutted softly. "I haven't started a game with you."

"That's a lie," I said, "but I'll remind you and advise you against starting one. The last time you tried to play a game with me you ended up enduring our queen's mercy, did you not?"

Gaspare had openly attacked me in court after I exchanged verbal insults with him. Renata had tortured him for it. The reminder didn't sit well with him, and his eyes narrowed beneath his bushy brows.

"So," he said, "becoming the slave-bitch-whore of our queen and the Dracule has at last gone to your head, little queen."

"Yes, Gaspare. That's precisely it. All the sex has gone from my groin and directly to my gargantuan head," I said, rising. "Now, if you'll forgive me, I've better things to do than to sit around and play repartee with you."

I turned my back on him, trusting Cuinn to alert me if he made any sort of threatening move. I didn't trust Gaspare at my back for an instant.

But Gaspare didn't have to attack me in the courtyard to bring me up short. "How many women are you sleeping with?"

I turned my head slowly to peer over my shoulder at him. "What makes you think that's any of your business, Gaspare?"

He smiled again, cruelly, arrogantly…coldly.

"Know this, little rabbit, were it not for your *skills*..." His smile stretched even wider as his eyes glistened darkly. "You would not have been so lucky."

I let out a deep breath. At last, it was happening to my face. He was trying to belittle me by implying that if I was not Renata's lover, I would have not survived the challenges, that I would not have survived his challenge.

I shook my head, unsure how to respond. In truth, Cuinn had aided me during my duel with Gaspare. Not Renata.

Cuinn gave no warning save to bark. His fur took on an orange glow, illuminating the night like a firefly. He rose up and slammed his paws down on the stone pathway that led to Gaspare, and the pathway rolled as if a small wave of water had set itself beneath it. Gaspare fought to keep his footing, caught off guard by Cuinn's magic.

Cuinn drew his ears back and he faced Gaspare. "Ye think it's been just your queen protecting her, do you? Believe if it wasn't for her you'd be able to do what ye want and hurt who ye want, do you?"

Gaspare's leather-clad hand went to the hilt of his sword. "Are you threatening me?"

I moved then and diverted his attention. Gaspare's gaze flicked from Cuinn to me and back to Cuinn. I touched the top of Cuinn's head, and a surge of strength and courage emitted off him and filled me.

I approached Gaspare, and as I did, I showed him exactly what I felt. I was not afraid. "For all your big talk, you don't have much bite," I whispered, and the night breeze carried my voice. It stroked awake the fire of something within me, and I felt my skin grow warm with the heat of its glow. "Gaspare." I raised my hand and he flinched when I placed my palm flat against his cheek. My power stretched open wide like a whirlpool in the center of my body. I felt it distantly, felt it reaching out to those nearby. I grabbed hold of the energy and narrowed it on the vampire in front of me, molding and shaping it into something more powerful than anything I had felt before.

And I felt it when it grasped Gaspare, felt it wrap itself around him like a dark void pulling, tugging, absorbing, making my skin crackle and head swim. I felt as if I stood in both positions at once, where Gaspare stood and where I stood. I felt his surprise and his struggle to fight it, to try to shield himself against it, to resist its call, and knew somehow that it was too strong for him to resist.

My power had never risen like this. It seemed to have grown stronger, wilder. I did not know if it was some byproduct of the soul bindings or if my power was really just growing on its own, but what it sought, it found and pulled from Gaspare as easily as a hand unravels a bundle of yarn.

Memories flashed in my mind, memories that were not mine. I saw a child's calloused and blistered hands. I felt the pain of blow after blow. I heard the screams of fighting voices and a younger child's cries.

They were Gaspare's memories, and I knew while I viewed them, he relived them. My power sucked him in and took us both to that place inside him full of helplessness and hurt.

When I came back to myself, Gaspare had fallen to his knees on the stone pathway. His chest rose and fell heavily beneath his velvet jacket as if he were about to hyperventilate. I laid my hand on the top of his bowed head, and when I spoke, the echo of power tinged my voice. "You are not a boy anymore, Gaspare."

Gaspare scrambled to his feet and away from me in a panic. "You had no right!" he yelled, his emotions unstrung to the point where he obviously didn't care if the others heard us.

I reached out to touch his arm and he whirled away from me, drawing his sword with a hiss. By the light of the moon, his eyes were wild.

"Gaspare," I said and my voice was as calm as I could make it. I tried to focus on drawing the energy back into the center of my body, of not reaching out to him again, though the power wanted that. I could feel it yearning to absorb whatever it could. "I will not fight you."

He raised his sword high between us. His hand trembled ever so slightly on the pommel. "Better you should fight me than ever try that again."

"You instigated this, Gaspare." A touch of anger flared within me, and I didn't question where it came from, whether it was his or mine. I harnessed it and I let Gaspare see it. "If you ever seek to harm me or mine, I will open you up from the inside out and I will spill you raw until there is nothing left." The power was still there, but it was paused as if someone had placed a stopper in the place where it rested. I knew all it would take was a thought to release it like silk in the wind. I moved into Gaspare's space, and this time, he gave ground. "I never sought to have any quarrel with you, Gaspare, but my days as a frightened Underling hiding behind the face of another's power have passed. Do you understand?"

I sensed Cuinn approach my side, his presence like a small flame of magic near my skin. Gaspare's armor of arrogance crumbled and he sheathed his sword with a shaky hand.

For the first time, I tasted the duality of my power. I had never realized until then that empathy could, in fact, be used as a weapon. It had never occurred to me that I could open someone so wide that I could bring all their inner shadows out to haunt them, that I could force them to face the beasts within themselves. Or the beasts who had chased them.

I knew myself in that moment. I could have torn Gaspare at the seams and turned his own inner demons against him. Somehow, I think he knew it too, and he was frightened of me.

He met my gaze one last time, and a part of him, I think, wondered just how far I could rip him open. I wondered as well.

"Epiphany," he said and took his leave with his tail tucked nicely between his legs before making his way quickly back to the castle, casting cautious glances over his shoulder at me until he was safely inside.

I released a sigh of relief and Cuinn pressed himself against my leg to comfort me.

"Cara mia." Renata's voice startled me, and I spun around to find her standing at the other end of the pathway near the bench where I had been sitting only minutes ago.

"How much did you see?" I asked.

"Enough," she said.

"Which means she's been there the whole time," Cuinn said.

Renata came to me and her palms slid across my cheeks. She buried her hands in my hair and bent her face low and kissed me, cupping the back of my head while she did it. At the touch of her lips, I opened to her, ignoring Cuinn's grumble of protest. Beneath the light of the moon, she pressed her body against mine and her kiss hardened, became something more ardent and deeper.

A world of yearning unraveled within me and I made a noise low in my throat. Renata broke the kiss to search my face.

"What is wrong, cara mia?"

"Nothing." I tangled my hands in her gorgeous hair and pulled her face back down to mine. "I missed you. Kiss me again."

She kissed me until the blood in my body thrummed for her, until I felt pleasantly light-headed and the dead gardens around us seemed foggy and unreal.

"I think we should request some privacy this evening." Her lips moved against mine as she spoke into my mouth. I groaned as her hands slid down my back as she pulled me tightly and possessively against her.

"Yes." I near-panted, my entire body set ablaze and aching for more of her, all of her.

Renata gave a low, purring laugh before she grabbed a handful of my hair and tilted my head back. I felt her mouth a second later as she nibbled a path down my neck and my knees threatened to give out under me.

"Mayhap now?" I moaned as she caught my skin between her teeth and bit lightly, teasing me on the cusps of her fangs.

Renata scooped me up into her arms and carried me back toward the castle. "A marvelous idea," she said and her smile managed to be both mischievous and intimate at the same time.

She carried me through the house and up the stairs. If anyone gave us strange glances, she made it abundantly clear when she closed the bedroom door behind us that she didn't care.

Renata lowered me onto the bed and instantly started to remove my clothing. I helped her by easing my shirt off and tossing it carelessly aside. I tugged at her gown, pulling it down to bare her beautiful shoulders. I pressed my lips against her skin, kissing and nibbling gently. She rewarded me with a sigh, and I turned my face into the bend of her neck and pressed my lips there, too, opening my mouth to catch her skin between my teeth. I drew my fangs across her skin and teased her as she had teased me moments ago.

Renata placed her hands on my shoulders and pushed me down against the mound of pillows. She stayed on her hands and knees, holding her body above mine as a dark brow arched exquisitely across her faultless features. I reached up to trace her figure and when she didn't complain or stop me, began working her dress down even lower.

Renata shook her head and laughed. "Cara mia, cara mia," she said in a voice that was almost a purr. She sat up and rose from the bed to disrobe, baring her gloriously nude body slowly. The sight of her deliciously bare coaxed a fire between my legs that nearly inspired me to lunge and pounce on her.

I refrained from doing just that and rose to my knees instead. Renata came to me and I touched her naked hips, traced the smooth plain of her stomach until the white mounds of her breasts hung over my hands. I bowed my head and kissed her, feeling her nipple stiffen under my tongue.

Renata placed a finger beneath my chin and I followed her guiding hand. She kissed me again, her mouth parting slightly as her tongue twined with mine in a dizzying rush of desire. She guided me back onto the bed and her lips trailed a path of petal soft kisses up the arch of my neck. "What do you want?" she whispered.

I buried my hands in her hair, crushing the waves in my fists. "You." I kissed her again. Her tongue filled me in another kiss that was sweet and slow like molasses. I stroked my hand down the waves of her silky hair and to the dip between her shoulder blades. I drew away from the kiss and whispered against her mouth, "Like this," I said, "sensual and heavy." I slid lower down her body until I could put my lips against her throat. I sucked her skin lightly as I reached for her hand. I found it and she allowed me to guide it to my thighs. "I want to feel and savor every inch of you."

The tips of her fingers played against me, threatening to part me but not quite finishing that last bit of movement that would put her in direct contact with the heated folds of my sex.

"Do you realize, cara mia, that this is the first time you have played the role of the seducer with me?"

I blinked, drawing back to see her more clearly. "Is it?" I asked.

She traced the slit between my legs and I spread them wantonly, trying to get her to touch me where I needed her most. When she didn't part me, I pressed more solidly against her hand. Renata drew her hand back with a knowing smile.

"A lot of good it's doing me," I said.

She laughed and worked her arm effortlessly underneath me, pulling me upright as she sat up high on her knees and nestled back against the pillows with me in her lap. "Oh, it's doing you more good than you think it is, my dear."

She tickled a path from my navel to my groin and I opened to her again. Her fingers slid into me with ease and I shuddered, catching hold of her shoulders and breathing a sigh against her skin. Renata touched me and teased me until I was drenched and ready to ride whatever part of her body I could swing my hips into. She laughed again as she traced a circle around my clitoris and I growled in frustration. She abruptly pushed inside me, forcing my spine to arch and thighs to tremble as my body contracted around her.

My nails scraped her skin as I fought to hold myself upright. I clung to her shoulders when she began to thrust harder, and the heel of her hand rubbing and pumping against me nearly made me lose my mind.

"Not yet," I begged, whispering the words against her hair. "Please, not yet."

Her fingers slowed to a stroking rhythm.

"What do you want?" she asked again, her voice gentle.

"Together. Come with me."

For a moment, the lovemaking stopped altogether as I sensed her working it out. Which position would be best given the difference in height between us?

I cupped her face in my hands and smiled. "Renata, you're over thinking it."

She laughed and the sound was genuine and joyous. "Mmm, no, I know just how I want you, dolce mia."

"And how is that?" I asked.

Renata rolled me onto my side as she rolled onto hers and faced me. She reached between my legs and spread me open again. She propped her long leg over mine and I found her sex with the tips of my fingers. My name fell sweetly from her lips before she buried a hand in my hair and forced me to hold eye contact with her.

"Open yourself to me," she said. "Epiphany, cara mia, open all of yourself to me."

I knew what she wanted and so I called to my power, releasing the will that kept it shackled deep within the heart of me. Renata released hers and her eyes awakened like dark moonlit waters and a spring blue sky.

She kissed me and we drank the sweet moans our fingers coaxed. We drowned and fell into each other, into the delicious murmuring waves of love, of passion, of power. When the orgasm came, we struggled to remain entwined. Renata locked her arm hard around my hips to keep me in place as my hips twitched. I fought to concentrate, to keep my touch against her while my climax threatened to consume me. I cried out, a small moan at first, and then another. Renata pressed her mouth hard against mine and I cried out in earnest.

When my orgasm passed, she tore her mouth from mine. I kept touching and stroking her, using the tip of my finger to bring her pleasure in just the way she liked. Her head fell back and her lips half-parted and then she came, her hips rocking forward into my fingers as she moaned, dragging her nails deep and hard across my lower back.

Afterward, we lay back, boneless. Tiny rivulets of blood trickled down my naked skin. Renata followed the crimson path with her hand.

"Did I hurt you?" she asked whilst she pulled me closer until the softness of her flesh was nestled comfortably against mine and she licked my blood from her fingers.

"No."

"Good," she said. Her hand swept through my blood and across the healed scratches. "That is very good."

The mark on my wrist grew warm before a light knock sounded at the door.

"It's Iliaria," I said.

Renata called out for her to enter and she did, closing the door with a quiet click behind her. "I thought to give you some privacy," Iliaria said.

Renata worked her thigh between my legs while keeping a grip on my hair. "It is most appreciated, Dracule."

Iliaria gave no other response save to nod in acknowledgement.

"Join us," Renata said and her tone was empty of command.

"Is that a request?" Iliaria asked. She didn't budge from where she stood near the door.

"An offer," Renata said, "nothing more. Suit yourself if you do not wish to share this night."

"Epiphany?" There was a thread of uncertain expectation in Iliaria's tone that made me turn to her. The yearning in her expression was raw and unguarded. "Do you want me to join you?"

"You didn't hear me protest, did you?"

"No."

"Then why do you stand there as if at any moment you will turn and leave?" I asked.

She stayed silent and I went to her and stood on the tips of my toes. I rested the tips of my fingers against her neck. "My hard-shelled Dracule, when will you realize that I cherish you no less?" I took her hand in mine and she let me guide her to the bed. "Yes, I want you to join us." I pulled at the blouse she wore and began unhooking the small metallic clasps that held it closed around her body. "I have missed you both immensely, incredibly. Why would you think for an instant that I would turn you away?"

She licked her lips, a sign of nervousness or uncertainty. "I do not know."

I freed the last clasp that held the blouse closed and pushed the material behind her back. I touched her then, placing my palms flat against the smooth expanse of her stomach. Her muscles rippled against my hands, but she didn't protest or draw away, and I didn't stop.

Renata moved up behind me. Her hand buried in my hair, grabbing a gentle handful as she guided me to move my head to the side. She took the skin of my neck in her mouth and nibbled lightly, sending a chorus of chills over my skin. Her mouth followed those little bumps to the back of my neck and lower.

Iliaria bowed her head and kissed me. The dance of her lips and tongue was slow and sweet, lighter and less deep than Renata's kiss had been. Renata's hands moved over my body and encouraged the honeyed song of desire to rise and sing through my blood again. She guided us back onto the bed and Iliaria's mouth followed mine until she knelt above me, craning her neck for my kiss. I wrapped an arm around her waist in effort to pull her closer.

She drew away as Renata's hands caressed down my hips and thighs.

"Did she hurt you?" Iliaria asked.

"Morina?"

"Yes." She cupped my face tenderly in one of her hands. "Did she molest you, Epiphany?"

The look in her eyes put a pleasant shiver in my bones. "No, no she did not molest me. Though, I sought to seduce and sway her, to no avail."

The corner of her mouth rose while that dark expression still lingered. "You tried to seduce her?"

I lowered my gaze, suddenly uncertain if what I had just told her was a good or a bad thing to have revealed. "Yes."

Renata clicked her tongue softly at my ear, making me flinch unexpectedly. "Surely, your loyalty to us is not so easily swayed, cara mia."

"I…" I closed my mouth and thought about my words before I spoke out of hand. "I had very few options left to me, my lady. I couldn't think of another way to escape."

Iliaria's expression became a near frightening thing. "You could have called me," she said.

I tried to read them both using my empathy and could not discern either of their intentions. As if they had discussed it, both had thrown up a wall to keep me carefully out.

I frowned and knew it bordered on pouting. "I can't tell...Are you really upset with me or are you both toying with me?"

"A little of both," Renata said, this time sounding amused. She dragged her nails over my stomach and I shifted beneath her hand. "I daresay, your misconduct while we were not present is enough to warrant punishment."

Iliaria grinned widely to reveal the canines on both her upper and lower jaw. Her tail swayed predatorily behind her where she knelt above me. "I daresay, indeed."

As far as punishment went, it was fairly exquisite. Renata laid me out on my back and pinned my wrists above my head. She held me while Iliaria crawled between my legs.

Iliaria set her thumbs against me as she spread me open. She licked me in a broad stroke. I gasped and Renata set her weight into the hold she had on my wrists. Iliaria lifted her head to gaze up the line of my body.

"It has been long since I have pleasured a woman this way. My apologies if you find my skills lacking." Her lashes fluttered closed before she bowed her head again. This time, even with the expectation of her tongue, I writhed when she buried her face in my mound and sealed her mouth over me. She drew me between her lips, lightly at first, her tongue flicking against me lazily and in a way that sent tiny flits of pleasure shooting up through my body.

Iliaria continued to make love to me with her mouth, carefully letting me feel the sweet glide of her fangs. She applied just the right amount of pressure, the right amount of sucking and licking to bring my breath short and make my body burn with the heavy longing of climax.

But she did no more than that.

"Mmm, do it slowly, Dracule. I want to watch you make her writhe and plead. I want her to beg you for her release."

In the end, I did. Iliaria teased me with the languorous rhythm of her tongue until it was a sweet torment that made me beg and fight Renata's hold.

No matter how long the time that had passed since she had pleasured a woman with her mouth, she blessedly was not lacking in skill, by any means.

Renata flung a leg over me to straddle my face and I raised my mouth to seal a kiss against her, shifting my head slightly to part her folds. Her body tightened at the touch of my tongue, but she gave the command coolly, "Now, Dracule."

Iliaria sucked roughly and I stifled a cry, setting my nails into whatever bit of nearby flesh my hands could find. Renata's hips pressed forward solidly against my face, encouraged by the flick of my tongue and my nails set into her skin. I drew her between my lips, tucking her lightly between my teeth. Iliaria's tongue danced against me and I fought the orgasm that threatened to overwhelm me, fought to please Renata with some measure of talent. Renata's breath stirred the air above me, short and clipped. Her hand touched the side of my head as she buried her hands in my hair. Her hips began to dance, and I bit down a little harder to keep from losing my hold.

She groaned above me, a sound that let me know I was close to going too far over the line between pleasure and pain. I flicked my tongue against the tiny bead of skin tucked between my teeth. Renata moaned, her head flung back and body rocking with the waves of her climax as she fought to stay on her knees above me. When the orgasm passed, her gaze met mine and she lowered her face to kiss me.

"Now, cara mia," she whispered.

I released my control and cried out. Renata sank her mouth down hard on mine again. She kissed me and her tongue played between my lips as Iliaria's tongue played between my legs. And this time, at the sensation of them both, of being filled by them both, the orgasm hit me in a hurricane of ecstasy.

CHAPTER THIRTEEN

The time came when I knew I had to confront Morina. The distance I had initially placed between us for peace of mind became a burden. After being forcefully bound to her and held as her prisoner, I still didn't want to approach her. Gratefully, the last day I spent in the dungeon was vague to me, like a broken and fragmented dream. There were bits and pieces I recalled. Unfortunately, my failed attempt at swaying her with my body was one of those bits.

I let out a breath and finished buttoning the red silk blouse Renata had brought for me. I tucked the blouse into a pair of lightweight black trousers that clung to my body and put on my boots as I perched at the foot of the bed.

Cuinn's ears pricked in attention. "I know I said ye should figure it out, but ye don't have to do this, Piph. You can let her rot."

"Cuinn." I knelt in front of him and stroked a hand down the back of his head. I raised my sleeve to reveal her mark upon me. "I have to; you know I do."

He got to his paws. "You're not doing it alone, then."

Emilio stood just outside her chamber doors. He brought me up short before I could enter. "Are you sure, lady?"

"Yes, Emilio."

He stepped to the side so I could enter. Though he had indeed spelled the room, he had not spelled it to keep intruders out, only to keep Morina from leaving her confinement. His magic pressed against me, flowing and tight. The pressure of it made my ears pop.

Had I been the one kept under magical warden, I would have liked it even less than the prison in which Morina had kept me.

I shut the door behind Cuinn.

Morina stood before the doors that led onto the balcony. She did not bother to turn around or give me her attention, though I knew she had heard me enter. She leaned against the frame and stared out into the night.

"Morina," I said her name, keeping my voice soft.

A stretch of silence unfolded between us and I tried again.

"So," she said at last without sparing me a glance, "the tables have turned and I am now your prisoner."

"You chose this, lady, not I."

She turned to face me and the air hissed through my teeth at the sight of her. She had taken off the patch and left her entire face unconcealed. A starburst of pink and white scar tissue decorated the hollow of her missing eye.

She turned back toward the balcony with a measure of cold grace. "Still, you are right to fear me, vampire."

"I think, Morina, you are more a danger to yourself than you are to me."

"Which makes me a danger to you," she replied coolly.

Cuinn sat by the wall behind the door. He remained quiet, I think out of respect and to allow me to handle the situation on my own.

"I don't think that's really what you want, Morina."

She turned back and glared at me. "And what do you know of what I want, vampire?"

A world of hurt and pain flashed across her face, briefly crinkling the flesh at the corner of her eyes. She tore her gaze from mine, perhaps thinking I hadn't caught it.

I raised my sleeve to bare her mark. "Release me, Morina."

"I cannot."

"Why?"

"It is a soul-binding," she said. "I cannot erase it. I cannot undo it. You don't get it, do you, vampire?" She came to me and reached out as if she would touch me. I refused to recoil in fear of her and her fingers trembled slightly in the air between us before she lowered her hand to catch my wrist. The nearer she was in proximity to me, the more her sigil tingled where it was embedded in my skin. She pushed my sleeve up to expose Iliaria's mark and I let her, intent on standing my ground. She traced the inky vines. "We're bound for eternity, you and your Dracule and I."

"Iliaria did what she had to do to try to save me from your hands. Would you condemn us all now in your plight of self-destruction?"

"I've thought of it."

"So, that is it, then?" I jerked my hand away from her. "What did Iliaria ever do to you to warrant so much of your hostility?"

Morina swept her hand outward to gesture at the room around us. "This," she said, her face drawn tight. "You have tasted the memories of this place, vampire. You know what happened here. None of it would have happened were it not for *her*."

"You blame Iliaria for what happened to Andrella," I said. It didn't make sense. And then I remembered Andrella's words, that Morina blamed herself and others out of a sense of her own guilt.

Morina grabbed me by the shoulders and her fingers dug into my skin. Cuinn got to his feet. I saw his ears flick back and put a hand up to let him know that I didn't need him to intervene yet.

"Do not ever speak her name to me, vampire. You've been toying with me the moment you learned of her and the tragedy that befell this place." Her fingers bit into my skin even more roughly and I groaned in protest. Her voice fell to a whisper. "How is it that every way I've thought to torment you does nothing more than bring me more torment?"

"Because somewhere inside of you, you know it's wrong."

"No." Morina shook her head. "No, I don't think it's wrong." She traced the line of my jaw as if she would memorize it. Her touch unnerved me, but the complicated expression on her face and the intensity of her gaze unsettled me more than that small touch.

"Why do you blame my lover, Morina? How is what happened here Iliaria's fault?"

"Your lover." She withdrew with an expression of disgust. "Your lover was the only one that knew, vampire. She was the only one I trusted to tell, and she betrayed me."

"That's a lie," Iliaria said, practically startling me out of my damn boots. She stood just inside the doors that led to the balcony and I wondered why I hadn't sensed her. I reached out to her, lowering my shields just enough to gain a taste and found that she shielded from me, so much so that even the sigil at my wrist did not trickle with warmth.

Morina's entire body straightened and stiffened like an arrow.

"Attack me if you wish," Iliaria said as she stepped more fully into the room. "You were always quicker to fight than you were to think."

An animalistic growl began to drum beneath Morina's ribcage.

"Be angry," Iliaria said, "but know this, Morina. I did not betray you. I am not the reason human men chose this place as their hideout. I did not go out into the human night and guide them here. If you want to know who did, you'll have to look elsewhere."

Morina turned her back on me but not before I felt the wave of emotion rise from the center of her body. It hit me and threatened to squeeze the air from my lungs. I suddenly felt light-headed and nauseous and fought to push against that emotional surge, fought to keep it outside of myself.

"You were the only one that knew!" Morina said and her voice was raw and unstrung. It pained me to hear it. "I trusted you. You were my friend," she said a bit more calmly as she tried to rein in her emotions. "I trusted you and you betrayed me."

"No," Iliaria said. "I give you my oath and I would have given it then had you not attacked me like a rabid beast in your grieving. I have never betrayed your trust, Morina. In the entire time we have known each other, I have not betrayed it, not once."

Even without the gift of empathy, I would have been able to tell that what Iliaria said was the truth. The surety of it was there in her expression, in the patient confidence of her stance. I didn't think she felt compassion for Morina's troubles, not exactly, but the bonds of old friendship made the situation complicated. As was everything to do with Morina.

"I would've helped you find the true traitor, Morina, had you not been so hasty to condemn me."

Morina rushed her then, a blur of onyx attire and ivory skin. She pushed Iliaria up against the wall and Iliaria didn't try to protect herself. She appeared unperturbed by Morina's attack.

"You know I didn't do it," she said slowly, as if she were trying to talk a madwoman from the ledge of her madness.

Morina growled and leaned in close. "You were the only one that knew."

"Can you give your oath on that with absolute surety?" Iliaria asked. "I don't think you can, Morina. You know as well as I how many of your cousin's spies liked to linger."

Morina growled but released her. Her tail whipped snake-like across the floor as she turned her back.

"Easy to blame my cousin when he is *your* enemy."

"Damokles?" I asked. "Damokles is her cousin?"

Iliaria stepped away from the wall but kept a watchful eye on Morina. "Yes."

I laughed. I couldn't help myself.

Morina startled at my laughter before giving me a venomous glare.

"You think that is funny?"

"I think, lady, the fact that you would blame Iliaria for your lover's death but not Damokles, well, it's ridiculous, quite frankly. Did you not say once that he killed his own sister, Iliaria?"

"He did," she said, "for bedding a vampire. He murdered her in her sleep."

"The court never found any proof of that," Morina said.

"No, they never found proof, but it is something the entire Regat knows, Morina. What happened when Andrella died? Who whispered in your ear that I had betrayed you? When you learned of her downfall?"

"Stefauni."

The name fell like a rock between them. I half expected it to clink and bounce lightly on the bare floor.

"Your cousin's closest ally," Iliaria said. "You've always been too easy to blindside, Morina. As much as I cared about you, discerning deception has never been your strong suit."

Morina made an expression as if she tasted something sour. "But it has been yours, Princess?"

Not only did Cuinn's ears prick at the word, my attention did as well. "Printessa," I said, "Princess." I shook my head, mumbling more to myself than anyone else in the room. "I do not know why I did not draw the connection sooner." I met Iliaria's surreal gaze. "Does she speak truly?"

Morina smiled then like a cat that had finally cornered its prey. "She did not tell you?"

"She does not need to know, Morina."

"That you stand in line to the Draculian throne? Oh, I think she does."

I did wonder why Iliaria hadn't told me. Yet, I also wondered what difference it would have made if she had. "I don't expect her to tell me everything, Morina. If you think to ignite a lover's quarrel between us, you won't."

Iliaria considered me. "You are not upset that I withheld information from you?"

I thought about it. "No," I said. "You may not have bothered to tell me who you really are among the Dracule, but you never outright lied about it either, for I never asked."

"Strange logic," Morina said, "to find your lover and ally keeping such intimate secrets and not care."

"Why should I give a fig?" I asked.

"Because," Morina said and she moved toward me again, "how do you know she is not using you to climb to the throne, little vampire?"

"The same way she knows how to expose the truth, Great Dracule." Cuinn got to his feet and came to stand beside me. "I think, Piph, it's time to use your charms to see if she's telling the truth."

"What do you suggest, Cuinn?"

He canted his head slightly and gestured to Morina with his snout. "Use your power and the binds between you," he said. "Those who have nothing to hide do not fear being exposed."

"Hmm." I touched his head, scratching idly behind his ear. "That's not a bad idea, Cuinn. What say the two of you?"

"What are you asking, vampire?"

"Do you think you can control your power enough to do it?" Iliaria asked me.

"I'm fairly certain I can."

"Then I will consent to it if it is the only way to prove my truth."

"How do I know you will not bend the truth, vampire?" Morina must have understood what I was going to try to do, though she didn't trust me enough to do it.

"Her power bends nothing, Dracule. It seeks and finds and brings things into the light; that is all."

"Are you saying she can share our memories?"

"Aye," Cuinn said. "That's exactly what I'm saying she can do. How badly you want the truth or not depends on the two of you."

Iliaria and Morina stared at one another for several long moments. Finally, Morina shook her head. "If you play me falsely, vampire..."

"I will not," I said. "You have my word."

Iliaria pushed away from the wall. "Let us do this thing and have no lies between us."

"You seem quite eager for someone about to have themselves laid bare before a vampire's eyes."

Iliaria didn't even bother to glance at her whilst she came to me. "I've laid myself open in other ways. I do not fear the truth."

I took the hand she offered and held the other out to Morina. With some hesitation, she took it. The instant her bare skin touched mine, the power flared to life between the three of us, and I found myself caught between the two of them. Iliaria's power rose around us like the wild night breeze. It tangled the curls of my hair. Morina's power mingled with it and made it something more crisp and icy. At that small touch of power, my control tumbled away from me. Empathy opened me wide until I could feel it like a living thing in the center of my body. It called and drew and drank the energy around it. I sank to my knees, only vaguely aware that the others followed me. Iliaria's grip tightened on my hand in a way that was almost painful.

"Focus, Epiphany."

I tried to focus, but I couldn't. Their energy overwhelmed me like a tidal wave that threatened to swallow me whole. Cuinn pressed his furred body against mine, and the wave receded enough that I could draw a ragged breath. I felt his paws at my shoulders a second before he laid his head in the bend of my neck, putting his fur against my bare skin. The storm stilled when Cuinn touched me.

"Now focus," he said at my ear. "Focus on one of them and let your power take what it will."

"Morina," I said while Cuinn ground me.

Morina's gaze met mine and she looked like a woman bespelled. She leaned toward me as if she couldn't keep herself from swaying into the call of my power.

Her lips met mine and I had a moment to think that they were surprisingly soft and gentle before the memories came unbidden. They hit hard and fast, drowning out the room and the sensation of her silken lips.

Too quickly, her memories passed. Too quickly for me to see and understand. Cuinn's voice flowed through my mind, *Slow 'em, Piph.*

All it took was a thought and the memories slowed.

Morina passed through two incredibly tall doors and into a room lined with small orbs of light. A hundred Draculian eyes turned to look at her from their round tables as she approached. I only had a glimpse of them before Morina knelt before the Dracule that sat on the highest throne. The Draculian queen wore no crown to mark her status. Only a collar of sapphire and diamonds graced her black furred body. A silver chain swayed from the collar when she leaned forward, a tear-shaped diamond sparkling like a star against the blackness of her smooth stomach.

The queen turned her angular face and looked to the Dracule standing beside her. As soon as Morina turned to look at her, I knew it was Iliaria. They were harder to tell apart in Draculian form, despite their variety of colors. But even without Morina's memories filling my head, I would have known her, would have recognized her by the way she moved as if the night itself had created her. There were subtle differences in facial structure and body that set the Dracule apart, but that special grace was Iliaria's alone.

Iliaria moved down the dais when the queen dismissed her with a gesture. She stepped down to meet Morina with her wings drawn back behind her, revealing the dark glory of her body without shame. A chain much like the queen's dangled at her hips. A smaller tear-cut diamond danced against the blackness of her left thigh.

I willed the memory to rush along and slowed it again when I saw Iliaria standing closer. The two stood on a balcony overlooking a dark and rocky landscape. I heard Morina tell Iliaria about Andrella as if the words had come from my own mouth. Iliaria listened, watchful and patient. Morina did not know what to do and she confided in Iliaria, telling her about Andrella wanting to leave her family to be with her.

"I cannot bring her back here," Morina said.

Iliaria shook her head. Witch or no, it was too dangerous for Andrella to live among the Dracule. The only safe way for Morina to be with her was to leave. It wasn't a response Morina liked, for Drahalia was her home and it was where she belonged. Morina was torn between her love of the witch and her loyalty to her homeland. If she left and the Regat knew, would she be able to return, or would she become an exile?

The vision sped along again and the perspective changed. I saw Morina then from Iliaria's height, Morina in Draculian form, her fur like white snow with dustings of ash and coal at the tips of her ears, traveling down the slant of her nose and eyes like artful makeup. Her gaze was whole and unscarred, black with a tint of crimson when the moonlight caught it. Morina left when they were done speaking and I felt Iliaria's concern and pity. She knew that if any of the others knew, it would put Andrella at risk. The possibility of their coupling being frowned upon was a high risk among the court nobles.

But Morina had made her decision. She would find another place to go with Andrella, even if she had to hide amongst the human world.

And Iliaria had made her own decision to keep Morina's secret. Iliaria remained on the balcony for some time after their conversation until she was interrupted by the presence of another.

"Printessa." The tall Dracule offered a slight bow as his ears swiveled flat against his dark skull. Something about the figure and his demeanor seemed familiar. At last, I recognized who the figure was before Iliaria addressed him.

"Tell my mother I'll join her in a while, Anatharic."

Anatharic bowed and disappeared beneath the archway he had come through. Again, the memories propelled forward in time. Iliaria dined with her mother, and when her mother inquired about what Morina had wanted, she made up some excuse about Morina seeking her hand. The queen seemed to believe it, as Iliaria had known she would, for most of the court thought them lovers anyhow. At one time, they had tried to be, until they had realized that though there was some love between them, their acts in the bedchamber were purely physical and not a romantic bond.

I came back to myself with Cuinn lying across one side of my body, his snout still buried in the bend of my neck. He got to his feet and moved away to give me room. Iliaria had pulled me into her lap and cradled my back against the front of her body.

"I can't hold it anymore," I said, feeling weightless and weak.

Morina released my hand.

"Just because you did not tell your mother does not mean you didn't tell anyone else in the Regat," Morina said.

"Surely," I said, holding Iliaria's arm around me, "if I could feel as well as see, you did too, and you know she didn't tell anyone."

Morina got to her feet and walked away to the far side of the room by the doors that led out onto the balcony, as if she wanted to put as much distance between us as she could.

"You have tasted my memories and still you call me a liar," Iliaria said, her voice low and hurt. I touched her hand with mine. "Let her believe what she wants, then." Iliaria helped me to my feet and I let her. "We have tried to show her truth. We can do no more than that."

"A sad day when the truth is wasted for a cherished lie," I said.

How could Morina not see the hurt she had caused in someone who had once considered her a friend?

Iliaria was still touching me and I caught a flash of Morina: Morina screaming, hurt and enraged, Morina challenging Iliaria before the court, Iliaria protecting herself, the crescent blades raised high as she drew one of them in a whirlwind of defense. Morina sank to the floor and shielded her eye with a hand. She screamed herself ragged in the memory, over and over, as if she would never stop.

The vision shattered when Iliaria stepped away from me.

"You do not need to see that, Epiphany."

"I didn't mean to," I said. "I'm sorry."

Iliaria directed her attention at Morina, who stared out into the night again as if she were alone in her room and had nothing better to do. Iliaria turned toward the door a second before I sensed someone on the other side of it. The door swung open and Vasco's panicked features came into view.

"Sorella, Great Siren," he said. He glanced around the room, as if looking for something.

"What is it, Vasco?" I asked. A sense of dread unfurled inside me.

"Where is Renata?" he asked.

"Is she not with Helamina or Augusten?"

"No," he said. He cursed under his breath in Italian.

The sound of the door downstairs opened and with it, the sound of several bodies moving quickly. Emilio came up the stairs at a run. "Father," he said. "Come quick."

The four of us rushed down the stairs and into the night with him, leaving Morina to her own company.

A wall of Dracule stood in our way, blocking us from whatever was on the other side of the wall they had formed. Iliaria pushed her way through their ranks, and when they noticed her, they parted to let her pass.

"Stay back," she said to me and though I knew she was simply being protective, I didn't like it. I followed her anyway, with Vasco at my back. Vasco's blade hissed from its sheath as he drew it.

Beneath the light of the moon, I was able to make out four figures across the stretch of land. One of those figures knelt, her skirts pooled around her body as the moonlight caught the waves of her raven hair.

My heart sank, and I stepped forward out of instinct.

Iliaria had stopped in front of me, and when I tried to move past her, she put an arm out to stop me. "No," she whispered. "Not yet."

"They have Renata," I said, feeling like the world was swaying dangerously under my feet.

It didn't make sense. How could they have captured Renata?

"You two," Iliaria said to Cuinn and Vasco. "Do not, whatever you do, let Epiphany through."

Iliaria strode forward and Cuinn and Vasco moved in front of me to block my way. I clutched the amber gem at my chest, my heart beating so hard it felt as if it would jump through my ribcage and onto the ground below.

"Damokles!" Iliaria yelled and her growling voice carried on the night air like a roll of thunder. "Come on, you coward!"

"You underessstimated me, Printesssssa." The hiss of Damokles's voice was a whisper on the breeze. He stood tall and proud between two other figures whilst Renata knelt on the ground by his side. One of those figures was shorter, and I realized they were much more human in appearance than the Dracule that surrounded them.

Damokles grabbed a handful of Renata's hair and jerked her head back until the moonlight hit the startling features of her face. Even from where I stood, blocked as I was by Vasco and Cuinn, I saw as her power blazed to life, saw her eyes shine like dark water and sky before she stood and shoved her elbow into his body so hard he staggered backward and lost his grip on her hair.

The move gave her a chance to flee, a split second to get away. It happened so quickly that I wondered if anyone else even noticed. But she didn't flee.

Why?

The human figure drew a hand back and struck Renata hard across the face. Renata's head turned with the blow, but she did not cower.

"Now," Iliaria whispered.

Augusten's guards stepped out from behind the wall of Dracule and raised their bows. Their arrows sang free, whirring and buzzing in a sound more menacing than Damokles's voice.

Iliaria raised a hand and lowered it. Emilio rushed forward and raised both his hands. White flames suddenly sparked to life at the tip of the arrows, burning and setting the entire field alight. Renata's eyes met mine from across the clearing, and I tried to push past Vasco and Cuinn to go to her. Cuinn tripped me and Vasco's arms slid around my upper body like shackles.

"No!" I screamed the word and fought against them.

Cara mia, Renata's voice spoke quickly in my head while I continued to fight and try to break Vasco's hold. *'Tis a game of chess. Use your wits. If the Dracule was going to kill me, he would have. I am safe. If he kills me, he loses all the vampires I have sired. I am sorry, my sweet,* her voice started trailing off, *this had to happen. The next move is yours.*

Wait! I didn't know if I'd thought it or yelled it aloud.

I tried to shake Vasco off with my elbows but couldn't. He had my arms pinned too tightly to my body.

"Halt!" Iliaria said. "Cease fire! They're gone."

Emilio waved a hand toward the fire that had spread quickly across the dead grass and the flames extinguished, making the night seem darker than it ever had before and leaving behind the smell of smoke. The field was empty. Renata, along with Damokles and his groupies, was gone.

I screamed again and Vasco pulled me in against his body. His mouth whispered words, words to try to console me, to try to comfort me.

"Colombina. Sorella," he said, and I felt him try to use his power to calm me.

My legs went out from underneath me and he let me go. I hit the ground repeatedly, screaming and trying to release the energy that welled up within me, the anger, the rage, the sorrow, the fear. I hit the ground until the sharp rocks tore the skin from my knuckles and bled me.

One of Augusten's vampires came forward, and I was distantly aware that Augusten had given her a command. Titania caught my wrists in her hands. She set her strength against mine.

"Epiphany," her words were harshly accented, "look at me, Epiphany."

Her power washed over me and made my blood run cold. It made me hesitate and raise my face to hers. The black irises in her emerald gaze swallowed me whole until I lost every thought and emotion and eventually, consciousness.

❖

I paced my chambers like a caged tiger. A thousand emotions raged through me at once: restlessness, listlessness, unease, fury, helplessness, longing. Renata's words were lost on me, for I couldn't think on them with a clear head. I cried. I screamed. I tore the room apart when my sorrow turned to the fine susurrus of wrath. I felt as though I should've known exactly what to do, and yet, I didn't. I couldn't figure it out.

I toppled the dresser and sent it splintering across the stone floor. I tore down the drapes that decorated the canopy and ripped them into as many tiny strips as I could, as far as the anger propelled me. I refused to see anyone and asked them all to leave me alone. After a while, they did, and I raged, alone.

I grew weak from refusing to feed. I knew I was punishing myself. I was punishing myself for not having a brilliant plan, for Renata getting captured in the first place. I was punishing myself for not knowing what to do or who to turn to. Queen Helamina came to speak with me when I turned Vasco away. I refused her as well.

"Is this what your queen would want, Epiphany?" she asked me, her stance proud and bold in all her silks and furs. "Do you think she would want you to starve yourself?"

"I need space and time to think," I said, my hands trembling. They didn't seem to want to stop.

Needless to say, Queen Helamina eventually gave up trying as well.

Later that evening I lay in bed, clutching one of the pillows to my chest. It smelled of Renata's scent. Had I any more tears to cry, I would have. As it was, my heart ached for her. I gazed at the fire burning in the fireplace and lost myself in the dancing flames in a sort of daze.

I didn't hear Iliaria enter. Even so, she made sure I saw her soon enough. She moved in front of the fire to block it from my sight and call my attention to her.

"Last chance, Epiphany," she said and her tone was colder and less sympathetic than the others had been. "Feed or be forced. I've already discussed matters with King Augusten. If you don't feed willingly, there are ways to make you."

I didn't care. I was lost in my own darkness and blinded by grief. Iliaria came to me and I lifted my gaze. She cupped my face in her hands and I tried to pull away from her.

She pulled me to my knees and pressed her mouth against mine. I growled and pushed at her chest. She broke the kiss. "Look at me," she said.

Angry, I refused and she used the grip she had to turn me to face her. Her other hand slid down my body. I closed my eyes. "Stop."

"No, Epiphany. Look at me."

"Why must you torment me, Iliaria? All I ask is to be left alone to figure out what to do."

"No, Epiphany. That's what the others are doing wrong. You don't need to be left alone, not in the state you're in."

I pushed at her chest again and the hand she'd placed against the base of my spine was suddenly as unyielding as stone. She gripped me tight against her, making sure I felt every inch of her body that pressed against mine.

"Do you love me so little to throw away all hope?" she asked.

"You don't understand."

"I don't, do I?" she whispered the words against my cheek. "I understand that she is your Siren. I understand the bond there, and I understand your love for her, Epiphany, but I also understand you in ways the others do not. I understand you're grieving, you're mourning, and that there's a strength inside you even you've yet to tap. You know this isn't the answer. You're not alone, Epiphany, and it's not just your lover who's missing. The others are missing their queen too."

I didn't fight her when her arms encircled me and she raised me off the bed.

"So get up," she said, "feed, take a bath, and get dressed." She set me on my feet and put her hands on my shoulders as if to keep me in place. "When you are done I want you to come down and speak with us as we try to devise a plan to rescue your queen."

Wordlessly, I nodded. Iliaria tilted my face up toward her again. She searched my gaze. "Will you do that?" she asked.

"Yes."

"Do you promise?"

"Yes."

"If you lie to me," she said, her voice dangerously low, "I will make you feed, I will make you bathe, and I will carry you downstairs kicking and screaming if I must. Do you understand?"

I sighed, knowing better than to call her bluff.

"Yes."

❖

Anatharic and others of the Dracule had gathered in the downstairs room, as well as King Augusten and Queen Helamina. There wasn't enough furniture for everyone to sit, so most of us stood. Vito, Vittoria, and Nirena stood on the side of the room against the wall closest to the door. Vasco and Emilio stood off to my left. Cuinn sat on the floor in front of me, and Iliaria stood nearby. Vasco and Emilio were paying rapt attention to Queen Helamina. Dominique stood in the corner looking as crestfallen and as lost as I felt.

I was not the only one that felt Renata's absence. I realized how selfish I had been, grieving by myself. I stood straighter and concentrated on the conversation at hand.

"The Dracule were to attack us here at the castle with an army, not a group to take your queen hostage," Queen Helamina said. "This means we understand less of their plan than we thought."

"More importantly," Vasco said, drawing her attention to him, "I think we should figure out how it is they took her. Capturing the Queen of the Rosso Lussuria is not an easy task, especially with so many of us gathered here. How did they do it? Did they infiltrate the castle and slip our guard?" He shook his head. "I don't think it likely, even working with witches. There are too many of us here not to have noticed *something*."

"A valid point," King Augusten said. "I agree. Unless someone here is working with the Dracule and has betrayed your queen... someone she trusts implicitly."

"Renata is no fool to trust anyone implicitly," Vasco said, "and if you are implying that I am a traitor or any of those she brought with her are, that's ridiculous. I think, signore, you forget her power. It is not easy to deceive a queen who can hear and discern your most intimate thoughts. To attempt to do so is unwise."

Indeed, it was. Their conversation got me thinking. If someone had tried to betray Renata, how would they have done it? Surely, she would have sensed their intentions if they had tried to lure her out of the castle or to a place where Damokles and his men could capture her.

The group discussed assembling a party to interrogate all those in the castle. There were those that argued against it, considering it a waste of time. Namely, the Dracule agreed that it was a waste of time, but Nirena, Vittoria, Vito, and Dominique also thought so.

"If King Augusten is right and someone is working with the Dracule, we are housing a spy," Queen Helamina said. "And any of our future plans will be laid to waste as well. We cannot harbor a spy. It's too great a risk. We're better taking the time to flush them out."

"What plans do we have left to us aside from trying to save our queen?" Dominique asked and there was a thread of heat in his tone as if he was becoming angry. "If we don't save our queen, all is lost for us. Maybe not for you, my lord, my lady, but for us. For the Rosso Lussuria, we are nothing without our Siren."

They began to discuss the matter more heatedly, and I tuned them out as I found myself distracted by my own thoughts. I moved to the fireplace and traced my finger through the dust on the mantel.

"Epiphany." Nirena's voice called me back to the conversation. "What are you thinking?" Her eyes narrowed inquisitively as she tried to assess me. The others turned to look at me as well and I ignored the expectation in their gazes.

"Nothing." I had thoughts aplenty, but none I was willing to share in their midst. None I was willing to share with everyone in the room.

Of course, it wasn't just them. Some of my thoughts I had not even had time to process myself, let alone share with those I trusted. I returned to my silence, they picked up their conversation again, and I allowed myself to drift on the tides of pondering. Renata had told me to rely on my wits, and so I tried to set aside my battered emotions and do just that.

When they were done, it had been decided. A party would be put together to interrogate all those within the castle. We left Queen Helamina and King Augusten to assemble their interrogation party.

Iliaria's shoulders were drawn tightly together as we ascended the stairs. I uttered Vasco's name under my breath and he and Emilio and Dominique followed.

Dominique closed the door behind them.

"Emilio," Vasco said.

Emilio went to the door and raised his hands, placing them against the door until the room filled with the weight of his magic.

"They will not hear us now. You may speak freely."

"Good," Vasco said and thanked him. "What have you thought of, sorella?"

I shifted my attention to Dominique and sat on the edge of the bed. "You were not with Renata when she was captured," I said, reiterating what I already knew. He nodded and I continued. "What did she tell you, Dominique? Where did she tell you she was going?"

"To speak with the Dracule privately," he said and I could tell he didn't understand why I questioned him.

He spared a glance at Iliaria and she shook her head. "Anatharic did not do it, if that is what you suspect. I will give my oath on his loyalty to me."

"I've seen his loyalty to you," I said. "I don't think he would do it, either."

"My lady," Vasco said, "I mean no offense, but it is far more difficult for Renata to read the intentions and thoughts of a Dracule than another vampire. Are you certain he would not betray us?"

"Very," Iliaria said, giving him a look that said, *tread cautiously*.

"Then, perhaps one of the other Dracule—" Vasco continued and I interrupted him.

"No."

"What do you mean, 'no' sorella? It is a possibility."

"No, Vasco. I don't think Renata was betrayed at all, at least, not without her consent."

"Are you saying that you think our queen, that your lover, handed herself over to Damokles willingly?"

"That's exactly what I'm saying, Vasco. Think about it, brother. You know Renata, mayhap not as intimately as I do, but you know she would have put up more of a fight than she did if she seriously hadn't wanted to be captured. As it was, she put up enough of a struggle to convince them that she was not being dragged away willingly."

"What makes you think this, colombina?"

"She spoke to me before they left," I said, trying to remember her words through my emotional upheaval. "She told me to use my wits, Vasco. The next move, she said, is ours." I shook my head. "I didn't understand it then. I didn't understand what she meant by it being a game of chess, but the more I think on it, the better I begin to understand her move."

"You really think this is a scheme of her own making?" Dominique asked.

"Don't you?" I asked. "She sent you away to allegedly speak with one of the Dracule, but who? And why would she not tell you who? If she was going to talk strategy with anyone, it would have been her." I gestured with a hand toward Iliaria. "I think it was a ruse to get you away from her so she could make her move. If you had known what she intended, you would have sought to stop her, I know that, Dominique. If I know that, Renata most definitely does."

Vasco grunted. "I am not trying to discredit your thinking, colombina, but why would she turn herself over?"

"You heard what Queen Helamina said. This changes things. Renata is changing the game and playing it on *her* terms. She must've figured out more than we know. She was right about Damokles not slaying her. If he was going to, he would have done it in front of us to make an example of her." I ran a hand through my hair to push it out of my face. A piece of the puzzle slid into place. "She's figured out what Damokles is after."

"Have you?"

"I think I just did."

"What is he after, colombina?"

"Us."

"But Damokles hates vampires," Iliaria said.

"Really?" I asked her. "Are we so certain of that? He marked Baldavino. He may not have come to his aid when we caught him, but he got close enough to form an alliance with him. He may hate us," I said, "but he wants us. If he didn't, he'd have slain Renata and with her, all the vampires she's created. The others talk of cutting off the serpent's head, right? All Damokles has to do to destroy hundreds of vampires is execute our maker." I gestured to Vasco and Dominique. "Yet, here we stand. And now, we know what he's really after. It has to be us."

Vasco touched a finger to his bottom lip. "So you're saying our queen turned herself over to change the game and reveal their hands?"

"Precisely."

"So now what?" Dominique asked.

"It's our move," I said. "We have to figure out a way to get Renata back."

"Aye," Cuinn said from behind me. "I've an idea."

"That would be?" Iliaria asked him.

"Send one of the Dracule you trust to find out where they're keeping her and bring her back."

He made it sound so simple.

Iliaria stubbornly shook her head. "No," she said. "It's too risky. Damokles will recognize anyone I pick to send.

"Bugger."

"Not necessarily," Emilio said. "Not if we find someone he doesn't know."

"He will recognize a vampire and he will recognize those that are loyal to me, witch. I will not risk it."

"I wasn't talking about them."

"Then what are you suggesting?"

"Someone new. Someone the Dracule won't recognize."

"If they're not Dracule, Damokles isn't likely to take them. Your magic is far-reaching, Stregherian, but even you cannot alter another's true form."

"No, I can mask it, though."

She shook her head again. "If you used a glamour, a Dracule would smell it. It won't work."

"There is someone with a power stronger than anyone in this room has. He can do what I speak of and his gifts run through the blood of both the Dracule and vampires alike. The only problem is that I don't know how to contact him."

"You're mad," Iliaria said incredulously. "Death? You're suggesting we find a way to contact the Angel of Death?"

"I am, lady. I cannot truly change another's form, as you said, but Azrael can. He holds the keys to life and death. He gave your king the ability to make the vampires." Emilio took his time in motioning at those of us that were vampires. "He has the ability to reshape them."

"Well bugger me in the arse," Cuinn mumbled. "The witch has got a point."

"And what makes you think that Azrael will listen, Stregha?"

"I'm not presuming he will," Emilio said, "but I'm not presuming he won't, either."

"The Dracule fell from his favor long ago," she said. "I am not so certain he will be keen on hearing us now."

"That may be well and true." His gaze that was such a mirror of Vasco's met mine. "But they are here and his power still courses through their veins."

An unspoken question lingered in his eyes. I thought I understood it. "I will do it."

"What?" Vasco didn't bother hiding his shock. "Do you know what you are saying, colombina?"

"Yes and no, but I will do it. I will beseech Death."

Iliaria grumbled under her breath and whatever she said was lost on me, for it was not in any language I understood. The intent behind her words, however, was quite clear.

She wasn't happy with my decision.

"He heard your king's cries once, Iliaria, and he took pity on him. He created us in the name of mercy. So," I said, "Let him hear mine and let's hope for the same clemency."

"You are sure?" she asked. "There must be some other way to retrieve your queen, Epiphany."

"Yes, I'm sure."

"You realize that what you're saying is that you are going to try and chase down the Angel of Death? Even if you do manage to get his attention, that could be a very dangerous thing to have."

"I know," I said. It might've been a fool's errand, but I had decided and was resolute in my decision.

What did I have to lose that I had not already lost in some way? I had faced death before. Mayhap, not as a physical entity, but his shadow had been thrown over my human life, and when I was reborn a vampire, I had passed through his veil.

I knew his power every time the sun rose and I did not wear Iliaria's ring. His very touch had both taken and given much to me.

Who better to beseech Azrael than me?

CHAPTER FOURTEEN

I made yet another pointless plea for privacy. Iliaria refused to leave me alone, and arguing with her only made her more resistant to my request.

"Do you even begin to know what you are doing?" Iliaria asked from where she stood on the other side of the bedroom.

"No," I admitted. "I obviously don't know how to contact Azrael, either."

"Then how do you suppose to do it?"

That was a very good question and I obviously hadn't thought that far. "Do you know?" I asked hopefully.

Her elegant brows furrowed thoughtfully. "There are only a few accounts of Azrael appearing to the Dracule throughout our history. Many of the texts were lost during the reign of King Theodosius."

"Lost?" I asked.

"Destroyed," she said. "There were once temples in Drahalia. King Theodosius ordered their priesthood disbanded and the temples burned when he took the throne."

"There were temples to Azrael?"

"To our entire lineage," she said.

"What about Azrael's priesthood?" I asked. "Surely, they would know. What happened to them?"

"They reintegrated into Draculian society. Those that were caught honoring our bloodlines were executed by Theodosius. When my mother took the crown, there was little for her to save among the ruins, and many of the old priests remained in hiding. Theodosius had turned most of our society against them," she said. "They hid their faith out of fear."

"So you wouldn't happen to know anyone that had once been a priest in Azrael's temple?"

Iliaria was dangerously silent, but I knew her.

"Iliaria?" I pressed her for an answer. "Do you?"

"Morina might know," she said at length. The firelight bathed the side of her face in darkness. "Her father was a priest."

I sighed heavily. "That's bloody fantastic."

Iliaria raised her shoulders. "Choose as you will, Epiphany."

"I suppose I must speak with her then, if she's the only one who might know."

Iliaria frowned, a line forming between her perfect brows. Cuinn muttered a complaint and rolled his eyes. I couldn't entirely blame him.

Seeking Morina's aid wasn't a task I relished.

I entered Morina's chambers to find her standing yet again near the balcony's doors. This time, she turned around when the door shut behind me. I'd asked Iliaria and Cuinn to let me speak with her alone and after much persuading, they had agreed, so long as they took over Emilio's watch at the door. If we kept our voices low, we hopefully wouldn't be heard, as we had no intention of sharing our plans with the others, especially if there was a spy in our midst. We'd already had Emilio provide us with a quiet place to talk earlier. It was too risky to ask him to call his magic yet again, and so Iliaria and Cuinn were also keeping watch.

"I need your help," I said and leaned against the door.

"Why?"

"My queen has been captured by your cousin and his toadies."

She didn't even look at me. "What makes you think I'll help?"

"I don't," I said.

"Then why do you bother asking?"

"Because I'm hoping that somewhere inside you, Morina, you won't subject me to the same fate you've been subjected to."

"What is that supposed to mean?" she asked, her voice dropping close to a growl.

"You know what it feels like to lose someone you love," I said. "Help me, please. If only for penitence for the harm you've already done."

"I haven't harmed you. I did not take your queen."

I moved away from the door as I spoke. "You brought us here, Morina. You brought me here. You left me to die with you. You dragged me into your prison and your hell. You've marked me. How can you stand there as if you have done nothing wrong?"

Morina shoved me up against the bedpost until the carved wood dug painfully into my back. "You came to me," she said lowly. "You put yourself between us. I would not have taken you, had you not approached me." She bowed her head and I turned my face from hers. "Now you are repulsed by me?" She stepped back, angry. "It was a ploy after all?"

"What was a ploy, Morina?"

"You were only trying to seduce me so that I would release you."

"What did you expect me to do?"

Her nostrils flared as she exhaled a breath through her slightly arched nose. "That is not an answer."

"What do you want me to say, Morina? Yes, I tried to seduce you so that you would release me."

"Was it feigned, vampire?"

I made a frustrated sound low in my throat. "I don't know what you want, Morina. You're infuriating, you're selfish, and you're filled with so much anger."

Slowly, the corners of her mouth rose. Her lips parted and she laughed, laughed until it rang from the ceiling like the tinkling of bells. She clutched her stomach and the post beside my head.

"And?" she asked when the laughter had subsided. "Is there more you'd like to tell me?"

"Yes," I said and I tried to push past her. Her arm straightened in front of me like steel. "I don't understand you."

"Good," she said. "I'm glad you don't. Shall I then tell you what I think of you, vampire? Should I tell you that you almost had me? Despite how infuriating I find you..." The tips of her fingers brushed my left hip and I flinched. "You almost succeeded. You almost had me."

I tried not to feel uncomfortable when her hand began to climb the side of my body, but I couldn't hide it. Morina saw my discomfort and it made her smile all the more.

"I wasn't trying to get you, Morina. I was trying to understand you. I gave up when you kept pushing me away. I tried to show you compassion."

"I don't want your compassion."

"I know."

She stepped away and I was grateful. I couldn't tell what it was about Morina, but something about her was infuriating, and yet, intriguing. As soon as I was certain I didn't like her, she said or did something or I saw a flicker of something inside her that made it hard for me to truly dislike her.

"Perhaps it would be easier between us if I hated you," I said, saying it aloud without realizing I was going to.

"I could say the same to you," Morina said. "Just being with you this short time has been torturous in more ways than one."

"She's still here, Morina. I wasn't doing those things to torment you. If you're going to blame anyone, blame Andrella."

She flinched when I said her name, as if I'd struck her with it.

"I'm sorry," I said.

"Sometimes," she said, and her gaze strayed back toward the balcony. "Sometimes, I think I can sense her."

"I can't remember everything that has happened." I raked a hand through my curls and stepped toward the doors she kept gazing at. "I can't remember if you really did force me to kneel on this floor and bathe in front of you, or if it was all a dream. I can't remember if seeing Andrella actually happened or if it was merely some kind of hysteria brought on by everything else that has happened."

"You've seen her?" Morina asked. "You never told me that."

"I thought I had."

Morina came to me and put her hands on my shoulders. "What did she say to you?"

"That you weren't always this way."

She recoiled, as if the words hurt her. I had a feeling they did.

I reached out and laid my hand on her arm. The white fabric of the blouse she wore was wrinkled and scratchy against my skin. "She asked me to help you."

"You cannot help me, vampire."

"Aye, that's what I kept trying to tell her."

Morina stared at my hand for far longer than was polite and so I removed it, uncertain what she was thinking.

"You do not hate me?" She didn't look at me when she asked.

"I want to. I've tried to. But I can't."

"Why?"

"You're like a wounded dog that bites the hand reaching out to help it, Morina. You're in pain and the only way you know how to deal with that pain is to lash out."

The tip of her tail rose and twitched in the air.

"I am sorry to say it, but it's true. You know it."

"Leave," she said. "I'll decide on the morrow if I'll help you or not."

She returned to the balcony doors and stood gazing into the night.

Quietly, I left.

I wasn't sure what Morina's intentions were, but one thing I was sure of, the Dracule were a harder lot to read empathically than any of the vampires I'd ever known.

"How'd it go?" Cuinn asked.

"She'll tell me on the morrow whether she's willing to help or not."

"That she did not outright refuse is a good sign," Iliaria said as she opened the door to my chambers. "Depending."

"Depending?"

"On if you really want her help. How much detail did you give her, Epiphany?"

"Not enough for her to use against us if she decides to turn on me."

"Good," Iliaria said. She knelt to toss another log of wood from the stack beside the fireplace into the fire. She sat back on her heels and placed her palms in her lap. "That is good."

Vasco knocked briefly on the door before letting himself in. "Queen Helamina will be questioning us personally," he said.

"Let her," I said. "She won't find anything."

Queen Helamina came to my chambers with Istania to question us. Vasco fetched the others and brought them to my chambers as well. Queen Helamina stood in the center of the room and questioned each of us one at a time. When Istania gave her nod of approval that we were telling the truth, she moved on to question the next person.

Needless to say, everyone had an alibi. Vito and Vittoria had been with Anatharic on guard duty outside the castle. One of Queen Helamina's men was able to confirm it. Nirena and Vasco and Gaspare had been downstairs with Istania and some of Augusten's vampires. Vasco vouched that he had seen Iliaria, Cuinn, and me disappear into Morina's room. He explained that when he had not seen Renata for some time, he went to find her, and when he couldn't, he felt something was amiss.

It didn't take as long as any of us had thought it would, thankfully. All of us were able to confirm our whereabouts, and so Queen Helamina wasted no time asking us further questions in vain. All save Cuinn, Iliaria, and I were dismissed. Queen Helamina turned to me when the others had gone.

"I have heard whispers, Epiphany, that you have been conspiring with the Dracule across the hall."

"I have gone to speak with her, lady, if that's what you're asking."

Her gaze narrowed suspiciously. "I am no fool," she said, straightening as if I'd accused her of being one. "Why have you been tiptoeing about?"

I raised the sleeve on my left arm. "As you can see, lady, I have been marked. I asked that she remove the metaphysical ties that bind us."

I felt no need to dissemble, for it was true. I had asked Morina to take back her binding. But whether Queen Helamina was our ally or not, I did not know her well enough to trust her with all of the truth.

"And why were you in her room when your queen disappeared and earlier this eve?" she asked.

"Well," I said, "if you must know, I visited the Dracule some days ago due to the issue she seems to have with my lover." I motioned lightly toward Iliaria, who tipped her head in confirmation. "This whole thing began based on a quarrel years ago."

"What is the nature of the quarrel?"

"The details are not mine to share, Queen Helamina."

"And you?" she asked Iliaria. "Will you tell me or will you pussyfoot as expertly as your lover? How do I now know the two of you have not conspired against your queen?" The last part she asked me.

A surge of anger whipped through me and made the muscles in my arms contract. "I would advise you," I said, "to never, ever, accuse me of such a thing. Renata is my Siren, lady. Not only that, but she is my lover and my queen. I would never, ever betray her, and you'd be wise to remember it." The emotion swam through me. It made my blood pump faster, my breath shorter and clipped. The thought of Queen Helamina trying to use her status to turn Renata's capture on me set my thoughts and blood on fire. "I could easily accuse you, Helamina. I could easily try to turn this entire situation about on King Augusten and yourself. But I have not, so please do me the courtesy of not turning it about on me and mine."

For several long moments, the room was bathed in an unsteady silence. The wood in the fire popped and crackled, seeming much louder than it should have. Queen Helamina assessed me while she stared at me, as if she would find the answers to her questions written on my face. I focused on making my expression as neutral as I could. Yet, the anger continued to burn inside me and I knew I couldn't hide it. Not entirely.

Queen Helamina inclined slightly. "Spoken like a queen, Epiphany."

"I don't care how it sounds. I have one concern, lady, and one concern alone and that *is* my queen." I stepped closer to her and Helamina stood still. "If I find that you have played us falsely, you will have not only the Rosso Lussuria knocking at your door but the Dracule we bear an alliance with. That, my lady, is all you need to know and keep in mind while you go about your investigation."

It was bold of me, to threaten the Queen of Ravenden, but it was the only thing I could think of to divert her from trying to pry into what I was about with the Dracule. I would not allow myself to overlook the possibility that Renata had been betrayed, whether she consented to it or no. If for some reason, someone in the castle had betrayed her, it could very well have been Augusten or Helamina, and that too was a possibility I would not overlook.

"Who of the interrogators assembled have questioned King Augusten and you?" I asked. "None, lady. You have both put yourself in a position to be the ones asking the questions, but who do you answer to?"

"I will answer to you, Epiphany," Queen Helamina said and her tone was calm and only slightly condescending. "I was with Augusten discussing a vision I have recently had about a Dracule I do not recognize. I have walked the halls of this castle and not one matches the appearance of the Dracule I have seen."

"And what do you think of this Dracule, lady? What else have you seen?"

"Nothing more," she said.

"You suspect this Dracule has something to do with my queen's whereabouts?"

"I do not know," she admitted. "I only know what I have seen and that is not much. I saw only its face in vision, its fur whiter than our skin, its gaze blacker than space."

"Did the Dracule have any markings, Queen Helamina?"

"No, it was perfectly and starkly white."

"None with me bear any resemblance to that," Iliaria said. "I can only tell you that we will keep watch for it."

Queen Helamina nodded and I asked, "Are we done?"

Helamina eyed me suspiciously. "You are quick to end this."

"You will not find the answers you seek here," I said. "I am quick not to waste your time."

"Then we are done," she said. "I may be Queen of Ravenden, Epiphany, but some of us sovereigns seek to protect one another."

"And some seek only to gain crowns and thrones, lady. I am no fool." I threw her words back at her. Queen Helamina gave no outward sign that it bothered her.

"Yes," she said, "some do, indeed."

She and Istania left and I breathed out a sigh of relief.

"Not sure that was in your best interest," Cuinn said.

"I think it was," Iliaria said. "Well handled, Epiphany."

"Aye, I didn't say it wasn't well handled," Cuinn said to her, "only now I'm not sure if the queen's more suspicious or infuriated with your audacity."

"You know what I have to say to that?"

"What?"

"She should not have begun to accuse me."

Chapter Fifteen

On the following day, Iliaria escorted the same Donatore woman I had fed from once before to my room. I fed again, choosing to drink from the sensitive skin at the bend of her elbow. She was compliant and as meek as a mouse. In a way, her demeanor reminded me of Justine, who often went quietly and willingly about the task of welcoming me and caring for me at Renata's behest. I did not ask the Donatore her name, nor did she ask mine. I fed from her and watched the flutter of her lashes while I did so. Her blood filled my body with warmth and when I was done, I drew away from her. Then, without an exchange of words, she was taken away and it was time for me to visit Morina.

I went alone again, leaving Cuinn with Emilio just outside the door to Morina's quarters.

"What aid do you specifically request of me, vampire?" Morina asked, her back turned to me. The arch of her wings relaxed behind her, the spurred tips curled as she rolled her neck. I wondered if she had gotten any sleep in the past several days and thought it unlikely.

"Iliaria tells me that your father was once a priest, my lady."

She turned and looked at me quizzically. "What would you need with a priest?"

"I seek to gain an audience with the angel Azrael."

Morina laughed. "And what makes you think I can help you with that?"

"If your father was a priest, surely you would know how to accomplish such a task."

"Perhaps I do," she said, "but what do I gain in turn for helping you, vampire?"

"Forgiveness. You have done me wrong, lady. Many times now. Yours are the hands that have set this wheel in motion."

"I do not care about your forgiveness, vampire, or anyone else's."

"I will try to help you find a way to see Andrella one last time," I said, mostly in desperation. I didn't know if I could do it, and I was careful not to promise her that I could, only that I would try.

Morina watched me long and hard.

"And what makes you think you can accomplish that?"

"I'm not promising that I can. I can only promise to try and make it so."

"That is an easy promise to renege on," she said.

"There are those around me that might be able to help, if you aid us with this thing. You cannot promise that your aid will fulfill my request, just as I cannot promise mine will fulfill yours. All we can do is try to help each other. I will give you my oath that I will try to help you to the best of my abilities if you will try to help me, Morina."

"How do you think Azrael will help you find your queen, vampire? That is why you wish to summon him, is it not?"

"It is, but how I believe he can help me, I'd rather not say."

"Because you are afraid I will expose you? You trust me so little?"

"In all honesty, you've given me little reason to give you my trust to begin with."

She blinked. "That's true, isn't it?"

"Aye."

Morina came close to me until there was only an arm's length of space between us. I gazed up at her much taller form and tried not to feel small. Truly, the Dracule were imposing in their height, even in the more human of their forms.

"There is a way, Epiphany." She looked both serious and thoughtful as she gazed down at me. I couldn't remember her ever speaking my name, and it surprised me. "The way is dangerous and you may not survive to keep your word to me."

"I will speak with the others and find someone to uphold my end of the bargain for me if I am incapable of doing it. What is the way, Morina?"

"The way is through his door, Epiphany."

I thought for a moment. "I have to die again."

"You must stand on the brink of life and death."

"Am I not doing that now as a vampire?" I asked.

Morina smiled slyly. "You stand with Azrael's gift filling you. You must relinquish that gift to him. Stand on the brink and call out his name."

"It's that simple?"

"Simple?" Morina asked. "What in the seven hells would make you begin to think it's simple? He may not answer you, vampire. He has not answered the Dracule for a very long time."

"How do I stand on the brink, Morina?"

"The priests of Azrael once practiced the art of bloodletting to commune with him. You must make of yourself an empty vessel, then you will find the brink, and there, you must call his name with your last breath."

It was impossible to tell if she was leading me astray. Though I sensed her words were true, for they made sense.

Of course, thinking they made sense didn't mean it wasn't a lie. Yet, if she was lying, she was a good liar.

"Thank you," I whispered.

"I would not thank me just yet, and you can thank me when you live to uphold your oath to me."

"I will do my best, Morina. You have my word."

"Fabulous," she said. "I pray you keep it, for if you survive and do not…"

She did not need to say the words to make the implied threat clear.

I nodded. "I will, Morina. I will do what I can to help you and I will inform those close to me if I fail and ask them to aid you in my place."

"Good," she said. "Now go."

I hesitated at the door. "If I fail and do not survive, will you live?"

"If I can shield from you, yes. But it no longer really matters."

I left and felt her gaze on my back until the door clicked shut behind me.

"Well, how'd it go this time?" Cuinn asked.

"I have my answer," I said, knowing my response was vague. I crossed the short hallway and opened the door to my room where Iliaria and Vasco waited.

When Cuinn joined us, I told them what I had to do. As I figured, neither was happy with the results. Yet, strangely, they did not try to dissuade me.

I told Vasco about my promise to Morina and he agreed to help me fulfill it or to see it followed through if I didn't survive.

"There is one condition, colombina," Vasco said. "I want Emilio with you when you do this thing."

"Agreed," I said and then looked at Iliaria. "Morina said that if I do not survive this, and she cannot shield, it will affect her. Will it affect you?"

"It might," Iliaria said.

"I almost dragged you down with me once, Iliaria. I don't want to do it again."

"That was my own foolishness, Epiphany. Not yours."

"I don't want to hurt you."

"We are Dracule," Iliaria said, "if I must shield from you, I will. Does that make you feel better?"

"Yes, a little. Are you sure you can, though?"

"Yes," she said.

"When she tried to save you, sorella, she threw every guard she had down to try to keep you alive." Vasco knew what I was asking, and he wasn't going to let Iliaria side step the truth.

"I don't want you to do that, Iliaria. Promise me you won't."

"When will you do this thing?" she asked.

"Tonight," I said. "I will do it tonight."

❖

Iliaria sat crossed-legged in front of the fireplace with one of her crescent blades in her lap. I remained true to my word to Vasco, and so his son Emilio was with us while Vasco took Emilio's shift outside Morina's door.

Iliaria brought my attention to her. "Once we begin, Epiphany, there is no turning back." She held the blade's pommel loosely. "Your body will not heal a cut from this blade. Do you understand?"

Wordlessly, I nodded. I understood.

"What about Cuinn?"

Cuinn jumped off the bed and tilted his head in thought as he approached. "I'll block ye from me, but understand, Piph, I won't let ye slip away entirely."

"I just need to find the brink, Cuinn."

"Aye," he said sadly. He didn't protest what I endeavored to do. He didn't need to for me to know that he, like the others, wasn't fond of my decision.

It was touching, how much they cared about me, even more so that they were willing to set their own feelings aside to allow me to do what needed to be done if we were to save Renata.

Strangely, I was calmer than I had anticipated, much more at peace with myself than I should have been given the circumstances. I tried to focus on letting go of all of my thoughts. Morina had said that I had to make myself an empty vessel and whether that was in reference to the bloodletting or my state of mind, I wasn't sure, but I thought it best to be cautious.

Iliaria carefully took my hand between her slender fingers. She raised my wrist upward and pressed the tip of the curled blade over Morina's name buried in the startling vines of her mark.

"Ready?"

"As I'll ever be."

She drew the blade lightly down my wrist, applying more pressure toward the middle of the cut. The claw-like tip parted my skin in a stinging song of pain. It sent a blaze of heat burning and twitching up the entire length of my arm, and I hissed at the rush of it, but when I tried to pull away out of reflex, Iliaria held tightly and raised my wrist to her mouth. It took me a moment to realize what she was doing.

"Why?"

She bent her head, her glossy hair tucked behind her small ear, revealing the perfect line of her neck and the pulse beating there. "I'll not have you bleeding all over the place. The others will smell it." She sealed her lips over the cut and drank my blood, her throat working as she swallowed. Her lips against my skin sent a line pulsing to my groin, and I tried to ignore the pull of her body. But it was hard to ignore her mouth on me, hard to ignore the way my blood seemed to flow more quickly as her tongue caressed the wound.

Her mouth continued to work at the wound, and I shut my eyes. The sound of my heartbeat pounded in my ears like roaring waters in my head. After some time, the beat slowed. Longer intervals passed between the beats, signifying how much of my blood she was taking.

Though I tried not to think, I couldn't help it. I remembered when Renata had given me the kiss of death. I hadn't been frightened at the sharp prick of her fangs or by her draining the life from me. I wasn't frightened now. My body felt heavy and my mind began to feel weightless as my lashes fluttered and my vision went out of focus. I had surrendered then, to Renata's kiss, as I now surrendered to Iliaria's.

I began to feel even more light-headed and then dizzy, and knew I was close. I forced myself to open my heavy lids, forced myself to watch Iliaria, to make her my anchor before the darkness came rushing in.

The edges of my vision were speckled with black stars. When I felt myself slip, losing my grip on the reality around me, I reached out with my thoughts. I thought of the angel's name, thought it until it was emblazoned like a beacon in my mind.

Azrael!

I felt his name on the tip of my tongue, threatening to break free of my lips, clenched just behind my teeth. The darkness at the corners of my vision exploded, and the last thing I felt of the world around me was my body falling into weightlessness and Azrael's embrace.

❖

I didn't know where I was. I felt strange. My head ached beyond belief, sending a cutting pain through the side of my skull. The room around me was dark, and I pulled the blankets up as if in a fog. I couldn't think clearly. I couldn't remember. I knew there was something I was supposed to remember. It seemed as though there was, but I looked inside myself and couldn't find it.

"Piph?" I recognized the voice, or at least a part of me seemed to know I should have recognized it, but why couldn't I recall the name that went along with it?

An orange glow bled to life in the darkness. It was bright and I shielded my eyes with a hand.

"It's me, Piph," the orange figure said while it came closer and closer to me. "Cuinn."

"Cuinn?" As soon as I spoke his name, my recollections kicked in. Memories of him came flooding back, and with them, Iliaria, Vasco, Emilio…

They came so hard and fast I bolted out of the bed, hitting the nightstand and sending an unlit lamp on top of it wobbling.

A door opened, spilling even more brightness into the room. Someone gripped me by the shoulders and began guiding me back toward the bed. My body didn't seem to want to work. As soon as my feet touched the floor, I lost my balance.

"Back," Iliaria said. "Cuinn, get back! You are hovering and crowding her. Come, Epiphany, lie back down…or sit…or something. There's something you need to hear and it's best if you not hear it on your feet."

I let her steer me with her hands and sat down on the bed. The blankets felt lumpy and uncomfortable beneath me as I laid back. Why couldn't I get comfortable?

I tried to sit up again and the room spun as if I'd had entirely too much to drink.

"What'sss wrong?" I tried to speak clearly and the words came out slurred and uncertain, my tongue as uncooperative as the rest of my body. Iliaria guided me to rest back against the pillows and still, I was uncomfortable. Something was digging into my back.

"Colombina," Vasco's voice flowed smooth and tranquil as he projected a sense of calm to me.

At first, I fought the touch of his magic. He laid his hand against my arm and I could barely feel it through the weight of my clothes. I was hot, hotter than I should have been. I started to panic and Vasco pushed out with his power again.

"Calm down, colombina, and we will explain. Take a deep breath," he said.

I did.

"Now let it out."

I shut my eyes tightly and exhaled.

"Focus on the beat of your heart, sorella, and only that."

My heart was beating rapidly. I forced myself to take the breaths that he had told me to, making them longer and deeper. My heart rate began to slow as I controlled my breathing.

"What do you remember of the night you sought Azrael?"

"Iliaria," I said. "Her mouth."

"And?"

"Iliaria drank me," I said slowly, as it still seemed more difficult than it should have to speak aloud. "I remember Emilio and Cuinn."

"And?"

"I don't know…I can't think."

"Vasco, just tell her," Iliaria said with a thread of impatience.

"Am I dead?" I asked.

"Your former self is," another voice said, a woman's voice. "Congratulations, vampire. It appears your dance with death was a smashing success."

Morina leaned against the bedpost with the black patch shielding her scarred eye. I made a face, trying to convey my displeasure, but it felt funny. My face felt strange. I raised my hand and Iliaria snatched it.

"Epiphany," she said.

I met her gaze.

"I do not know what you said or what you did, but Azrael has answered your request."

I tried to glance down at her hand on my arm and she moved her other hand to bring my gaze back to her face.

"Not yet," she said. "You do not remember a thing about Azrael?"

"No, why? What happened?"

"Bugger it all!" Cuinn exclaimed. "Just tell the poor girl!" He leapt onto the bed. "You're one of them now." He motioned with his snout to Iliaria. "You're Dracule, Piph. You asked and received."

I blinked. I wasn't sure I'd heard him right, and if I had, I wasn't sure I believed it. I felt strange, but wouldn't I know if I had changed that much?

Cuinn must've seen the disbelief on my features, for he snorted and said, "Get a mirror."

"You are going to send her mad," Morina said, but not like she really cared.

Iliaria let out a heavy sigh and released me. She held a mirror. "It is true, before you doubt. Remember that what you see here is only what is true now. It may not always be so."

She held up the mirror. I managed to catch a glimpse of myself and no more than that, for as soon as I saw the white fur, the angular face, and fathomless eyes—

My heart lurched with panic and I scrambled from the bed, though Vasco and Iliaria tried to contain me.

It was a mess. I was a mess, a mess of the tail I paid little heed to, a mess of wings I didn't know how to use, a mess of the slightly bent legs that I had not yet learned how to maneuver.

If it weren't for Iliaria, I might've taken all three of us to the floor. As it was, she pulled me down and sealed her arms tightly around my midsection. "Stop, Epiphany! Stop fighting it!"

I tried, but every instinct within me told me to fight, to panic. Every fiber of my being told me it wasn't *right*.

For some reason, Queen Helamina's vision came to my mind.

"It'sss me," I said.

"What is?" Iliaria asked.

"Helamina'sss visssion."

"Sì," Vasco said. "We kind of noticed that."

I slumped against Iliaria, defeated. "Tell me."

Vasco understood. "You died, Epiphany. Iliaria drank you empty."

"Vasco begged me to interfere," Emilio said. "I couldn't."

"Neither could I," Cuinn said. "Nothing we did to try and pull ye back worked."

"I thought I had lost you," Iliaria mumbled against my neck, tickling my fur with her lips. "I lost control. I couldn't stop drinking. I'm sorry."

"What elssse?"

"Azrael came," Emilio said. "We could see him. He stood over you. He knew what you sought and he gave you what you asked."

"Why?"

"Love, I think," Vasco said. "He did not explain why. He barely spoke to us, sorella. He only said, 'For turns of the whole moon, she will have what she asks.'"

"*Four*," Cuinn corrected him. "As in, four months. He took the cloak from his back and wrapped you in his magic," he explained. "In four months, he will return you to your former self."

"Where are we?"

"Azrael wrapped you in his darkness," Iliaria said, stroking my back like you'd calm a child. "When his darkness began to fade, we saw that he had indeed changed you. I too remembered Helamina's prophetic vision. We feared she would turn against us, so we've brought you somewhere safe."

"Who elssse isss here?"

"All of the Rosso Lussuria, save Gaspare," Vasco said. "We decided to leave him behind just in case he goes shouting wolf."

The corner of my mouth tugged in a smirk. "Wissse."

"Aye, I didn't disagree with it," Cuinn added. "Bit of a whiny bastard, that one."

"Anatharic will be here shortly," Iliaria said.

"I ssstill do not know where we are."

"We're in a hotel room in the human world," Vasco said. "And don't worry, Emilio's warded and spelled the place. No one will know we're here."

Morina snorted.

"Why isss ssshe here?"

"We had no choice but to bring her," Iliaria said.

"Aye, she threatened to squeal on us if we didn't," Cuinn added with an accusatory glance toward the Dracule in question.

"Don't sound too thrilled," Morina said sarcastically.

"Anatharic and I will teach you how to use this body." Iliaria gratefully changed the subject. "Are you able to stand?"

"I think ssso."

She helped me to my feet, and though I still felt like a drunken sailor on a swaying ship, her hands on my arms helped me to remain upright.

"Use your tail for balance, Epiphany."

"How?"

"If you focus, your body will react. It's a lot like moving the rest of your limbs. Think about it and it will happen. Your wiring just hasn't sorted itself out yet."

She was right. When I focused on *trying* to move it myself, it did. Left, then right, left, then right…

I knew I made a strange face at the sensation. "Odd."

"You'll get used to it."

I swung it a bit roughly and nearly lost my balance again. I reached out to catch myself by gripping Iliaria's arm and accidentally stretched a wing outward.

Iliaria laughed. "It's a bit like watching a newborn colt, sorry," she said when I glared at her. "In time, they'll become just another part of you, but for now," she started guiding me back toward the bed, "rest. Sleep. It's something your Draculian body needs."

She dismissed the others, all save Cuinn, to an adjacent room. Iliaria climbed into bed beside me.

"Try your stomach," she said, noticing when I began fidgeting and trying to get comfortable.

I rolled onto my stomach and felt the node of flesh between my legs pressing against the mattress. I rose up on my arms with a gasp.

Iliaria laughed again and stroked a hand down my back, between my winged shoulders blades. My fingers curled in pleasure and with them, the spurred tips.

"Just lie down," she said. "Try to ignore that."

"Awfully bleedin' hard."

"Is it?" she asked with a mysterious smile. "So soon?"

I gave her an impatient look, but lay back down on my stomach, a bit more cautiously this time.

"Not like *that*," I grumbled.

Another trickle of laughter fell from her lips and I closed my eyes, burying half my face in the pillow. "I'm hot."

"You're supposed to be. You're Dracule now, no longer a vampire."

"Couldn't Azzzrael have made me hairlesssss?"

"A bald Dracule?" Iliaria asked. "That'd be an odd sight and I think it unlikely that you'd fool Damokles that way."

I groaned unhappily.

Iliaria stroked my ear and it tickled insanely, making them twitch wildly as I tried to avoid her. I felt them flatten against my skull, tugging the muscles near my forehead whilst I frowned.

"We'll teach you to change your form," she said. "When you're ready...for now, sleep, Epiphany."

She started to leave and I laid a hand on her arm. "Ssstay with me, pleassse."

"I will," she said as she curled her long body against mine. "I promise."

❖

I stretched, relishing the mists of sleep that clung to me. After two hundred years, I'd forgotten how good it felt to sleep normally instead of dying at dawn. The stretch alone felt incredible, sending a tendril of pleasure unfurling from the center of my body and spreading through every inch of me. My ears sank back as my toes curled, and I yawned.

A triangle of sunlight cut through the hotel bedroom and I ducked down low and instinctively in the bed.

"Good morning," Iliaria said as the thick curtain over the window swung back into place. "You need not fear sunlight, not as one of us."

I managed, albeit a bit uncertainly, to get myself upright.

I clambered out of the bed in a mess of limbs and wings, holding on to the bedpost for balance. "May I?"

She gestured to the window with a smile softer than any I'd ever seen on her face before. "By all means," she said, and came to help me.

I pulled the curtain aside, and the light was too bright. It made me squint and draw away as it sent a shooting pain through my eyes and into the back of my head.

"Let your eyes adjust, Epiphany." Iliaria gently steered me back toward the window. She drew the curtain aside herself. "Close them."

I did and the light beyond sent an orange glow behind my lids.

"Open them, slowly."

It took a few tries, but after a while, my sight did adjust to the brightness beyond the glass.

We were some stories up. Below us was a world of healthy and lively green grass. Tall and sturdy trees with wide leaves dotted the rolling landscape. The sunlight caught on a pool of water at the edge of a tree line. It danced and rippled off the blue metallic surface where ducks and white swans swam. A mother duck with a startling crown of iridescent plumage led her chocolate and yellow ducklings up to shore. The boat of her tail danced behind her as she led them, happy as could be.

"You will notice your vision is better than that of a vampire in this form," Iliaria said, though I sensed she wasn't sharing deeper thoughts.

I nodded, for I had noticed. It was not that my vision appeared weird in any way, only that the scope of it seemed wider. The colors below came to life more vividly than those any artist's brush could give birth to.

Iliaria handed a wad of black cloth to me. "Put this on," she said. I unfolded the cloth to find a pair of trousers cropped just above the knee. Iliaria had to help me dress, and when she was finished, she said, "Come." Her hand squeezed my shoulder briefly before she turned to slide open the two wooden doors that led to the adjoining room. She led me into the room where we found Anatharic and Morina waiting. Anatharic, as usual, was in his Draculian form. Morina was still in the more human of hers, though she had changed her garb for a pair of leather breeches and a blouse over which buttoned a figure-flattering vest.

"Where are the othersss?"

"They're in the basement." At my expression, she said, "I told you we would teach you. Emilio has spelled the entire hotel and its grounds. We are safe here."

"If you're going to fool Damokles, you need to know how to move like one of us and not like a gangly fawn," Morina said.

Iliaria showed me soon enough what they were talking about. She moved throughout the room, shifting furniture and placing it just so. She moved a high-backed chair from its spot in front of a desk and placed it just catty-corner to it. A sofa was pressed up against the wall by the door.

When she was done, she turned to Morina.

"Since you wanted to help," Iliaria said, gesturing at her with a hand.

Morina kicked off her knee-high boots until she stood barefoot.

"This is how you should be able to move," Iliaria said. "Watch closely."

Morina drew in a breath and let it out slowly. As soon as the breath left her body, she was moving. She ran toward the round-back chair and leapt on it, catching the corner of it with the tips of her toes. Her wings fanned out to slice the air as she continued to move. Every part of her body worked in perfect harmony, her tail swayed for balance and her wings cut and cupped the air to aid her movements. After she caught the corner of the chair, she stepped onto the desk, and from that, the nightstand beside the bed. I thought she would simply walk across the bed, but she did not. She turned and danced, nimble and swift like a ballerina on her feet. Her hands caught the thick wooden post before she swung herself around to walk right across the top of the footboard. The footboard creaked beneath her weight, but she was not on it long before she threw herself to the sofa, walking along the narrowest part. She left herself little room to stand, but she did not need it. She used her fingers and the spurs of her wings to penetrate the sheetrock of the wall and climbed upward toward the ceiling.

Iliaria tilted her head back as Morina flattened her body against the ceiling. Her long white, gray, and black hair hung loose before she dropped herself. She swung her body into the fall and landed flat on her feet.

Not a piece of furniture was out of place when she was done. The only damage done were the holes she had created to climb. Morina stood to her full height. "If you're not careful when climbing, you'll pull the entire ceiling down on top of you. Remember not to create your holds close together."

Iliaria said, "Now watch Anatharic."

Anatharic stepped up and did what Morina had done, with only a few alterations to his movements to compensate for his less humanoid form.

When he was done, he dropped silently and deadly behind me, only creating a small disturbance in the air.

"You try," his voice hissed.

I had memorized their pattern and so started as they had. I made a run for the chair and misjudged my jump, sending it toppling over.

Morina laughed while Iliaria set the chair back upright.

"Again," she said.

Again. It was something I ended up hearing over and over for the next several hours.

Again, again, again...

Finally, I got to the point where I made it to the bed, and then I slipped on the footboard and had to start all over. *Again.*

It was night when I made it through the entirety of the course they had set for me. It looked simple, watching them do it, but in action it was far more difficult than it appeared. Where Morina and Anatharic had done as minimal damage to the room as possible, I'd accomplished removing great chunks of sheetrock from the wall and ceiling.

But at last I got it, dropping to my feet and the ground below in an ungraceful heap.

"That was good enough," Iliaria said, a thread of tiredness in her tone as if she were the one who had been trying to get through the makeshift course repeatedly and not I.

"The others should be awake now."

"Sì," Vasco said from the doorway between the rooms. "Awake and seeing that you've been busy." The corner of his mouth raised in a half smirk as he assessed the destruction and bits of debris on the floor. "I guess it's a good thing after all that we are not really using this room. How do you feel, sorella?" he asked me.

"Exhausssted." The tip of my tongue flitted of its own accord and I groaned. "Frussstrated."

"We'll teach you to change your form soon enough," Iliaria said. "Right now, you need to get used to the Draculian tongue. You're too obviously irritated by it."

No surprise there.

Chapter Sixteen

With six floors of rooms, the hotel was larger than I had anticipated. The hallways were wide, lined in a rich, creamy carpet that complimented the wood paneling and off-white walls nicely. It was far more extraordinary than anything I had seen in the Sotto, or even in my life as a mortal. Everything in the place seemed new, and though we cared for our belongings and our furnishings, they were usually from centuries past.

Morina and Iliaria turned a corner and we followed them when they stepped into a lift. I found that if I did not think about it, if I just did it, walking was not so complicated.

Iliaria pressed a button when the doors slid closed and the lift dropped. The sudden movement made my stomach feel as if it were trying to crawl to another location in my body. When the lift stopped, I clung to the metal rail that lined the box.

Vasco asked with some amusement in his voice, "Surely, you've read about these, sorella?"

"I've read about a great many thingsss," I said. "It doesss not mean I want to try all of them."

"I take it you won't be coming back to play in it?"

I shook my head, still feeling mildly unsteady when we stepped out into another hallway.

"It's not so different an experience than jumping," Iliaria said. "At least with the lift it's a controlled experience."

"By whossse ssstandardsss?" I asked.

She laughed at that.

Cuinn trotted ahead. "I didn't mind it."

"Of course not, Fata," Nirena said. "Your kind has long been fascinated by the advances of human technology."

He didn't disagree with her; instead, he continued to lead the way, his fluffy tail bouncing behind him as he trotted to a tune that only he seemed to hear. Cuinn seemed strangely cheerful.

"A Dracule smiling," Nirena said, "that's rather unsettling."

"Sssorry," I said, not really sure why I was apologizing but doing it anyway.

Cuinn led us through a massive dining room filled with round tables covered in white cloths and back to the hotel's kitchen. Emilio moved about the large space with ease, leaning over and making things beep annoyingly. The smell of cooked meat made my mouth water.

At my questioning look, Iliaria asked, "It smells good, no?"

"Yesss."

Vasco scrunched his nose up in distaste. "Not so much, no."

Emilio cleared off space on a long metal table and gestured for us to sit.

"It's not for you, vampire," Morina said.

I wondered how Vasco, Nirena, Vittoria, Vito, and Dominique were to feed. Severiano had also been left behind. I suspected Vasco had decided who would and would not accompany us, and I thought he had decided well. Head of the Cacciatori or no, I did not trust Severiano as much as the others.

Emilio was a splendid host as he set about arranging glasses before each of the vampires. The Dracule shared their blood, even Morina opened a vein, though as she did so she held my gaze, as if making sure I noted her kindness.

While they drank, Iliaria told me more about the Dracule.

"We have to eat solid food. A diet that's high in iron and protein," she explained. "Meat, mostly. Though there are some foods you should steer clear of."

"Like?"

"Dairy," Morina said as she folded a cloth napkin over her thighs. "The Dracule are naturally lactose intolerant."

"We're nursed on blood till our fangs erupt, not a mother's milk. Also, most plant-based foods do not sit well. You could try them, of course, if you're so inclined. Your Draculian body will not reject anything quite like a vampire's would," Iliaria added.

"Will it?" I asked Vasco and he comprehended what I asked.

"She's never tried food since she was reborn," he explained to the others. "Sì, I will show you. Emilio?"

Emilio set a small saucer with a little cut of meat on it before Vasco.

Vasco picked the tidbit up between his thumb and index finger and plunked it into his mouth. As soon as the food passed his lips, he gagged violently and the morsel fell back onto his plate.

"And to think, we always thought of you as a lady of impeccable manners," Nirena said as she sipped blood from her glass. She stared at the meat on Vasco's plate with disgust.

Vasco took her teasing in stride. He picked the morsel up again. "Would you like to try it, Nirena?"

Nirena raised her glass. "No, thank you."

Emilio took the plate away, chuckling as he returned to check the food.

"What elssse?" I asked Iliaria.

"Garlic," Morina said, inclining forward on the aluminum countertop. "Avoid it."

"Isss it poisssonousss?"

"No."

"Then?"

Iliaria touched my shoulder lightly. "You'd best not find out. At least, we'd appreciate you not trying."

"I think it gives 'em flatulence, Piph."

My ears swiveled of their own accord as I wondered if that was really what it was. At my expression, Morina laughed and offered verbal confirmation. "Just avoid it like the plague," she said. "It's not something we digest well."

Emilio kindly brought our plates with well cooked slices of delicious meat served on top of them. "Unseasoned," he said. "I've been listening, sorry."

Iliaria thanked him and encouraged me to eat by pushing my plate closer to me. Even though I was no longer a vampire, I was hesitant to try it. Two hundred years of feeding like a vampire made me suspicious of trying something new.

Eventually, my stomach outweighed my hesitancy and I dined with the others. The meat was juicy and metallic on my Draculian tongue. It was delicious, but when I began to chew, I found it was not easy keeping the piece in one place in my mouth and ended up nearly choking on it.

Iliaria was in near tears by the time she leaned over to offer me a suggestion. "Guide it to the back of your mouth, Epiphany. Like this. Anatharic," she said.

Turning to look at Anatharic gave me more of an idea of what I appeared like trying to eat. Granted, he had the hang of it better than I. He turned his head at an angle to guide the piece away from his fangs and against the row of teeth closer to his cheek. His ears flattened against his head while we stared at him, as if he wasn't enjoying being watched.

I shook my head. "And I thought walking wasss a challenge." I sighed and resigned myself to chewing and swallowing my food any way it wanted to go down.

Iliaria finished before the rest of us, and when she was done she took her plate to Emilio. She leaned into him, her mouth inches from his ear, and whispered words low enough I couldn't hear them.

"Yes, lady. I'm still working on it."

"Good," she said, "let me know when you've made some progress."

"I will."

I pushed my plate away when I was done with it and Iliaria touched my upper arm.

"Come with me," she said.

I rose and followed obediently. In the hallway on our way back toward our room, I asked, "What wasss that about?"

"Oh," she offered, almost absentmindedly, "he's working on figuring out where Damokles is hiding and where your queen is."

In that moment, it occurred to me that out of all those with us, Iliaria was the one who had taken the lead in regard to our situation.

She seemed to be making most, if not all, of the decisions since I'd woken.

"You're still intent on saving her, aren't you?" she asked, searching my face.

"Yesss, my lady."

Iliaria's hand rested on the handle of the door as she halted just outside the room. "It's not going to be easy, Epiphany. You are Dracule now thanks to Azrael, but you still have to fool Damokles into thinking you're really one of us and that you're someone who believes as he does."

"I think I can manage it."

"Do you?" she asked, her head tilting as her long black hair fell to frame her porcelain face. "Epiphany, you do not have a cruel bone in your body. Dracule like Damokles are bloodthirsty and cruel. In order to do this thing, you must become everything you are not."

"I will do what needsss to be done."

She looked doubtful but opened the door to admit us to the room beyond. "Sit on the bed," she said as she motioned idly with a flick of her wrist. "There's more to learn, then."

And so she began to teach me of the Draculian tongue, which I found curling and complicated. When I faltered on a pronunciation, she pushed me.

Again.

I grew increasingly frustrated with the unfamiliar alphabet.

"You have to learn everything, Epiphany. There are no shortcuts in this. If you want to fool Damokles, you must learn to read our hand, you must learn to write it, and you must, above all, learn to speak it without hesitation and uncertainty. Again," she said.

I focused on the web-like and spidery figures she'd written on a tablet of paper and tried to sound their letters out, to put it all together. I daresay, it was more difficult than when I had learned to read as a child.

"My name isss Epiphany," the Draculian language tumbled sloppily off my tongue, and I frowned and said in English, "We ssshould change that."

"Keep your focus," she said. "We'll figure that out later."

Hours passed until a light tap sounded at the door and Vasco peeked in. "Still studying?" he asked.

Iliaria leaned her head back against the bedpost and rubbed her temples. The tilt of her head exposed the smooth expanse of her throat and perfect line of her jaw.

"Yesss," I grumbled unhappily.

"May I borrow her for a while, Great Siren?"

"She needs to learn," Iliaria said, though she sounded tired.

"She's spent the entire day and night learning. Surely, she can resume her lessons on the morrow?"

She sat up straight and then nodded. "Fine. Epiphany, go."

I went with Vasco and found Cuinn in the hallway with him.

"What are we doing?" I asked.

"You'll see, sorella," he said with an impish smile.

Vasco and Cuinn guided me down the long hall and several flights of stairs to the ground floor. Vasco opened a door near the stairs and spoke as we walked through. "She's intent on teaching you a lot, but perhaps we can be of some assistance in other realms."

I didn't know what he meant, until I took in the sight of the room and the large pool of water in the center of it.

Cuinn rushed past me, practically flying on the tips of his paws as he jumped and launched himself in the air above the water. He landed with a riotous splash and paddled back up to the surface, his orange head bobbing as he swam.

I couldn't help it, I laughed. That, too, felt strange.

Vasco unbuttoned his shirt and let it fall.

He ran to the pool, leaping and arching his long arms out in front of him as he dove and swam the pool's length underwater. The surface broke as he stood and pushed his long hair out of his face. His nipple piercings caught the light as he smiled widely.

"Come on, sorella."

"Vasssco, I don't know if I can."

He swam to the steps and emerged. It took me a moment to realize he was coming for me.

"What are you doing?" My ears flattened and I felt my tail swing in an uncertain twitch behind me.

"One way to find out!" Cuinn yelped with glee. "Throw her in! We'll see if she sinks!"

I looked past Vasco's pale shoulder to glare at the frantically paddling fox.

"Watch it," I warned him.

Cuinn sniggered before taking up a chant that encouraged Vasco to throw me in. Vasco stepped forward and I stepped back warily.

"You better not," I said.

Cuinn called out from the pool. "What? Being turned into one of them made you a scaredy-cat? Here kitty, kitty! Come on, furball, the water's fine!"

Vasco took another step forward and his roguish expression told me that if he got his hands on me, he would throw me in. I sank to all fours and he hesitated.

Cuinn had taken up a song while he swam in merry circles, continuing to egg Vasco on.

"I once knew a scaredy-cat, who thought she couldn't swim, till me ol' mate Vasco hoisted her up and decided to throw 'er in!"

I glanced up at Vasco and gestured as inconspicuously as I could by nudging my head toward Cuinn in the pool. He seemed to understand, and as his grin split more widely, he gave the barest of nods.

Cuinn was still singing, though I no longer focused on the words that he barked and yipped. The damn Fata had gone bleedin' bonkers and seemed thoroughly distracted by continuously swimming in circles while he sang like a drunkard.

When Cuinn made a small loop that brought him closest to the edge to us, Vasco took a single step back to get out of my way. I didn't think. I lunged forward, my ears and wings flattening to my body and my tail catching the air behind me.

Cuinn turned his head. His eyes grew large as he realized what was about to happen and he yelled, "Shite!" and tried to paddle rapidly in the other direction.

I leapt off the edge, and for a moment, I was airborne. And then I fell. I landed mostly on top of Cuinn, his words gurgled as his head went under water. He pushed at me as we sank to the bottom, his paws drumming repeatedly into my midsection as he sought to kick me off. I tried to swim, to push back to the surface, but the water enveloped me. The wings stretched out from my back and caught the water even as I tried to push against it.

I flailed and tried to figure out how to gain on the surface while Cuinn cursed bubbles beneath me. A hand gripped my shoulder and an arm wrapped around my waist and I was hauled, spluttering, from the water.

Iliaria glowered as she dragged me unceremoniously to the side of the pool. "You idiots," she hissed. "What in your right mind made you think the Dracule can swim?"

"We were just trying to have some fun," Vasco tried to explain.

Iliaria didn't seem to care about his explanations. She turned her vividly angry gaze on him. "Drowning her is fun? Really?"

Cuinn sputtered as he struggled to climb out of the pool, his nails ticking on the hard concrete as he flopped onto it. "Alas, me hearties. She sinks, she sinks indeed." He coughed and spat a mouthful of water before he shook from head to tail.

My fur was wet and plastered uncomfortably to my body. The shorts Iliaria had given to me dripped as she seized me by the elbow and hauled me to my feet.

"They meant no harm," I said.

She jerked on my arm in attempt to guide me toward the door.

"Iliaria!" I hissed, protesting and pulling against the strength of her hold. I wasn't a child to be scolded.

She used the grip she had on my elbow to bring my body up against hers. "You're done here, Epiphany."

At the expression in her eyes, I shuddered. Something dangerous and commanding lurked in her gaze, more dangerous and commanding than anything I had seen in her when she dominated me in the bedroom. I could tell she was angry and had no intentions of budging.

But I saw something else, a hint of fear mingled with the displeasure of her gaze.

She loved me.

Iliaria loved me, and since she and Renata had rescued me, I had not paid much attention to her feelings. Equipped with such knowledge, I found it difficult to defy her. I nodded and obliged when she led me back to our room.

I knew Iliaria cared for me, but I had not really acknowledged how deep that caring went. It was something I should have known, I should have acknowledged sooner, and a part of me felt guilty for failing to see it. She had tried to protect me. She had tried to save my life by offering up her own. In spite of how harsh she had been, I knew she meant well. I was her dragă, and I had failed to understand what that really meant.

What thanks had I shown her? I hadn't given her fear of losing me any consideration at all. I would have survived drowning, but perhaps all it took to rattle her was the thought. Perhaps I had been too close to death too many times recently.

My focus when she had saved me had been mostly on Renata. Though we had shared a bed together, I had not pleasured Iliaria. I had not told her how much she meant to me. I had made love to Renata while Iliaria made love to me.

I sighed and looked at her. Iliaria's shoulders were tense. She wasn't looking at me. I touched her wrist and she stepped away from me to walk to the far side of the room.

"Iliaria," I tried. "I'm sssorry."

She ignored me as she sat on the edge of the bed with a flop.

"Iliaria," I tried again.

"For what, Epiphany?"

"I've neglected you."

"What are you babbling about?" She turned to face me.

"I feel like I've been ssso focusssed on Renata, I've made you feel neglected."

"I'm fine."

I knelt at her feet. I put my furred hands to the side of her thighs. This time, she looked puzzled. I don't know what propelled me to do it, but I began to slide my cheek across her knees.

"Epiphany," Iliaria said, amused. "Are you trying to claim me with your scent?"

I hesitated. "I don't know, actually."

She touched the tip of my ear and it tickled. I ducked my head and her fingers sank into the fur at the back of my neck. She grabbed me by the scruff and pulled up roughly, until our faces were only an inch apart.

"Take off the shorts," she whispered, her breath tickling the fur of my cheek.

For a moment, her request caught me off guard. "Why?"

"Need you ask? Take them off."

I unhooked them, wiggling my hips to send them from my limbs and to the floor below. I kicked them off and freed my tail.

"Another lessson?" I asked.

"Yes," she said. She moved behind me, her hands sliding through the fur at my hips and up my sides.

She pressed the front of her body against the back of mine and that one little touch was all it took to send pleasant sensations bolting through me. Iliaria's hand dipped down my stomach and my knees grew weak with the knowledge of where it was going.

She cupped me in her hand gingerly, and my head rolled back. Steady and pleasurable warmth suffused my limbs and made my body ache in a way that had nothing to do with pain. The node of flesh between my thighs awakened at her touch, pulsating with blood and desire.

"I told you I would teach everything you need to know about the Dracule," her voice whispered breathily against a particularly sensitive spot of my neck. "We can skip this lesson, if you're squeamish." I shuddered as she applied a bit more pressure. "If not," her voice took on a purring and dark edge, "I'd be more than happy to show you."

Even if I had been squeamish, the murmur of desire rushing through me was too strong to ignore. The idea of Iliaria taking me, any way she pleased, sent a thrill of excitement through me.

"How do the Dracule make love?" I asked.

I felt more than saw the dark smile that spread across her lips. "Get on the bed, Epiphany, and I will show you."

I crawled up on my hands and knees and waited. I heard her move behind me and turned to find her in all of her slinky Draculian glory.

"In thisss form," she gave a rumbling laugh at my slightly surprised expression. "Oh yessss, we fuck in thisss form. There isss alwaysss a dominant and sssubmisssive," she explained. "The dominant ssslipss behind like thisss." She used her knees to guide my legs apart. Though I was Dracule now, Iliaria was still taller in her Draculian form than I was in mine. She guided my wings to rest loosely outward before she bowed her body over mine. Her hands came to rest just above my shoulders as she bridged over me.

I felt her face against the back of my neck and she growled. The growl rumbled against my skin and sent tiny jolts of electric desire down my spine. The muscles in my back twitched uncontrollably in response.

She shifted her hips and pushed against me, pressing her sex against the damp folds between my legs. A shaky breath left me, and I grabbed at the blanket, feeling my claws unsheathe as I did so. The sound of cloth tearing beneath my claws was loud and strangely erotic.

Iliaria's mouth opened and she bit me. The bite made me groan and arch my spine to press my butt into the cradle of her hips. She growled around the mouthful of my skin, and this time, those tiny jolts of pleasure made my muscles jump in a way that was almost painful. Her teeth pressed harder, her fangs drawing pinpricks of blood.

A frustrated growl built low in my throat. "Pleassse."

Iliaria growled again and bit down until she sheathed her canines inside of me. The bite immobilized me and slowly, her hips began to move behind me. The Nod Dragoste between her legs brushed my sex as she pressed against my entrance and continued to roll her hips. It felt as though I would die from the need that was building inside me. Her hips rocked forward. She penetrated me and I cried out at the sensation of it, a rumbling sound spilling from somewhere inside of me. I had taken her inside me before and found that though Draculian women were slightly more equipped, such an act worked incredibly well for foreplay. With the position she had chosen, she was able to sheath more of herself inside me than I had been able to riding her in my human form. I would not spend myself, but knew by the tremor that ran through her hips that she would.

"Pleassse," I begged.

She released the back of my neck and I felt her straighten behind me. She placed her hands on my hips and began to push and pull my body back into hers.

"When I am ready."

The gentle sway that connected our bodies before she guided us apart again was sweet torment. The memory of Renata and her olisbos swam behind my closed lids, and it hurt to recall the particular memory that rose: Renata behind me, piercing me rough and sudden, the way her expert hips thrust as she pushed inside of me as deeply as she would go—

It was not fair to Iliaria, thinking such thoughts while the small knot of her sex buried shallowly inside me. I pushed the thoughts from my mind and concentrated on the moment. Iliaria's thrusts quickened and helped bring me back to the present moment as my body reacted, muscles tightening. I felt her body react to mine. She shuddered as she approached the crest of her climax. She took her pleasure from me, and while she did, every sexual sense within me ignited and threatened to consume me. I wanted to roll onto my back, to rub my sex against her so that I could spend myself in wild frenzy.

But I didn't. In spite of the crippling need, I remained complaint.

Her hips thrust harder as she began to lose her control in the crescendo of lust. She plunged inside me, pushing as far as she could go. Her hands clawed at my hips and became deadly points that held me in place with their threat alone. She thrust inside me one last time, her body bowed, her hips pressed hard against me. My body tightened in reaction to her touch. The cry that fell from her lips was a sound caught somewhere between a moan and a growl.

She released me and I fell to the mattress. My sex pressed stiffly against it, and I groaned, raising my hips slightly as I found myself on the verge of a pleasure so sharp, it brought tears to my eyes.

Iliaria touched my cheek with a human hand.

"You were spectacular," she said.

I groaned to express the agony I was in and she laughed. "Hmm, we'll have to do something about that."

Flipping me onto my back, she sank down on top of me and her sex burned hot and wet against mine. Her wings stretched out behind her and she threw her head back as she began to ride me, guiding my sex between her delicate folds. The orgasm came in a rush, the touch of her sex against mine unleashing the hell fire that burned within me. Outward and outward, the pleasure spread, until I cried out at both the sight of her above me and the touch of her between my legs.

Iliaria collapsed on top of me, catching herself with her elbows. She raised her lower body. The knot between my legs pounded as if my heartbeat had transferred to it.

"I want you to learn how to change," she murmured. "Now." That one word was spoken with delicious command and promise.

"How?"

She caught me roughly by the jaw and forced me to look at her. The wild and hungry expression she wore just about undid me. "You have but to think it and will it be so."

Iliaria's face moved toward mine and I realized she was inclining for a kiss. "Give me your lips, Epiphany. Give me your body."

Uncertainty flowed through me, though I wanted to give her what she asked. I wanted to feel her soft lips mold to mine in a kiss. I wanted to feel her fleshy breasts crush against mine and not the bedamned coat of fur between us. I held that longing in my mind, held tightly to the memories I had of my vampiric body until it felt as though I had convinced myself of the reality of them.

Iliaria drew back and spoke my name in soft amusement.

"What?"

She laughed and reached a hand out to touch me. Her hand sank into the curls at the base of my skull as she guided me up. I startled, surprised as her hand wound gently in my hair and she laughed again. "Not so difficult, you see."

"I did it?"

"Yes."

"I didn't feel anything."

"Why would you? Come here," she said.

The gray carpet was lush against my bare feet as she led me from the bed. The air kissed my skin and relief rushed through me as Iliaria guided me to the oval mirror.

She stood beside me, securing an arm about my waist. "You see? Azrael seems not to have taken all of you."

I looked relatively the same, but different. The gray of my eyes was struck through with branches of the same onyx lightning that decorated Iliaria's and Morina's gazes. My hair spilled in the long mass of mahogany curls that it always had. The wings that stretched from my back were ivory and pink, matching the pale shade of my skin. In human form, the wings felt heavier than they had before. I stared at my reflection and traced the small tuft of white fur that shielded my groin.

"How do I change back?" I asked.

"You change back the same way you changed. You will it and make it so."

I brushed her cheek and locked my arms around her neck. "Kiss me."

"Gladly." The word was barely discernible in the purr that tumbled from her. She did and her tongue parted my lips in a kiss that was warm and inviting. She cupped my buttocks and lifted me against her, our sexes brushing briefly before I wrapped my legs around her hips. My sex stiffened against her stomach as I buried my hands in the silky fall of her hair.

I broke the kiss and fell back and only Iliaria's hands kept me pinned to her body and not sprawled in a heap on the floor.

"Are you ever satiated?" I asked. "I feel as though I'll never get enough. Is that normal?"

She laughed lowly as she knelt on the bed with me in her arms. "The Draculian appetite is a voracious thing."

I never realized until then how much self-control she exerted. I had known that in many ways, she held back, but I never reckoned the half of it.

Iliaria sat me down in front of her. She pushed the hair back from my face, her touch and expression gentle. I raised my hands to cup her jaw, sliding my thumbs down the sturdy bones of her face to her neck. Her pulse beat against my thumbs before I smoothed my palms down the jagged slants of her collarbones.

I cupped her breasts in my hands and her nipples hardened at my caress.

I drew her into my mouth, my blood humming pleasantly and encouragingly. I sank my mouth down on her, careful not to draw blood with the points of my fangs. I traced that tiny knot of flesh with my tongue and Iliaria groaned. I slid a hand down her body, massaging her while I tended to her breasts with lips and tongue. When she growled in frustration, I pushed past the knot between her thighs and eased inside her. Iliaria raised high on her knees, her body arching as she flung her head back to expose the wondrous line of her pale neck. I coaxed her with my hand, catching her breast between my teeth and tugging lightly. Her body clenched around my fingers and I curled them, pressing into her deepest corners. I repositioned my arm, just enough that my palm brushed the hard knot of her sex.

Iliaria trembled slightly and said in a husky voice, "You're going to make me spend myself again."

I moved my other arm between our bodies while I nipped the sensitive skin at the top of her breast. "That's the point," I murmured, brushing my lips over the silken skin stretched over her sternum and to her neck. I stayed inside her, repeatedly stroking the spot that seemed to encourage her thighs to tremble. I traced her sex with my thumb and Iliaria moaned for me.

Her lips parted as I stroked her, her gaze meeting mine briefly before I licked her, flicking the tip of my tongue in a dance against her erect nipple. I sank my mouth down on her, and this time, sucked hard, pricking skin on the cusps of my fangs.

Her hips twitched and bucked, her body tightening under my hands and mouth. I quickened my movements, sliding my free hand down her body, I tugged lightly on the hardened knot between her legs. Iliaria's back arched again as her hands gripped my shoulders. Her nails cut into my skin and I groaned, my grasp tight around her.

She came in a shuddering dance under my hands. Her lips trembled against my neck in a long growl as she came. When her climax subsided, she kissed my neck, nibbling and sending gooseflesh along my arms.

I withdrew and her hips twitched and her breath caught short at their withdrawal. I brushed aside the silken curtain of her hair. Iliaria gazed at me with a lazy and satisfied smile.

"Well done," a voice called deviously from the doorway between the rooms. "Exceptionally well done."

Iliaria's eyes narrowed into angry slits as she turned to glare at the intruder.

Morina stood in the doorway, her slim yet curvaceous body propped against the frame, her dark coat fanned out around her as she gave a crooked smile. "My, my," she said theatrically, "perhaps I should have fucked you when I had the chance, after all. If only I had known you'd the skills of a prized courtesan."

"Watch your tongue, Morina," Iliaria growled. "Jealousy and regret do not become you."

Iliaria guided me back on the bed with a hand on my shoulder and one at my lower back. The move forced my spine to bow and my breasts higher than the rest of me. Iliaria smiled again. Only this time, it was not for my benefit. She pressed her mouth against the skin at the base of my sternum and licked a wet line upward between my breasts in obvious show.

Show or not, at the touch of her tongue, I suddenly wasn't concerned with the fact that Morina stood watching us.

Iliaria sealed her mouth over my breast and sucked until my skin prickled.

A grunt sounded from Morina's direction. "Flaunting your toy, Iliaria. How diplomatic."

Iliaria sank lower on my body, her mouth leaving a trail of hot kisses across my stomach and hips. I fell back against the bed and her arm slipped out from beneath me. Her mouth brushed past the snowy fur between my legs. Her warm breath against my sex stirred me to arousal again.

"You wouldn't," Morina said.

"Watch me," Iliaria said as she took me into her mouth.

I cried out and clawed at the blankets. Her mouth was hot, so hot, and I was not sure if I would burst or burn with the pleasure. That brilliant tongue stroked me broadly, fluttering tentatively at my tip in a way that made me writhe and cry out again.

I forced myself to open my eyes and watch her, to watch the up and down motion of her head as she sucked and a thousand nerve endings fired off through my body in an unyielding orchestra of delight.

My breath was shallow and my chest heaved. I shut my eyes, curling my hands into fists and balling them in the coverlet.

Another grunt from Morina's direction inspired me to look at her. She leaned back against the door, her coat unbuttoned to reveal her attire. Her trousers were tight enough that I could see the slight swell of her Dragoste underneath.

She met my gaze as she slid a hand down her body. An air of defiance surrounded her, but her eye was filled with a hunger so fierce it made the breath hitch in my chest.

Iliaria prolonged the orgasm. When she felt my legs begin to tremble, she drew back and slowed her pace just enough to keep my climax at bay. I glanced away from Morina long enough to find that Iliaria watched her, too. I knew in that moment that though the pleasure might have been for me, the show was for Morina. Iliaria made love to me to possess me, to state her claim, and prove that she could touch me and pleasure me while Morina could do nothing more than watch.

Instead of upsetting me, her dominance thrilled me. Iliaria buried her fingers inside me and I rose off the bed, crying out again.

There was movement from the doorway and I turned again to find Morina still there, still watching. She had unhooked the top clasp of her trousers and her hand disappeared under the waistband. By the slight movement underneath the fabric, I knew she pleasured herself.

I forgot everything she had done or said to me, everything but that moment when I'd been chained to the wall and felt her sex awaken against me, felt the flame of desire leap between us both. I found myself wanting to know what Morina looked like without her clothes on. I wanted to watch her pleasure herself, wanted to see just how her body reacted to the sight of Iliaria pleasuring me.

Morina held my gaze in a stare both passionate and defiant. Her hand did not still as she thrust her hips forward, reclining against the frame of the door as her lips parted, the tips of her fangs glistening in the lamplight.

Will you? I thought, moaning as Iliaria did something with her tongue that raised me half off the bed again. *Are you that bold, Dracule?* I wondered.

I hid nothing in my expression while I held Morina's stare. I wanted her to drop her trousers and show me what she was doing to herself. I slid my hands up my body and cupped my breasts, tugging lightly on my nipples. Morina seemed encouraged at the gesture. A grunt fell from her as her hand struggled more vigorously beneath her breeches.

Iliaria's mouth became a vise around me as she sucked, calling my attention back to her. I placed a hand on her head and the flicks of her tongue against me increased. I cried out, twining my hand in her hair and jerking her head back as the orgasm tore through me.

A long moan sounded from Morina's direction, but before I could turn my head to see, Iliaria climbed my body and caught my mouth in a hard kiss. When she broke the kiss, Morina was gone.

"I'm sorry," Iliaria said as a line creased across her forehead. "I shouldn't have used you to taunt her."

"Don't," I said. "Don't apologize. You were spectacular. You should never apologize for that."

"And you, my dragă…" She hoisted me up into her lap and her sex stiffened against my buttocks. *My dragă*, she'd called me. The possessive intonation in her words gave me a sense of excitement and belonging. "You were curious about her," Iliaria said, her voice soft as she searched my face.

"Yes," I admitted, seeing no reason to lie. I traced her brow and let her see what I felt in my heart. "But I love you, Iliaria, and she is no threat to what I feel for you."

"Do you promise?" she asked and a pang went through my heart as I thought of Renata. When I had first taken Iliaria to my bed, Renata had fairly much asked the same thing of me; that I would not revoke my love for her and give it to another. I hadn't. I still loved Renata. I'd simply come to love Iliaria as well.

"I think our hearts are capable of more love than we give them credit for."

"What do you mean?" she asked.

"Even if I fell for Morina," I said and added, "which is unlikely, but even if I fell, do you really think I would love you or Renata any less?"

"I like to think you wouldn't," she said, tracing my shoulder.

"I swear to you," I whispered, "I wouldn't. I've fallen in love with you, Iliaria, and it hasn't in any way belittled the love that I feel for Renata. I love you both."

"I want to make love to you until we collapse and sleep with exhaustion," Iliaria murmured against my mouth.

I cupped her face in my hands. "Then we shall."

It was not pity, nor was it necessarily the insatiable well of desire within me that inspired me to agree to her request. It was love, and the thought that, at some point I would leave. I would leave her behind not knowing if I would survive to come back to her arms.

Iliaria laid me back across the bed and we made love, again and again, until our muscles were weak, our minds cloudy, and our bodies entirely spent. She wrapped her long body around mine, one of her legs flung over me. She played with my hair, making me relax.

"I miss her too," she said when I was on the verge of sleep.

"Renata?" I asked, just to be sure.

"Yes." She tousled my hair rather playfully. "Pesky though she can be, somehow, we fit you, and somehow, in that way, we fit together." After a few moments, she asked, "Does that make sense?"

"Yes," I said as I pulled her arm more snugly around me. "I think it makes perfect sense."

Iliaria pressed a kiss against my temple and tears stung at my eyes. "It's a good thing the Dracule aren't monogamous, isn't it?"

she asked with a chuckle. "You're able to cling to one of us, but you're not whole without both of us. I know that, Epiphany."

I laughed, though something in the statement made me sad, too. Her tenderness undid me and she held me while I cried. A heavy melancholy fell over me. She was right. I was not whole without Renata. Without her, it felt as though a piece of me was missing, a large piece that I went about my day trying to ignore.

I would not be whole until I had the two of them again, until both of them held me in the safety of their arms.

I buried my face in the bend of Iliaria's neck, inhaling the musky incense scent of her. "I love you."

She cupped the back of my head in her hand and drew me closer. "I love you too."

She wrapped her arms around me tightly and I sank into her strength and protection.

My sweet Dracule, I thought as I traced tiny circles over her lower back, *you've no idea the gift you've given to me or how, in some way, you've helped to redeem us all.*

To find one great love during the course of one's lonely existence is a truly remarkable thing. To find two great and passionate loves was more than I could have ever asked for. Silently, I made a vow…

As long as I lived, I would never let anything come between us. If I had to learn to fight, to kill, and to cheat to protect what the three of us had, I would do so gladly.

CHAPTER SEVENTEEN

The sound of running water woke me. I stretched before shambling out of bed to see what Iliaria was doing. I found her in the small bathroom beyond, propped on the edge of a porcelain tub.

"A shower would be easier given the wings," she said with an affectionate smile, "but I figured you'd prefer a bath."

I pushed the untamed curls of hair out of my face and nodded. The door to the bedroom opened and I stepped out to see who it was.

Vasco's eyes widened when he saw me. He stood frozen with his hand on the doorknob before he quickly lowered his gaze. "Sorella..."

"What?" I asked.

He motioned at me with a hand.

"Oh. Oh!" I snatched the crumpled blanket off the bed and used it to cover myself.

Vasco chuckled. "Grazie, colombina. I feel strangely like I should say something more."

"Sorry, Vasco." I couldn't stop the laughter that bubbled up from within me. "That's probably not the first thing you want to see in the evening."

He gave a dashing grin. "No, but I can certainly say I see what keeps our queen and that Dracule of yours interested."

"Is that a compliment?"

"Sì, I'm trying to make the situation less awkward." He rolled forward on his booted feet and asked in a teasing whisper, "Is it working?"

"A bit, though perhaps you should knock next time before entering a woman's bedchambers?"

He raised his hands in the air. "My apologies, sorella." He motioned at me again with a sweep of his arm. "I did not know you strutted around…"

"I just woke."

"Sì, but I've never known you to sleep in the nude," he said.

"I don't often die in the nude, if that's what you're asking."

"You do now?"

I raised my hand to indicate Iliaria's ring on my finger only to find it wasn't there. "Well, no. The ring," I said, suddenly realizing it was gone.

"Azrael probably has it," Iliaria said from behind me. "Considering you don't need it as a Dracule."

I nodded and Iliaria asked Vasco, "What do you need?"

He straightened in a way that reminded me more of his courtly appearance than how he interacted when it was just us. I don't think he was trying to make amends, per se, so much as simply showing her the same respect he would have shown to Renata.

"All's ready when the two of you are."

Iliaria nodded and Vasco dismissed himself. He stepped out of the room, but not before he pretended to tip an invisible hat to me.

"He's acting odd," she said.

"He just got a surprising eyeful of lady bits and assumes you're still mad at him for nearly drowning me, I think."

She chuckled. "So it's true, he is like your brother?"

"Of course, what else would he be?"

She shrugged. "Just curious."

"You didn't think there was something between Vasco and I, did you? He doesn't like women, and if you didn't know, I'm not particularly fond of the male anatomy myself. I told you, I was a virgin when Renata took me."

Iliaria took me by the wrist and led me gently into the bathroom beyond. "You've never been with a man?"

I shuddered. "No, absolutely not. Have you?"

"No." She tugged at the blanket around me and I released it. The blanket fell to the floor as her hand slid down my side to cradle my hip. "Hmm, so technically," her arm slid behind my back as she brought us close together, "you're still virgin flesh." She buried her face in the bend of my neck and began nibbling on my skin. I released a heavy sigh and reached up to hold on to her shoulders.

"Again?" I asked, pretending to be surprised. "So soon?"

Iliaria picked me up and carried me to the bath, her lips tickling the lobe of my ear. "Yes," she murmured between nibbles. "I promise, it's better than swimming."

It most certainly was.

Freshly bathed and clothed, we descended to the lower levels of the hotel to continue my training. Thus far, Iliaria hadn't asked me to change my form, for which I was thankful. It was so much easier moving about on human feet rather than the slightly bowed and claw-tipped legs of the Draculian form. Though the wings still felt heavier on my human frame, my balance was greatly improved.

I wondered which form Iliaria preferred. I asked her when we passed through the lobby. She considered my question.

"Honestly?" She shook her head. "I never really thought about it. I'm comfortable in both." The corner of her mouth curled slyly. "You prefer this one, don't you?"

I grinned. "How did you guess?"

She laughed and shook her head again, the long braid of her hair dancing past her waist. I reached out to wrap that braid around my hand when she caught me by the wrists and pulled me back against her.

"You've got to stop distracting me, Epiphany."

"*I'm* the distraction?"

She held me tight, her arms closed around me like shackles. I could feel her heartbeat against my spine. She rested the side of her face against mine. "You will have to change form," she said. "You need to learn to fight in both."

"I know."

She released me and gave me a playful push from behind. "We've more training to attend to."

She opened two gold doors at the end of the hall and we stepped into the ballroom beyond. Anatharic pushed off the wall when we came in, his dark wings folded around his body. He bowed and used his head to gesture toward a table upon which he'd placed a row of weapons. Iliaria opened the long brocaded coat she wore and drew the crescent blades of the Dracule. She motioned toward the table with the tip of one.

"We should begin now, so we're not at this all night."

I took the blades they offered, not knowing who they originally belonged to. I hefted them and found that they were heavy yet strangely well-balanced in my hands.

They showed me how to use the blades first by slow-motion example. Both made their footwork and dancing blades appear easy and effortless as they circled each other.

I found, as with the obstacle course they had set for me, putting their instructions to action was not as easy or effortless. If the blade wasn't held just so, a person risked losing it entirely. Iliaria stood behind me and the line of her body followed mine as she walked me through the motions as we sparred with Anatharic. She showed me how the curled edge came in handy for disarmament as well as a thrust-pull motion that would deal quite a bit of damage.

She swung outward to prove her point, using the hook like a claw before she jerked it backward. "Do you see?"

Slightly distracted by the heat of her body, I nodded.

She seemed satisfied and turned to Anatharic. "Go easy on her," she said before she took a seat next to Vasco and Cuinn.

Easy was not exactly how he went. Anatharic held his blades aloft and crossed his arms in a loose X shape in front of his body. I stepped up to face him, and as soon as I was within arm's reach, he launched a full-out wildly slashing attack. I raised my blades to block him, constantly turning my wrist to turn the blade so that he could not catch hold of it and disarm me.

He pushed me backward across the marble-tiled floor, his elongated ears drawn back in fierce concentration. Frustrated, I ducked his next swing and skittered some feet away from him. I threw my blades down in a clatter.

"Epiphany, what are you doing?" Iliaria asked with a thread of annoyance.

Anatharic's ears swiveled uncertainly. I kicked the blades with my booted feet and said, "Come on, then."

Anatharic shrugged and obliged. His right blade made an arch toward my face, and I used my speed to escape the shot. I reached out with an open hand and slammed my palm into his wrist. The hit to his wrist was too sudden for him to react, and when I hit him, his arm flung away from his body.

It caught him off guard for the split second I needed to slip past his defense. I stepped into him and brought my knee up hard into his groin. Anatharic's body bowed forward out of reflex and I grabbed him by the shoulders and shoved, using my weight to steer his momentum.

Anatharic fell in a heap on his side and I fell on top of him, lowering my head to his chest. With muscles I wasn't used to having, let alone using, I whipped my tail up in a semicircle behind me and lowered the barbed tip against his cheek.

"If you're going to go for a killing blow that way," Iliaria said, approaching, "You're going to have to make sure you have the force behind you to follow through with the throw."

Anatharic wiggled beneath me and Iliaria ordered him to be still. He did.

One of her hands touched my lower back and the other cradled my right hip. "Like this," she said, "follow my hands." She pulled back on my hip and I went back with her. The move was strangely intimate and I tried to ignore it. "And forward," she said, and her hand at my lower back encouraged me forward. "When you come forward with it, throw your upper body forward and then down, so that you don't end up putting a barb through the back of your own head. Got it?"

"Got it."

She helped me to my feet.

"Not bad," she said. "But you still need to have the basic knowledge of the blades and the footwork. It's something we learn at a young age. If you don't have that and Damokles forces you to fight your way into his ranks, he'll know something's amiss."

"Surely, not all of the Dracule are such fine warriors?"

"Every Dracule knowsss how to usssse the bladesss."

"I haven't seen Morina use them." In fact, I hadn't seen Morina at all since she disappeared from our room.

"She knows how," Iliaria said. "That's the point."

Anatharic and Iliaria shared their blood with the vampires before Iliaria and I retired to dine in our room. Emilio brought up a metallic rolling cart with plates of food. Iliaria handed a large bowl to me and I found that whatever it was, it was very good and only lightly seasoned. Large chunks of beef and potatoes drowned in a savory and peppery broth. Emilio handed us a basket with a loaf of bread and Iliaria tore a piece off and handed it to me. I dipped the bread in the broth and practically moaned at the deliciousness of it.

"Well?" Emilio asked.

"It's quite good," I mumbled around a bite of bread. I swallowed so that I could speak clearly and dabbed at the corners of my mouth with a cloth napkin. "You've already helped us so much, Emilio. You didn't have to do this."

"Ah," he said, smiling almost shyly. "It is my pleasure, lady. It is as much for me as it is for you."

"Have you not tried it yet?" I asked.

"I will eat later."

"Nonsense," Iliaria said. She placed her bowl on the nightstand and rose to move the armchair under the window closer to the bed. "Sit."

"I wouldn't want to intrude," Emilio said politely.

"Sit," she said again, raising her bowl. This time it was clear it wasn't an invitation, but an order.

Emilio joined us and we enjoyed a quiet conversation with our dinner. He asked about his father and we spoke at some length about Vasco. I told him how good Vasco had been to me when I most needed a friend, but it was obvious when speaking with Emilio that I did not need to say such things for him to respect Vasco. I could tell that he already did.

He told us about Savina and how she never spoke of him, how he had asked as a child about his father and was given the same cold silence repeatedly, until one day, he just stopped asking.

"She despises him," I said. "She's hurt, which in a way is understandable, but she's also blind."

"I know," Emilio said. "My mother clings to any slight she perceives. It's petty and childish, but that is who she is." He shrugged and took a bite of his soup. "I cannot change it. I've tried."

"We can't change people," I said. "We can love them, we can despise them, but we can't change them."

"Indeed."

We finished our meal and Emilio bid us good night. He took the tray and dirty dishes away with him. I got the door for him as he guided the cart from the room.

"You look so like your father," I said.

Emilio blushed. "Is that a good thing, lady?"

I nearly snorted. "Aye," I said. "He's a handsome one, your father. Many a vampire among the Rosso wouldn't mind keeping his bed warm. Women and men alike."

With that, he blushed a brighter shade of red and took his leave. I closed the door with a laugh.

"Flirting, Epiphany? I thought you didn't fancy men."

I felt my brows rise practically into my hairline. "That is Vasco's son we're talking about, and that, my Great Siren, was not flirting."

"It sounded like it to me."

I bent and touched her arm. "If I was flirting, my lady, I would have done this." I slid my palm lightly up the length of her arm before I ruined the seriousness of the gesture by fluttering my lashes absurdly.

Iliaria laughed and grabbed me by the shoulders. She rolled me onto my back on the bed and tackled me. "You little minx," she growled and nipped at my throat.

"Minx?" I asked, pretending to be appalled. "I'll have you know, I'm quite the lady."

She settled down on top of me and pinned my wrists above my head. "Oh, really?" she asked, but not like she believed me.

"I am."

"I'd dare to argue that." She grinned wickedly.

"I said nothing about the bedroom. A lady doesn't always have to be a lady there, you know."

"Thank goodness for that."

"I'd be more inclined to thank Renata." I smiled.

"Well then, perhaps I'll get her a fruit basket to show my gratitude."

The idea was so ridiculous that I laughed until my belly ached. I could only imagine the look on Renata's face if Iliaria were to actually follow through with the gesture.

In time, we slept, and the following day Iliaria gave me a more in-depth explanation of the workings of Draculian society. At the head of the society, there was always a king or a queen, much like with the vampires. Only, unlike the vampires, where a single clan was governed by a single monarch, below the throne the Dracule were broken up into smaller groups, houses where an individual was chosen to lead and answered to the queen for the entire house. Iliaria explained that it gave those that wanted a taste of power a position to be in it. In essence, they became miniature kings and queens for the group or house they represented.

To make certain I couldn't be caught off guard, Iliaria taught me some Draculian history, along with some cultural norms. Though I would only be Dracule for a short time, it was fascinating.

The Dracule descended from a line of beings they referred to as the Mal'akh. Once, the Mal'akh had been favored by their God, held in high esteem for their passionate natures. Iliaria explained that, in the beginning, it was their passionate natures that had pleased their One God. Yet, in the end, it had been their fall from grace.

The Mal'akh walked the earth among mortals, instructed by the One God to teach them how to cultivate the land, to weave, to build, to defend and protect. The Mal'akh taught the first tribes to provide for themselves and to live in harmony with nature. But living among the mortals ignited other passions in the Mal'akh, passions that the One God frowned upon. The Mal'akh began to take the mortals to their beds.

"The One God overlooked it thinking that the Mal'akh would remember their purpose on their own," Iliaria said. "But being a passionate and hedonistic folk, they did not and it was not long until mortal women held within their wombs the seeds of their couplings. The One God could not turn his back on such an abomination, and so he ordered Azrael to destroy the bastard children that grew within the mortal women. He sent the sword of his right-hand, Gavrille, to lead an army to retrieve the Mal'akh. Yet, as with everything the Mal'akh did, they fought the advances of Gavrille and his army with unrestrained passion.

"They knew they could not win against the One God's forces, but they refused to give up. They gave Gavrille's army no other choice but to overpower and destroy the Mal'akh. Azrael, with his orders from their God to destroy the Mal'akh's offspring, waited until he heard a woman's screams of labor. The babe was born and the woman, having learned his name from the teachings of the Mal'akh, begged him not to destroy her child. Azrael held the child in his arms and where the One God saw a monstrosity, Azrael saw the same unwavering passions of the Mal'akh reflected in the strange child, and swayed by their passion and a mother's love, he refused to destroy the babe."

"That was the first Dracule?" I asked.

"Yes. Azrael and the last remaining Mal'akh created Drahalia and took the babes there to hide them from the One God's sight. Only three of the Mal'akh survived Gavrille's invasion. The others were captured or destroyed. Adara, Ephraim, and Keshet raised the babes that Azrael brought to Drahalia as their own, in honor of the Mal'akh that had fallen prey to their God's cruelty."

"What happened to the three remaining Mal'akh?" I asked.

"No one knows," Iliaria said as she traced a line across my bare stomach. "The Dracule grow fast and we learn quickly. It is said that when the first-born came of age, the Mal'akh saw in him the same sense of honor and echoing passion that they saw in their brothers and sisters. He ruled Drahalia for a time with the Mal'akh by his side, and then one day, they vanished."

It was a beautiful story and I was hard put not to believe it, for I saw in the Dracule before me the same passion she had spoken of in the Mal'akh, the same fine vein of heroism and hedonism that had lured them down the path of love and carnal delight.

But a thought occurred to me when she told her story and I gave voice to it. "If the Mal'akh were able to take mortal lovers to bed," I said, thinking out loud, "they didn't experience the bloodlust?" I asked. "Is that not something they inherited from the Mal'akh?"

"Some say the bloodlust is a part of a curse their God placed on the Dracule when he learned of the babes Azrael refused to kill."

"What did the Mal'akh look like?" I asked. "And why wouldn't the One God, if he was a God, have destroyed the Dracule himself? Not that I'm too keen on the idea, mind you."

"Some say like us, some say more beautiful. Some say their God cursed us to appear as we do, some say we inherited our appearance from the coupling of mortal and Mal'akh." She offered a sharp shrug. "As to why he did not destroy us, I do not know. Some believe a blood curse was placed upon us in hopes that we'd destroy ourselves, which didn't work, if that was the case."

"What do you think?"

"We are what we are," she said. "Whether it is curse or inheritance, that is what I think."

The days passed and my more physical lessons resumed. Yet again, I sparred with Anatharic and Iliaria to better improve on my footwork and fighting skills. Iliaria made me practice in both forms. When she saw that I continued to struggle in Draculian form, she pressed me even harder to wear it and practice in it.

I grew exhausted though I slept and ate. Lesson after lesson, I learned the Draculian tongue, recitations, penmanship, blade work, agility, all of these things and more as the days passed in a dizzying haze of lessons. I worried that I wouldn't remember all of it and that she was pushing too much into my head at once, but Iliaria persisted, and yet another week of lessons passed. She taught me to *evanesce*, to visualize a destination and use my abilities to go there. The experience made my body tingle uncontrollably afterward, as her mark used to on my skin. Iliaria ensured me that I would get used to the sensation, though I found it highly unlikely.

Finally, the day came when she woke me with news that Emilio had found Damokles. Such news tightened my chest as fear and excitement both surged through me. I asked her when I could go only to learn she still was not satisfied that I was ready.

Almost an entire month passed in the human world and I began to grow anxious. I remembered what Cuinn had told me about Azrael. *Four months.* I had four months as a Dracule to find and rescue Renata.

And an entire month had already passed us by. Renata had been a prisoner for too long, and I was becoming impatient. A few days later, Iliaria's curriculum changed.

"We must work on your disguise," she said. "If you are to infiltrate Damokles's ranks, we must work on your story."

And so we did. Iliaria gave me false names for my parents and came up with a believable history that I was an unlucky child born in the sin and slums of Drahalia's Noapte Quarter. I sat on the bed cross-legged while she explained the dark cobblestone streets and crude shops in great detail and when she was done, she had me repeat it to her in full detail, down to the services offered, the illicit brothels and pub houses and the faces of their clientele.

"Who is your mother?" Iliaria asked me in the Draculian tongue.

"I was born to Batya and Chaim," I replied smoothly.

"Their occupations?"

"Merchant rovers, they stole and sold whatever goods would bring them fortune." Iliaria and I both agreed that if I was the offspring of a sort of Draculian gypsy folk, Damokles would be less able to confirm their existence, or rather, their lack thereof. Too many faces passed through Noapte Quarter. It would make the task of finding two in particular difficult, if not impossible.

Iliaria told me to stay in Draculian form so that I would gain confidence in it. The Draculian language grew on me. I found the soft lilt and curl of it beautiful and fascinating the more I heard it and the more I used it. For a week, Iliaria verbally chastised me whenever I slipped into English.

After a tiring day of blade-twirling and even fancier footwork, Iliaria woke me the following evening with news that she had invited Cuinn and Vasco to dine with us in our room, and although Vasco did not eat any of the lamb stew that Emilio had made, Cuinn nibbled on pieces of meat that Emilio had set aside for him. We conversed quietly about nothing much. Several times, I found myself slipping habitually into the Draculian tongue. When I did, Iliaria gave me a look of sadness and pride.

I was ready.

We both knew it.

Vasco caught it, too. "When?" he asked.

Iliaria turned to me for the answer. "Tomorrow, I think."

We ate the rest of our meal in silence.

Iliaria and I spent our last night together making love. The satin of her fur slid against mine as our groins brushed to send a wave of heat and pleasure coursing through us both.

Her hands gripped my buttocks. "Come back to me," she whispered, her voice tight.

I shuddered as the climax built between my legs. "I will try, I promisse."

"Don't try." She clung to me as I held her. "Jussst do."

The goldenrod glow of the late afternoon sunlight shone through the thick curtains that covered the window. Iliaria's tall frame was nestled beside me, her arm draped loosely over my hip. Carefully, I climbed out from beneath the covers and worked my way into a pair of black velvet trousers. The trousers were less troublesome to pull on over my tail than the shorts had been, as a small clasped opening snapped closed above it to secure the material. The bathroom tile was cold beneath my feet as I struggled with the blouse. I still had not quite gotten used to dressing myself in human form. The wings, whether the blouse had slits that hooked below them in the back or not, were still difficult to work around when it came to getting dressed. After some fuss, I managed to secure the tiny hooks and sighed with relief. No doubt, Iliaria would chastise me for me changing form, but on my last day with the others, I wanted to feel more myself in my skin.

With all the training and lovemaking, it felt as though I'd had little time to do aught else but prepare for this day. The one time Vasco had tried to pull me away and give me a reprieve from the task hadn't gone as well as planned.

I stalked the hotel hallways, inclined to be alone with my thoughts. Truly, a part of me didn't want to leave the safety we had established here. I wasn't the type of person drawn toward reckless adventure, let alone the type to undertake the task of walking boldly into the heart of danger and a nest of intrigue. If at all possible, I tried to avoid such things. But with Renata captured, I couldn't avoid the coming fight.

I thought of her with a surge of heartache and longing. No doubt, she had felt my death when Azrael had changed me, and I could only guess of what she thought, let alone endured, at Damokles's hands.

I stopped before the window at the end of the hallway to watch the last strands of light filtering through.

This whole plan is madness.

It had been madness from the beginning when Renata had turned herself over in order to tip their hands. And now, due to her impulsive stubbornness, I had to find the courage within me to go in after her.

I wasn't even sure how I would do it. Iliaria and I had discussed many things, but we hadn't specifically decided on how I would work my way in and gain Damokles's trust.

I sensed someone behind me and turned to find Cuinn. "I thought I'd sensed ye out here."

"Cuinn," I said. I turned my back on the window and slid down the wall beneath it to sit on the floor.

Cuinn came to me and propped his chin on my knee. "Aye, your thoughts are heavy, lass."

"They are," I admitted as I stroked the fur between his ears. "I wish you could go with me. You've more courage than I."

"Ye know why, lass? I don't question myself," he said matter-of-factly. "Ye've got to trust your instincts, come what may, and then with whatever comes, ye've got to trust 'em again."

I fingered the amber stone that hung from the makeshift collar about his neck. "How am I to do this thing, Cuinn? I can speak their tongue, I can move and fight like them now, but when it comes down to it, what am I to really do? Just walk into Damokles's midst and claim to join him in treachery?"

"Aye," Cuinn said, "if ye cannot work your way in undetected—"

"I'd much rather work my way in undetected."

"I've been thinking about that." Morina strode toward us in the same black trousers and white billowy shirt and dark overcoat she'd worn for the last several days.

"And?" I had not seen her since she had watched Iliaria and me make love, and I wondered how she thought of me now.

"I will take you."

"You said that you weren't working with Damokles."

"Yes," she said, her face an expressionless mask, "I did, but that's not to say I won't begin working with him. If I take you, I can ensure that you stay alive long enough to keep your promise to me."

Cuinn had risen to his feet when she came forward. His ears had slicked back to his skull as if he were ready for a fight to break out between us.

"And what makes ye think we'd trust ye to go with her and that ye'd not expose what she's about?"

"I could have exposed you already," Morina said. "And yet, all of you are still here, unmolested and unharmed. Dracule or no, Epiphany, you're somewhat smaller than the rest of us and easy pickings for someone more dominant. You may not be very fond of my idea," she gave a toothy and predatory smile, "but if I take you as someone that belongs to me, you're less likely to be a target for someone more dominant."

"If you haven't been working with Damokles all this time, what makes you assume he'll trust you?"

"I have my ways," she said. "Damokles knows of my hatred for Iliaria, and more than likely he has heard from his spies that I was being held prisoner in the castle. He will believe that I seduced you, one of her followers, into rescuing me and that I turned you against Iliaria and her vampires. He doesn't know that I know her side of the story."

"Why the sudden change of heart?" I asked. When I had tried to show her Iliaria's side of things, she still hadn't believed them.

"I have my reasons," she said and again, her voice was cryptic. The expression she wore, however, intrigued me now. Dark knowledge lingered behind her eye. Images of her hand pulsing at her groin, of her lips half-parted and her back arched against the frame of the door swam to the surface of my mind and I looked away.

"I will help you save your queen, Epiphany. Is that not enough to gain me some of your favor?"

My mind raced as I tried to understand what she meant. I raised my head. "And what favor, my lady, do you seek from me?"

"You know what I want."

"I thought I did," I said. "Now I'm not so sure."

The air grew tense between us. I had bargained with my body before, and fortunately, it had not turned out to be so terrible a thing. I had gained Iliaria's love and protection in the bargain. And though there was no love between Morina and me, there's no question I was curious about her in many ways.

She was quiet long enough that I was sure she wanted it, that I was certain she would request me to repay her by warming her bed. I felt queasy. I wasn't certain if it was from nerves, apprehension, or excitement, or a combination of all those things.

"Your promise," she said, finally. "I want you to keep it. That is what I want."

"That's all," I said. "If the others agree to it, we will do it your way."

Morina didn't say another word. As she had so many times since the day she had taken me as her captive, she walked off when she was done talking to me.

"You're playing with fire, Piph." Cuinn brought my attention back to him as he settled down against my thigh again.

"Why do you say that, Cuinn?"

He snorted. "I'm no idiot, ye know. It'd take an idiot to have missed what just happened. Ye've already got two women in your bed," he said. "Do ye really want to add a third? Especially *that one*?"

I placed my index finger beneath his chin. "Don't give me that look."

"Don't tell me ye were seriously considering it. Lugh's bollocks, woman. Taking a tumble with that one's about as good for you as rolling around naked in brambles."

"You think she's that bad, do you?" I playfully ruffled his ears.

"You're too quick to let your groin do the thinking," Cuinn said. "If there's anything I know about women, it's that that one has thorns and you're beginning to seem a little too eager to be pricked by them. I say again, Piph, you're playing with fire."

When it came down to it, didn't I already play with fire? Neither one of my lovers was particularly meek or mild, though a streak of unexpected tenderness flowed through them both. He made a disgruntled sound low in his chest and rolled his eyes. "Of course, you're gonna play with it anyway, whether I advise you to or not. Like a cat to curiosity." Cuinn grumbled, "Bleedin' masochists, always courting danger."

"I never said I would take her to my bed."

The look he gave me told me plainly he doubted I wouldn't do just that.

I shrugged. Morina hadn't asked for my body in the bargain, and since she hadn't asked, I wouldn't give it. On the other hand, if she did ask, I wasn't sure what I would do.

Cuinn and I decided to go downstairs and found Emilio keeping himself busy in the kitchen. He raised his head when we entered and gestured toward a porcelain teapot. "There's tea if you'd like any," he said.

I grabbed a white mug and made myself a cup. Iliaria hadn't said anything about tea, and if there was one thing I wanted to try before I became a vampire again, if I survived to become a vampire again, it was tea.

Sadly, I took Iliaria's advice and did not add milk. I raised the brim of the cup to my mouth and took a small sip to test it.

Emilio must've caught something in my expression. "Do you like it?" he asked.

I took another sip more slowly, letting the hot beverage sit on my tongue. I tasted cinnamon and a hint of orange, licorice, and clove, and something sweet like vanilla.

I swallowed and finally said, "It's not terrible."

"English?" he asked.

I nodded.

"Ah," he said, as if that explained everything. "What generation? Your accent is easy to place but your vocabulary…"

He wiped his hands on a towel after setting some dishes out to dry.

"What do you mean?" I asked.

"*Aye?*"

I motioned toward Cuinn. "That's his doing."

"Aye," Cuinn said with a mischievous twinkle.

Emilio continued to make idle conversation with me as night fell. I offered to help him prepare dinner, and when he declined, I took a seat to watch him while he worked. He moved around the kitchen as if it was a place he was comfortable in, and I began to understand why he didn't mind making food for us so often. For whatever reason, he really did seem to enjoy it. He hummed quietly while he worked, adjusting dials and pressing buttons, seeming undisturbed by an audience or by the modern human technology. But then, he lived in the mortal world. I was the one out of touch with it.

Iliaria and the others came down just after nightfall. Iliaria was in her human form again, with a pair of tight-fitting black trousers and a silk top that left one of her shoulders bare.

One of the round tables from the ballroom was brought in, and all of us sat around it while we dined.

Dominique, who had mostly kept to himself since our arrival, finally spoke to me. "I'd rather go with you, piccolo."

I smiled at the nickname. Vasco had once explained that technically, it was *piccola,* a term of endearment for *little girl,* but I much rather preferred the sound of *piccolo* and being compared to the small woodwind instrument. Dominique must have discerned as much for he never tried *piccola* on me.

"I'm sorry, Dominique. They would recognize you as her guardsman."

He knew it, of course. I was stating the obvious, but still, I knew it didn't eradicate his wish to go with me.

"We'll find a way to keep our hands busy here, brother," Vito said as he tossed an arm over Dominique's shoulders.

"We can only hope she is successful," Vittoria added as she lowered her glass.

"It is not that I do not believe in you, piccolo, but this thing you undertake is a dangerous mission to run into all on your own," Dominique said. "If something were to happen to you, our queen would have our hides."

I laid my fork on my plate. The chicken Emilio had made was nice, but my appetite for it waned with the conversation.

"Actually," I said at some length, "there's a matter I wish to speak with all of you about."

And so I did. I explained to them Morina's plan, though she had not come down to dine with us and reinforce my words. Iliaria surprised me by not immediately protesting as I had feared she would. She appeared thoughtful, her brows slightly pinched.

"If she's true to her word, it's not a terrible plan. But if she's not true to her word, it's a large risk. Are you willing to take it?" Iliaria asked.

"It seems safer than walking in alone, doesn't it?"

At that, even Vasco agreed. "It does. Yet, I fear you have forgotten that this is the Dracule that kidnapped you to begin with, colombina."

"I do not forget, Vasco. Shouldn't I give her the chance to redeem herself if that's what she seeks?"

Iliaria looked skeptical. "You really believe Morina is trying to redeem herself?"

"No, I think she has her own agenda. In fact, I'm certain she does, but I do believe she was being honest when she offered to help. If I go in under the guise of being her pet and Damokles knows her abhorrence of you, it's a far more believable story."

"If she sticks to it," she said.

"If I don't," Morina said from the doorway, "Epiphany wouldn't be around to keep her word to me, would she? I'd very much like to see that promise upheld."

"Technically, the others have offered to aid you in my stead if something were to happen to me. I hadn't thought about it up till now, but if we don't succeed, you still have your promise."

"You," she said to Emilio and pointed a finger at him, "if something were to happen to the girl, would you still aid me?"

Emilio shook his head. "No."

She stuffed her hands in the pockets of her coat and lifted her chin. "And you?" she asked Vasco.

"No," Vasco said, his eyes narrowing.

"So you see," she said, "I have nothing to gain by harming you."

Iliaria pushed her chair back to rise with a daunting expression. "If this is a trick, Morina—"

"I'll give you my blood oath if that makes you feel any better," Morina said, not sounding thrilled about it.

"Do it."

Morina bit her wrist and flung her hand outward, droplets of her blood staining the tile at Iliaria's feet. "You have my oath that I will not let any harm befall her at my hands or another's."

The droplets of her blood sizzled as if from some unseen flame before they dispersed, leaving no trace behind.

"Epiphany," Iliaria said at last. "You will go with Morina."

"A little blood and you suddenly trust her?" Nirena asked.

"A little blood and a little magic," Iliaria said. "Morina knows the consequences of her actions if she attempts to break the oath now. She has bound herself to it."

"Terrific," Morina said but not like she meant it. "Now that you're satisfied, we'd best be on our way soon. I'll let you say your good-byes."

She motioned for Emilio to follow her and they left the room. So many expressions surrounded the table, pity, curiosity, sadness, and fear.

"Well," I said, "I suppose this is it."

Chapter Eighteen

I liaria's kiss still lingered on my lips. I had said my farewells, mostly to Cuinn, Vasco, and Iliaria, but to the others as well, though our parting did not inspire such sweet sorrow as leaving those I loved behind. It was a strange thing to leave without Vasco and Iliaria by my side, and even stranger to leave without Cuinn, who had been part of me for so long.

I didn't cry when I bid them farewell. I wouldn't let myself, though my stomach was twisted into knots and the thread of anxiety wound tight within me. I trusted that Emilio had told Morina what she needed to know about Damokles's whereabouts. Her arm rested at the base of my spine as we stood in the ballroom.

"You should change now," she said.

I focused my will when I felt Morina summon the mists of her magic around us. Before I could change my mind, I found myself untethered from the ground I had been standing on while the world drifted away in a sheet of fog.

Morina's arm tightened around my waist to help me keep my balance. The ground was solid beneath my feet as her power fell away to reveal the landscape around us.

The sky stretched above us, a faded cerulean that peeked through melancholic gray clouds. Fiery strokes of sunlight penetrated through the places between the clouds, illuminating a sparkling veil of mist and casting imposing shadows across the terrain. I stepped away from Morina and she caught my arm as I tried to navigate the rocky, uneven ground.

"Thisss isss Drahalia?"

"Yes," she said, her speech clear, as she had remained in human form. "This is the wildlands of Drahalia."

As far as I could see, it was nothing but rocks. The land consisted solely of dark boulders, some larger than others. Most of the boulders were jagged, only a few created smooth slabs of stone to walk on. Dark mountains jutted sharply above the rocky wasteland to serrate the sky, their façades imposing and so uneven they appeared impossible to climb. A few of their peaks disappeared into misty clouds.

"The sssun sssetsss in the eassst?" I asked.

Morina released me and started making her way carefully across the uneven landscape. I followed and slipped on jagged stones.

"Yes," she turned back to watch me as I tried to find a way, albeit precariously, over the rocks. "You don't intend to walk the entire way like that, do you?" Something close to amusement flashed across her face.

I slid and shifted my weight to my other foot as I nearly fell into a crevice between two larger stones. "Do you have a better idea?"

"Try all fours. It's really not as difficult as you're making it to be. At the rate you're pussyfooting, we're not likely to be there for days."

I sank to all fours and found that she was right; it was much easier to crawl and climb through the rocks than to continue the uncertain dance I had been doing. I used my tail as Iliaria had taught me to do to maintain balance when I leapt from one boulder to another. The force of the leap threatened to send me skittering through the rocks, but I managed to catch myself.

Morina had no trouble whatsoever with the treacherous terrain, even in her human form. She moved without hesitation, as if she instinctively knew where to step. Stones crunched beneath her boots as she swung a leg over a short wall of boulders, and I followed, pouncing from rock to rock when I encountered ones that were too big to leap from.

After we had walked for some time, the landscape began to smooth out and I was able to walk beside her. The ground was still uneven beneath my clawed hands and feet, but the rocks were smaller and less complicated. We walked for what seemed ages. The night sky was a bright cloak of moonlight and stars.

"We've been wandering for hoursss," I hissed. "You didn't think to drop us sssomewhere clossser...why?"

"Impatience is not a virtue, Epiphany. You'll get us there no sooner complaining."

Irritated at the chastisement, I closed my mouth and decided to walk the rest of the way in silence. Some hours after nightfall, we reached an edge where the terrain sloped down into a valley. Morina came to a halt and pointed to the darkness below. "There," she said.

The area she indicated looked like a large gathering of rocks. Once my head made sense of it, I realized it was a building composed of the same rocky material we traversed. It was well camouflaged in the dark. With so many mountains and rocks, it was easy to mistake the pile as part of the mountain range from a distance.

Morina led the way down the hill. No torches marked the entry, but Morina found it, a small door of gray wood nestled between jutting stones. She placed three solid knocks upon it, and that queasy feeling returned to churn at the pit of my stomach.

❖

The Dracule that admitted us was by far larger than any of the Dracule I'd ever seen. He had to be a good nine feet tall, if not taller. He opened the door and Morina pushed past him, obviously not unsettled in the least by his stature.

"Where is he?" she asked.

The Dracule's ears swiveled. His voice, when it came, was a low, hissing grumble. "Thisss way." He strode forward and started down the darkened hall.

Apparently, he recognized Morina. Why else wouldn't he attack us on sight?

He kept his imposing back to us as he led us down the lengthy hallway. Here and there, torches flickered to provide substantial light to see by. I stayed on all fours, deciding in that moment that

I'd simply follow Morina's lead. I kept my head low as we walked around a sharp corner and down another hall.

"I can find my way from here, Bastaille."

The Dracule sank away from the doors ahead of us. "Sssuit yoursssself, Morina."

Morina flung open both doors and stepped inside. Inside the room, we found ourselves surrounded by a dozen Dracule that were suddenly armed and on their feet. Morina strode between them with a swagger in her step, her tail flicking behind her with dangerous confidence.

She strode toward a tall figure slouched in a throne at the far end of the room. A woman moved up beside the figure, as if to protect him, but not quite. Her dark hair framed a round face. Her green eyes narrowed as she raised a hand. She didn't have wings, and she was very much human. The figure on the throne touched her wrist and the woman lowered her arm.

"Morina," Damokles hissed.

"Hello, cousin," Morina addressed him in Dracule.

The tension in the air built like a tsunami threatening to break over us. I stayed close to Morina's heels, not quite on them, but close enough that no one in the room would think I wasn't with her.

Though, I wondered if such a bold statement of association was in my best interest.

"Come to join usss at lassst?" Damokles asked, idly twirling a chain that hung from his neck around his clawed fingers.

"As a matter of fact, I have."

Damokles made a noise low in his throat, a Draculian chuckle of sorts. He leaned forward, and the intensity in his ominous gaze seemed as though it'd burn a hole through Morina.

"I told you that you couldn't do it on your own. Lassst I heard, the vampiresss had reclaimed what you'd ssstolen and imprisssoned you, cousssin."

I prayed silently to whatever Gods there might've been that the ears of Damokles's spies only heard so much. If he knew of the mark Morina had placed upon me, things would be bad. Very bad, indeed.

But apparently, he knew very little.

"How did you essscape, cousssin?"

Morina stepped aside to reveal me. She brushed the arched curve of my wing. "I have my ways. You should know that."

And so, our plan began to play out in earnest as Morina swung into motion. She told the story believably, so believably that had she told it to me, I too would've fallen for it.

She spoke of Iliaria with distaste, making it sound as though she truly sought his aid in her mission of vengeance. One by the one, the Dracule around us relaxed. Even Damokles leaned back as he listened.

"Well, cousin?" Morina asked him. "What say you?"

Damokles curled a finger and a Dracule covered in smoky fur stepped forward. "Yesss, massster?"

"Alahard," he said. "Find my cousssin and her pet a room."

"My king, do you think it wise?" The woman who stood beside Damokles said it quietly, but not so we couldn't hear it. Damokles's ears flattened back against his skull as he glared at her. She lowered her gaze. "I meant no disrespect, your lordship."

"Hold your tongue," he growled in threat. "Our arrangement can be a temporary thing, vampire."

She stepped away from him but turned her attention to us, her murky green eyes flashing with anger.

Alahard obeyed his king's orders and escorted us from Damokles's makeshift throne room.

In spite of his initial distrust, Damokles welcomed Morina and me into the kingdom he had established for himself. Morina advised me against wandering about on my own, and I found myself relying on skills I'd acquired both among the Rosso Lussuria vampires and under Iliaria's guidance. I stayed close to Morina's side at all times, shadowing her as inconspicuously as I could. To my surprise, my endeavors to remain unnoticed were successful. The Dracule often spoke freely to Morina, and a great many of them paid no mind to my presence, either because they truly believed I was just her pet or because they really didn't care who I was to begin with.

Two days after our arrival, Alahard returned with a summons from Damokles. If Damokles had any spies among the clans assembled at the White Lady's castle, they weren't very good ones. It became apparent in their conversation that he truly didn't know how Morina had gotten free.

"What do you know of the vampiresss?" he asked, his head tilting toward her.

"They're gathering against you."

Damokles chuckled, the sound odd and drumming in his chest. "Asss I sssussspected. Good."

I was tempted to ask why it was such a good thing, but kept my yap closed. The last thing I wanted was for Damokles to begin focusing his attention on me.

"I have sssomething to ssshow you, cousssin. Sssomething I think you will find very pleasssing."

"I wait with bated breath," she replied in a snarky tone.

Damokles showed no irritation at Morina's sarcasm. If anything, it seemed as though the bitterness in her attitude was expected and the norm between them. Damokles led us through a rectangular room and down a flight of stone steps.

He pushed open the door at the base of the stairs. The room beyond was set aglow by a single burning torch that he took from its place on the wall and held aloft in one of his clawed hands. I fought to mask my rising sense of unease, continuing to keep my head low as I followed the Dracule more deeply into the room beyond.

Damokles stopped in the center of the hall and raised his torch so that the light fell on the cell blocks around us. Beyond the crisscross of metal bars, my mind slowly began to take in the reality around me.

"Behold, cousssin," he hissed boastfully, "my conquessstsss."

Morina walked a circle around him as she peered into the holding cells. I followed her with my gaze, reminding myself that Damokles was with us and not to let any expression pass through my features or my body. Dracule or no, the slightest uncomfortable twitch of an ear could give away my discomfort and potentially expose us both.

A hundred or so vampires were imprisoned beyond the bars like dogs in a kennel. Their bodies were hunched and slack, their eyes glazed and empty. What had he done to them?

Morina's face was a hard mask, though the corner of her mouth curled in a secret smile. The expression sent a shiver through my bones.

"Well done, cousin, but might I ask what you intend to do with a bunch of starved vampires?"

One of the vampires closest to the bars of a cell near me raised her head with an effort. The shackles behind her clinked as she shifted her position lightly. Her desolate gaze met and held mine behind strands of straw-like hair.

"Aaah, but there'sss more, dear cousssin. Thessse are only the vampiresss that refusssed me when I took their queen. There are othersss that have been ussseful."

Damokles breezed past me and waved the torch near the vampire staring at me. He hissed, "Ssstupid ssswine!" and she sank back further into the cell, turning her face and shielding it in the curve of her shoulder from the embers. Her attire was tattered and torn as if she'd at one point been in a physical fight, and though she had healed, her clothing had not.

My muscles twitched with the urge to intervene, to stand between Damokles and the vampire he verbally abused.

I thought of Renata and a hollow feeling gripped my heart. *My lady*, I thought, as I crawled away from Damokles and closer to Morina, *this threat is indeed greater than we thought.*

I wished that somehow, somewhere, Renata could still hear me. Knowing she couldn't, not while I was a Dracule, I hung my head in dismay.

Damokles kicked the bars and the metal rattled. A few cells down, someone screamed, sharp and startled. It hurt to hear it.

Damokles chuckled again. Morina's hand touched my head and I flinched. With Damokles's back turned to us, she shook her head lightly. I knew something must've showed in my posture and I steeled myself. I raised my head and refused to look away, refused to show anything, most especially how much I loathed Damokles. My ears slicked back against my skull of their own accord.

"You sssseee?" he asked Morina as a smile stretched unnervingly across his feline face. "It isss only a matter of time until they break. Then they will be of ussse to me."

Damokles made his way to the far end of the cellblock. He rapped on the door and a Draculian guard from the other side opened it to admit him.

I descended cautiously to find two other guardsmen posted at the bottom of the stairwell. The walls faced us in an octagonal pattern. It reminded me almost of the Elders' chambers in the Sotto, if it hadn't been for the heavy metal doors and the small barred windows. The place was very much a prison.

"Here," Damokles hissed again and motioned with a flourish. "My greatessst trophiesss."

He seemed quite to enjoy bragging, and Morina indulged him effortlessly. She walked the perimeter of the room with her head held high. I stayed put, waiting for her instructions like any good *pet*.

"Hmm," she murmured, "seems as though you've already done most of the hard work, Damokles. How can I be of service to you, cousin?"

"There are more," he said, no longer boasting and prideful. "I need more."

"For what?"

"Ssso glad you asked." He moved closer to her and his voice dropped an octave. "How would you like to rule with me, cousssin? How would you like to sssee the beginning of a new era and the fall of that ssshe-bitch'sss mother?"

The smile Morina gave unsettled me in its wicked sincerity. She fingered the patch over her eye almost idly, as if it bothered her. The gesture drew Damokles's attention to it.

Morina said fiercely, "I'd love to."

I couldn't help but wonder if she actually meant it and hoped silently that she would not betray me. She turned her attention to me, then, and held out her hand. "Would you like to see, little pet? Would you like to see what has befallen those nasty vampires?"

I took the hand she offered and rose to my feet. Morina steered me by the elbow as she gave me the opportunity to gaze through the narrow windows.

Each cell we passed, I tried to school my face, to prepare myself for what I might see, though I had my back to Damokles. Each cell was dark but not dark enough to conceal the lifeless figures shackled along the walls.

Part of me prayed I wouldn't find Renata in such a state, strung up and left like an empty vessel, Damokles's precious trophy queen chained to a wall.

Anger flared in me.

Morina's hands moved intimately on my body, sliding through my fur and cradling my hips as she guided me to the door in the middle. Her lips brushed my ear as she whispered, "What do you think, pet?"

I gazed through the slit and into the cell beyond. On one wall, I made out the figure of a man chained at wrists and ankles. The shadow of his head lolled forward as if he were unconscious. On the other, another figure was bound. I tried to look away when Morina pressed the tips of her fingers into my skin, and I knew with a sinking feeling that there was something she wanted me to see.

I stared at the figure more intently then, studying the shadowy outline. Strands of hair hung in waves about her face and heartache and desperation gripped me. *Renata.*

She did not raise her head, either because she did not sense me there or because she was too weak to do so. I traced the curves of her figure over and over, trying to be sure that my mind was not playing tricks on me. And then Morina steered me to the next cell and the next, though I stared into them in a sort of detached daze.

"Hmm?" she prompted before releasing me. I sank back to all fours and kept my gaze on the black stone under my feet.

I nodded in false approval, hoping Damokles would not see through my façade.

"Doesss ssshe ssspeak, Morina?"

"Rarely, dear cousin." She gripped my neck tightly. "But she approves, don't you? The vampires were not very kind to her. They deserve what they get, don't they?"

"Yesss."

My response seemed satisfactory enough as Morina and Damokles began to converse in hushed voices as we ascended the stairs and left the dank prison behind us.

While they talked, I listened to their conversation, trying to follow along and only missing a few words here and there. I learned that Damokles planned on sending a party out to retrieve another clutch of vampires, another trophy queen. He had his sights set on a clan somewhere near a town known as Jasper. Carried away by my thoughts, I lost track of their conversation.

Somehow, I had to find a way to get past Damokles's guardsmen. Becoming a guard was the only way I could think to get close to Renata without arousing suspicion.

I wondered what Iliaria would suggest and another idea dawned on me. I shook the thought away nearly as soon as it entered my mind. If I challenged one of his guardsmen, it would raise suspicion…or worse. I could get myself killed in the process.

How then was I to gain access to the cellblocks? The answer eluded me.

Damokles continued to give Morina a guided tour of his stronghold. There was a dark beauty to the place, a sort of gothic resonance that made it cold and yet strangely warm. Damokles boasted almost thoughtlessly, as if such boasting was merely reflex to him. Whether he trusted Morina or no, he was proud of the world he had made for himself.

And given his hatred of vampires, there were an awful lot of them mucking about. We passed several in the winding halls, going about whatever daily tasks Damokles and his henchmen had set for them. They kept their heads down until we had passed. A few of them looked up only when they thought our backs were turned, and I caught the same resounding hatred I felt echoed in their eyes. When they noticed me, many of them glared with the contempt of caged tigers.

They were vampires, Azrael's gift given out of love and mercy, twisted and caged by Damokles, who had taken that gift and turned it into something it wasn't meant to be.

I watched one of the vampires out of my peripheral; he was garbed foot to head in gray fur pelts and kept a careful watch on us as we passed. Damokles came to halt. "What are you ssstaring at?" he hissed.

The vampire replied in a language I didn't understand. The dark halo of hair around his face and deep blue of his eyes put me in mind of Vasco, and his memory clawed at my heart. If only Vasco was here, I thought. He would know what to make of all this and what to do about it.

Damokles raised his hand as if to strike the vampire. The vampire stood unflinching as his features blazed with challenge. He did not care if Damokles struck him. In fact, he seemed to invite it.

Damokles followed through on his threat, striking the vampire across the cheek hard enough that his head whipped sharply to the side. I thought he would stop there, but he didn't. Damokles continued to strike him until the vampire was on his knees. Damokles grabbed a handful of his dreadlocked black hair and kept beating him.

Morina casually cleared her throat. "Cousin?"

Damokles seemed to come back to himself for a moment as one of his ears swiveled in her direction. He flung the beaten vampire away and left him to fall in a crippled heap on the floor.

"Asss weak asss they are," he hissed and returned to Morina's side, "their defianccce continuesss." A tremble of rage or disgust shuddered visibly through him, making his tail lash behind him like the angry end of a whip. "Ssshall we continue?"

"If it pleases you, cousin."

They carried on down the hallway, and I remained where I was. Damokles did not turn to look at me, but Morina spared a glance.

She touched Damokles's arm to bring him to a halt before she strode back to me. She knelt and placed a hand beneath my chin to lift my gaze to hers. "Go back to our chambers and wait for me."

"Yesss, my lady."

I waited until they had rounded the corner at the end of the hall to turn back to the vampire. Surely, Morina didn't really believe I was ready to lock myself away in a room and wait idly for her.

I had a better idea. I checked the length of the short hallway in which I stood, glancing down each of the three halls that branched off it to make sure no one was there.

I went to check on the unconscious vampire. He didn't rouse when I stood beside him and so I nudged him with the back of my hand.

The vampire caught my wrist. I caught a flash of something in his hand before he raised it toward my midsection. I jerked my arm and rolled away from him.

I rolled onto my feet, kneeling with one hand on the cold stone beneath me. The vampire stood before me holding a makeshift knife made of stone in his right hand.

I drew my ears back. "Idiot!" I said in English, trying to keep my voice as low as I could make lest we be overheard. "I'm trying to help you!"

His jaw clenched as he glared at me. "Why would you help a vampire?" Thankfully, he kept his voice low and spoke clear enough English that I could understand him.

I thought of Damokles's guardsmen and my aspirations to gain access to the dungeons. If there was a better plan than enlisting the aid of my brothers, I didn't see it.

"I cannot talk long," I said, listening intently in case someone approached. "But sssufficcce it to sssay, I want thisss hell no more than you do." I inched toward him and he raised the knife in warning between us and I paused. "Will you help?"

"What trickery is this?"

"No, not trickery. Will you rissse and aid your kind in their time of need?" I asked. "You have three ssseconds to decccide." I sank back, counting silently in my head. On the third second, the vampire nodded sharply. "Good."

"What do you plan?" he asked.

I ignored his question, because I honestly hadn't thought that far. I asked, instead, "Are there othersss among you that will aid usss?"

He nodded again, his brows knitted.

"Ssseek them, quietly," I said.

Confused or not, the vampire agreed, and I slipped from the hallway in search of our room.

Time. A good, developed plan would take time to set into motion and unfold. Time I didn't have.

The more conquests Damokles's made, the closer he came to his goal of overthrowing the Draculian Empire. He planned on using the vampires to aid his cause.

Well, I planned on using them to aid mine. Cuinn, I thought with a slow smile, would be proud.

I made it back safely to our chambers and awaited Morina's return. While I waited, I perched on the edge of the small bed and pondered my encounter with the vampire. I turned the tiny knob on the lamp beside the bed, giving the flame more wick to burn and sending a brighter light throughout the room. I still hadn't figured out exactly what I would do with the vampires that agreed to help me. Would the vampire I had spoken with recruit them quietly? I certainly hoped so. Even more strongly, I hoped that he asked only those he trusted. I wasn't foolish enough to believe that none of the vampires had joined Damokles out of self-interest.

I rolled onto my back, careful of the wings stretched beneath me. *What would Renata do?* I repeated the question in my mind, as if the answer would come to me if I asked myself over and over. *Renata.* I exhaled loudly. I was so close to her and yet she was still beyond my reach. Every impulse and instinct in my heart told me to run to her.

But I couldn't. I restrained myself because if I ran to her I would only expose myself, and any notion of a plan would be thrown out the window. Damokles's guards would apprehend me, or worse. I had to play along with Morina's game and my guise and hope that my reckless impulsivity in the hallway with the beaten vampire didn't cost me dearly. I played the scene over and over in my mind, becoming nearly paranoid about it. Had someone been listening? Surely, Damokles had placed spies to keep watch on us, or did he trust Morina so completely?

As soon as I thought it, I knew better.

Damokles's trusted his own brilliance to hold Morina to his plan. He was arrogant and the encounter with the vampire was just a childish temper tantrum. I stood and paced the room, trying to keep my mind distracted and my heels from itching with the urge to be closer to Renata.

How was it I still seemed to get strong feelings about others without the empathy? I hadn't realized until I thought about it that I still relied on my senses, though they were not as acute as my power when I was a vampire.

Was I leading myself falsely to believe that the vampire in the hall would truly aid me? I didn't think so. His hatred for Damokles was too sincere and he had not bothered to conceal it. I thought of the vampiress behind the bars of her prison.

The prisoners would be of little use to me unless they were fed, but how was I to feed them? There too, I couldn't fathom how to feed them without getting caught. I passed by the slightly ajar door of the closet in my pacing and it occurred to me we didn't have any new clothing with us. I sighed at the distracted thought.

Mayhap, I was not as adept at conspiracy as I thought. Surely, if I were, I would have come up with a dazzling plan by now, or at least, a better and more passable one than I had.

A hand clamped over my mouth as someone yanked me backward in a steel grip. Panic sang through my limbs as my pulse increased.

"Ssshhh, don't startle the entire keep by screaming." The familiar voice behind me lilted with amusement.

I jerked my arms up and peeled her hand off my mouth. "What the bleedin' hell are you doing here?" I whispered. My heart hammered in my chest and I took slow breaths to calm down.

Iliaria, garbed from shoulder to foot in her black and gold brocaded coat, smirked devilishly at my surprise. "You really didn't think I'd simply let you go and walk in here alone, did you?"

"You're going to get yoursssself killed!"

"And you're not?" Her perfect brows arched high.

"How did you get in?"

"Ah, that," she said. "He's not had his little witchlings spell the place to keep any of us from evanescing in and out."

"Where are the othersss?"

"Near enough," she said, then added in response to the look I gave her, "They're not here, if that's what you're asking."

"Morina ssshould be here any moment," I said.

"Have you found *her*?" Iliaria asked, ignoring my comment and searching my features.

"Yesss, ssshe'sss being held with othersss. Damoklesss hasss left them ssstarved and weak ssso they cannot fight or defend themssselves."

"How many rulers?"

I tried to remember their silhouettes and to recount how many there had been. "Eight...nine...ten..." I shook my head. "I'm sssorry, I can't remember."

"And what of the vampires?"

I told her then of the vampires I had seen caged and how Damokles had starved them in order to weaken them. I knew their numbers were higher than those of the royal trophies Damokles kept. I also told her about my encounter with the vampire in the hallway.

Iliaria didn't seem to approve or disapprove. She weighed my words carefully, a frown forming across her pale forehead as she deliberated. "What do you plan to do if your vampire succeeds in recruiting others?"

"I hadn't thought that far," I said, feeling a bit silly.

Iliaria reached for me and drew me up against the line of her lean body. "Well, I have," she said and pressed her lips against the fur of my forehead.

"And?"

"A coup, my dragă." Her lips tickled my fur as she murmured against me. "You've already set the makings of it in motion. Await my word." Her hand slid down the side of my body. "I will return to you when it is safe."

A sound came from the hallway beyond my door and I shifted my attention to it. I felt Iliaria step away from me, but when I looked back to find her, she was gone, leaving no trace that she had been standing in front of me seconds before.

The door opened as Morina entered.

"Were you talking to someone?" she asked as she closed the door behind her.

"Myssself," I said, knowing that we had kept our voices low enough that no one, not even a Dracule would have heard us unless they had their ear pressed to the door.

Morina seemed satisfied with my answer, but cast me a warning glance. "Careful doing that here, Elpis."

"Elpisss?" I blinked, uncomprehending.

"*Pet* only goes so far," she explained, going to the closet. I heard her remove her boots. "Remember the name and get used to it."

"But why *Elpisss*?" I asked. "You couldn't have come up with sssomething better than that?"

Morina emerged barefooted. Her feet were silent on the stone as she set about unbuttoning her white blouse in front of me. "Because," she said, "I like it."

I shrugged.

"Haven't read much Hesiod, have you?" Morina asked as she lifted the patch from over her eye and drew it back against her hair.

"Apparently not," I said, trying to understand and failing.

"Pandora's box." She freed the last button on her blouse. The shirt gaped open from neck to stomach, revealing the smooth porcelain skin and soft swell of her breasts.

I stared at a corner of the room.

"Surely, you've heard of Pandora's box?"

"Yesss," I said, trying to recount the story behind my lids and not the sight of Morina undressing. "The box wasss filled with all the plaguesss of the world, wasssn't it?"

"And the spirit Elpis, the personification of hope."

Though she said little in the way of explanation, the thread of kindness in her voice made me look at her, only to find that Morina had turned her nude back to me and disappeared into the closet to retrieve something else.

Hope. Why had she seen fit to give me such a title? Did it bear personal significance, or was it simply reflective of the task I undertook to free my queen and the vampires Damokles sought to use?

I was still wondering when Morina emerged from the closet in a pair of billowing silk pants and a matching long-sleeved top.

"Where did you get the clothes?" I asked a bit suspiciously.

"If you haven't noticed, we're not the only females." She cocked a brow at me. "Distrusting me so soon?"

I lightly shook my head and let it go. The only clothes I had were the ones on my back, the pair of dark shorts and a lightweight tunic tailored to fit over my wings. The Draculian body wasn't made for clothes, but that had not stopped Damokles's Dracule from wearing lightweight cloaks or breeches to cover their private bits. Damokles himself wore a dark wrap around his hips to shield his groin.

I slid into bed beneath the stiff sheets and blankets and tried to find a comfortable position. I wouldn't risk changing into a more human form here, in case someone in Damokles's keep recognized me.

Given the width of the bed, there was little room between Morina and me, and even when I lay as straight as an arrow, I could feel her body inches from my own.

In time, the tedium of my thoughts lulled me to sleep.

❖

Morina and I broke our fast in the breakfast hall, dining among the other Dracule. Vampires scattered throughout the room, placing servings of meat on the plates before us. Morina and I ate in silence while the other Dracule around us whispered to each other in their curling tongues and hissing voices. I felt a body brush my arm as someone leaned forward to place a goblet next to my platter.

The vampire I had spoken with in the hall gave me a blank and empty stare before he moved on down the table, placing a goblet before each of the Dracule.

I ate the seared meat before me without worrying what I looked like. Considering most of the Dracule ate in much the same animalistic manner, it seemed only burdensome to try for any more grace than my form would allow.

Morina raised her glass and brought it to her lips. She met my gaze wordlessly when she set it aside. I took a small swig and felt immediately sick to my stomach.

Vampire blood. I recognized it by the strength of its metallic essence and would've wagered that this was how Damokles kept his vampires weak and under control. He did not waste their blood; he bled them, weakened them, and shared their life's essence with his Draculian horde. I took another sip and some of the blood dribbled into the fur down my chin.

I observed the Dracule around me and wondered if Damokles had bled Renata to feed them? Somewhere down the row of tables, did one of his men drink *my queen's* blood? I knew I didn't, for I had tasted her blood so many times before I would've recognized it the instant it hit my tongue.

A susurrus of rage hummed through me and I downed the blood in the goblet at a gulp, uncaring of the red lines that dripped from the edges of my mouth to stain my white fur.

I hoped the vampire had done as he agreed. I hoped he had talked with others that despised the Dracule so that we could get our plan moving along. Iliaria wanted to stage a coup. I prayed we had enough vampires to pull it off.

When we finished breaking our fast, Morina went her way and I went mine. I did not bother asking her questions about where she went, figuring that if she was going to betray me and cast me to Damokles's traitorous hands, she would have already done so and if she decided to do so, what could I do to stop her? I wandered the halls aimlessly, with no clear destination in sight. I memorized the winding patterns and used the location of the torches and chambers to navigate and try to map the place out in my head.

"You," a woman's voice called when I rounded a corner and passed by a sitting room. "You," I heard the voice behind me as she scampered to catch up. "What are you doing?"

I turned on my slightly bent legs and tilted my head to the side. The vampire who had stood beside Damokles's throne eyed me with suspicion. The dark curls of her hair were clasped at the nape of her neck and she wore a gown of white and gold that made the green in her eyes less drab and more vibrant.

Given her obvious loyalty to Damokles, I replied, "Nothing, lady."

She moved closer and tilted her head back slightly to look me in the face. I stared down at the vampire with what I felt was a perfectly neutral expression.

"Something about you seems familiar, Dracule. Have we met before?" She extended her arm and traced a finger down the cloak of my wings.

"No, lady. I'd remember if we had." I blinked slowly.

"Are you sure?" she asked, inclining as her nostrils flared slightly.

"Yesss."

Another Dracule appeared in the hall.

"*Lucrezzzia.*"

She turned to him and they stared at one another while I tried to control my face. I wasn't sure what I felt. I was surprised, but only a little. I had suspected Lucrezia had survived, I just hadn't expected to come face to face with her and not recognize her. It had to be her, of that, I was sure. It certainly explained the unease that settled in my stomach around her. A different body or not, perhaps my own instincts had been trying to tell me all along.

"What is it now?" she asked with familiar agitation.

"Damoklesss wishesss to sssee you."

Lucrezia turned back to me with an inscrutable expression. "We'll meet again, Dracule."

Carefully, I bowed my head until the sound of her slippers and skirts slithering across the stone floor disappeared back through the doorway and she was out of sight.

Somehow, Damokles has used the witches in this, I thought, certain that it was the only way Lucrezia could've survived execution. I had seen Renata pierce her heart and lop her head off myself. I remembered Dante when they had brought him back to the clan, the X cut across his chest, the same target the sadistic bitch had carved into my back years ago. His broken mind…

How had she retained her power? How had she broken Dante's mind in her new body? *The Kiss of Madness* had been one of Lucrezia's powers when she had been among the Rosso Lussuria. I could grasp that a witch might have somehow used a spell to transfer her spirit to a new body, but her powers with it? How was that possible? Were our powers tied to our spirits? Why hadn't I seen any of Damokles's witches lurking about?

I continued my investigation of the lair, my thoughts heavier than they had been in days. My mind was boggled with ideas, none of which were helpful and all of which only led me to asking myself more and more questions.

For instance, why hadn't I seen any of the Rosso Lussuria vampires? If Damokles was taking our queens and kings and using them to manipulate us, why hadn't he managed to take the Rosso?

Queen Helamina and King Augusten. It was the only logical explanation. In order for him to gain the Rosso, he had to gain our ally rulers as well, and he didn't stand a chance attacking three clans at once. That must be why he was biding his time…

I traversed the dark and narrow hall, preferring to keep to the shadows and move as quietly as I could. A good thing, I reckoned, as I didn't want to call another's attention as I had Lucrezia's.

I passed by a line of doors when I heard voices come from the third on the right.

"You said she was mine," Lucrezia said, obviously displeased and upset.

"Ssshe isss yoursss when I am ready to give her to you," Damokles hissed in a voice that held matching heat.

"You can't even get your hands on the Rosso Lussuria. They're too heavily guarded for you, Damokles. They've outsmarted you by forming alliances. You can't even break their queen. What do you think you're going to do with the whole clan?"

Damokles slammed something down with a heavy bang. "Sssilence! I told you, vampire, your ssstay in that body can be temporary. Do not tempt me."

"I can break her," Lucrezia said eagerly. "I can break her and make her a puppet for your hands. Why will you not give me the chance to prove myself to you, to our cause, Damokles?"

There was the sound then of someone's breath being squeezed out of them, followed by Damokles's slithering tongue. "When I give an order, you obey, vampire. Do you understand?"

There was no response save for the sound of a table's legs as it scraped across the stone floor. And then, "Yes."

At the sound of approaching feet, I moved quietly as I backed myself further in the cloak of shadows. Lucrezia emerged from the room, her shoulders high as she stomped off in the opposite direction.

I retreated from the hall before Damokles or anyone else emerged to catch me eavesdropping.

CHAPTER NINETEEN

"You do not speak much to me," Morina said pensively from where she sat in the leather armchair tucked against the wall.

Her comment caught me relatively unaware, as I hadn't expected that she'd been paying any attention to me. I finished folding the quilt down toward the foot of the bed. With a pelt of fur, the quilt was too heavy to sleep with most nights, and thus I preferred sleeping with only the sheet. If it hadn't been for comfort's sake, I would've slept without the sheet too, but I enjoyed the small sense of security it provided.

I raised my head. "You do not ssspeak much to me, either."

Another bout of silence stretched between us and I peeled off the lightweight tunic I wore. I didn't bother to remove the shorts that Iliaria had given me. Fur or no, I wasn't eager to sleep in the Draculian equivalent of *nude*. And I couldn't bring myself to take fresh clothing from the closet.

Her statement was true. It seemed that when we did speak to one another, our conversations were always brief. If I asked her a question, Morina answered it in as few words as possible. I released a sigh. How was it I was able to discern more about complete strangers than I was about the woman who slept in the same bed? Around the others, she played the role of my lover convincingly, going so far as to offer affectionate touches that implied there was more than there really was between us. But when we were alone, she was succinct in speech and guarded in her mannerisms. That same detached demeanor she had presented to me when she had taken me as her prisoner came tumbling down as she barricaded her real self.

I slid beneath the sheet without pressing her, though I spared a glance to find she had set aside the book of Draculian verses she had been reading. She leaned forward in her chair and gazed at nothing in particular.

If she wanted to talk, I told myself, she would. I must admit, a part of me found it exasperating the way she attempted to strike conversation by making an idle comment, only to let it die off again.

I felt the mattress dip beneath her weight when she climbed in beside me. Darkness unfolded as she extinguished the bedside lantern. The heavy silence between us pressed against my chest and made it feel tight.

What did she want from me? I couldn't discern it. If she disliked me so, why did she offer to be my escort? Why did she swear on her life to protect mine after everything she'd done to me in her pursuit of vengeance? Did she only offer her aid because she finally realized Andrella's death was Damokles's doing and then only to get even with him? Or because she was so desperate to see Andrella just one more time?

I found myself drowning in the well of my emotions. I longed for Renata and Iliaria, to be nestled sweetly between them, to feel the line of their tall bodies against mine and their arms around me again. How was it that I felt more alone with Morina than I would have without her?

I choked back a sob, shut my eyes tightly, and buried my face in my pillow. I would not cry, not over this, not over Morina's mind games.

Her words were soft beside me. "I do not know how to talk to you."

"You do well enough around the othersss."

"That is different."

"I know," I said bitterly. "It'sss jussst pretend."

"No," she said, "it's more than that."

I raised enough to find her pale outline in the dark. She'd removed the patch from her eye and left it on the bedside table. "Then what isss it?"

"I don't know," she said and it seemed to me that she did know. She just evaded telling me the truth.

I rolled back onto my side, intent on ignoring her.

Morina growled lightly and whispered harshly into the dark. "You are so frustrating."

I shot up then. "I'm frussstrating?" I leaned into her and hissed. "*I'm the one that'sss frussstrating here?* You can't even follow through and have a complete conversssation with me!"

"Keep your voice down," she said. "We may not have spies trailing us about, but I'd rather not wake and rouse anyone's interest."

I let out a huff and narrowed my eyes. How dare she call me frustrating? I wasn't the one constantly dancing from foot to foot, trying to hide behind an invisible stone wall, and skirting subjects.

"If you remember, lady," I kept my voice down, as requested, "you took me. You ssstarted thisss."

"And are you ever going to let that go?" she whispered in exasperation. "I'm here with you now. I'm sticking my neck out for *you*."

"Oh, ssso you can ssstick your neck out but not the ressst of you?"

"What is that supposed to mean?"

"I don't know," I said heatedly. "You claim to be risssking your life for mine, you make your promisssesss and give your oathsss, and yet, look at how you treat me, Morina. You act asss though you really couldn't be bothered to hold even one sssimple bloody conver—"

Her hand slapped over my mouth to silence me and I glowered, heat rising to my cheeks beneath my fur.

"I told you to keep your voice down," she said without bothering to remove her hand. "Do you want everyone to hear us? What you think of me, I cannot help or change. If the fact that I'm here with you now isn't enough proof, I don't know what else to do."

"Proof of what?" I grumbled, resisting the urge to roll my eyes.

She lowered her hand and shook her head. "Nothing," she said. "Go to sleep."

"No." I rolled on top of her without thinking and caught her hands.

Morina's attention snapped back to me and I heard the breath hitch in her throat. A warm sensation built low in my belly as we gazed at one another. Her eye was wide, showing a bit too much white. I knew I had surprised her as much as I had myself.

"I'm sssorry," I murmured and began to draw away.

Morina's hands tightened on mine and I hesitated. "Wait," she said, her voice drawn tight as if she were choking.

"Why?"

"I want you."

An emotion that I'd tried to bury somewhere deep inside me came unfurled like a dragon rousing from its slumber. I was suddenly very aware of Morina's body beneath mine, conscious of the rise and fall of her chest beneath the silk sleep shirt.

"I don't know how to seduce you or win your favor," she whispered, and the fluttering in my chest increased. "I don't know how to gain your forgiveness for what I've done to you and yours when I'm *not* sorry. If I apologized to you, it would be a lie. I'm not sorry I took you as my prisoner, *Elpis*." Morina touched my face uncertainly. Her expression of confusion and want nearly undid me. Unthinkingly, I leaned into her touch, into the tenderness of the hand she offered. I covered her hand with one of my own and turned my mouth into her open palm, parting my lips and dragging my skin across hers.

Morina trembled almost unnoticeably beneath me. "You frighten me."

"Why?"

"Because you were right," she touched my thigh tentatively while keeping her eye closed. "You remind me of her."

"But I'm not her, Morina. I never will be," I said, trying to keep my tone tender but honest. If what she looked for in me was Andrella, she wouldn't find her. I couldn't replace her and I wouldn't try to.

Morina rose and buried her hands in the fur of my neck. She brought my face down to hers and slid her cheek across mine until her face was buried in the bend of my shoulder.

I stiffened uncertainly, a thousand battles warring inside me as my emotional and logical self conflicted. A part of me remembered the woman who would have done anything to hurt Iliaria and harm anyone that got in her way.

Morina drew back, her voice small, "Do I repulse you?"

I shook my head, lightly. She didn't. And yet…

I didn't know what to do. A part of me wanted to draw away from her, to not let any sense of closeness happen between us, to not forge any more intimate ties or bonds with her. What had she really done to redeem herself and gain my trust? At any moment, she could still turn against me.

I remembered Cuinn's words, *"Ye've already got two women in your bed. Do ye really want to add a third? Especially that one?"*

How would Renata and Iliaria feel if I took Morina to my bed, if I let passion come between us? Was it fair to them? Iliaria had already made it abundantly clear that I was *hers*.

"What is it?" Morina asked.

"I can't, Morina. Not yet."

At first, it appeared as though she would protest, but then that guard settled once more between us.

I touched her face, tracing the starburst of scar tissue just below her eye with my thumb. "No," I said, "don't withdraw. I'm not rejecting you entirely."

"*Entirely*," she said and snorted. "That's good to know."

"If thisss isss what you want…" I pressed my hips to hers, and even through our attire felt her sex kindle against mine. "I can't give it to you yet, not completely."

Morina's hips moved against me as if she could not help herself. A shuddering sigh fell from me at the contact. The slight friction of her body against mine sparked heat between my thighs and I cursed the passionate Draculian nature that encouraged me to release all thoughts and caution and to surrender to the call of flesh.

Morina kept moving against me, and though the request was on the tip of my tongue, I didn't say it. I didn't ask her to stop. Her hands moved to my hips and when I looked down at her, her expression was pained. Her hand moved from my hips and fumbled with the clasp of my shorts. The muscles of my stomach jumped at the nearness of her touch. If she got her hand past the material and touched me, in truth, I wouldn't be able to stop.

Summoning all my willpower, I caught her hand in mine and drew it away from my groin. "I can't."

She recoiled and turned away from me as if I'd hit her. I shut my eyes and focused on changing my form. We had spent enough nights under Damokles's nose that I was certain we wouldn't be interrupted if I didn't stay in it too long.

Morina turned back to me when she felt me change. She gazed up at my naked torso with hunger in her eye.

"And so you seek to torment me?" she asked.

"No," I said, and when she reached up to touch my breasts, I caught her wrists to stop her. "No, I'm not trying to torment you." I slid down her body and between her thighs. "I can't give myself to you just yet, Morina. I hope you understand, but this…" I worked the laces of her breeches open. "This I can give to you."

Comprehension dawned on her features and her lips parted as I drew her breeches down her thighs to expose her sex. I couldn't give all of myself to her, for so many reasons, but there was one thing I could do.

I ran my lips down the shield of snowy fur at her mound. I moved lower, angling my head and pressing a feather-soft kiss against the tip of her sex. Her sex and the rest of her body responded immediately at that small touch, stiffening in arousal as she raised her arms above her head and caught hold of the headboard.

I gazed up at her and asked, "Do you mind?" I recalled how adamantly against such an act Iliaria had initially been.

Morina shook her head, apparently not sharing the same qualms. "No."

I settled comfortably between her thighs and explored the folds of her heated flesh with my fingertips. I traced her Nod Dragoste and admired how her body reacted to my touch, how her muscles constricted as the pleasure echoed and unraveled through her limbs.

"How long has it been, Morina?" I whispered against her sex and the muscles in her stomach rippled beneath her shirt.

"Since Andrella."

I traced a finger against the underside of her sex and her hips rocked slightly. Her sex glistened in the dark with the dew of her desire, and I eased my fingers through that sacred honey and inside her.

Morina groaned and rose slightly off the bed, her hips pressing against me. I slid another finger inside, and her muscles constricted and fluttered against me, kindling a fire that burned low in my own body. I felt myself stiffen against the mattress and resisted the urge to grind my lower body into the bed.

I parted my lips against her and traced her with my tongue. Morina moaned for me, her grip tightening on the headboard.

"May this be worthy of breaking your long fast," I said and closed my mouth around her.

The wood of the headboard creaked under her hands and I sucked lightly, licking the length of her sex in long, sure strokes. I curled my fingers inside her and used them to mimic the broad strokes of my tongue against her sex.

Morina raised her hips and I sucked her. Every muscle in her body tensed as she clasped around me. Her back arched and I had to lower my face to keep her sex sheltered in my mouth. I drew back with her between my lips and she cried out as I submitted my mouth and hands to her pleasure. I coaxed her body with gentle strokes and soft sucking until her legs began to tremble. Her climax built and quaked through her, and when she spent herself, she came with a closed-mouth moan.

I withdrew from her and got to my hands and knees to crawl from between her thighs. I didn't know what to do afterward and so I lay down in the empty spot where I slept and slid my arm beneath the pillow, remembering to focus on calling the Draculian form back to my mind. The shorts I wore were suddenly snug again and I drew my ears back against my skull. I heard Morina lace her breeches before I felt her against my back.

"May I hold you?" she asked, stroking her hand down the bend of my neck, across my shoulder, and down my spine.

"Yes," I said, trying to ignore the pulse that throbbed between my legs.

Morina curled her body against mine and draped her arm loosely over my waist, as if she wasn't certain if I would let her leave it there.

I did, and it seemed as soon as I closed my eyes, the sexual tension drifted away as sleep welcomed me in her embrace.

❖

An ear-splitting sound echoed throughout our chambers. Morina threw back the blankets with a curse and stumbled out of bed quickly to don her attire. Groggily, I sat up, swiveling my ears in the direction of the sound. It came again, a loud, piercing blow that bounced off the walls. The air vibrated with its burst.

"What isss that?"

"An alarm," Morina said as she tugged on her boots. She spared a hurried glance toward the door. "Get up."

Another sound rode the air, the familiar clang of steel on steel. I climbed quickly out of bed and pulled on my tunic, tying the ribbons beneath my wings and trembling as the adrenaline started to rush through me.

"What'sss happening?"

"I don't know," Morina said. "But one of Damokles's men has sounded an alarm."

The door burst open and my heart leapt into my throat.

Vasco stood in the doorway with a wild grin on his face, a sword held loosely in his right hand. Cuinn pushed past him to enter the room.

"What're ye doin' just standing there?" Cuinn asked. "Get your arse up and go save your queen!"

As if in a daze, I blinked. Surely, I was dreaming. Iliaria had told me she'd return again, but she hadn't returned to tell me anything of her plans or what our next move would be.

"Colombina," Vasco said. "It's time. We have to go."

He strode into the room and grabbed my elbow to emphasize the importance of his words. I blinked and tilted my head as I followed him out into the hall.

"Where is she being held, colombina?"

"Vasssco, why are you here?"

"Helamina and Augusten refused to wait. We have to act now," he said. "Damokles's vampires can only hold the Dracule at bay for so long."

A growl sounded from behind us. One of the Draculian guards sank low on all fours, as if ready to launch an offensive attack. His lips drew back in a snarl as he hissed.

Morina was suddenly between us and the Dracule. "Go!" she shouted. "Get her out of here, now!"

She was unarmed and I hesitated to leave her. Vasco used his grip on my wrist to steer me down the hall and I went.

"They're thisss way," I said, the ice in my limbs finally seeming to melt as I gained my bearings. Renata, I thought, finally.

Cuinn, Vasco, and I rushed down the winding halls and to the dungeon rooms where the vampires were being held. We had no trouble making our way to the dungeon itself, but as soon as we burst through the door, Damokles's guardsmen were upon us.

Vasco was graceful and light on his feet as he rushed the Dracule in a blur, drawing his sword in an arch and slicing open his belly. The second Dracule set his attention on me and raised the two crescent blades in his hands.

"Traitor!" he spat the word at me and rushed me, giving me no time to think.

I reacted out of instinct when his blades crossed in a slashing motion near my midsection, leaping back in time to feel the disruption in the currents as his blades flashed past my stomach. I flexed my hands and unsheathed the sharp claws.

Our fight broke out in earnest. I was distantly aware of the rhythm of Vasco's boots scuffing the ground and knew he struggled to cripple the Dracule that attacked him.

Cuinn started to move in front of me, to place himself between me and the Dracule, but I sidestepped him and charged.

The Dracule raised his blades to swing both at me in an arch and I slid between his legs on the stone floor. I caught the base of his tail in my hand and sprang to my feet as the vampires and cells around me blurred. I pushed off the ground and lunged for the Dracule's back, using his own barb like a blade as I drove it through his ribcage. The Dracule gave a sharp cry and went to his knees. I pushed against the resistance of the furred body beneath mine, shoving the barb in as deeply as it would go.

In a red haze of fury, I lost myself. I slashed at the body beneath mine, tearing skin and fur with my claws as if I would dig a hole in his body to climb through. The smell of metallic blood filled the air and spurred my frenzy. The Dracule raised his arms to protect himself and I dove toward his neck, biting and tearing away the skin and arteries in a shower of blood. I thought of Renata and the vampires they had abused.

Someone touched my back and I turned, snapping and narrowly missing a pale arm.

"He's dead, colombina," Vasco said. "He's dead. You can stop now."

I blinked and gazed down at the motionless body beneath mine. A pool of blood spread out from his body like a blossoming flower. At some point, I had ridden him to the floor. My white hands and knees were covered in the Dracule's blood. The taste of metal was everywhere inside my mouth.

I drew away and turned my attention to the vampires behind the bars of their prisons. Those strong enough and conscious enough to realize what was happening had moved closer to the bars, their eyes filled with an eager light at the scent of blood.

"We have to free them," I said.

"Not yet," Vasco said. "If we free them now we'll have to fight them off of us."

He gripped me by the shoulders. "Where is Renata, colombina?"

The two guards had emerged from Damokles's trophy room and left the door wide open. I led Vasco and Cuinn through it.

"They're in here," I said. I flattened my ears and scanned the room for a set of keys to open the dungeon doors.

Vasco shot a question to me with a glance and I explained, "Keysss, we need keysss."

"Nay, we don't," Cuinn said. He approached the first cell on the left and rose on his back legs. He opened his mouth and blew into the small keyhole. The lock tumbled open with a click and the heavy door swung open.

Vasco and I yanked the shackles out of the stone walls and lowered the kings and queens one at a time. Most of them were too weak to stand, let alone attack us for our blood. When we got to Renata's cell, I went to her side and took her down. She fell into my arms, unconscious, and I took her weight, cradling her tall body against mine.

I turned to Vasco when he lowered the man across from her. "I think they're too weak to get out without help."

"Vasco," a voice hissed from the steps as we emerged from the dark prison. Cuinn had unlocked all the doors, but we had not made it to the last two cells. I cradled Renata close to my chest as a figure descended the steps and stepped before us in a gown of white and gold like some terrible, demented angel.

A look of confusion crossed Vasco's face as he didn't recognize the dark-haired woman. She turned to me with an expression of venom I had seen her wear so many times before in open court.

"You," she said. "I knew you were bad news."

"Vasssco," I said, "take Renata."

"You won't be taking *her* anywhere."

The glint of a sword winked like a threat in the dark.

I drew back my lips in a snarl as Vasco took Renata's weight.

"Want to bet?" I sank to all fours and growled, tail lashing behind me. "I think it'sss time we sssee jussst how permanent that new body of yoursss isss, Lucrezzzia."

I lunged and she swung her sword to force me back. My claws ticked on the floor below me as I tried to find an opening in her defense. When I found it, I lunged forward again and Lucrezia deftly blocked me and drove me back again.

"I have no fight with you, Great Siren, if you step aside," she said in a low voice that did not reveal the fear I smelled emanating from her. She was afraid of me. She was afraid of all of the Dracule. I remembered her fear when she had learned I wore Iliaria's mark.

I used her fear to my advantage, taunting and testing her defense.

"Ssso you think," I hissed and lunged again, this time catching her sword hand in mine. I used all my strength to slam her back against the wall. I took both her wrists in my hands and pinned her body with mine, slamming her sword hand roughly into the wall until her grip loosened and the sword fell with a clatter.

Inches from her face, I whispered, "I told you once, Lucrezzzia, to be wary of the powersss you chassse."

She stared at me uncertainly, in a lack of recollection and recognition.

I drew back, still pinning her with my body so that she could not get a leg up between us to kick me off or cause me harm.

Against a Dracule, she couldn't fight me off. I changed before her and felt the cruel smile that spread across my lips.

Lucrezia's eyes flew open even wider and this time, she began to struggle. "You wretched little whore!" she spat.

"Ah, ah, ah," I pushed against her and slid my mouth across her cheek. I nipped her skin, letting her feel the threat of my upper and lowers fangs. "He promised her to you, did he?" I asked. "You'll never have her, Lucrezia. No matter how many bodies you find to call home, you will never, ever touch a hair on her head."

She glowered at me, her eyes burning with the same mad power I had seen so many times at court. The same power I had seen her turn against Renata before Renata had killed her. The same power she had used on Dante and broken him with.

A growl built in my chest and beat against my ribcage. "I will take great pleasure in this." In the space of a heartbeat, I released her right wrist and flexed my hand, driving my nails into the yielding flesh of her stomach.

Never, never in my life had I found pleasure in causing another pain. Never had I understood cruelty or the sweet rush of violence, the taste of vengeance. I had spent a great deal of my existence trying to avoid such things, trying simply to survive the cruelty and violent greed of others. In that instant, I relished her agony and screams.

She tried to fight me and I thrust my arm forward, pushing my fingers more deeply inside her. The meaty brush of her organs caressed my knuckles, the intimate glide of blood like a woman's desire on my skin. I twisted my arm and pressed it higher, another scream, and another. Lucrezia's body writhed helplessly, her eyes rolling back into her head as if she would faint. I felt her beating heart, the meat thumping rapidly against my hand. I curled my fingers around it and pulled. Veins and other things ripped and popped, fraying and tearing as she screamed so loud I feared my ears would burst with the sound.

I drew her heart out of her chest and stepped back as she fell to her knees.

Lucrezia's hands rose to clutch at the wound. Her mouth opened as she gasped for air, as her body struggled to survive without its most vital organ.

Though I had pulled her heart free of her chest, the blood-slicked gob continued to beat in my hand. I went to Vasco and my queen and held Lucrezia's heart up between us, ignoring the startled expression he wore.

"Wake her, Vasco. Wake her with the blood of Lucrezia's heart." Obligingly, he took the heart from me and I turned back to Lucrezia.

Cuinn sat some feet away from Lucrezia's feebly struggling form. "You want me to gnaw off her head?" he asked, craning his neck and glaring at her. I hadn't known the Fata had a taste for blood, but I had a feeling he'd enjoy chewing her head off.

"No," I said. "No, I have better plans for her, but I will need your assistance."

"Gladly, lass."

I grabbed a handful of Lucrezia's hair and jerked her away from the wall. She raised her hands in protest, but the blood and organ loss had made her too weak to defend herself.

I dragged her up the stairs and into the center of the room between the prison cells. I released the clutch of her hair, letting her head fall to the stone floor.

"Open them, Cuinn."

One by one, he forced the barred doors open with his magic. The vampires gazed at me uncertainly, their hunger warring with their fear, as if they thought it was some sort of trap.

"Come, my lovelies." I gestured to Lucrezia at my feet. She shook her head from side to side, her eyes pleading with me not to do what I was about to do. I held her gaze and said coldly, "Your dinner awaits you."

I turned my back and heard the *clink-clink* of the vampires' shackles as they emerged from the cells. Lucrezia somehow found breath to scream when they fell on her. I glanced back to see the mob of starved vampires moving like one beast on top of her.

One of the vampires, the female with straw-like hair, shuffled forward on her knees. When she knelt a few feet away from me, she bowed her head.

I nodded at Cuinn, who moved cautiously behind her and broke the hold of her shackles.

"What will you when this is done?" she asked me, blood smeared in a half-mask across her lips and chin.

"Take her head," I said whilst the others continued to feed in a frenzy to break their long fast.

The girl smiled fiercely before tilting her head in another measure of respect. "It will be done, Great Siren."

I watched as she rose to her feet and peeled the vampires off Lucrezia to gain hold of her head. The vampires didn't fight her; they simply shifted and moved like a pride of lions on a carcass and found another place to feed. One of them licked the blood from the stone floor and another raised her head, her nostrils flaring animalistically as she began to crawl toward the fallen Dracule. She dragged the Dracule's body into the cell, leaving a trail of blood behind as she offered the blood left in his body to those in the cell too weak to stand.

The straw-haired woman twisted her arms and I heard the sick crack of Lucrezia's spine as she ripped her head from her body.

I descended the steps to find Renata stirring in Vasco's arms. He sat on the floor with her upper body cradled in his lap. Her lashes fluttered open as she reached up to grab a handful of his shirt.

"Epiphany," she whispered my name and I sank to my knees beside them.

"I'm here," I said, touching a lock of her wavy hair with bloody fingers. "I'm here, my queen."

I took the heart from Vasco and asked Cuinn, "Can you do something with this?"

"Aye, I can."

I set the heart in front of him. Renata's hand curled around my arm and Vasco and I helped her to her feet.

Cuinn's eyes narrowed and a plume of smoke rose from Lucrezia's heart. A small flame ignited before it consumed and scorched the heart, leaving nothing but ashes behind. The smell of cooked meat permeated my senses.

It was done.

Renata took my hand in hers and turned me to her. She placed her palm flat against my cheek and I nuzzled my face against her skin.

"It seems you've much to tell me, cara mia." Her thumb grazed my lower lip as she drew it down to glimpse my fangs.

"Yes, yes, I do."

"We need to retreat." Iliaria stumbled down the steps, and fear lodged into my throat at the way she limped. I went to her, helping her down the last set of stairs. "Queen Helamina and Augusten have announced a retreat. We have to go," she said, "now."

"Can you travel?" I asked. "How badly are you hurt?"

"I'm fine," she said, though she winced as if something pained her. Anatharic was suddenly by her side, helping me to hold her upright.

"We can travel, but not far," he said. "Iliaria," it was the first time I had ever heard him use her name, "Printessa, we must go to your mother."

Iliaria looked as though she was about to argue when Morina and Emilio descended the steps.

"So we will," Morina said. She shot Iliaria a stubborn glance. "Don't argue."

"What about the other vampires?"

The straw-haired vampire appeared at the top of the stairs. "We will tend our own," she said, descending. "You've done what you could. Let us tend to our lords and ladies. We are not without means of escape."

Renata's arm slid about my waist. "Cara mia," she said and I nodded.

Morina and Anatharic guided us into a group and with Iliaria, they combined their power. Cuinn leaned against my leg as the dungeon vanished and my insides lurched with the rush of magic and, as a group, we headed for safety.

Chapter Twenty

Queen Basmathe, Iliaria's mother, offered us sanctuary. We arrived in the midst of the throne room, interrupting whatever politics had been taking place before our arrival. Basmathe descended the dais, the silver chain marking her status swinging brightly in the light. She caught sight of Iliaria in our party and summoned a healer without hesitation.

I stood outside the infirmary, waiting with Vasco and the others to hear word on Iliaria's condition. Dominique, Nirena, Vito, Vittoria, and even Gaspare waited with me. Renata, Queen Helamina, and Augusten had gone to meet privately with Iliaria's mother.

Renata knew as well as I what Damokles had been planning, and no doubt, she told the king and queens of how he was gathering an army to try to take the Draculian throne.

We had not overtaken his keep, though we had, with the vampires' help, forced his numbers to dwindle. I hoped silently that the vampires we had freed made it out alive. Without their aid, Damokles's numbers were too small to overthrow Basmathe.

Still, in his arrogance, I knew it would not stop him from trying to reassemble his army. There was still the matter of the clan he had prepared to strike and take. I feared we had only accomplished slowing his progression.

The healer emerged, a cloth of white silk around her gray hips. "Ssshe will sssurvive, though the barb grazed her lung. Let her ressst for a while."

Morina emerged from the ornately carved double doors at the end of the hall. Renata stood beside her and turned to meet my gaze as Basmathe escorted them from her chambers.

The Draculian queen towered above Renata, which said something of her height.

"Isss that her?" she asked, her obsidian gaze coming to rest on me.

"Yes," Renata said.

Basmathe moved past Augusten and Helamina and came to stand before me. Morina followed at her heels quietly, her cheeks and hands still stained with blood.

Basmathe reached out to touch me and I forced myself not to draw away. Instead, I sank to my knees on the marble floor. "Great Siren," I whispered and bowed my head.

Basmathe made a sound low in her throat and said, "Get up."

I did.

"Ssso, you are the one Azrael has blesssed?"

"Yes, my lady."

"The one who bringsss the whisssspersss of treachery and war?" Her ears turned outward, the black fur of her head glossy in the firelight.

"Yes, my lady."

"And you are my daughter'sss lover?"

At that, I tensed, unsure how to respond.

Basmathe gave a purring laugh and said, "It isss jussst a quessstion, girl. Answer me."

"Yes."

She touched my cheek. "Sssee, that wasssn't ssso hard, wasss it?"

"No, my lady."

"Thank you," she said and I found myself at a complete loss.

I raised my brows. "For what, lady?"

"Not only have you brought word of Damoklesss's treachery, but you have brought her back to me." Her gaze slid to the door of the infirmary. "I had hoped one day ssshe would return, even if againssst my command."

A flicker of fear rose within me and Basmathe caught it. "You are sssafe," she said, "as isss my daughter." She tilted her head sharply to the side, as if inspecting me. "I learned long ago why ssshe lied." She turned and fixed her attention on Morina. "Ssshe did sssoo to protect you, Morina."

Morina bowed her head. "And you cast her out for it."

"Yesss," Basmathe said, her voice crawling like a chill through the hall, though her eyelids shuddered closed in what I thought was regret. Her shoulders rounded as she straightened and said, "It hasss been decided. Your clansss will ressside here under my protection until we eliminate Damoklesss's threat entirely. There isss plenty of room to keep you all asss we prepare to march to war to defend both our sssidesss."

With that, Queen Basmathe folded her leathery wings around her tall frame and entered the infirmary to speak with her daughter.

Clearly dismissed, I went to Renata's side.

Well played, cara mia. She offered her arm and I took it whilst Basmathe's guards led us to our quarters for the night. When I realized Morina was not with us, I came to a halt and Renata stopped with me.

Morina stood alone by the infirmary, the patch in place over her eye and her hands buried in the pockets of her coat. I met Renata's beautiful gaze and watched as her brows arched high in question.

"She helped me," I said. "If it wasn't for her, I don't know that we'd be here right now."

It was true, though Iliaria had gone off on her own plan. Morina had been the one to sneak me in under Damokles's nose. She had been the one who had distracted Damokles while I asked the vampire he had abused to gather those he could to rise against their captors. Vasco had explained to me that Iliaria had presented herself to them and swayed them by informing them she worked with me. Helamina's and Augusten's men and the rest of those Elders and vampires with us had begun the fight with Damokles's Dracule. But Iliaria had thrown it into motion from the foundation of my plan.

Without Morina's help, I might not have survived finding a way in for any of our plans to be executed. The vampires might have still joined Iliaria in our fight, but they would have been unprepared for the coup.

Renata assessed Morina and finally asked. "Will you join us, Dracule?"

Morina glanced uncertainly at me and I shrugged. It was not my decision to make.

"We've much to discuss," Renata added and then glanced at me in bemusement. "More than I had initially anticipated, apparently."

We made it to our room with Morina following silently at our heels and settled ourselves in. Renata kept touching me with an expression of soft wonder and amusement. She traced the curve of the wings arched from my back. "Is it permanent?" she asked.

"No, my lady. Azrael merely loaned it to me."

She seemed to find that highly amusing and laughed. The sound made my heart light and I curled into her, burying my face in the bend of her neck.

I felt her attention slide to Morina. "And her?" Renata asked. "Is she on loan as well?" Her voice was light with amusement.

"I cannot withdraw my binding on her," Morina said. "When Azrael grants her true form back to her, she will still bear my mark."

Renata buried a hand in my hair, running her fingers through it. "Hmm," she mused. "Have you taken her to your bed, Epiphany?"

"Partly."

"Partly?" Renata's brows arched exquisitely again.

"Wait," Morina said. "I have a bargain for you."

Renata seemed more interested than I to hear it. "Yes, Dracule?"

Morina kept her eye on me as she spoke. "I will release you of your oath to me…"

"On what condition?" I asked.

"On the condition that you do not cast me aside," she said, and her voice was strained.

"You'd sacrifice your opportunity to see Andrella one last time to stay with me?" I asked, disbelief making my blood hum dizzily.

"Yes," she said and sank to her knees. She bowed her head, the curtain of her tri-color hair shielding her face from our view.

Andrella's words flowed through my memory: *You can save her from herself.*

I met Renata's steady gaze and she sighed. "Far be it from me to complain about a harem in my bed."

Morina raised her face at that and Renata gave her honeyed laugh.

"Mmm, you bed her, Dracule, you bed me. Still interested?"

"And Iliaria," I said.

"And Iliaria," Renata echoed. "If she agrees."

"Yes, if she agrees," I said.

Morina's eyelid flickered. "Yes," she said, only a bit uncertainly after hearing our stipulations.

Perhaps, it wasn't just me who could save Morina from herself.

❖

Some hours later, I stood with Morina outside Iliaria's room. Renata had gone to see her and requested that we remain out in the hallway. Morina was quiet, as usual. Renata emerged and nodded to me, indicating that I enter.

I slipped into the room with Renata behind me and found Iliaria resting against a mound of pillows. Her upper body was bare save for the material wrapped around her torso. She held her hand out to me and I went to her, crawling carefully atop her and pressing my lips against hers.

Iliaria smiled softly and winced as she tried to adjust the pillows behind her.

"Here," I said, "let me." I propped the pillow more solidly behind her back and helped to guide her against it.

"Renata has told me of Morina's request."

I sat back on my heels beside her. "And?"

"I have some conditions of my own."

Renata went to the door to admit Morina as if the two had planned it. Morina appeared highly uncomfortable and crossed her arms over her chest.

"What are your conditions?" she asked Iliaria.

"Be my friend again," Iliaria said. "We've wasted all of these years fighting over nothing."

The request took Morina by surprise. Her crossed arms relaxed to her sides. After a moment, Morina pushed the patch covering her scar back into her hair. "You did this, Iliaria."

"In defense," Iliaria said as a sly smile quirked at the corner of her mouth. "Besides, it makes you look more dangerous, in a bad-girl sort of way."

Morina scowled. "I didn't come here so you could ridicule me."

"I don't think she is," I said and motioned at her face with a hand. "It kind of does have a certain appeal."

"If we are to make this foursome work," Iliaria said, "all of us must find some common ground. Renata and I have already established ours with each other, but you and I, Morina, we haven't been friends in a very long time. I'd like to be again."

"I will try," Morina said.

"I don't expect it to happen overnight," Iliaria said. "We had something good once."

A flush rose to Morina's pale cheeks and Iliaria grinned.

I rested my head carefully on Iliaria's shoulder. "How long were you lovers?"

"A while," they both said.

"It was purely physical," Iliaria said.

"It was," Morina added. "But still—"

"Not bad?" Iliaria cut her off. "Those better be the words about to leave your lips, Morina."

Morina stared at her brazenly. "And if they weren't?" she asked, but it was obvious she was toying with Iliaria.

Iliaria's arm slid down my back as she raised my shirt. "I'll remind you that you pleasured yourself while watching Epiphany and me together."

Renata moved toward the bed and slid in behind me. Her hand folded over Iliaria's against my lower back. I felt Renata's breath against my cheek. "Cara mia," she whispered playfully. "What have I missed, hmm?"

Before I had the chance to reply, her mouth sealed over mine and she teased my lips open with her tongue. I moaned at the touch of her, at the exquisite feel of her.

Iliaria grunted beside me as Renata's tongue danced with mine and I sank back against her shoulder. "That's not a fair thing to do in front of a woman who's crippled."

Renata drew back, her eyes sparkling mischievously. She turned toward Iliaria and caught her mouth in a kiss. Iliaria made a noise of surprise and raised her free arm as if to push Renata away, but she didn't. She lowered her arm and returned the kiss with a fervor that sent blood humming directly between my legs.

Renata broke the kiss with a triumphant smile. "Mmm." She touched Iliaria's glossy hair. "Better?"

Iliaria's eyes burned with a heat that I'd never seen her direct at Renata. She turned that smoldering look on me and said, "Almost."

I went to her, discerning what she desired of me and offering my lips as she kissed me as passionately as she had Renata.

"Now it's better."

I reclined against her uninjured shoulder and snuggled down, curling my leg over hers. Renata spooned me and rested her face against the side of my neck.

Morina hadn't moved from her spot just inside the room. She stood-stock still as if she wasn't certain what to do. Iliaria must've noticed the same slight etching of pain and longing in her, for she held out a hand.

After several moments, Morina came to the side of the bed. She took Iliaria's hand in her own and fell to her knees with a choked sound that made my heart feel as though it was cracking. She pressed her forehead to Iliaria's hand and breathed, "I'm sorry."

Iliaria raised her face and wiped the tears from her good eye. "I know, Morina," she said. "I know."

Gingerly, she guided Morina into bed with us, trying not to jostle her injured side. Iliaria held her loosely while she cried and I reached out to stroke her arm with Renata's comforting presence against my backside.

Some people are really bad people, like Damokles and Lucrezia, but the Dracule in our bed was not one of those. Sometimes, the people we think are bad are merely misguided by their pain. They disguise their wounds, but deep down, they can be saved.

The future was unforeseeable, though it was like to be fraught with danger with Damokles still alive and seeking to lay claim to the Draculian throne.

But now, in this moment with these strange, beautiful women, I was as happy as I could possibly be.

And one thing I was certain of, we would fight to protect what was ours.

About the Author

Winter Pennington is an author, poet, artist, and closeted musician. She is an avid practitioner of nature-based spirituality and enjoys spending her spare time studying mythology from around the world. The Celtic path is very close to her heart. She has an uncanny fascination with swords and daggers, and a fondness for feeding loud and obnoxious corvids. In the shadow of her writing, she has experience working with a plethora of animals as a pet care specialist and veterinary assistant.

Winter currently resides in Oklahoma with her partner and their ever-growing family of furry kids, also known as, "The Felines Extraordinaire."

Books Available From Bold Strokes Books

Speed Demons by Gun Brooke. When NASCAR star Evangeline Marshall returns to the race track after a close brush with death, will famous photographer Blythe Pierce document her triumph and reciprocate her love—or will they succumb to their respective demons and fail? (978-1-60282-678-6)

Summoning Shadows: A Rosso Lussuria Vampire Novel by Winter Pennington. The Rosso Lussuria vampires face enemies both old and new and to prevail they must call on even more strange alliances, unite as a clan, and draw on every weapon within their reach—but with a clan of vampires, that's easier said than done. (978-1-60282-679-3)

Sometime Yesterday by Yvonne Heidt. When Natalie Chambers learns her Victorian house is haunted by a pair of lovers and a Dark Man, can she and her lover Van Easton solve the mystery that will set the ghosts free and banish the evil presence in the house? Or will they have to run to survive as well? (978-1-60282-680-9)

Into the Flames by Mel Bossa. In order to save one of his patients, psychiatrist Dr. Jamie Scarborough will have to confront his own monsters—including those he unknowingly helped create. (978-1-60282-681-6)

OMGqueer edited by Radclyffe and Katherine E. Lynch, PhD. Through stories imagined and told by youth across America, this anthology provides a snapshot of queerness at the dawn of the new millennium. (978-1-60282-682-3)

Coming Attractions: Author's Edition by Bobbi Marolt. For Helen Townsend, chasing turns to caring, and caring turns to loving, but will love take five steps back and turn to leaving? (978-1-60282-732-5)

Oath of Honor by Radclyffe. A First Responders novel. First do no harm…First Physician of the United States Wes Masters discovers that being the president's doctor demands more than brains and personal sacrifice—especially when politics is the order of the day. (978-1-60282-671-7)

A Question of Ghosts by Cate Culpepper. Becca Healy hopes Dr. Joanne Call can help her learn if her mother really committed suicide—but she's not sure she can handle her mother's ghost, a decades-old mystery, and lusting after the difficult Dr. Call without some serious chocolate consumption. (978-1-60282-672-4)

The Night Off by Meghan O'Brien. When Emily Parker pays for a taboo role-playing fantasy encounter from the Xtreme Encounters escort agency, she expects to surrender control—but never imagines losing her heart to dangerous butch Nat Swayne. (978-1-60282-673-1)

Sara by Greg Herren. A mysterious and beautiful new student at Southern Heights High School stirs things up when students start dying. (978-1-60282-674-8)

Fontana by Joshua Martino. Fame, obsession, and vengeance collide in a novel that asks: What if America's greatest hero was gay? (978-1-60282-675-5)

Lemon Reef by Robin Silverman. What would you risk for the memory of your first love? When Jenna Ross learns her high school love Del Soto died on Lemon Reef, she refuses to accept the medical examiner's report of a death from natural causes and risks everything to find the truth. (978-1-60282-676-2)

The Dirty Diner: Gay Erotica on the Menu, edited by Jerry L. Wheeler. Gay erotica set in restaurants, featuring food, sex, and men—could you really ask for anything more? (978-1-60282-677-9)

The Marrying Kind by Ken O'Neill. Just when successful wedding planner Adam More decides to protest inequality by quitting the business and boycotting marriage entirely, his only sibling announces her engagement. (978-1-60282-670-0)

Sweat: Gay Jock Erotica by Todd Gregory. Sizzling tales of smoking hot sex with the athletic studs everyone fantasizes about. (978-1-60282-669-4)

Missing by P.J. Trebelhorn. FBI agent Olivia Andrews knows exactly what she wants out of life, but then she's forced to rethink everything when she meets fellow agent Sophie Kane while investigating a child abduction. (978-1-60282-668-7)

Touch Me Gently by D. Jackson Leigh. Secrets have always meant heartbreak and banishment to Salem Lacey—until she meets the beautiful and mysterious Knox Bolander and learns some secrets are necessary. (978-1-60282-667-0)

Slingshot by Carsen Taite. Bounty hunter Luca Bennett takes on a seemingly simple job for defense attorney Ronnie Moreno, but the job quickly turns complicated and dangerous, as does her attraction to the elusive Ronnie Moreno. (978-1-60282-666-3)

Dark Wings Descending by Lesley Davis. What if the demons you face in life are real? Chicago detective Rafe Douglas is about to find out. (978-1-60282-660-1)

sunfall by Nell Stark and Trinity Tam. The final installment of the everafter series. Valentine Darrow and Alexa Newland work to rebuild their relationship even as they find themselves at the heart of the struggle that will determine a new world order for vampires and wereshifters. (978-1-60282-661-8)

Mission of Desire by Terri Richards. Nicole Kennedy finds herself in Africa at the center of an international conspiracy and is rescued by the beautiful but arrogant government agent Kira Anthony—but can Nicole trust Kira, or is she blinded by desire? (978-1-60282-662-5)

Boys of Summer, edited by Steve Berman. Stories of young love and adventure, when the sky's ceiling is a bright blue marvel, when another boy's laughter at the beach can distract from dull summer jobs. (978-1-60282-663-2)